THE TRIA

# The Rise of an
# HEIRESS
### PART ONE

**PAULINA PANY**

The Rise of an Heiress by Paulina Pany

paulinapanyauthor.com

Copyright © 2022 Paulina Pany

All rights reserved. No portion of this book may be reproduced in any form without permission from the publisher, except as permitted by U.S. copyright law.

Cover by Ashton Taylor Creative

Editing and Formatting Services by Miss Eloquent Edits

ISBN: 979-8-9869598-0-1(print)

ISBN: 979-8-9869598-1-8 (ebook)

Printed in United States of America

First Edition

The Rise of an Heiress is work of fiction and should be read as such.

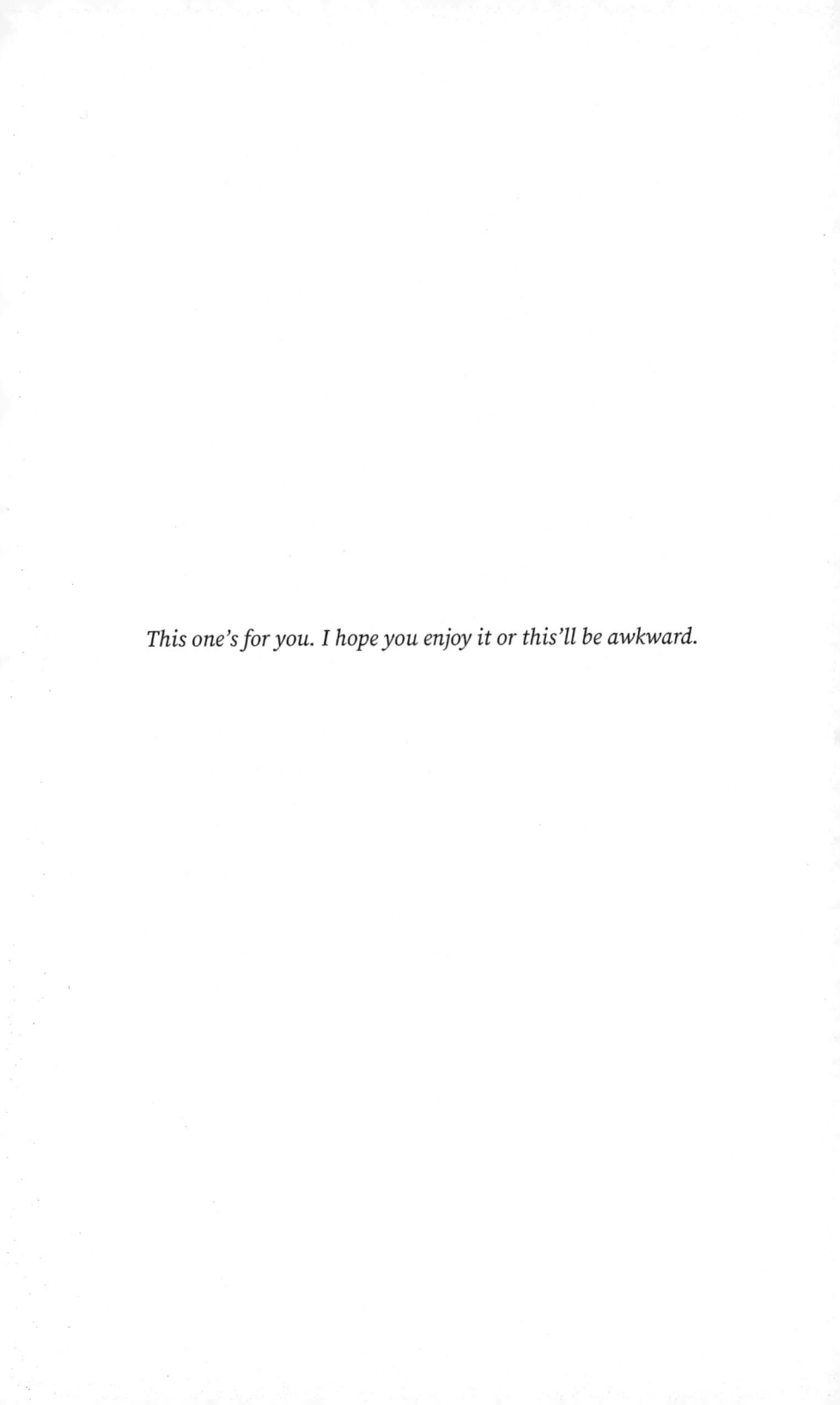

*This one's for you. I hope you enjoy it or this'll be awkward.*

# Author's Note

Dear Reader,

First and foremost, I want to thank you for choosing to read The Rise of an Heiress and thank you for giving my first couple a chance.

As someone who is well-versed in dark mafia romance novels, I felt there was something missing, something I was desperate for. I knew what I wanted, but my searches came up short.

Actor Dax Shepard once said, "Make the movie you want to see." And with those words, I made it my own. I set off to the tell the story I wanted to read.

I played with the idea of The Triad Series for many years and finally had the courage to take the plunge, and here we are. Those words kicked off my journey with The Triad Series. Writing this novel was a deeply personal and emotional experience, and I hope you enjoy the first part to this couple's story as much as I did writing it.

With gratitude,

# Content Warnings

Your safety is top priority to me. This content is 18+ and reader discretion is advised.

Please see below for potential triggers:
- Death of parent(s), spouse(s), child (off page)
- Death and murder (on and off page)
- Graphic depictions of sex
- Graphic depictions of violence, torture, and death
- Explicit language
- Mentions of cancer
- Kidnapping/Attempted Kidnapping
- Use of weapons
- Use of illegal substances

# Family Trees

Warning: Potential Spoilers

## Liu Family Tree

Peter Liu (Dragon Head, deceased) + Nina Violante (formerly Liu, née Li, deceased)

↓

Anya Liu (Triad Heiress/Princess)

(Alias: Natalie Yang)

## Delucci Family Tree

Giuseppe Delucci (Former Capo, Retired) + Marcella Delucci

↓

Sebastiano "Bash" (Capo)

Niccolo "Nico" (Consigliere)

Lorenzo "Enzo"

## Violante Family Tree

Cesare Violante (Capo) + Luciana Violante (deceased)

↓

Dominic (Outfit Heir)

Donatella "Donna"

# Contents

| | |
|---|---|
| Prologue | 15 |
| Chapter One | 19 |
| Chapter Two | 29 |
| Chapter Three | 45 |
| Chapter Four | 55 |
| Chapter Five | 75 |
| Chapter Six | 87 |
| Chapter Seven | 95 |
| Chapter Eight | 103 |
| Chapter Nine | 113 |
| Chapter Ten | 123 |
| Chapter Eleven | 135 |
| Chapter Twelve | 149 |
| Chapter Thirteen | 155 |
| Chapter Fourteen | 163 |
| Chapter Fifteen | 167 |
| Chapter Sixteen | 179 |

| | |
|---|---|
| CHAPTER SEVENTEEN | 187 |
| CHAPTER EIGHTEEN | 195 |
| CHAPTER NINETEEN | 213 |
| CHAPTER TWENTY | 225 |
| CHAPTER TWENTY-ONE | 231 |
| CHAPTER TWENTY-TWO | 237 |
| CHAPTER TWENTY-THREE | 255 |
| CHAPTER TWENTY-FOUR | 259 |
| CHAPTER TWENTY-FIVE | 263 |
| CHAPTER TWENTY-SIX | 271 |
| CHAPTER TWENTY-SEVEN | 283 |
| CHAPTER TWENTY-EIGHT | 293 |
| CHAPTER TWENTY-NINE | 303 |
| CHAPTER THIRTY | 307 |
| CHAPTER THIRTY-ONE | 313 |
| CHAPTER THIRTY-TWO | 327 |
| CHAPTER THIRTY-THREE | 335 |
| CHAPTER THIRTY-FOUR | 341 |
| EPILOGUE | 347 |

# Prologue

## SIX YEARS OLD

*First*, Daddy, and now Mommy's gone, too, I think as I sit in the living room. Several people are here, at our house. All in black. Everyone looks sad. I'm sad, too.

*I'm all alone. I have no one left.*

"You'll always have me," Dom says as he sits next to me on the couch.

How could he always read my mind?

I look at my blond-haired, blue-eyed, too-tall-to-only-be-eleven-years-old step-brother, "Promise?"

He places his hand over mine in my lap. "*Sempre.*" He kisses my forehead. *Always.*

After the funeral, Papa had me come to his office, which he's never done before. They're yelling, but I don't understand what they mean. Papa is arguing with the buff, dark-haired man I had seen earlier. I didn't see his face. My vision is always blurry with tears now.

The day went by in a blur. I'm falling asleep in the chair as I wait. Why won't he let me go to bed yet?

"You have to put her first!" the man yells from the other side of the door.

"What do you think I'm doing, Bo? You think this is easy! I have to!" Papa yells back.

They speak in hushed tones. I only hear raspy whispers, then the door springs open. My gaze is focused on the floor when the dark-haired man gives me a hug, but I still don't look at his face. When the man leaves, only then does Papa's face soften before he speaks.

"Let's go in." He gestures with his arm for me to walk into the office. I sit on the couch by the fireplace. He follows and bends down to his haunches, giving me a long hug before he grabs my face with both hands and kisses my cheeks. I look at his face, and it looks like his eyes are full of water.

"Mia dolce bambina." *My sweet little girl*, he says. "This is very important. You are going to live with a new family in New York."

I knew it. He was going to send me away. I'm not his daughter.

"You don't want me anymore now that mommy is gone?" I ask him, casting my gaze down as my eyes well up with tears.

"No, amore mio." *My love.* He holds the sides of my arms before he continues. "That's not why. It's not safe for you anymore in Chicago."

"I don't want to go. I want to stay here with you and Dom and Donna. I'll be good, I promise," I sob.

"I wish you could, but I need to keep you safe. Do you understand?" he tells me, holding my cheeks, wiping my tears with his thumbs.

I shake my head. Papa is the only father I'd ever known. Daddy was murdered when I was just a baby.

"You must be strong, bambina. Do this for me. You are going to live with your new parents in New York City. It is the only way I can keep you safe. Can you be strong for me?"

"Will I ever see you again?" I ask, sobbing.

"Of course." He chuckled. "We will visit you often, and you'll still spend summer holiday with us. This breaks my heart, but it is the safest." He squeezes my hands.

"Okay." I nod, taking a deep breath. "I can be strong."

I want to be, at least.

"That's my girl. Now, this part is very important. You must listen to me." He lifts my chin with his finger. "You can never let anyone know who you are. Ever. Under any circumstances."

"But—"

"What did I say about being strong?"

I nod. "I will be strong."

Dom and Donna, my step-siblings, sneak into my room. Dom is five years older than me, my self-appointed protector. Donna's two years older than me, my best friend. I spend my last night in Chicago, in the only home I've known, crying myself to sleep, while Dom holds me close and Donna holds my hand.

"This isn't goodbye, Sister," Donna whispers with tears in her eyes. "We'll see each other all the time," Dom promises.

The next morning, I get into the car and walk away from my life.

# Chapter One
## NATALIE—PRESENT DAY

"Are you even listening to me?" Maya asks, breaking through my thoughts.

Bringing my gaze back to her, I say, "What? Of course!"

I must've zoned out.

She takes a bite of her salad, rolling her eyes. "No, you're not!" She laughs. "Hellooo? It's your birthday! Come on, pay attention!"

Maya Villanueva has been my best friend since we met at NYU. I was a freshman, and she was a sophomore. We ran into each other at a mixer and hit it off immediately. We are total opposites. For starters, she's strikingly gorgeous, with glowing dark golden skin, long curly black hair, curves every woman envies, legs to die for, and extremely extroverted. *Honestly, what's it like being God's favorite?* She's always in an assortment of colors; her outfits are always bold and bright. She loves yellow, hot pink, emerald-green, royal-blue, and purple, all at once. Somehow, she makes it work.

I'm the opposite. Short, petite—but with my training, my body is pretty toned. My long, straight, black hair goes to my butt, and I stick to mostly neutrals—pink is always my go-to color if I need a "pop" of color. I'm not that girly or boring, I just don't want to—can't—draw attention to myself. I'm not introverted, but with the way I was raised, I definitely had an acute sense of danger, while Maya doesn't have a cautious bone in her body.

And then there's the secret. I can't afford to make a mess. I can't be myself, whoever she is. Sometimes, I feel like I'm living a half-life, going through the motions but not really experiencing it.

"Oh, is your hottie of a *best friend*—after me, of course—coming into town?" she inquires, as if she's talking about a stranger and not someone she's known for years.

Maya is asking about my step-brother Dominic. She doesn't know he's my step-brother. No one does. Everyone just thinks the Violantes are close family friends.

"Gross, Maya. I'm eating. He's not hot. But, yes, he's never missed a birthday. He'll be here for two weeks. Donna is coming, too, next week, with Cesare," I respond, plucking a piece of chicken from her salad.

"Oh my god, he *so* is! I wish I had an *old family friend*," she says with air quotes, "that stayed in touch with me like he does. You know he's in love with you, right? When are you gonna tap that?"

## Rise Of An Heiress

"I'm gonna stop you right there." I put my hand out to gesture for her to stop talking as my food nearly came back up. "Nobody says 'tap that' anymore, and he is certainly not in love with me. I promise you that. He's like a brother to me."

She throws her head back, laughing.

I don't blame her—or anyone for thinking so. He has a protective streak people, sometimes, mistake for jealousy and romantic feelings. He has quite the temper at times.

"I love when Donna comes into town. I'll have to text her so we can coordinate your big night. Don't you worry that pretty little head of yours. I have everything planned. And if you're *just friends,* then you wouldn't mind if I took him for a ri—"

"Don't! Stop!" I pretend to gag. "And not because I like him. You can have him. I just don't need the details."

Cringe.

Blood couldn't make us closer. He's one of the only people who knows the real me, even the darkest parts. He knows all my secrets, mainly because he had witnessed most of them, but he's as loyal as they come. He's also terrifying when he wants to be, which works in his favor. As Cesare Violante's first born, he is going to be the Outfit's next capo. *Boss.* Cesare is my stepfather, my Papa, and even though I'm Chinese-American, the Italian mafia raised Dom, Donna, and me. This isn't even the biggest thing we're hiding.

Donatella or Donna—unless you want your fingers chopped off—and I are as close as sisters could be. She's not your typical mafia princess. She's not docile by any means; she's tough, outspoken, and sharp as a tack. She'll take your eye out without batting a lash, then turn around and bake the best damn cake you've ever had. She's a math and economics genius, which is why she and Maya get along so well. I'm convinced Donna could single-handedly control the stock market if she wanted to.

You'd never guess how we were raised by looking at her, though. We never dare speak of our real lives to outsiders, non-mafiosos.

So, every day, I pretend. Only three people in the world know the real me: Papa, Dom, and Donna. The only family I've ever known.

"So, when does Dom land?" Maya asks, breaking me out of my thoughts again, picking up a piece of shrimp off my plate with her fork.

"He gets in this evening, and we're going to dinner at—"

"Ming's. I know, sweetie. It's Thursday," she says with a smile.

"You should come with us!"

"As much as you know I'd love to, I can't. I still have so much to do with this conference at the university." She lets out a sigh.

Even though Maya's a year older, I had finished in three years, so we finished undergrad at the same time. We both attend Columbia, where I'll be wrapping up my law degree in a month, while she finishes her Masters in Economics before moving on to her PhD. My dream is to become a criminal lawyer, for criminals, of course.

"Oh, right. How's that going?" I ask.

"Really well! I know it's not your thing, but I'd think you'd really enjoy it. We have a lot of trailblazers and business leaders coming to speak. That could help, since you want to work for the Violante family's businesses."

*Right.* I told her I wanted to work for them, and she assumed I meant as a corporate lawyer, but I just never corrected her.

"I'm going to try. I've been so busy looking for fellowships and studying for the bar. I don't even know which way is up."

"You have nothing to worry about. You're one of the smartest people I know. Seriously, do you even try?"

Before I can get out a syllable, she looks at her watch. "Ugh, well, I have to get going. It was so nice seeing you! Can't wait for your birthday!"

"Just a normal night out, Maya," I say to her as she packs her things.

Completely ignoring me, she snaps her fingers like she had just come up with an idea and opens her mouth. "Oh, hey, you should invite Jeremy out. He's totally got the hots for you."

"I told you I'm not interested in Jeremy."

He definitely has a crush. It's not that he's not attractive. No, it's because of who I am—marriage, kids. The whole nine yards were never in the cards for me. I knew that from a young age, so there was never a point in getting attached to anyone. I could never marry a non-mafioso. It would be too dangerous, nor could I marry into the Outfit. I was an outsider to them. The orphan. Marriages outside of the house you belonged to only happened for business purposes and forming alliances. I have no power. I'm nobody.

"Just think about it. You don't have to marry the guy. One night won't kill you!" She winks at me, and with that, she's off. Maya's always been a free spirit. She can convince me to do anything. It was hard saying no when I secretly craved adventure and chaos. Papa calls us Trouble One and Trouble Two. I laugh to myself as my phone buzzes.

>Dom: Taking off, see you soon birthday girl!
>Me: FYI Maya's planning.
>Dom: Shit, I'll beef up security.
>Me: I can't tell if you're joking.
>Dom: With all the shit you two get into, this is not a joke.
>Me: LOL you mean all the shit she gets me into!
>Dom: Yeah, I'm pretty sure you both getting stuck on Long Island at 3 a.m. was your doing.
>Me: Omg, that was one time! Whatever, just text me when you land.
>Dom: She's going to ask for my credit card isn't she?
>Me: *shrugging girl emoji*
>Dom: *eye roll emoji* Bring the Porsche when you pick me up, I'm driving.

As I gather my things, I think about how strange my life is and the circumstances that resulted in this. As a Chinese-American girl brought up by the Italian mafia—strange is an understatement.

My real father died when I was a baby—life in the underworld and all—and so did Dom and Donna's mom—car accident. My mother remarried Cesare, the real love of her life. Life threw another wrench my way when she got cancer.

Cesare tried to raise me as his own, but it was too dangerous being an outsider. Not because I wasn't Italian. Anyone who wasn't born or married into the Outfit was considered an outsider. That's how it is with all mafia syndicates. With my mother's passing, most of the Outfit men didn't see me as one of them anymore, especially since I was, technically, born into another crime organization. I couldn't go back to my mother's family. She was labeled a traitor after marrying Papa. So, after she died, Papa thought it'd be safer for me to have a normal life in New York with my adoptive parents. No one knows I was adopted except for Papa, Dom, and Donna. The secrets never end.

## NICO

"Can someone explain to me what the fuck happened?" my brother Bash said in his calm voice, which meant he was anything but calm.

Three of our men stood there silently, looking like Larry, Curly, and fucking Moe. Three goddamn stooges. Their eyes meeting everything but Bash's, like they were fucking five-year-olds getting ripped into by their mothers. Not made men.

"Someone better speak now," I said, my patience wearing thin by the second.

How the fuck did these idiots manage to lose $20 million worth of *product*?

"It was the Outfit," Joe blurts. "We had the shipment ready to go, and they ambushed us at the docks."

"Why the hell would the Outfit attack our docks if they need access to our harbors for their businesses?" I ask.

This doesn't make any sense.

"They wanted the shipment. They made off with most of it and destroyed the rest," Rafaele chimes in.

Fucking hell.

"You sure it was the Outfit?" Bash asks.

It seems he's thinking what I'm thinking. Once upon a time, the Outfit had been a pain in our ass, but they haven't been an issue for at least two decades, since shortly after our father became capo. Why now?

"Had to be. They used their typical M.O.—cyanide bombs and tranquilizers, spoke Italian, which was stupid. Who else is remotely strong enough to think they can take us on?" Joe answers.

"Did you actually see their faces?" I ask.

They all shook their heads.

"They had ski masks on," the third guy, whose name I can't remember, replies.

"We gotta look into this. We need proof." Bash looks over at me.

"I'll take care of it," I say as I walk off.

"Nico, I don't want you shrugging this off to get laid. This could mean war," Bash calls after me.

I wave my hand without turning around. No shit. I know this is serious.

And so my work begins. I love my job. Our father recently retired, making Bash the capo of the Cosa Nostra, King of the

## Rise Of An Heiress

East Coast. Naturally, the title of consigliere, his right-hand man, fell upon me—Prince of the East Coast—the brains. That was always the plan since we were boys. My brother is a monster and a good talker, which made him good for business and our public image, but he needed me for my skills. I'm a damn good hacker, and I intend to learn everything about the Outfit. Where they sleep, what time they shit, and all their mistresses' names.

My family owns the East Coast, and since we own most of the shipping harbors, it was easy to get a cut from all the other *businesses* that want to get their products in and out of the country, with our legal global logistics company easily being our main cover and bringing in billions.

I love this life. Live and breathe it. I thank the Lord every day that I was born into this world.

# Chapter Two

### NICO

"AAAHH!" the ugly fucker screams as Dante pours water over his head.

Dante wears a sinister smile on his face as he removes the towel from Ugly's head.

"Are you ready to talk?" I ask.

He spits in my face.

Dante punches him in the face.

*Okay, the hard way it is.* Adrenaline surges through me as I crack my neck. I'm in my element.

Staring at the pathetic fucker, who is now tied down to a chair in one of our club basements, I can't help but snarl. This low-life makes me sick. Did he really think he could rat us out?

I move over to the table off to the side and examine my options. Pliers, hammer, blow torch, various-sized knives, brass knuckles, and a ton of others to choose from. I grab one of the knives and turn back to Ugly. His eyes grow wide, and he shakes more violently. Another rush of excitement passes through me.

Dante walks over to the table and grabs the pliers and brass knuckles. We circle the idiot. Finally, I stop and place the knife over his hand. He can't move, though he tries. Too bad his arms are strapped down in the chair.

"Tell me who convinced you to turn on your own brothers, and maybe I'll let you keep your fingers," I say as I graze the knife over his fingers.

"Fuck yo—AAAHH!"

Before he can even finish, I slice three of his fingers clean off. He lets out a cry, but Dante shoves a towel in his mouth and punches the idiot across the face with the brass knuckles.

"He thinks he can just narc on us and *then* disrespect us, Nico?" Dante says to me in mock amusement.

I grab some needles lying on the table and make my way back to the ugly rat.

"They always think they can outsmart us." I twirl the knife between my fingers. I take the towel out of his mouth, while Dante pulls Ugly's head back and holds the pliers up to his eyeball. "Tell me, what was more important than the Omertà promise!" I scream in his face.

Omertà is the promise all our men had committed to and had to recite during their initiation to become a made man of La Cosa Nostra. *Our Thing.* It's an oath of silence, an oath to family and brothers that we would never sell out and talk to outsiders. Basically—*the first rule about fight club is: you do not talk about fight club.*

# Rise Of An Heiress

The guy doesn't say anything. I shove the towel back in.

"I think you forgot who we are. *Who I am!*" I slowly push the needles under the nails of the fingers on his good hand one at a time.

I may come off as an easygoing man sometimes, but I am not the one you want to cross. Bash was the one who could always compose himself in any situation. Not me.

"AAAHHH!" Ugly tries to yell through the towel as Dante springs on him and pries the pliers into his eye.

I pick the drill up that was sitting by the chair, switching it on and off to test it so the traitor could hear. The rat pisses himself. This shouldn't take long. Dante pulls the towel from the guy's mouth.

"You better start talking."

Before he can respond, I drill into his kneecap with a delicious crunch. His cries are so loud my ears are ringing. When I finally feel satisfied, I turn the drill off, and the idiot spills.

Apparently, he had found himself in some debt, and someone approached him with money in exchange for information about our shipment. Fucking coward. He'd been with the Cosa Nostra for twenty-five years. This isn't new, though. Loyalty is getting harder and harder to come by. We knew it was him; he was the only one who knew which shipping compartment had the product.

I drill into his other knee, and it doesn't take long after that for the idiot to pass out from either the pain or blood loss. I don't give a shit.

"Take care of this," I say to Dante, which is code for: *kill the fucker and call clean up.* "Meet me in my office when you're done."

As I head to the showers, I send a quick message to my brother.

*Me: It's done.*

*Bash: Good.*

* * *

Later that afternoon, I'm sitting in my office, looking at spreadsheets for the clubs, when Dante walks in with a smile on his face like he had won the lottery.

"What's gotten into you?" I ask, pulling out two glasses and a bottle of whiskey.

"It's just a good day," he says as he sits. "Got to torture and kill a guy. Been a while."

"It's been a week, Dante." I laugh at the crazy fuck, handing him a glass.

"That's a long time for the enforcer," he says, like I'm the idiot, and sips his drink. "I think I'll call up Jamila with the nice tits tonight, you know, to celebrate. Maybe Sophia will be free." Dante wiggles his eyebrows.

I cringe at the thought. Sophia is your typical, stuck-up, two-faced Manhattan socialite bitch—entitled, will never work a day in her life, another social climber, desperate to marry to maintain her lifestyle. Considering who my family is, that makes me her type. I'm not a commitment guy. Even if I were, her voice sounds like nails on a chalkboard. Not that it would matter, anyway. I'd never marry an outsider.

## Rise Of An Heiress

In this life, you get married for tactical reasons, to start the next generation of Deluccis. Bash has the bigger chip on his shoulder, being capo. But as consigliere, you still have expectations to meet in the Cosa Nostra. Marriage is a duty. In the underworld, they're rarely a reflection of love and always a display of power. My parents got lucky, as their marriage was arranged. They both wanted it.

I'm not holding out. I'm not a romantic. I leave that shit to our youngest brother Enzo, the emotional one. I'll do what I have to because it's my job. If it'll make the family more powerful, then I'm all for it.

"I'd rather go find one of the whores we employ than go anywhere near her. Anyway, I need you to look into the Violantes for me."

"The Outfit? What did those fuckers do?" He pours himself another glass.

"We got word that they're fucking with our shipping harbors. There was an attack earlier, and I want to know who was behind it and why."

He nods and takes another sip. "Seems odd. They're not desperate."

"I agree, but we can't leave any stones unturned, and we gotta start somewhere." I rub my thumb on the rim of my glass.

"You got it, sweet pea." He finishes his second drink and stands to leave.

I shoot him a glare, and he laughs. The bastard and his nicknames.

Later, I'm still in my office when my phone chimes. An image is attached of a tall, built, blond man getting into a white Porsche Cayenne.

I know exactly who it is.

> Dante: Nico—check this out, Dominic Violante just landed at JFK.

What the fuck is a Violante doing in New York for a non-business trip? And it's Dominic Violante out of all of them. His father is capo of the Chicago Outfit, and he's next in line to take the throne. They come into New York for business and to get access to our harbors, but they shouldn't be entering our territory unannounced.

The Violantes rule over the Outfit. They're one of the most powerful Italian families in the U.S. Their influence stretches from the East Coast to the Midwest and in parts of Italy. The Outfit's involved in the usual underground trades, including gambling, extortion, money laundering, and drug trafficking, cushy nightclubs, shell corps, and art galleries covering them up. But that wasn't their crown jewel. The Outfit was heavily involved in politics, where they had us all by the balls. We all have one big super power. Policy is theirs, just like global trade is ours. And we all had used each other—or "worked together"—when convenient. The Outfit are the only ones who are close competition. But we've been at peace.

> Nico: Follow him, I'll catch up.

Grabbing the keys to my Range Rover, I head down to the parking garage of the club.

## Rise Of An Heiress

*Seriously, a Violante in New York?* I have to admit: the guy has some fucking balls entering New York so soon after an attack—that or he's the biggest idiot alive. It doesn't surprise me. Most men who in our world always feel they need to prove something.

Violante is lucky I didn't look into him right away, or he never would've made it off the airstrip.

I pull up Dante's location on the monitor and head toward the moving dot on my GPS. A text pops up on the screen.

*Dante: Some girl picked him up. She was practically bursting at the seams. Could be a secret lover.*

*Me: Who the fuck says lover?*

*Dante: What? Chicks dig it.*

This fucking idiot. Dante's been my best friend since we were in diapers. Not only that, but he's one of the Cosa Nostra's best trackers, which is why he's our enforcer. It's his job to hunt anyone who has debts with us, not to mention he's an expert in hand-to-hand combat and not a bad hacker, either. Instead of texting back, I hit the call button on my steering wheel.

"Hey, lover," Dante answers seductively.

I ignore him but can't help but laugh. "What do you know?"

"Not much, except she's hot as fuck. Long black hair, toned legs, and—"

"Not the girl," I say, irritated. Dante was always looking for the next piece of ass. "Did you get anything on Violante?"

He chuckles. "Not yet, but they're close. She all but threw herself at him. She could be useful—might know something. Looks like they're heading to dinner. Want me to keep watch?"

"Follow them, and I'll meet you to take over from there."

"Sounds good."

"Later, man."

Before I could hang up, Dante spoke again. "Oh, and Nico?"

"What?"

"I love you, baby."

I laugh. "Fucking hell."

"Say it back!" he yells back, feigning anger.

"Love you, too, jackass." I hang up but not before I hear him making kissing sounds on the other end.

The bastard was so easygoing you'd forget he'd been a made man since we were both sixteen.

I pull into a parking spot across the street. Not long after, I spot the white Porsche. Dominic and said woman walk up to the restaurant.

*Well, fuck.* Dante wasn't lying. She's a fucking smoke show. She's shorter than my usual type, maybe five feet flat, with high cheekbones, plump lips, and black hair so long I could wrap it around my fist multiple times. She's in a short skirt, tight blouse that shows off her curves in all the right places, and heels that showcase her legs. She has a smile plastered on her face, and I can't help but notice the dimple on the left side of her cheek. I also couldn't help but notice how she looks at him like he's her hero.

*Poor girl. Did she know he was next in line to inherit one of the most powerful mafia syndicates in the states?* Sucks when the innocent get sucked into this world.

I pull out my phone to take pictures so we can run them through my system. I'd know every dirty secret about this mystery woman in no time. I send them off to Dante.

## NATALIE

"I'm so excited you're here, Dom!"

I couldn't contain my excitement. I love my brother, though you'd never guess he was my brother.

He's a six-foot-three Italian man. Muscular and large, not quite as buff as our Papa, who's built like a tank, but he's getting there. Blond hair, blue eyes, his arms covered in intricate tattoos. He's attractive, but he's always been just Dom to me. Women constantly check him out and ignore me or give me the death glare, assuming I'm his girlfriend. Gross. He's never paid them any mind. He's not into relationships. Romance was uncommon in the underworld, so he didn't see the point in getting to know women. Typical made man. Although, I do think he secretly hopes to find love one day. He's mentioned how my mother and Papa used to interact a few times.

"Me too, sorellina," he replies, opening the door to Ming's for me.

Ming greets us. You'd never guess he was a chef, since he looks more like an MMA fighter, but who am I to make assumptions? Chefs can be in great shape, too.

I've been coming to this restaurant with my adoptive parents, since I was seven, and he's always here to greet me. I come here almost every Thursday, so it's no surprise. Sometimes, I don't even come to eat. Ming feels more like family, so sometimes,

I'll drop something off for him or talk to him. He's more like a surrogate father. I'm closer to him than my adoptive dad.

"If it isn't my favorite girl!" Ming grabs me into a bear hug. "Looking good, man!" he says to Dom as he pats him on the back.

The server brings our food out immediately. "I already knew Dom would be in town, so I went ahead and made your favorites, so it'd be ready when you got here. It's your birthday, so no waiting for you."

Touched by his gesture, my heart feels full.

"Thanks, Ming," I say as I sit, taking a drink of water. "My birthday isn't until next week, though, so you better keep this charade on until then!"

"Please don't spoil her." Dom rolls his eyes, and I try to kick him from under the table, but I miss.

"Shut up, Dom!" I throw a paper towel at him.

"I think she's the only person on Earth who can get away with speaking to you like that." Ming laughs. Dom and I quickly share a look of suspicion. Before we could react, Ming went on. "Besides, you and your father spoil this girl enough."

Dom shakes his head.

We enjoy the rest of dinner with easy conversation. Dom and Ming talk about getting together to work out while he's visiting. I tell Ming about school and Maya's birthday plans for me.

We leave the restaurant, and I can tell something's bothering Dom, so I ask, "Okay, what's going on?"

"What do you mean?" he answers, acting clueless.

"Really? We're going to do this?"

He opens the car door for me, and I slide in. When he gets into the driver's side, he's silent for a moment and doesn't turn the car on.

"Has Papa reached out to you?" he asks tentatively, eyebrows pinched.

"About my birthday? No, why? And why do you seem so nervous?"

Silence lingers as he ponders his thoughts. Then he heads to my apartment.

"It's nothing. We've just had some strange things happen in Chicago lately. He's been meaning to check up on you and make sure everything is okay."

"Should I be worried?"

"No." He pauses. "But if you see anything—anything at all, no matter how small—I need you to promise you'll tell me."

"Uhm, okay. I promise."

We sat in silence the rest of the way home.

## NICO

After the happy couple eats dinner, they head back to what I assume is her penthouse. I know this because I'm on a rooftop across the street with a perfect view into her place. What did this girl do for a living? Was he paying for this? It isn't unusual for made men to take on outsiders as mistresses.

They turn on the TV and watch shit reality television the rest of the evening. They might be happy, but they sure as fuck were boring. All I know is, if I had her alone, we would not be spending the night watching TV. My cock hardens just thinking about what I'd do to her. *Fuck. Get it together. She could be the enemy—or worse, an innocent who's about to get caught in the crossfire.*

When I get home, I hop in the shower. As the hot water soothes my body, all I can think about is the dark-haired beauty. I wrap my hand around my cock, hoping this would help get her out of my system.

* * *

The next day was business as usual. I woke up at six a.m. to get in my daily workout. I had breakfast on my balcony, taking in the New York City skyline I love so much. When I get out of the shower, I see a missed call from Dante. I've been waiting for him to get back to me about the mystery woman.

My phone rings just as I was about to return the call. I tap the answer key, and before I could utter anything, Dante is on the other end.

"Excuse me, where have you been?" he says in the worst impression of an angry woman.

"Sorry, dear. I was in the shower and just about to return your call, but you beat me to it," I reply. *Why do I encourage this*?

"Don't let it happen again!" he yells in a huff.

"Dante, you're getting way too good at this. Is there something you'd like to share with the class?"

Cackling on the other end, his voice goes back to normal.

"I got the information you wanted on our girl."

*Our girl*. I don't like that he called her that. I push that thought and my unexpected feelings aside, not ready to dissect that.

"And?"

"Not much, but it could be something. Some of it doesn't make any sense."

"Come over and let's talk. I don't want to do this over the—"

Before I could finish my sentence, my doorbell rang.

"Already ahead of you, man!"

I hang up and make my way to the front door. I key in the code, and it slides open.

Dante saunters in, all six-foot-two of him, with coffees in hand. We look alike, but I'm taller, and we both have dark hair and olive skin, except his hair is longer, and his eyes are hazel.

"What did you find?" I ask as we head into my office.

"What, no 'hello, how are you' or 'you look very handsome today?'" He gestures toward his body with our coffees still in hand. Ignoring him, I take a seat. He walks over to the desk and puts them down.

"Pft, guess not," he mumbles, pulling out a flash drive.

He plugs the drive into my computer, and an image of the woman I'd just been fantasizing about the night before lights up my screen. A professional headshot.

"What am I looking at, Dante?"

"Patience, man." He rolls his eyes.

"You know that's not in my vocabulary, so let's get on with it."

He put his arms up in surrender. "Okay, okay. There's really not much about her. Natalie Yang, born April 22, 1997 at New York Presbyterian in Brooklyn." He switches over to a photo of a newborn Natalie in her mother's arms, while her father holds them both and smiles at the camera. "So, she'll be twenty-five next Friday. Grew up in the Upper East Side. Parents are Jet and Nora Yang."

When I don't respond, he takes it as his cue to continue.

"She went to private schools, attended NYU, graduated early, and is now at Columbia Law."

"Okay, she's smart. Get to the part where it doesn't make sense, D."

"All right, all right. So, her parents are college professors at NYU, and I know that's decent money but not private school and Upper East Side money. She went to school debt-free and has had her own penthouse since she turned eighteen."

"You think someone is funding her lifestyle?"

As I suspected, it could be Dominic.

"There's no other way. Plus, I've checked her bank statements, and a questionable amount of money gets wired to her from an untraceable account."

I roll my eyes. "You should have started with that. Nothing is untraceable. But that is weird." I make a note to look into it and set up alerts on any movement on her end. "I'll keep an eye on her. I have some meetings at the clubs today. I'll catch you later."

"All right, man," Dante says as he heads toward the door, but before he leaves, he turns. "I was right, though, wasn't I?"

"About what?"

"She's hot." He wiggles his eyebrows. I flip him off. "Maybe I'll just go up and talk to her, flirt a little, and see what I can get out of her. I'm sure she won't be able to resist my charm." He smirks, adjusting his collar.

The cocky asshole.

"Stay away from her until we know more," I order, not liking the idea of him talking to her.

"You're no fun," he says as he exits.

I sit back in my chair. Mystery amounts of cash. Close with the Violantes. *Who are you?*

# Chapter Three

### NATALIE

JAB. JAB. CROSS. KICK. DUCK. HOOK.

"Nice!" Stephen yells as he lands with a thud.

I stand over him, a proud smirk on my face. I reach down to help him up.

"Natalie, you're making a lot of progress," Stephen says as he catches his breath.

"I feel like you're going easy on me," I say as I walk over to grab my water bottle.

"I used to, but it's getting harder and harder to go easy on you. You seriously just took me by surprise there." He pats me on the back.

Stephen's been my trainer for the last five years. I had a few before him, but none are as good. My Papa insists Donna and I learn how to defend ourselves. She can throw a punch, but she's stopped training when she turned eighteen.

I couldn't stop, though. I get this amazing rush, like I'm on top of the world when I'm fighting. I feel powerful and in control. The killer workout is a plus.

"We'll pick this up tomorrow. I'm gonna try some new techniques and exercises with you. Seriously, good job," he says as he runs off to the front of the training center to greet his next client.

After a hot shower, I'm in desperate need of some coffee before I head to class. As I type in my mobile order and make my way to the café right off campus, my thoughts wander to summer before my eighteenth birthday, when we were in Italy, as we were every year.

\* \* \*

*"You have fifteen minutes to complete this drill. First one to make it to the end wins," Papa instructs.*

*Papa sets up courses, which get harder each year. He wants us to be prepared. This year is different; we'll be using live ammunition. That explains why one of the soldiers handed us bulletproof vests.*

*I stare off into the lush clearing with the ocean gleaming in the background. Making mental notes of the space was now scattered with targets, obstacles, and booby traps about half a mile long. Papa owns acres of the island of Sardinia. His men had set up obstacle courses for us each summer to make sure we'd get practice should we ever need it.*

*"Shall we make a bet?" Donna smugly suggests.*

*"The two losers have to wire a hundred thousand dollars each to the winner?" I recommend.*

## Rise Of An Heiress

"Nah, we need something priceless. Winner gets to tell the two losers to do anything for the rest of the summer," Dom challenges, coming up from behind us.

Donna and I share a look before I glance back up at Dom. "Deal."

"Let's go!" Papa barks, snapping us out of our laughter.

He's in boss mode. It always amazes me how he can transform from the doting father to the don. The boss.

My siblings and I get into position and take our marks. Dom snaps his head side to side to crack it, while I stretch my quads out and Donna stretches out her arms. I scan the area once more, noticing opportunities of hidden traps. Several men were instructed to hide behind the barriers and had been ordered to attack at full force. Papa was not messing around. I know there's a sniper hiding farther down. I wonder if he was instructed to shoot at us and if either Dom or Donna noticed.

As I prepare to take off, my ears roar, and my senses spark. I've never felt more alive than when I'm in the middle of action. Though I'm not sure how true that is, seeing as I've never actually been put in a situation to use these skills.

Papa shoots his gun into the air, and Dom and Donna take off. I take another second to see where the soldiers pop out from, finding the best path to the end of the course. Donna is met with resistance while Dom has already taken out two men before I move. I run past Dom and over the haystack.

A bomb is planted somewhere. When I finally spot it, I grab it. It's crazy, but I have a plan. I rush past one of the wooden barrels, and a soldier jumps out. Before he can move, I throw the dummy bomb, and smoke plumes from it, blinding him. I have to keep moving. A *gunshot goes off, and the grass by my feet erupts—definitely has a sniper. Thanks, Papa.*

*Ducking, I see an opening. As I take off into a sprint, another soldier barrels at me, knife in hand. Kicking him in the stomach, I block his swing, but the man is huge and barely stumbles. He has a baton on his belt, so I fake a right hook to his face and grab it with my left hand. Before he can process what happened, I whack him over the head with his baton. He's too big to take down, but while he's trying to regain his wits, I bolt. The sniper shoots again, and out of irritation, I shoot right back at him. I can't help but laugh as he falls out of the tree with a grunt.*

*Glancing around, I spot Dom battling out with another soldier. I don't get to watch for long, as strong arms wrap around me. I throw my body forward and use the soldier's weight to take him with me. I stand over him and point my gun at him, then shoot into his vest-covered chest.*

*Another bomb goes off, and I look over to find Dom is about to reach the end, already doing a victory dance.*

*I have no idea where Donna is.*

*Without thinking, I point my gun at my brother and fire two shots, one into his bulletproof vest and another into his arm—just for shits and giggles. He stops his little dance and lets out a cry as he falls backward. He looks for the source as I sprint to the end, eyebrows pinched.*

*Donna comes out of nowhere, rushing to the end of the course after me. Her lip is busted, but she's wearing a huge grin. I smile from ear to ear.*

*Dom lost.*

"You fuckin' shot me!" he yells incredulously.

Before I come up with a comeback, Papa runs in our direction, yelling, "Serves your arrogant ass right! You make a mistake, you get killed!" He beams at me before shaking his head at Dom. Donna and I break out in laughter.

"Looks like you lose!" I sing-song back at him.

"Well done." Papa regards us but shoots daggers at Dom. "You can't get cocky, or that can be deadly. You're going to be capo, you need to start acting like it." He inspects Dom's arm. "You'll be fine. It's a flesh wound. Go get it cleaned up."

And without another word, Papa was off.

Dom fixes his glare back on me. "You could've killed me!"

"Nonsense, Dom. I'm a better shot than you. If I wanted to kill you, I would have. I grazed your shoulder on purpose. Besides, you're wearing a vest." I pat his back with a smug grin before walking away.

Donna follows suit, and we saunter off laughing.

Before we head toward the villa, Donna yells, "I think I'm craving cannoli"—she turns to our brother—"made from scratch."

"You didn't win!" he calls back to Donna.

\* \* \*

"Medium cold brew with oat milk and honey!" the barista calls out, breaking me from my trip down memory lane.

Smiling to myself, I walk up to the counter to grab my much-needed iced coffee and take a sip before sitting. Its coolness rushes down my throat, and my body comes alive. As I move through the cafe, I spot an open table outside. It's a cool April morning in New York City, just nice enough to sit outside. It's been a while since we've been able to be outside like this in the mornings, so I take full advantage of the empty table.

I'm scrolling through my phone, catching up on emails and texts, when I hear a male voice call out for me. I redirect my attention up, and green eyes stare back at me.

"Oh, hey, Jeremy. What's up?"

Maya's right. He's attractive. Dimpled smile, dirty blond hair, big green eyes. He looks exactly like an old-money New York City bachelor should. A little too polo and preppy for my taste but handsome nonetheless.

"Just seeing how your paper for Milovich is going?"

"Ugh, it's a nightmare. What do you think?" I laugh, covering my eyes with my hand.

Jeremy laughs. "Same. Shit's giving me hell."

"It's just busy work. What was yours on again?"

"Immigration," he answers lightly. "Yours is on RICO, right?"

"Yes."

Of course, I chose the topic ironically.

"That's cool." He pauses and rubs the back of his neck. "So, I was thinking maybe we could get together sometime and work on our papers together? I know they're different, but maybe we can bounce some ideas off of each—"

"Excuse me," says a deep voice from behind me.

I turn to the darkest, deepest eyes I've ever seen, accompanied by thick black lashes. His jawline and high cheekbones could cut a diamond. The man has gorgeous olive skin with short, dark facial hair contouring his sculpted face. He's in a long-sleeved shirt, but I can see tattoos peeking up from his collar, and he has some on his hands, too. I wonder if he's a model; we have no shortage of those in the city.

"You dropped this," he says, handing me my wireless earbuds, standing to his full height.

That's weird. I could've sworn they were zipped up in my bag.

"Thank you," I reply breathlessly, reaching for them.

We stare at each other, then a cough breaks me from the trance. I look back over at Jeremy. I forgot I'd been talking to him.

"It's no problem at all," the handsome stranger replies as I look back at him. "Have a nice day." He smiles, but it doesn't reach his eyes.

*Hello, Mr. Tall and Mysterious.* My mind screamed danger, but my body had other thoughts.

"I'm sorry. What were you saying, Jeremy?"

"Oh, just that we should get together and work on our papers together."

"That sounds great. I have to go, or I'm going to be late." I stand to gather my things. "But I'll see you in class this afternoon?"

"Of course." He nods with a sweet smile.

I speed-walk toward the campus to get to my class on time.

## NICO

There she is, right in front of me, sipping her morning coffee. Oat milk and honey, what an odd combination. She doesn't notice me. She's playing on her phone. I sit at the table next to her, and some preppy douche approaches her. They must know each other. *I wonder if I can get her attention.* I look down, and her bag is within arm's reach. I unzip the bag and grab the first thing I can feel. Earbuds. These'll do.

Before I can interrupt them, I hear "RICO," and that piques my interest immediately. She's writing a paper on The Racketeer-Influenced and Corrupt Organization Act? *Interesting.*

Maybe she's using the Violantes to extract information out of them? Damn, she's one hell of an actress if that's the case. I was even sold when I saw them outside of the restaurant the other day.

Barely listening to their conversation, I can tell Preppy has a crush and is trying to ask her out. It's kind of painful to watch but amusing.

This is my opportunity.

"Excuse me," I say to her, her black eyes shooting into mine as she sucks in a breath. "You dropped this." I hold her earbuds to her, wondering if she felt the jolt of electricity I did.

She looks at them like there's a mystery to be solved. I use the moment to take in her features. Her long dark hair and eyelashes that fan over her cheeks, silky skin that's mostly covered by a long sleeve blouse and jeans, and full lips.

Damn, she's stunning.

"Thank you," she says.

The fucker coughs.

"It's no problem at all. Have a nice day."

I watch her for the next week. So far, I know she wakes up early and goes to a building with no cameras inside. I'm assuming it's one of those private gyms that doesn't allow cameras. Which is a shame. She has a killer body. I'd love to see her use it at the gym. Well, I'd actually like to see her use it in other ways, but I'll take what I can get. Afterward, she goes to class or studies. She owns that Porsche but prefers her Audi e-tron Sportback.

She spends a lot of time with one of her tall supermodel-looking friends and some other classmates, usually studying on campus or grabbing drinks. I've come to learn that Preppy is actually named Jeremy. Jeremy van der Sar. His family is old money. I've seen him get handsy with her a few times, and I get this unfamiliar rush of possessiveness I don't like.

She hasn't spent too much time with Dominic, a quick lunch here and there. She frequents that Chinese restaurant every Thursday, according to her bank statements. Nothing seems unusual, except for the large sum of money that consistently shows up in her account.

I've had men tailing Dom, too, but he's been quiet. It's making me anxious. It's like he's genuinely here to see this woman. Hell, he doesn't even sleep with her. He's been staying at a hotel all week.

Are they just friends? I haven't seen anything sexual yet. I'm oddly pleased by this. But she definitely means something to him. I can tell by the way he looks at her. I need more answers, and I'm tired of waiting. Dominic is a hard no. He'd be too difficult to grab, and even if we were successful, there'd be consequences. We really don't need a war right now.

But her? Her, I can break. I almost feel bad. *Almost.* But it's not enough to stop what I'm about to do.

It's Thursday, and I order Joe, Rafaele, and the third guy—whose name, I learn, is Mario—to make a grab for the girl. They have strict orders to wait until she's leaving the restaurant to make the grab. If she's a regular and doesn't show up, I don't want to draw attention to it. I know Dom will be four hours north for the day—I tapped in on his phone conversation. Son of a bitch is a bitch of a hack. But soon, we'll have her, and soon, we'll have answers.

"Don't forget to disable the cameras," I tell them before walking off the club's empty dance floor and back to my office.

These morons better not fuck this up. They're already on thin ice after what happened at our shipping docks. If they can't handle a small woman, I'll have to kill them.

I spend the day making sure our spreadsheets are up to date. Legal and *not so legal*. We've recently acquired a new nightclub, The KA.RA, and will be using this new location as our new main office. The owner was forced to sell when he owed too much money. We got this place for a steal. Great timing, too. Too many cops sniffing around the old one. A lot of them are on our payroll, but plenty still think they can change and make a difference. Fucking pricks.

After compiling a list of names of people who owe us money, I send it to Dante. As our enforcer, it's his job to ensure we get those payments. It's also his job to take care of it if they can't pay us back.

In the evening, I finish a late dinner at one of the restaurants that pays us for our protection. I expected confirmation from Rafaele about the job by now. I've been checking my phone every ten minutes for the last hour. Nothing.

## Chapter Four

### NATALIE

The week has gone by in a blur. Between class and studying, I barely have time to breathe. But Maya has plans for my birthday Saturday evening, and I'm ready to let loose. I wonder what trouble we'll get into this year. I wouldn't put it past her to have new ideas. It's Thursday, so I came into Ming's. I walk in and freeze at the sight.

"Surprise!" a number of voices yell.

Ming stands with the staff and has a giant cake with sparkler candles going off. They sing, "Happy Birthday" to me, and I blow out the candles. I look at the beautifully decorated cake and wish for more out of life.

I'd have to unpack that later.

I stick around, catching up with the staff who watched me grow up, but I don't eat anything. I wasn't in the mood for Chinese, but not going in on my usual day just didn't feel right.

"How's the birthday girl doing?" Ming asks, coming out from the back.

"I'm good, Ming. You really didn't have to do all that, but I'm so touched," I say, pulling him into a bear hug, even though he's more bearlike than I am.

He wraps his big arms around me. "Nonsense. You come here so much you practically pay the bills. Do you have any fun plans this weekend?"

*Hopefully meeting a handsome stranger and having hot birthday sex.* It's time. I had ended things with this guy I'd been seeing six months ago after he expressed his feelings of wanting more. However, I need this dry spell to end, and hopefully, this is the weekend.

Cutting myself out of my thoughts, I say, "Maya is taking me out Saturday night. She has a whole day planned for us."

"That makes me nervous."

"You and me both." I laugh.

Maya was trouble—a good time but trouble.

"But she assured me it'd be low-key. Spa day and dinner with her and Donna, then a club where Dom will meet us. She said she's getting too old." I rolled my eyes.

We were just heading into our prime, for crying out loud!

"Well, I hope you meet a nice man soon so you can settle down and stop getting into trouble. You're too smart to get involved in all that nonsense."

"I don't need a man, Ming. Besides, something tells me, man or no man, trouble will always find me," I joke.

I thought I heard him say "you have no idea," but it's so quiet that maybe it was all in my head.

"Anyway, I'm exhausted, and I have a long day tomorrow, so I'll see you next week. Thanks for the cake," I say as I get up and grab my purse.

"You, too. Happy birthday, *Natalie*."

He's always said my name like it was foreign on his tongue or from some inside joke I wasn't in on.

After hailing a taxi, one comes out of nowhere. Thank God. I'm so tired I could fall asleep standing.

The taxi driver rolls in the wrong direction before I can give him my address, so I blurt it out. He doesn't listen.

"Hey, I said my address is the other way."

Unease settled in my stomach.

He doesn't respond. Just as I'm about to poke his shoulder, he floors the gas and makes a sharp right turn, whipping me back into the seat.

"What the hell are you doing?" I yell. "Let me out right now!"

He swerves through traffic and makes another sharp right turn, then slams on his brakes.

We're in an empty alley. Shit.

Tires screech, and I look for the source. Two black SUVs with tinted windows pull up. Chills covered my body. They found me.

My ears grow foggy, as they always do, when a wave of adrenaline rushes over me. But something new takes over, too. My mind flips a switch. Everything slows as the sound drowns out. I tap my smart watch to alert Dom that something is wrong.

He had a panic button installed on my watch and phone in case of an emergency.

I snatch my Beretta out of my purse. I usually don't carry weapons on me, but with the attacks going on, Dom said I need to protect myself. Thank God I listened to him this time.

Without thinking twice, I aim and shoot the driver in the head as the door to the back seat opens. I turn to my right, kick the guy in the face as he reaches for me, and shoot him in the forehead, too.

The door behind me opens, and the third man grabs me by my hair, dragging me out. I let him pull me out of the car so that I could swing my elbow back into him then slam my head back into his. I had to act fast and get him down—if he learns I can actually defend myself, he'll put his defenses up. That's the one thing a lot of men do. They underestimate women, but I'm not mad. I'd use it to my advantage.

As I try getting away, something slams into my head. Next thing I know, strong arms are around me. Fuck. Now I see why Papa and Dom insisted Donna and I take on combat training. I need to make sure he doesn't get the upper hand, or I'm screwed.

When I pretend to give up, he relaxes. Idiot. As he does, I use his arms to pull my legs up with all my core strength and wrap them around his head. I use his own momentum to flip him and slam him to the ground. He wasn't expecting that. Good. I can practically see the birds chirping around his head as he's taking in what happened. Before he can gain any composure, I shoot him right in between his eyes.

I scan the alley, pointing my gun out, looking around for more men.

"Only three?" I say to myself as I roll my eyes, of course.

They assumed I'd be an easy target. Papa made sure people knew little of my existence. No one knew I was an expert shooter and fighter. Not that I've had a real opponent until now. As annoyed as I am that they underestimated me, I am grateful because, with any more men, I would've been fucked.

Looking at the dead bodies in front of me, I examine my damage. The adrenaline has my hands shaking as I take photos of their license plates. My phone rings—Dom. I tap the answer button.

"Fucking shit, Nat. I've been worried out of my goddamn mind. What the fuck happened? I'm on my way to your location now."

"Sorry," I say, catching my breath. "I think I'm in shock. I didn't hear my phone. I was leaving Ming's and got into a taxi, and two other SUVs showed up, and they tried to—"

"FUCK!" he screams into the phone, causing me to pull it away. "What did they say? What did they want? Do they know who you are?"

"The hell, Dom. Do you think we just sat around in a circle trading each other's secrets while painting each other's fingernails? I didn't ask questions. Shoot first, remember?" I rub the sore spot on my head.

Seriously, what did he hit me with?

"You killed them?" He sounds impressed. It never failed to amaze me at how quickly he could calm down.

"There were only three." I sigh, scanning bodies again as if expecting they'd come back to life.

"I'm proud of you, but this isn't good. Who were they?"

"First of all, are you coming to get me? Because I have no idea if there's more of them lurking around, and I'd rather not be here when the cops show up. You don't seem worried or in a hurry at all. Second, I'm sending you photos of their plates."

He laughs. "I'll be there in two minutes. I'll have the clean-up crew come deal with them."

"No," I blurt. "I want whoever sent them to find the bodies."

"Ice Queen," he replies.

At the time, I didn't realize how true his words really rang.

I take a deep breath. "I've never actually had to kill for real before, Dom."

"Fuck, I know." He sounds regretful. "I have your location pulled up. I'm a minute out. You're lucky I came back early. Fuck. You're lucky."

The fog I was just in lifts as Dom pulls into the alley. He's mad again. So much for calming down. He stares at the photos I'd sent him as I put on my seatbelt. He runs it through some software he had our hacker and his best friend, Franco, develop.

"Fucking hell." He hits the steering wheeling.

"They found me, didn't they?"

I didn't even want to say the name. Having grown up with the mafia, I know Papa wanted to keep as much of this world away from me as possible. He told me only what I needed to know and made sure I could fight off any potential attackers, but that was it. Of course some things slipped through.

*Rise Of An Heiress*

"Triad?" he asks, looking at me cautiously. He pauses before looking back at his phone. "Not sure I sent the images over to Franco."

"They don't look like they could be Triad, unless they were hired. Could be Russian or Italian, but I didn't get a good look," I say as I run my hands through my hair.

"Plates come up blank. If it's not them, the only other people it could be is the Cosa Nostra. It's possible they know you're in New York."

"What do you mean, they know I'm in New York? I grew up here."

"Yes, but you grew up as *Natalie*."

He didn't need to elaborate. Dread fills me.

"What would the Cosa Nostra want from me? I thought there's been peace for decades now? That's why it was safe to bring me here," I press.

"It was until now, apparently. Maybe the Triad hired them. Rumor has it they're low on manpower right now," Dom replies with a sigh as he drives us to my penthouse.

"What could they want from me? I was just a kid back then. I'm nothing now."

"That's the million-dollar question."

Before my parents died, they were part of the Triad, a secret Chinese society heavily powered by organized crime, going back thousands of years—according to the legends. The Triad still rules most of Asia, but the U.S. sanction broke off to be independent seventy years ago. At one point, they were known for having the best stock in illegal or banned firearms. They also produced the best assassins. I'm not too sure on what they do now, but over the years, word got around they aren't as strong.

I didn't grow up around the Triad, so the Cosa Nostra could use me as bait. Papa changed my name when I was little so I could grow up with a normal life, apart from this world. My mother was ruled a traitor, but I had no other connections to the Triad, so getting a hold of me would be useless.

As I settle into my penthouse, Dom heads into my office to make a few calls. I knew it would be awhile, so I pour wine and take a bath. Dom is getting ready to leave as I enter the living room.

"You heading out?" I ask him.

"Yeah." He nods. "I'm just waiting for Matteo and Tony to get here," he says as he fixes his jacket.

"How did they get here so fast?"

Matteo and I've had a noncommittal *thing* for the past few years. We live in different states, so it was just whenever we'd see each other on holidays. He doesn't have much going on upstairs, but he sure knows to use what's beneath the belt.

"They've been here the whole time, just out of sight. I can't come to the city alone. That would be suicidal. I'll have them stay with you, and we're setting up more security in your penthouse, so we know exactly who enters and exits the building. You'll be safe."

"Thank you." I walk up to him and wrap my arms around him.

# Rise Of An Heiress

He takes a deep breath as we stand in silence. "Sempre, sorellina." *Always, little sister.* Papa made sure I was fluent in Italian.

Just then, there's a knock at the door. Dom looks into the peephole before opening the door. Matteo and Tony walk in, clad in their signature black-on-black ensemble, decorated with their tattoos all over their muscles. Matteo winks at me, and Dom and I roll our eyes. Tony nods, always all business.

"Tony, I want you up here guarding her door. Matteo, downstairs in the lobby."

Tony agrees, while Matteo smirks. I try to hold back a laugh. Dom knew about Matteo and me, and he didn't like it one bit.

"All right, I'm out, Sis." He kisses my forehead and turns to his men. "Matteo, Tony, we've got some guys coming in tonight to relieve you from your shifts in the morning. Until then, don't move and don't let anything happen to Nat, or I'll have both your balls nailed to the back of a semi with you still attached."

## NATALIE

"I'm sorry, what?"

Maya nearly falls out of her chair as I tell her what happened at lunch.

Well—I may have left out the part where they were mobsters and just told her it was a mugging and that there was only one of them, not three. I would rather say nothing, but I can't not explain the extra security detail following me around. I also don't mention the bodies I left behind . . . allegedly. So many lies.

"If you're too shaken up, we don't have to go out tomorrow." She grabs my arm.

I look over at her. As always, she's in a colorful ensemble with bright lipstick.

She probably thinks I'm freaking out after I don't answer her right away. I was shocked when it first happened. But I don't feel bad about it, and that's what has me twisted in knots. The blood lust. It's addicting. I *liked* killing those men. Not only did I feel strong, I felt a high. I felt more in control of myself than I ever had in my entire life. Sometimes, I wonder what I'd be like if I didn't have to bury that part of myself.

I shake myself out of my own thoughts before Maya panics.

"No way," I say casually. "After the week I've had, I need to get out more than ever. And I need to get drunk."

"Oh, good," she says, clapping, "but only if you're sure! Seriously, I wouldn't be mad if you'd rather stay in." In the same breath, she follows with, "We should totally pregame tonight."

I laugh, shaking my head. "I don't think that's how pregaming works, Maya."

"Sure it does," she says with a wink.

"Well, either way, I can't. Donna and Cesare are flying in today, so I'm having dinner with all of them."

"I think it's so amazing that Cesare takes care of you as if you were his own daughter."

She doesn't know the irony of that statement. She knew I wasn't close with my adoptive parents, who she thought were my real parents. They're good people. They've just been through some trauma.

## Rise Of An Heiress

"The conference starts next week. Are you excited?" I ask, eager to change the subject.

It works like a charm. She doesn't pry any further and goes off about the upcoming conference Columbia was hosting, for which she was on the board. She knew I didn't like talking about my family. Not that it was bad—it was just hard to keep a story straight if she knew too much, and she definitely couldn't know the truth.

\* \* \*

Later in the evening, I'm with Donna in the penthouse suite at the hotel she, Dom, and Papa are staying at. We're rewatching our guilty pleasure, Gossip Girl, a show we could recite by heart.

Dom and Papa have been chatting in the office for what feels like hours, and I can't help but feel like the other shoe is about to drop. Some sort of doom is coming. I'm trying to stay positive, at least for my birthday. Everyone came out for it.

"You want to know what the most unrealistic part of this show is?" Donna asks as she shovels popcorn into her mouth.

"Do tell," I respond.

Neither of us bother to look away from the screen.

"Not one mafia storyline. I'm genuinely surprised the mob never made an appearance in any episodes with these egotistical billionaire types—you know how many of those people Papa has in his back pocket. You expect me to believe Serena didn't once get tangled up with one?" Donna huffs.

I laugh at her assessment. We spend the afternoon catching up on life. We haven't stopped talking since they got off the plane this afternoon. It's good to have Donna around. It's nice to just be myself.

I never had that with my adoptive parents. They were kind, never abused me, but there was always the giant elephant in the room. So, when I was eighteen, I moved out. I didn't see the point of staying; we weren't a family, and their job was to keep me safe until I was an adult. We still talk now and then, but I'd never actually be *their* Natalie.

Just as I was taking a trip down memory lane, someone knocks and opens Donna's door, breaking my train of thought. Ronnie, Papa's right-hand man, comes in.

"Natalie, the boss would like a word with you."

Donna and I look at each other.

"Don't worry, it's probably just your birthday present!" She pushes me off the couch with an encouraging smile.

I nod and head into the office. The sinking feeling is back.

When I walk in, I find Cesare sitting at the desk and Dom sitting on the edge. Definitely not my present. By looking at their expressions, I have a feeling my life would change. I stop at the door, too afraid to step farther.

Papa gestures to the seat in front of him and Dom. "Mia dolce bambina, please sit."

Suddenly, I'm taken back to the moment Papa told a six-year-old me he was sending me away.

Dom looks angry, which wasn't new. But he also looks anxious. That's what worries me.

"What's going on?" I ask as I sit.

Papa knows I hate beating around the bush. As if he could read my mind, he spoke again.

"So direct and to the point." He laughs.

His eyes wrinkle around the corners, emphasizing his age. He's always been the big, scary, handsome protector. Don't get me wrong—he still is, but the years are showing on him now. In my mind, I still see a man in his early thirties, not fifties. Dom sighs and rubs his face. I look at him and back at Papa, waiting for someone to speak.

"What do you remember about your mother, amore?"

That was another thing. He's never addressed me as Natalie, not once in almost twenty years.

"She was beautiful. Always laughing. She called me princess. And you two were in love. She was a traitor for marrying you, which is why I can't go back and had to change my name," I say.

"Yes, we were in love," he said, smiling as if he were recalling a memory. "And a princess, you are." He pauses. "It's time you learned the truth. The whole story."

"Whole story?"

"It is no secret that your mother and father's marriage was arranged and so was mine to Luciana's."

Dom and Donna's mother.

"What does this have to do with me?" I work on keeping my heart rate down.

"When your father died, it is true that your mother and I got married because we were in love, but we also got married for tactical reasons. Otherwise, the Outfit wouldn't have allowed it. We wanted to give you your best chance."

"My best chance?"

"Because of who you are." He pauses. When I don't respond, he continues. "Your father was Peter Liu."

My mouth goes dry, and my heart rate jolts. I knew that my birth parents were part of the Triad, but I didn't realize my parents *were* the Triad. King and Queen. Peter Liu was the dragon head of the U.S. Triad. He was also known as "The Mad Dragon" because of his sick and twisted mind games. He was a patient man. Could play the long game. A true master at psychological warfare. I didn't know much of that world, but Peter Liu was infamous. Everyone knew who—what Peter Liu was in the underworld.

"You said my father's name was—"

"I lied," Papa says.

*I'm a Liu? What the hell . . . This whole time, I thought my real last name was Cheng.*

"So, if my father was the head of the Triad, then that would make me . . . ?"

"The heiress," Papa replies. "Your mother was not a traitor. That's not why they want you dead. I lied about who you were to protect you. The less you knew, the better, but before Peter died, he knew he wanted you to be his heir."

Now that's a surprise.

"He didn't care for a boy after you were born. The moment he held you in his arms, he knew you were special," Papa says, smiling fondly. "Your mother agreed, so after he died, she intended to honor his wish. But you both needed protection—not everyone in the Triad was supportive of a woman becoming the boss. We got married, and the Triad and Outfit formed an alliance. Our main concern was that you were protected at all times so that you could, one day, take your father's place. But then she got sick."

Grief falls over his face before he snaps out of it.

"And things changed," I say, void of emotion.

"Yes. When she died, her brother, your uncle Andrew Li, took it as his chance to take over since Peter had no siblings and no other living relatives. Andrew put out an order for your assassination. He hired the Bratva to do it, so it wouldn't get back to us, who was responsible. One of our moles, of course, informed me, so I came up with a plan to let Andrew believe he succeeded."

*He hired the Russian mafia?*

All the pieces were falling into place, all the answers to the questions I've been too afraid to ask. He always said growing up in the Outfit would have been too dangerous for me, but this made more sense. It's why he sent me away, why I had to change my name, and why I wasn't allowed back in Chicago. But everything I knew was a lie to cover up an even bigger lie.

"That's why you sent me to live in New York?"

"Yes." He nods.

"So, why are you telling me all of this now?"

"We believe the Cosa Nostra has connected the dots on your identity since Dominic has arrived in town."

"But he's been here hundreds of times?" I asked.

"I have word that they believe the attack on their docks a few weeks ago was us."

"Okay, but that doesn't answer what they want from me. Should you even be here, Papa?"

Dom finally spoke up. "They don't know he is here. Only me. And we don't know what they want yet, but we're looking into it. My guess is, they think if they get their hands on you, they can use you as leverage with the Triad, so they can form their own alliance. The Triad is weak right now. They're bleeding money and owe a lot of favors. The only thing keeping them afloat was their black-market weapons. If the Cosa Nostra can catch them, they can take over their territories and the trade of illegal arms."

"You think they want to take over the drugs and weapons trade?"

"Those drugs and weapons get shipped worldwide. The Cosa Nostra own most of the harbors. They want to take over internationally," Cesare answered.

"The Triad has deep connections in New York and Chicago; it would be a smart move on their part." Dom added.

"So, what happens next?" I ask.

Papa pulls out a folder from the desk drawer. "Nothing yet. But you need to be vigilant." He places four images on the desk. "You need to memorize their names and faces."

"Why can't you just email this to me?" I ask, looking over the images.

"Because of this guy." Dom points at the third image in the row.

My eyes practically fall out of my head.

The text under it says *Niccolo 'Nico' Delucci—consigliere.*

## Rise Of An Heiress

My heart does this pitter patter thing. *What the hell. It's Mr. Tall and Mysterious from the café.*

Fuck. I've heard the name, but I had never paid the Deluccis any mind. A simple Google search would've saved me a lot of trouble. Everyone in NYC—hell, the East Coast knows who they are. To the outside world, the Deluccis are multi-billionaire business owners. To the underworld, they are the Cosa Nostra, one of the most powerful Italian crime syndicates in the nation.

They have complete control of the East Coast. It was easy for them to attain, considering they owned all the docks on this side of the states—at least, that was their legal cover. They also owned most of the clubs and had a solid grip on the construction industry. If the Cosa Nostra didn't own it, someone was paying them for their protection. If you wanted anything in or out, you'd have to go through them. While they have several enemies, only an idiot would go against them. Even Dom—most of the time, when he'd come to visit me—would use the business as a guise, so he wouldn't raise suspicions. It was too risky to fly under the radar all the time.

He's the "consigliere" of the Cosa Nostra, the advisor—meaning, he's the brains.

I study the image. It's obviously an older one from a few years ago. I can see it in his face, and the tattoos don't quite go up his neck just yet. He's still handsome. His whole family is. No wonder they're always being written about. I shake my head to stop myself. *Snap out of it. He's the enemy.*

"He's also one of the best hackers out there and probably the one that ordered the grab on you."

*Fan-fucking-tastic.* Something is definitely wrong with me. Telling them about my encounter with him won't make a difference and will only set Dom off.

Papa points to the first image. "Giuseppe Delucci, he just stepped down, and now, his eldest"—he points to the second image—"has taken over as capo."

The name under it read, "Sebastiano 'Bash' Delucci."

"This is Dante Borelli, their enforcer."

I take in the images. Luckily, I have an excellent memory; it doesn't hurt that they're attractive. *Jesus, I'm going to get myself killed.*

As I'm taking all of the information in, a thought occurs to me, and my heart feels like it's going to split. My adoptive dad, while kind, didn't love me, and the only other dad I've known is Cesare.

"You were only raising me to take over the Triad?" I look at him.

"No," he says firmly. "If I had it my way, I would've kept it from you forever. But I knew I couldn't rob you of your birth right. My plan was to tell you after you graduated. I wanted to give you the tools so you have the choice. If you want to claim the Triad, I know for a fact there are still Triad members who are loyal to the rightful heir and that the Outfit will also stand by you. The choice is yours, bambina. But I will tell you, there's not much of an option anymore if they know who you are."

"What do you mean?"

"If they know you exist, Andrew will stop at nothing to make sure you're dead. You either die or you take over," Dom answers.

"How do I know they won't kill me when I take over?"

"You don't." They answer at the same time.

*Well, that's lovely.*

"And if I don't want to be the dragon head and just want a normal life?"

Papa answers this time. "He won't let this go. You're a loose end."

Dom walks me out of the room as I'm still processing. Once we're outside of Donna's door, he stops and grabs my shoulders.

"We won't let anything happen to you. We'll be there for you. *I'll* be there for you." I nod and look into his eyes.

"Sempre," I whisper.

He pulls me into a hug. A real hug. We stand in silence before I join Donna.

The rest of the evening has me reeling over this new information about my life. Everything I know is a lie. I thought my dad was just a soldier and that I'd been put into hiding because my mother was a traitor. I knew Papa had a reputation, but I'm really starting to see the extent of his true colors. I wasn't angry; I know he did all of this to protect me.

What kind of fucked up situation is this? Was I really going to have to take over? If I choose to walk away, what would I do then? Change my name and move again? Would I have to cut all ties from my family? I shoot down the idea the moment it crosses my mind. Absolutely no way am I leaving my family behind. Papa and Dom are right. I don't have a choice.

This isn't something I can run from anymore.

I have to kill Andrew Li and take over or die. The question is how?

# Chapter Five

NICO

Three dead bodies.

Three dead bodies, all with a single bullet hole in each.

Who is this woman?

"I'm going to fucking kill her," I say, scanning the scene.

I'm standing over three fucking dead bodies. Luckily, the cops are on our payroll, so they clear out fast enough.

"I want to see the security footage," I demand, knowing the cameras are disabled.

Being so fucking pissed, I'm in the mood to be a dick, so I'm going to be unreasonable. Did I mention the three dead bodies?

"Pulling up the footage now," Dante replies, typing on his laptop in hand.

"Wait, no one disabled the cameras?" I ask.

"They fucked up. Idiots. No wonder she took them down so easily."

"She did?"

I know it was her, but still not willing to accept it.

"Take a look." Dante hands me the laptop.

I pull up grainy video footage. It looks like the taxi pulled up to the SUV, as planned. Idiots—how hard is it to follow simple instructions? I practically spoon-fed them this mission. I'm glad she took them out.

I watch the screen, mesmerized by her speed and grace. She shoots Joe, who was in the driver's seat, before Mario and Rafaele get to the car. Damn, she's fast. She shoots Mario right in the forehead as he opens the door—no hesitation. I can't help but be impressed. Rafaele drags her out of the car, and she manages to get the upper hand and takes off. He throws his shoe at her. His fucking shoe. I take a deep breath as I watch this embarrassing encounter continue. As he goes to grab her, she uses her whole body and knocks him on his back, shooting him in the forehead. Damn. For a tiny thing, she's got some fight in her. She took them out in four minutes flat. And she knows how to use a gun. *Rein it in, Nico. She just killed three of your men. Why are you complimenting her?*

I pinch the bridge of my nose. Those fucking ass heads. I'm only glad she killed them, so I don't have to waste time and energy doing it myself.

"She's feisty. A pint-sized goddess of destruction," Dante says admirably, looking over my shoulder.

I look over at him. His eyes are glazed with lust. I don't like it one bit.

"She could be an assassin. That would explain the money," Dante suggests.

*Fuck, this is the last thing I need.*

"At this point, I wouldn't rule out anything. She's clearly well trained, and we can't make a mistake like that again," I say as I take in the scene again. "We'll keep surveilling her until we know more." I shove the laptop back at Dante and storm off. "Delete any evidence of this and clear up the bodies." I head to my car and start the engine.

"Done," Dante says.

## NATALIE

"Okay, wow . . . I think I look hot?" I say, gazing at myself with my hands on my hips.

Swiveling, I check out my attire in my floor-to-ceiling mirror in my closet.

"Holy fuck. Nat. I wish I had your legs," Donna says as she stands next to me, applying her mascara.

Even after all these years, my name didn't sound right coming out of Donna's mouth. I can't help but roll my eyes because Donna, much like Maya, is one of the most beautiful women I'd ever seen.

Like Dom, she's tall, blonde, but has gentler features and literally looks like an angel. Especially tonight. She is wearing a skin-tight, white, strapless jumpsuit that left little to the imagination, with feathers etched across the top, and killer white stilettos.

"Donna, you're like eight inches taller than me?" I look at her like she's crazy.

"I should have never stopped training."

Catching her slip up, we pause, locking eyes with each other in the mirror. Thankfully, Maya didn't pick anything up and quickly interrupts our silence when she pokes her head into my closet. She straightened her hair tonight, so we know she's serious.

"You do not *think* anything. Natalie, you *do* look hot. And welcome!" she says as I roll my eyes.

Not only is she my best friend, intelligent and gorgeous, but she has a talent for hair and makeup, with the best fashion sense. She also looks amazing tonight in her more colorful attire, compared to Donna and me. Maya is in a very short puff-sleeved orange-and-fuchsia dress that ties at the waist with a plunging neckline and stunning lime green stilettos that would no doubt cause a riot.

"Shots!" Maya yells like she can't contain herself anymore, running to the kitchen.

"Yes!" Donna calls out, following her.

"I'll take one!" I yell back, fixing my lipstick.

As Maya and Donna make themselves comfortable in my kitchen, I look back at myself in the mirror. I'm wearing a champagne minidress that could pass as a shirt covered in Swarovski crystals. It falls mid-thigh, just under my butt. It has thin straps and a deep neckline and falls loosely around my body, but it's slightly see-through so you can still see my curves. I have a lace bustier and tiny matching shorts that might as well be underwear. I choose sky-high nude strappy pumps. At five foot even, I need all the height I can get. I remind myself that I'm a normal twenty-something, not some psycho who had just murdered three grown men. Donna hands me my shot and a lime from over my shoulder. The three of us stand in front of the mirror, laughing.

"Cheers to twenty-five years!" Maya exclaims, raising her shot in the air.

Donna follows suit. "Buon compleanno, bella!" *Happy birthday, beautiful!*

We clink our glasses and throw our shots back.

## NATALIE

We pull up to one of the hottest clubs in the city, The KA.RA just half-past eleven p.m. After two more shots of tequila, I feel buzzed.

"Okay, so Dom got us a table in VIP. It's all under my name, so we're all set," Maya says, walking backward but facing us.

We head straight to the doors, ignoring the line.

"Wait, I thought you planned this?" I ask.

"I did. But I made him pay for it, duh!" she says, nudging my shoulder. "Besides, I knew if I brought it up, he'd pay for everything." She smirks.

"Where is our idiot brother, anyway?" Donna asks, looking around.

"He'll be here later," I respond as Maya talks to the bouncer.

A stunning brunette hostess with the biggest boobs I've ever seen leads us up the spiral stairs. The club is live tonight. Colorful lights stream around the room as the DJ blasts music. Our bottle service girl introduces herself to us and pours three glasses of champagne, then opens a bottle of tequila for us.

I'm going to regret this in the morning.

I look around and find Matteo and Tony already in the VIP section, who are standing at either exit just in case something happens.

"Oh, I'll be right back. I told Max I'd meet her," Maya yells into my ear, getting up.

Max's name is Meixiang. She's a Chinese-international student who's finishing her PhD in Chemistry. She's currently looking for a job to become a pharmaceutical scientist so she can stay in the states under a work visa. She's a literal genius.

"Tell her she can join us!" I yell back.

"I will, but it's not really her scene!" Maya runs off.

"Let's dance when Maya gets back!" Donna yells as she pours us each another glass.

Two men approach. One looks like he had just graduated high school, while the other wouldn't even make eye contact with us. The younger-looking one opens his mouth, but before he could utter anything, Donna shoots him the death glare from hell, and they both scramble.

We would eat them alive. How did they even get up here? As they make their escape, Maya appears.

"You're totally getting laid tonight," Maya yells over the music. "You look so hot!"

## Rise Of An Heiress

"Oh, yes, please. Let's find some hot, delicious men whose lives we can ruin." Donna claps.

We finish our champagne and shimmy to the dance floor. As we head down the spiral staircase, Maya hands me a small bag of pills.

"Where did you get these?" I ask, surprised—though I really shouldn't be.

This *is* Maya.

"Max! She's been making her own special concoction of shit to earn some extra cash," Maya replies before popping a pill in her mouth.

"No thanks!" I hand her back the bag, remembering the conversation I'd had with Papa and Dom earlier.

I don't have any qualms with drugs, but I can't risk it at a time like this.

"Suit yourself," Maya says as she shoves the bag into her clutch. "I can't believe she hasn't snatched up a job yet."

"I don't think you can stroll in and be like, 'Hey, guys, I have this drug that could be borderline lethal, definitely illegal, but it makes you feel good. Trust me—I've tested it on all my friends! Hire me,'" I reply sarcastically, and Maya huffs into a laughing fit.

As we make our way to the dance floor, a group of men with a table pull us in. Bachelor party. The guys are wasted but a total ball to be with. They offer us shots, and we clink glasses to congratulate the groom. They have a bachelor weekend bucket list, and one of the items is to convince a woman to flash them. Maya, of course, takes them up on the offer. As the group is mingling, I feel a set of eyes on me. I look over to my right, and a very tall handsome man is walking my way. As he gets close to me, I realize who he is.

"Hi," he says, nodding.

"Hi," I say back.

Brushing hair behind my ear, I pretend to be shy, taking in his features. He's tall, tan, and lean. His long dark hair is pushed back, and he has a gorgeous set of hazel eyes. I'm looking for any visible weapons, but he probably thinks I'm just checking him out. I want to laugh. Men always underestimate women. I can't let him know I recognize him.

"Dante," he says as he sticks his hand out. "Can I get you something to drink?"

The enforcer for the Cosa Nostra. This can't be one of their clubs, can it?

Maya's eyes widen from behind him as she mouths, "He's cute!"

Looking away from her, I stifle a laugh to glance back at him and take his hand. "Natalie."

He then looks around and back at me. "I'm sorry, but I have to go."

"What was that about?" Donna asks as he walks away.

"No idea," I reply as we look in the direction he jets toward.

# NICO

*Dante: Spotted.*

    *Me: What?*

    *Dante: My future wife.*

# Rise Of An Heiress

Dante sends an attachment with the last text message. It's an image of the dark-haired menace herself in the flesh.

*What the fuck, she's at our club? And what the fuck does he mean his future wife?* Another unjustified wave of jealousy courses through me. I leave my office to head to the VIP section so I can see for myself.

Looking at one of the tables, I see *Happy Birthday, Natalie!* written on the plaque we have for our guests to spend a certain amount of money. *How did I miss this?*

I call over the hostess.

When she arrives, I order, "Let me see a list of the reservations for tonight."

She unlocks her tablet without question. Swiping through, I recognize one of the names. The reservation is under her supermodel-looking friend's name: Maya Villanueva.

After walking to the railing, I look down and spot Dante talking to our mystery woman. Just as I'm about to threaten him, Bash comes over on our head piece. Thank God because I wasn't sure what I was going to say. I just knew I didn't like him talking to her.

"Dante. You're needed in the basement," Bash says.

He doesn't need to explain further. He was capo, and when he says *jump*, you don't ask *how high*—you're supposed to just know. This usually means there's either someone who needs to be taken care of or they're already dead, and their body needs to be taken care of.

## Natalie

I'm not sure how long we dance. The music is just right, and I'm having the best time. An attractive man has his arms wrapped around Maya as they "dance" on each other. If I'm not *Auntie* Natalie in nine months, I'd be shocked. Donna knows better than to let anyone touch her while Matteo and Tony are present. Plus, Dom could show up at any moment if he isn't already acting as security from VIP. I dance with a few guys, but I send them off when they get too handsy. In the distance, Tony and Matteo look eager to step in, hands on their concealed guns.

So dramatic.

After having a few drinks on the dance floor, I have to use the restroom. I point back upstairs at the girls, and they nod and join me. We head back up to our table in VIP, where Dom is waiting. He hugs me, picking me up in one of his big bear hugs.

"Happy birthday, sorellina," he yells as he spins me.

"Thank you!" I say, stumbling as he sets me down.

Women glare at me and ogle my brother from out of the corner of my eye.

"Are you having a good time?" he asks.

"Yes, I'm having so much fun!"

"Drink all of it," he orders as he pours a glass for Donna and Maya.

Thirsty—although not drunk—I down the glass. I need to slow down. I don't want to lose too much control.

Dom, Maya, and Donna hug and fall into easy conversation. They pour more drinks as I excuse myself to go to the restroom.

## Rise Of An Heiress

There's never a line in the VIP restrooms, and for that, I'm thankful.

I wash my hands, then check my phone, responding to some happy birthday texts. As I exit the restroom, I relax after this week's revelations but then I feel a shift in the air. I halt. A chill whisks through the hallway, alerting the hairs on the back of my neck. I look up from my phone and lock eyes with *him*.

Nico Delucci is standing, tall and sexy as sin, in the dim hallway, leaning against the wall. I should've left the minute I saw their enforcer.

I'm able to get a better look at him this time. Older than the photo, short facial hair that made him even sexier. He's also bigger now, if that is possible. If only this man wasn't trying to kill me. He stands proud, clad in a gray suit and a white button-up that hugs him in all the right places—that also does nothing to hide his protruding muscles. If he flexes, he'll rip his whole wardrobe off.

Admiring his ink, I scan his arms and neck. I'm sure ink covers his torso, too. I lick and bite my lips. *Fuck, I hope he didn't notice.* I make eye contact with him. *Shit, he totally noticed.*

What should I do? Don't panic, for starters. Do what you always do. Pretend to not know anything. I throw on my best smile—if there's anything I'm good at, it's a poker face.

"Excuse me," I say, scooting past him.

He doesn't budge.

Brushing him as I pass definitely helps.

I look up at him, and he just looks me up and down. Twice.

What is he, six-foot-four? I'm maybe five-four in these heels.

Lust is blown in his eyes. Or maybe desire—the desire to kill me.

Fuck. I killed three of his men. Of course he wants to kill me. Now he's here to personally do the job he'd sent them to do.

# Chapter Six

## NICO

*D*oes *she not know who I am?* I've seen her twice now, and she hasn't reacted. Her face doesn't scream panic; it's screaming for me to take her. Make her mine.

Fuck. I only meant to watch her tonight. To see her in person. But that dress. That sad excuse of a dress. I saw Dominic arrive, and he just had his hands on her. He must not know the Cosa Nostra just took over The KA.RA; otherwise, they wouldn't be here. Regardless, I can't stay away from her.

I take in her whole body. Twice. Our eyes meet, and she's caught me checking her out. Oh well. She did it first. Possessive rage boils inside me, seeing her out in a dress like this. I didn't want anyone else looking at her, especially Violante. I couldn't keep my eyes off her from the moment I saw Dante with her. Neither could every other douchebag in the club. Although trying not to smash every man's skull into the wall who talked to her or even looked at her, I realize I have no right to feel this way, and I hate her for it.

When I saw her talking to Dante after I told him not to, I really thought I was going to shoot my best friend. I told myself it was because he could've compromised everything, but I knew that was a lie. I could kill her right now. Girls go missing from clubs all the time.

She tries to get past me, but I don't move. She's blushing. Fuck if that wasn't cute. She either really has no clue as to who I am and wants me, or she's one hell of an actress. She could be an assassin. I should let her go, but I can't.

"You're the girl from the coffee shop. What brings you out here tonight?"

She smiles. Christ. That fucking dimple.

"I'm surprised you remembered. It's my birthday," she says sweetly.

I'm almost convinced she's as innocent as she looks. *Damn, she's good.*

Bending forward, I grab her right hand into mine. She gasps as electricity jolts my body. I wonder what she sounds like when she's gasping for other reasons. I know she feels it, too. Her chest heaves, but I force my eyes to stay on hers.

"You're not easy to forget." I bring her hand up to my lips and kiss the top of it. "Happy birthday." I bring her hand back down but don't let go.

She doesn't pull away, either.

God, she smells good. It's intoxicating. She smells like a sexy mixture of amaretto crème, cherries, something floral, and her own intoxicating scent that is just hers and hers alone.

"Thank you," she replies breathlessly before biting her bottom lip and taking in a deep breath, but she doesn't break eye contact.

Moving toward her, I give her a chance to back away, but she doesn't move. She stiffens her spine as she looks up at me. *Is she fucking with me?*

"You're so beautiful."

I catch myself leaning into her. Fuck. This is a mistake. But all I can think about is how badly I want to kiss her.

Before I know it, that's exactly what I'm doing. She doesn't push me off, but she doesn't kiss me back, not right away. Placing a hand behind her neck and one on her back, I pull her to me, deepening the kiss.

Finally, she opens for me, and I let my tongue explore her mouth. She tastes amazing. Now I'm wondering where else she could possibly taste good. My cock strains through my pants.

Her body relaxes as her arms come up to run her fingers through my hair, and I forget all thoughts of who she is or why I'm here with her. I back her into the speakeasy we use for storage behind us. To my displeasure, she tenses and pulls away. For a second, she looks like she's about to bolt but then she looks around. I keep my arms firmly around her.

"How did you know this was back here?" she asks, breathless.

And fuck if that didn't make me want her more.

"I own this club," I reply, not taking my eyes off of her as she takes in the room.

I'm still cautious of her. I don't know if this is an act and she's going to pounce at any moment. She's still holding onto my biceps, and I can't help but smile.

She looks back at me and tilts her head to the side, surprise etched on her face. Maybe she really doesn't know who I am. I'm too turned on to think. My cock was going to get me killed one day. I pull her into me, not wanting any more distance between us, and force my mouth back onto hers, harder this time. She moans into my mouth as she kisses me, small hands running through my hair. I walk her back into the wall and move my hands just under her ass to pick her up. She immediately wraps her legs around me. Her body feels good against mine, like she was made for me.

She glides her hands across my back, neck, and chest. I know she is wet. All I had to do was reach down. After snaking my hand up her back, I grab a fistful of her hair, giving me access to her neck. With my other hand, I massage her breasts over her dress, and she moans as I kiss a trail down her neck, taking in her scent. I pull away to look into her eyes. Lust. I move my hands down her body slowly, giving her a chance to stop me. She grinds her hips into mine, and I take that as approval to keep going.

My mouth is back on hers, and I reach the paradise between her legs. She's soaking as I push her panties to the side and use two of fingers to spread her wetness to her clit. She moans into my mouth again. I press my fingers inside of her.

# Rise Of An Heiress

Fuck, she's tight. She's perfect.

## NATALIE

Oh my god. I could kick myself. How did I not know this club belonged to the Cosa Nostra? This had to be a new development. Dom wouldn't have allowed it otherwise.

*And what the fuck am I doing? Well, I know what I'm doing, but what am I doing?* This could be a setup. But he feels so good with his body pressed against mine.

I have a death wish. If I die right now, I absolutely deserve it.

He can't be pretending. You can't fake a hard-on like this. As if he can read my mind, he presses his length against me. I know he's hung. I'm making out with the man who's tried to kill me. The man who's tried to kill me has his fingers inside of me right now. *They feel so good.* I'm so hot I can't even think. How long have I been gone? I hope no one comes looking for me.

I should tell him to stop and run for dear life. But I don't want to. He feels and smells so good. Like someone took the deep depths of the ocean and the coastal winds and mixed them with pines and mahogany.

I want this. I want him.

I thrust against his fingers as they enter me, and his palm rubs my clit. I let out a moan. Thank God no one can hear us over the music.

"Fuck," I cry.

Needing more, I work my hands down his torso and unzip his pants. He stops what he's doing and looks down at my hands. I look back up at him.

I can tell he's thinking, *To fuck or to kill?* He's making a choice. I can see it in his eyes. I don't even give him a chance to change his mind.

"I want this." I breathe out and press my lips against his.

"What is it that you want?" he asks against my mouth, smirking.

I bite his bottom lip. "I want you inside of me."

He kisses me again but pulls away too soon.

"Nico," he says as he adjusts my legs around him.

"What?" I blink at him, stupefied.

Too much is going on at once.

"My name. Nico. What's yours? Since I'm about to be inside you," he says with a smirk as he reaches into his pocket and pulls out a condom.

*Oh God, that smirk.*

My whole body is on fire. "Natalie," I barely whisper.

He doesn't take his eyes off me as he rips open a condom wrapper with his mouth, the other holding me in place. He adjusts his pants, and his cock springs out, ready to play.

Holy shit. He's huge, hard, and beautiful. *Did I just call his cock beautiful?* As he puts the condom on, I realize there's no fucking way that's going to fit inside of me. I stiffen, my eyes wide.

As if he could read my mind, he laughs and kisses me. He's rubbing himself against my wetness now. I let out another moan. His kisses trail up my jaw until he's at my ear. He lines his cock up at my entrance and pauses. I'm fighting for air at this point it's so hot.

Then he whispers, "You'll take it."

I become wetter at his words, and he pushes his length into me as he growls.

"Oh god!" I cry out, grabbing his back, digging my nails and heels into him as I take in his size.

He doesn't move. He looks into my eyes. Our mouths are lined up as we breathe each other in. We stay there for a moment. Then he kisses me, but he still doesn't move his hips. I kiss him back and wiggle my hips against him. I need more. More movement. More friction.

"Please, Nico. Move." He smiles against my mouth and moves slowly. In and out. Stretching me out.

"Fuck, so tight," he lets out, quickening his pace.

"So good," I breathe out. It's the best I can do as he fucks me against the wall. I'm so close I can feel it.

"Come for me," he whispers in my ear as he wraps a hand around my throat.

For a second, I think he's actually about to kill me like this. I can't think of a better way to go.

"Fuck, I'm gonna—" I try to get out.

"Me, too," he says with hitching breaths.

He speeds up. I'm so close. I can feel myself coming undone. I'm just about—

BANG. BANG. BANG.

Someone knocks at the door. Nico slams into me as he grunts before stopping. *Did he just—?*

"Nico! Bash needs you out back."

"Fuck." He pulls his head away and looks at me, still inside me.

For a moment, we still don't move, panting.

BANG. BANG. BANG.

"Nico! Now!"

He stares at me like I had pissed him off, like it was my fault someone chose this very moment to knock. He pulls out of me, setting me down. I look down. He definitely finished. That made one of us. I'm still adjusting my dress as he's walking toward the door, zipping himself up. He throws the condom in the trash. I'm still leaning against the wall, processing what had just happened.

He reaches for the handle, but before he opens the door, he says, "Have a good night," without even looking back at me.

Then he's gone.

# Chapter Seven

### NATALIE

I'm so humiliated about what happened with Nico Saturday night that I didn't even bother telling Donna or Maya what happened. I told them I took forever in the restroom because I got sick. I'd rather die than tell them I had sex with the consigliere of the Cosa Nostra, the man targeting me and my family.

The worst part—I've been so hot and bothered since that night. It was like having a wet dream only for your alarm to go off right before you finish—only it wasn't a dream. It was very, very real.

Our encounter is all I can think about. I never felt so alive. Was it so hot because I knew who he was and he knew who I was and it was forbidden? God, I was so close to having the best orgasm of my life. Of course it was interrupted. Because I'm me. These things only happen to me.

I've been staring at my final paper for four hours because I can't concentrate on anything else. I thought our traditional Sunday brunch with Maya and some college friends would distract me but nope. I'm hot, bothered, and hungover.

By Tuesday afternoon, I wasn't any better. I tried taking care of myself, but that only left me feeling more unsatisfied. I can't even pay attention during lecture. It doesn't matter if I want him. I can't have him, and if he did come back, it'd only be to kill me.

Shaking my thoughts out of my mind, I try to focus on my paper. School should be my focus, not some guy I met at a club who's trying to kill me. As if my life weren't complicated enough, I'm learning the truth about my parentage, and now having to make sure the Triad *and* Cosa Nostra don't get me. I cannot get involved in anything emotional.

## NICO

"Have a good night." Have a good night? You fucking prick.

Saturday night is still haunting me. I'm a fucking idiot. I should have stayed away. I don't know what possessed me to get up to follow her. To talk to her. Kiss her. Fuck her. Actually, I did. It was me envisioning Dante talk to her, flirt with her. And the smile she gave him. I wanted that smile.

I knew I wasn't prepared to grab her without any witnesses, and I definitely was not expecting to fuck her in the storage closet. It was her damn long dark hair, the matching dark eyes, those killer legs I had dreamed she'd wrap around me, and her scent. I don't know why it turned me on to watch her kill our men. But she'd fit right into my world. I wouldn't have to shield anything, like most of the men do with their wives. I'm a moth, and she's the flame. I want her. *Strictly physical, though,* I try to tell myself.

What has gotten into me? Never had I imagined what kind of woman I wanted. I fucked them, and that was it. If I ever got married, it'd be for tactical reasons. I tried to stay away after Saturday night. That lasted about a day, which is why I'm on a rooftop across from her building, just like I have been every day since Sunday.

My phone rings, and I pull it out of my pocket. Dante.

"Tell me you got something." I ask as I look into binoculars like a damn stalker.

"I might have something I'm not sure it's worth looking into."

"Did you find who has been sending her money?"

"That's the thing. I'm pretty sure it's the Violantes. It has to be, but I have no proof. They hid their tracks well, man. So, the question is—"

"Why are the Violantes so invested in this girl?"

"Exactly. She could be an assassin for them. She's not Italian, so it wouldn't draw any attention."

"Maybe. She can't be a love child. I imagine Cesare's current offspring wouldn't be so fond of her," I say, taking a seat on the roof.

Not to mention she's not half Italian, as far as I can tell. I pause for a moment.

"It's worth looking into," I say into the phone.

"You got it," Dante replies.

Just as a hang up, my phone dings again. It's a text from my brother, Bash. I don't hear from him as much now that he's taken over as capo. He needed me to finish a job for him on Saturday, the job that interrupted my storage closet hookup. He's been so busy he hasn't even followed up.

> Bash: Is it taken care of?
> Me: Can you be less vague? You talking about the girl or the Saturday night?

My phone lights up with Bash's name. I answer.

"What are you doing texting that shit? It's a simple yes or no," Bash yells into the phone.

"Our jammers are impossible to get through, Bash. Calm down. No one can break through my security. And, the girl—well, I'm still working on it." I omit some details for obvious reasons. "And as far as I'm concerned, Saturday night didn't happen."

I had to refer to the body I had to dump and not the deadly angel I was with.

Fuck. I couldn't think about her without getting tied up in knots. Never thought I'd see the day. I'm not cocky—scratch that, I *know* I am. But I'm only cocky about it if I know it's the truth, and I've *never* had a problem getting a woman off before.

Fucking Dante had to come knocking on the door right as I came and right as she was about to. I made a mental note to kick his ass during our next training session. I could tell by her face she didn't finish. And like I goddamn sixteen-year-old, I got my fix and told her to "have a good night." That's how she'd remember me.

"Are you even listening, Nico?"

Shit, Bash is still on the line. This girl is a distraction, to say the least.

"Yeah, I'm listening. No one saw me. We're good. Now I have to go." I hang up.

I'm probably the only person who could get away with hanging up on Bash. Even our little brother, Enzo, wouldn't dare.

Fuck. I've been off my game lately. All because of this raven-haired obsession of mine. I let out a deep breath, not realizing I've been holding it. Before my mind can wander further, her lights flicker on.

Examining her place as she walks in, I notice her penthouse is luxurious. Too nice for a college student. She might be getting a law degree, but she isn't working. Floor-to-ceiling windows. Neutral tones. Large fireplace in the living room and both bedrooms.

She's dressed in a sexy silk blouse and tight black pants that did wonderful things for her ass. She drops her bag on the counter and stretches her neck out like she'd had a stressful day. *I could help with that. Calm the fuck down, Nico.*

She checks her phone as she pours a glass of wine. I should check her phone again. It's usually nonsense from her friends, nothing telling. Then she unbuttons her shirt, and my mouth goes dry.

My pants suddenly feel tighter. So much for calming down.

Her button-up is now completely open, exposing a pink lace bra. I imagine using my knife and cutting it off of her.

She reaches behind herself and removes a gun from her back, a knife from her pants, and another knife from her shoe. She takes another sip of wine, finishes the glass, and pours herself another.

The fuck? Was she packing the other night? No way. Her outfit hardly covered her, and it was see-through, for crying out loud. She must've had security at the club. She very well could be an assassin.

She takes the gun and wine into her room as she undresses. *Smart girl.* She takes off her pants, leaving her in just the button-up, bra, and matching underwear.

My hard-on is at full mast at the sight of her. I have to adjust my pants. At this point, I have to fight the urge to not rub one off on the roof.

She strolls to her claw-foot tub and turns the water on. She pours a bottle of what I'm assuming is bubble bath into it. Disappearing into the closet, she leaves the water running. I should definitely look away. Surveilling her is one thing but watching her bathe is another. She reappears in a robe that barely covers anything and grabs a book and her glass before she turns the water off. As she's about to get in, she stops suddenly and makes her way to the front door.

Standing at the entrance is one of her guards I've seen her with. My blood is boiling. I have no right to be jealous, but I don't care. What the hell is she doing answering the door dressed like that? I can't hear what they're saying, but it looks like he's trying to make a move on her. She obviously knows him, though she doesn't seem interested, but I couldn't give a shit.

## Rise Of An Heiress

Goddammit. I should've demanded she couldn't leave the room and told her to wait until I came back so I could devour her pussy and make her come until she lost her voice from screaming my name. But that would have made her run off faster, screaming for the hills.

My boiling blood scalds my veins as he places a hand on her arm. Why's he so familiar with her? He moves a stray hair behind her ear and looks like he's about to lean in and kiss her.

*I think the fuck not.* I've seen enough.

Planning to hack into her apartment building's alarm system, I open my laptop. "Not so fast."

Proud, with a smug smile, I hit a button, and just like that, the fire alarms go off. The whole building will evacuate. But I can't ward men off of her forever.

I need to act—fast. Maybe just one more time. Maybe I'm only thinking about her because we have unfinished business. Is my ego really that sensitive? This woman has me in fucking knots.

# Chapter Eight

### NATALIE

My focus is all over the place. Last night did not go as expected. I planned to just take a bubble bath and read for enjoyment for a change, but with Matteo showing up unannounced on top of the fire alarm going off and the building having to be evacuated, I'm exhausted. We couldn't go back into the building for hours—as if my mind wasn't foggy enough, thanks to the hot Italian psycho after me. Let's add lack of sleep to the mix.

Even though I lost hours of sleep, the alarm going off was a blessing in disguise. I know exactly what Matteo showed up for, and I had zero interest in entertaining any of those ideas. I'm starting to think no one will excite me the same way Nico does. I push the thought out of my mind.

Itching for class to be over, I want to throw a pity party in a room when I feel it again.

The room stills, and the hairs on my neck stand. I try to resist, but I can't. I turn and make eye contact with none other than Nico Delucci, who is sitting in the back of my lecture class, staring right back at me. I turn my head back to the front quickly. No one seems to notice he's walked in.

Pretending to pay attention to the rest of the lecture, I feel it's difficult to focus while accepting these are your last moments on Earth. His gaze is burning into the back of my skull.

I can't just get up and leave. I'm at the front of the class, so it will draw too much attention. I'm scared he'll threaten to take out the whole room. *Would he*? God, why now? Why didn't he just off me Saturday night? Dammit. I slept with him, and now he's come back to kill me. Serves me right for being such a fool.

Jeremy's sitting next to me. Oh god. I hope he can get out of here before this guy takes us all out.

What feels like hours was actually only fifteen minutes, and class finally ends. As I'm packing up my things, I feel a large warm figure sit next to me. Goosebumps prickle my body, but I keep packing, as if I didn't notice.

"Natalie, want to grab a bite?" Jeremy asks, eyeing the man next to me curiously.

"Stay," he said quietly into my ear, in a demanding tone

Like a fucking moron, I listen.

"Uh, no, you go ahead, Jeremy."

I need to get him as far away from here as possible. He eyes me warily and leaves.

Nico waits until the classroom is empty. There goes all my witnesses, probably for the best. He gets up, and his steps drag toward the door. I hear him lock it and pull down the blinds behind me.

The lecture hall is small. Suddenly, it feels smaller and hotter. I think the air is dissipating, too.

He walks to the front and sits on the teacher's desk. I need to distract him. He's obviously attracted to me.

Before I could stop myself, I blurt, "Am I in trouble, professor?"

I could slap myself. I'm about to die, and my go-to tactic is role-playing? I don't even like role-playing. Well, there's no going back now.

"I know my paper was late. But I really need an A."

*God, did I really just say that?* I shoot him my sweetest smile. I've committed to what I just started, and clearly, he's caused me to lose brain cells.

He doesn't say anything. I can tell he's making a decision again. To kill me or not to kill me? My breathing becomes frantic with every second he's silent. Finally, he opens his mouth.

"What are you willing to do to earn your grade?" he asks, adjusting his cufflinks.

*Oh my.* This, I was not expecting. He's playing along. I feel like the wind has been sucked right out of my lungs as heat moves to my core.

"Anything," I say, breathless.

"Anything?" He raises his eyebrow, and he somehow gets ten times hotter.

"Yes." I try to come off as seductive, but I'm sure I just sound like a desperate school girl.

"If I asked you to take your dress off, would you?"

My core tightens. "Yes."

His eyes narrow. "Yes, *professor*, you mean."

I have to squeeze my legs together. I can feel myself getting wet, my core aching.

"Yes, professor."

"Stand up," he demands, getting up from the desk. "Turn around, put your hands on the desk, and bend over."

## NICO

My cock hardens at her words. *Am I in trouble, professor?* I like it. I like it a lot.

She's in a flowy, lacy pink-and-white dress that stops mid-thigh. *Damn, she's beautiful.* She's bent over with her hands on the desk, as I demanded. Something tells me she's not always this accommodating.

I'm painfully hard at this point. My pants are about to rip. Everything in my body is telling me to just pull her dress up and fuck her until she's screaming my name, begging for release, but I want to see how far she's willing to go.

"First, I'm going to punish you," I tell her as I undo my belt and bring my lips to her ear. "Then you're going to earn your A." I drag my fingers up her thighs before lifting up her dress and pulling her panties down.

She swallows. The sight is beautiful. Her pink lace panties are see-through, and her round, perky ass is just asking to be spanked, bitten, and caressed. All of which I intend to do.

I press my body into her from behind and pull her hair. My erection rubs her ass. She gasps as I kiss her neck and breathe the sweet scent I've already become obsessed with. Amaretto crème, cherries, flowers, and her. It's addicting.

"Do you understand?" I ask. Waiting for her consent.

"Yes," she replies.

SMACK! I whip my belt on her bare ass as she cries out.

"Yes, what?"

"Yes, professor," she replies.

"Will you be a good girl?" I ask her, rubbing the spot my belt just took.

"Yes, professor."

SMACK! She moans, and her breathing picks up. She loves this. SMACK! She moans louder. I love how responsive she is.

"Are you going to turn in an assignment late again?"

"No, professor." She gasps.

SMACK! I smooth my hand over the red mark on her ass cheek. "Good girl."

"I thought you said you were going to punish me," she says breathlessly, then looks over her shoulder at me and smirks. "Let me know when you start." *Fuck it all to hell.*

"On your knees," I tell her as I unzip my pants.

She gets on her knees, and there's something about her at my mercy that made my cock ache even more. I pull out my cock, stroking it in front of her face. She licks her lips, staring at it. I could get used to this sight.

"Yes, sir."

"I believe we left some things . . . *unfinished* the last time we saw each other."

Her eyes widen, and her cheeks flush pink as she looks like she's pondering our last encounter. I have a lot to make up for.

"Open your mouth."

She parts her lips.

I push the tip of my cock into her mouth slowly. She licks and sucks, grabbing onto my thighs for support. I use one hand to guide her head and the other to wrap her hair around my fist. I groan out loud. Fuck me, this is heaven. I watch as her head bobs around my length, her cheeks hollowed out as she sucks, her noises pushing me over the edge. I'm about to explode.

"Fuck," I cry out, "that feels good."

She sucks harder and faster. I almost can't take it anymore.

"Stop," I command.

She listens and licks the tip of my cock before pulling back completely. She looks up at me with a triumphant smile, the little minx.

I nod to the teacher's desk. "On the desk, legs spread."

She does as she's told and sits on the desk, leans back on her elbows, and spreads her legs wide. My mouth is watering at the sight of her glistening pussy, with her dress bunched up at the waist, wet from sucking me off. She is fucking perfect. She pants as I approach her. I stand between her legs and lean over to kiss her.

The tip of my cock is now sliding over the wet slit. She wiggles her hips and moans. I pull back and can tell she's getting frustrated. I get on my knees in front of her, my eyes never leaving hers. I kiss up the inside of her thigh, skip over her pussy, and kiss down the other thigh. She's squirming now. I can tell she needs more. She wanted a punishment. I'll give her one.

"You won't come until I grant you permission."

"Yes, professor."

I press my lips on her clit, kissing her before I suck. She moans as her head falls back, her legs wrapping around my head. She looks beautiful when she's lost in what I'm doing to her. I use my tongue to lick her entrance and slowly move up to her clit. God, she fucking tastes good. She grabs my hair and thrusts her pussy into my mouth. As I devour her pussy like it's my last meal, she moves faster and moans louder. If anyone is outside of the classroom, they can definitely hear her. I reach up to pull her dress down. Releasing her tits, I palm them. She's close, and I stop just as she's about to release. She looks at me incredulously.

"Not. Yet," I tell her as I take her nipple into my mouth. She moans as her nails dig into me, begging for more. I work my way back down to her pussy. She jerks as I rub my tongue over her throbbing nub.

"Remember the rule." I devour her pussy, licking up every drop of her arousal. "Tell me what it is," I command.

"No coming until you give me permission," she pants.

I insert two fingers inside of her, and she tightens around me. My lips never leave her pussy. Her back arches.

"Oh, fuck!" she cries out, putting her hand over her mouth.

I continue to fuck her with my tongue as I reach up to move her hand away.

"I want to hear you," I say to her as she looks down at me.

"Yes, professor," she breathes, and I go back to eating her pussy like it was my job. "Oh god, oh fuck!" Her legs quiver.

"Say my name," I demand.

"Nico!"

I like hearing my name on her lips, especially for this reason.

"Good girl." I suck on her clit.

"Oh my god! Ah!"

Her pussy tightens around my fingers.

"No. Not yet." I pull my head back and stop moving my fingers, smirking at her. She huffs out in frustration. "Have you learned your lesson?" I ask, rubbing my hand up and down the outside of her thighs with my lips right at her pussy as I talk.

"Yes!" she cries out.

I smile and laugh against her pussy, kissing her clit. Slowly, I work my tongue back on her slit. She's pulling my hair harder now, searching for more friction. She's getting close again. I edge her more and more. Her legs tremble again as she chases her orgasm. I pull away.

"Nico!" she whimpers.

I look up at her as she looks down at me, eye brows pinched. The sight is beautiful.

"Beg," I tell her before grazing her pussy with my lips, stroking her with my tongue.

"Please. I need to come."

"I'm not sure your punishment has been severe enough," I tease, not easing up on her pussy.

"Yes, it has, please. Make me come," she pleads, nails digging into the edge of the desk.

I kiss my way up her body that's still trembling and desperate for an orgasm, stopping on each nipple before I plant my mouth over hers, letting her taste herself off of my lips.

"You're going to let me fuck you now," I state.

Fuck, I want her so badly.

I pull out a condom and put it on in record time. I don't give her a warning as I thrust hard inside of her, and she cries out.

"Fuck!" We both yell at the same time.

I thought her mouth was heaven; I lied. This is heaven. Her pussy was made for me. I thought if I fucked her out of my system, it'd be easier to kill her when the time comes, but I was wrong.

"Nico, I'm going to come, please," she pants.

"Your cunt is so tight. And wet," I say as I pull back and glide back into her.

"Ah, for you," she gasps.

I move torturously slowly, allowing her to get used to my size. It's taking everything I have to restrain myself. I want to fuck her so fast and hard. She rocks her hips against mine.

"Faster," she pleads.

She doesn't need to ask me twice. Increasing my pace steadily, I fuck her hard and fast, desk shaking and scraping against the tile floors. We're both cursing and yelling.

"Come for me," I finally tell her.

She cries out my name as she comes. I swear I see stars as I explode inside of her. This was how it should have been the first time.

We lay there, panting for a minute. Me on top of her. I kiss her neck and work my way back up to her mouth. Our tongues clash as our lungs fight for air.

What was it about her that made me want to kiss her? I usually didn't care for it during sex, but with her, I wanted more. I wanted everything.

A sexy whimper falls from her mouth when I finally pull out of her to adjust myself and throw the condom into the trash. She doesn't move right away but follows my movements with her eyes. I motion for her to sit up. Without a word, I pocket her panties and readjust her clothing. She doesn't fight me.

We stand in the silent classroom. She walks over, grabs her school bag, and nods. I stare at her, but I don't say anything. I watch her as she walks away, like she couldn't leave fast enough. Something pink on the floor catches my eye.

## Chapter Nine

NICO

"Can you run this for prints?" I ask my Uncle Ricky, walking into the back lounge room of one of our clubs.

Looping my finger into the pink water bottle's loop, I hold it up. Won't want to mess with the fingerprints.

My Uncle Ricky is our tech guy, my mother's brother. He could do anything, and if he didn't know how, he'd learn. But scanning prints he could do in his sleep. I notice Bash on the lounge chair.

"What's that?" my brother asks.

"Hopefully, that Natalie girl's prints. I stole her water bottle and want to see what we can pull from them," I say as I walk over to the table Uncle Ricky is sitting near and set it down.

"Great idea," Bash says as he gets up and walks over.

"So, you think you can do it?" I ask Uncle Ricky.

"Is that a serious question?" Uncle Ricky pipes back, with his thick Long Island accent as he grabs his kit and pulls on gloves.

He examines the water bottle. "Give me ten minutes."

I nod. Bash pours me a glass of whiskey, and we sit back down, allowing Uncle Ricky to work.

"Do I even want to know how you got that thing?" he asks.

"Nope." I smile.

"You better not do anything stupid, Nico," he demands.

He's the capo right now, not my brother.

"Relax, man. She was at a cafe and left it behind." I lie, definitely not telling him what really went down.

My mind immediately drifts back to the last hour, when I had the best sex of my life. I don't know what it is about this woman that makes my brain short circuit.

"This is weird," Uncle Ricky says, breaking my train of thought.

And I'm glad he did. Otherwise, I'd have to explain a random boner to my brother.

"What?" Bash asks, standing. We walk back over to Uncle Ricky. "Her prints are unreadable."

"What does that even mean?" I ask.

"I've scanned them a bunch of times. It just says 'error,' like the system doesn't even recognize them as fingerprints."

"So, what? She like an alien or something?" I ask sarcastically, irritated.

"What prints does she have to get her license?" Bash questions.

"That's the other thing I thought of, too. When you look her up, the prints on her files don't match the one from the water bottle," Uncle Ricky answers.

"Are you sure this is hers?" Bash asks, looking at me.

"Yes. I watched her pick it up and drink out of it and put it back down," I answer.

"Then, whose prints is she using?" Uncle Ricky asks.

"You and Dante, look into her some more. Nothing's adding up, but there's bound to be a mistake somewhere. Don't know why this girl comes with more questions than answers, but we need some soon," Bash instructs Uncle Ricky.

He nods as Bash and I leave the room.

"You still good to go to the gala this Friday?" Bash asks me.

"Ah shit, forgot about that. Yeah, I'll be there," I reply as we walk outside.

He's talking about the annual Black Rose Gala, the most exclusive event. I don't want to go, but Bash had already accepted the invitation to meet with one of our new "business associates."

"Good," he says as he pats my back. "Now, remember, it's just a low-key ass-kissing event, schmooze the right people, so we can get our construction projects approved and on time. *Don't* cause a scene. Most of the men'll be kissing your ass anyway since they'll need access to our docks."

"When do I ever cause a scene?" I ask sarcastically.

"Bastard," he laughs, shaking his head as he gets into his Maserati before driving off.

## NATALIE

"I can't believe you're going to the party of the year tonight! I'm so jealous." Maya screams as she beats my face with a beauty sponge.

I'm going to the Black Rose Gala tonight, and if you're a New Yorker, you know it's bigger than the Met. Hell, *Hell*'s easier to get into than the Met.

Dom blackmailed one of the hosts with images of him participating in the Outfit's illegal side of business. Dom was then added to the list with a plus one once he heard Sebastiano Delucci was going. Usually Papa would go, but since Dom will be capo soon, Papa thinks this is a good opportunity for him to network. We're also going to see if there's any talk of the Cosa Nostra's plans. Dom didn't bother letting them know he was going to be in attendance, since they'd make it obvious they already knew he was in New York.

"You know I don't care about these things, Maya." I roll my eyes.

I really don't. I try to stay away from high-profile events out of fear of being recognized, which I know is ridiculous, since nobody knows my secret. But a small part of me is actually excited to be attending a party only a select few gets invited to.

"I know, which is why I'm going to try to rein in my green monster and not make you look like a clown on purpose," she says, maneuvering through a rack of dresses my stylist had sent over.

## Rise Of An Heiress

She's helping me with choosing an outfit and with my hair. What can't this woman do? I could hire someone, but for some reason, I only like the way Maya does my makeup.

"How very kind of you," I say sarcastically.

Maya puts me in a form-fitting black silk gown with a very low back and high slit. It goes up the length of my leg to my hip bone. I have to be strategic about my underwear placement all night. And my gun. She puts my hair in an intricate, loose updo. I don't wear makeup every day, but I love when Maya does my makeup. I feel like a queen when she's done with me.

\* \* \*

We've been at the ball for about an hour now. Dom is connecting with a lot of people, but we're not hearing anything useful for our problem. No sign of Sebastiano yet. I'm sort of nervous there's going to be a brawl. Nevertheless, I play the dumb socialite and get nothing but gossip.

I try not to cringe when Dom tells people I'm his date. It just feels wrong and sick. I know he feels the same way, too. If you didn't know him as well as I did, you'd never be able to tell. We're both pretty convincing to others that there's something going on between us, especially every time he leans in to kiss my temple. But I can feel his body tighten and jaw flex every time he says the word *date*. It's kind of funny at this point. I never thought I'd see him squirm so much.

A shiver runs up my spine, and the hairs on my neck stand at attention. *Oh god. He's here.* I don't even have to turn around. My body knows it. I look around, pretending to look for a server. Through my champagne glass, I sip, looking at those dark eyes that lock onto mine from across the room. My mind has been reeling about what happened the other day. Seriously, what the hell was that?

He looks furious. He must've come in his brother's place tonight. Some blonde is clinging onto him, talking his ear off, but his focus is, unfortunately, on me. Is he going to kill me now? I cannot play this game much longer.

I'm still not sure what happened back in that classroom. I thought for sure I was a goner. For a moment, I thought it was a dream, but the ache between my legs proved it was all too real. The only thing I know is that I want him more than I've ever wanted anyone before. *You don't even know him.*

"Are you cold?" Dom asks, his arm around my waist.

I look at my arms and notice I have goosebumps. "Uh, no." I look back at Nico.

He looks like he's ready to kill someone, and I follow his gaze. It's on Dom. Oh, crap. Is he here for Dom? His face goes from angry to something else. Murderous.

I can't breathe. I need air, so I excuse myself and run up the venue's stairs. There's an outdoor garden somewhere up here.

When I finally locate it, I can breathe. I take in a deep breath and admire the night sky. The city's too bright to see the stars, but the moon is still beautiful. I hear footsteps freeze. I know it's him behind me. Good. As long as he's away from Dom, I don't care what he does to me.

*Rise Of An Heiress*

## NICO

I've been talking with some millionaire suit-types all night, and I'm ready to smash my skull into the wall. They see my tattoos and think I'm an idiot, like we don't have more money than them and like I didn't just hack into their accounts. I know who's cheating on their wives, has off-shore accounts, second families, and who's losing more money than they pretend to make. On top of that, Sophia spotted me the minute I walked into the lobby and hasn't left my side since. I'd tell her to fuck off, but I can't risk burning bridges with her father—at least not yet.

It's all the same surface-level conversations, people laughing at each other's dry jokes and bragging about their accomplishments, trying to one-up the other. I can't pay them any mind. Nope. I'm too busy watching Dominic fucking Violante grope Natalie, the woman who ruined sex with anyone else for me. I don't know why I'm raging with jealousy right now, but I am. And seeing that fucker's hands on her like she belongs to him, I could rip his throat out right now without a second thought.

*Who is he to her?* Can't be a boyfriend if she just had one of his soldiers over. Unless she makes this a habit of sneaking around. Fuck. How did I get this deep? I've compromised everything. My phone rings, pulling me out of my thoughts.

"What?" I say, not even checking who it is.

"Black vans just pulled up out back. Plates come up blank. No one's come out," Dante tells me.

"Vans? You think they're trying to pull something on us?" I ask.

"No, I don't think they're dumb enough to do it here and now with Dominic inside. I think either he's the target or you are. Maybe even both."

"You think?" I ask, irritated.

"We found some things earlier—can't get into it now. I'm waiting for Uncle Ricky to confirm. I'm just calling to tell you to be vigilant and don't fucking do anything impulsive or stupid." He pauses. "Did you see her?" Dante's pitch heightens.

"Who?"

I'm officially annoyed.

"Natalie. She's a vision."

No, not annoyed. Pissed off.

"Yeah, I saw her. Didn't notice," I say, lying.

"Well, I did. I swear, when this is over, I'm go—"

"Do your job, Dante, and stop drooling over some woman," I yell before hanging up.

At that moment, she takes off in the direction of the garden. I shrug Sophia off, and I follow Natalie. She's moving quickly. What's she up to? Are those vans outside hers? I pull out my phone to text Dante.

*Me: Make sure the car is on standby.*

I find her in the courtyard. She's admiring the garden and the night sky, and I can't take it anymore.

"You make a habit of cheating?" I bark.

"What?" Her head shoots in my direction. She looks at me like I've grown a second head.

## Rise Of An Heiress

I don't blame her, but I don't care.

"Your boyfriend know you fuck other guys in clubs and in between classes?"

She jumps back like I had just smacked her. But her shock turns to anger. She stomps right up to me and slaps me.

"Don't you dare question me!" she screams.

I wipe my face with my palm before looking back at her. "Who is he to you?"

I couldn't stop myself from asking. This question had been eating at me since the moment I laid eyes on her.

"You're one to talk. Go back to your *date*. What I do is none of your damn business. We don't even know each other," she yells back, crossing her arms, drawing my attention to her breasts.

She isn't wearing a bra, and the cold air isn't helping. Her nipples were practically begging for attention.

"I think I know you very well." I walk closer to her as she backs up.

I scan her body up and down. She looks like she wants to slap me again; I like this fire in her. Nothing at all like the good girl in the classroom.

"It was just sex"—she glares—"it was good, but that's all it was. You don't get to come in here and question me so you can—"

Just sex? Fucking liar. I grab her and bring her mouth to mine. She only resists for a second before relaxing into my embrace, wrapping her arms around me. I kiss her hungrily, taking in her scent, my new obsession. As I walk us behind one of the tall hedges so no one can see us, my lips never leave hers. Lost in her kiss, I cup her ass and lift her. Her legs wrap around my waist. *Will I ever fuck her in a bed?* That's if I ever see her again. More and more, I'm realizing this woman is dangerous for me with each encounter.

Gunshots and screaming interrupt my thoughts, and I pull away. I look around for the source, not setting her down. *Shit, what's going on?* C-4 wasn't the Outfit's M.O. This was more on track for . . . *The Triad.* Fuck. I turn back to face her, and instead of finding her eyes, I'm met with the barrel of her gun. *Where the fuck was she hiding a gun?*

"I'm going to ask you one time." I hear the click as she turns off the safety. "Are you playing me?" she asks, stone-faced, eyes devoid of emotion.

All innocence washed off of her.

*There you are.*

## Chapter Ten

### NATALIE

I swear, if anything happens to Dom, I will ruin him. *I'm such an idiot*! I'm still holding my gun in between his eyes as I think about my next move.

He doesn't budge.

"Talk," I demand through gritted teeth with my legs still wrapped around his waist. When the bloodlust hits, I turn into someone I don't even recognize. I can feel it now. I love it.

"So, you *do* know who I am," he says, with that stupid, sexy smirk.

The bastard is smirking.

"And you know who I am," I say, keeping the gun I had strategically hidden dead still.

"Actually, I don't," he answers matter-of-factly.

I press the barrel against his forehead.

"Put the gun down, baby. Before you hurt yourself."

*Baby?* The smug bastard.

He leans back and puts his hand over the barrel, like his hand will stop my bullet from smashing his skull in.

Adrenaline is running through me now. The gun feels so right in my hand. I realize how good this feels, so I pull my hand back. I can't risk shooting him without any witnesses. People are running around like crazy. So, I pistol-whip the side of his face.

His head flies back, but he still manages to put me down gently. "Fucking hell, baby!" he yells, holding his head.

"Not your fucking baby." I hold my gun back up to him. "Start talking. Did you set me up?" I'm filled with rage, but somehow, I'm calm.

"What are you talking about?" he asks, rubbing the side of his face.

That'll definitely leave a mark.

I smile to myself before another explosion booms. He looks over to where the sound came from, and I didn't give him time to think. I squat, kicking my leg out to knock him down on his back. But he's quick and only stumbles slightly. He grabs and pulls me in, giving me a chance to knee him in the balls.

"Fuck!" he screams as he bends over.

I turn to run. Someone is shooting, bombs are going off, and I need to find Dom. I need to make sure he isn't hurt—or worse, dead.

Not long after, a pair of arms grab me. I swing my legs back, knocking him down. As I try to get away again, something snags the bottom of my dress, bringing me down. I'm attempting to army crawl now, but he climbs on top of me, flipping me onto my back.

"If you thought you could fuck me to distract me enough to kill me, baby, you thought wrong!" he says, pinning my hands down.

*Kill him? Who was shooting if not his men?*

"What are you talking about? You followed me and kissed me, you jackass!" I scream, writhing in his grip.

"Don't act like you didn't like it. You kissed me back," he says, panting with that stupid smirk still on his face.

I push my hips into him, and as expected, he relaxes, and I'm able to push him off enough to knee him in the stomach.

*Men.* I scramble up and run down the hall toward an exit, looking for Dom.

As I'm running down the corridor, another explosion erupts, and someone's firing gunshots at me.

*Well, fuck. At least I know who the target is now.*

Someone pulls my body down, and I turn. Nico pulls me down behind a pillar, and I elbow him in the nose.

"Get away from me!" I yell, trying to get away.

His head swings back. "Jesus, fuck! What'd you do that for? I just saved you!"

Man, he's good. I'm almost convinced he's trying to help me. He grabs my arm and pulls me in so we're face-to-face.

"You're making it really hard not to hurt you," he says.

"Fuck off!" I spit in his face and run off.

Or at least I try to. I only make it a couple of steps before I look back to see him tailing me.

Before he could grab ahold of me, a crash whips through the air, and my body is suspended. Shattered debris and glass from the wall flies. I land hard with a thud, knocking the wind out of me. My vision blurs as the rubble settles on top of me.

"Wǒ zhǎo dào tā le." *We found her,* I hear a deep, raspy voice say . . . in Mandarin?

Papa made sure I learned Mandarin. At the time, he said I needed to know how to speak the language to stay in touch with my roots. Now I know the real reason: in case I ever decide to take over the Triad.

I try to look around, but everything is spotty. My whole body aches. I can barely hold my head up. Nico is passed out about twenty feet from me, but he's coming to. He's starting to move again. Two men appear in masks, standing over me. One slaps me across the face. This motherfucker.

"Dāng wǒ men tīng shuō gong zhǔ hái huó zhe de shí hòu, wǒ men dōu bù xiāng xìn." *When we heard the princess could still be alive, we didn't believe it,* the man says, taking off his mask. "Dàn nǐ zài zhè lǐ." *But here you are.*

"What?"

This can't be happening.

The second man also removes his mask, and the last thing I see is a gun coming toward my face, and everything goes black.

## NICO

A bang goes off, and next thing I know, I'm on the ground. When I realize what happened, I look around for her. *Shit, why was she so fucking stubborn?*

## Rise Of An Heiress

I look to my left, and I see two men standing over her, speaking a language I don't understand. One of them slaps her across the face and takes off his mask. *He's fucking dead.* I reach for my gun as they say something else to her. The second guy takes his mask off, too, and pulls his gun in front of her face. He doesn't shoot her but connects the butt of his gun to her head twice. I shoot both of them. One in the head and one in the chest.

I get up and make my way over to her. She's out cold. I hear the one I shot in the chest gasping for air. Without looking twice, I shoot him in the head.

I pull out my phone to call Dante. "What the fuck are you doing, man? Get the fuck out of the building. What's taking you so long?"

"Call and get the jet ready. We need the doc, too. I'll be out in a second. We're going to The Castle."

The Castle, our nickname for one of our safe houses.

Fuck, my body was sore. Not to mention I have the worst headache because this fun-sized bundle of terror used me as her personal punching bag. I made a mental note to talk to her about this later. Right now, I need to get us out of here. She's clearly the target. Nothing is making sense.

I pick her up and run. Dante is barking orders on the phone, waiting out front in an unmarked SUV. I place her in the back seat and get in with her. Dante takes the passenger seat.

"Drive! Now! Take us to the airstrip!" I yell at the driver, and he floors it.

I'm assessing her damage. She's pretty banged up but nothing that won't heal in a few days. At most, it's a concussion. She'll be sore and have some bruises to treat. Once I know she's going to be fine, I take my phone out.

"Jet's ready to go, man. Who's coming?" Dante asks from the front seat, inspecting the girl beside me.

"Just us, my brothers and a few soldiers. Call Enzo, I'll call Bash."

We arrive on the strip thirty minutes later. As I enter the jet with the woman in my arms, Bash, Uncle Ricky, and Gerardo, our *family* doctor, are already sitting on a luxury tan couch across from a large flat screen TV. The minute they spot me with Natalie in my arms, he gets up to join us with an irritated look on his face, but I can see the sliver of curiosity.

Dante follows me as I place her in the plush tan seat next to me and buckle her up. She's still out like a light. Bash and Dante sit in the seats facing ours. I put my jacket over her, not wanting her to get cold or risk any of the other guys checking her out. *Again, what the hell am I doing?*

Gerardo moves to Natalie, shining a flashlight in her eyes, making sure her injuries aren't too serious. He pulls out a vial and syringe. Before I can stop myself, I grab him by the shirt.

"What the hell are you doing?" I bark in his face.

"It's a mild sedative to keep her asleep until the plane lands. I imagine we don't want her waking up mid-flight," he replies, unfazed by my outburst.

And he had a point. The last thing we needed was for her to wake up while we're 30,000 feet in the air.

## Rise Of An Heiress

"She has a concussion and will have one hell of a headache when she wakes up, but she'll be fine. The sedative will wear off by the time we land." I narrow my eyes at him before releasing his shirt and sitting down across from my brothers.

Gerardo finishes tending to Natalie before quickly moving to take his seat. Darting my eyes between them, I'm grateful nobody has said anything because I don't know what to say, either. I could've just left her and minded my business. Instead, I dragged the Cosa Nostra into her drama. But we'd have answers, at least that's what I tell myself.

Enzo, our youngest brother, and a few others are the last to join us. He scans our seats, his eyes lingering too long on our guest before he plops in the seat across the aisle next to Uncle Ricky. Any time we call for the safe house, we follow a no-questions-asked policy until we know everyone's safe. I send him a death glare, and he just sends back a crooked smile.

We stay quiet, but once the plane is in the air for a while, I pick her up and take her to the private bedroom in the back. When I come back out, both of my brothers, Dante, and Uncle Ricky stare at me with a mixture of incredulous and curious looks on their faces, obviously waiting for answers.

"What?" I ask no one in particular as I take my seat.

Bash snaps his fingers, and the flight attendant brings us all glasses and a bottle of whiskey.

"You gonna tell us why we're being called to the safe house and why that girl is in your possession"—his gaze shifts to the door and back to me—"*unconscious?*" Bash asks me as he pours us all a glass. I realize how it looks. I took her, and now I'm on the run.

"Yeah, the fuck happened back there, man?" Dante says.

"It was the Triad. Crashed the Black Rose. Two men came after her, and I think they were speaking Mandarin, but I can't be sure."

"That makes sense," Dante states as he shares a look with Uncle Ricky before sipping from his glass.

"Care to elaborate?" I ask.

"Dante and Uncle Ricky found some . . . things on her. We weren't sure at first, but if what you're saying is true, then the pieces just fell into place."

"What the hell is going on?" Enzo piped up.

We hadn't told him the full extent of our assumptions on what went on at our shipping docks. I catch him up to speed about the attacks, our suspicion of the Violantes, and Natalie's mysterious appearance.

"Shit," Enzo says. He takes a drink. "So, why is she on this jet with us? It sounds like she's the one they wanted. Are we protecting her now?"

"I'm not sure. We have more questions than answers. Need to make sure she's not a threat," I say.

Enzo looks at me curiously. "So, you bring her on the plane with us?"

"Uncle Ricky. Dante. Tell us what you found," Bash ordered, ignoring Enzo, in capo mode.

"We think she's Triad," Uncle Ricky answered.

"I figured that much out," I respond, rolling my eyes.

"Well, she is, but she also isn't," Dante replies cryptically.

"Okay, this isn't confusing at all. So, why are *they* trying to kill *her*? Aren't they on her side?" I ask.

"I think I know the answer to that. I wasn't sure, but what you said about what went down tonight pretty much confirmed it," Dante replied.

"Go on . . ."

My patience is running thin.

"Did you know that Cesare Violante had a second wife?" Dante asks.

"No," Enzo and I say simultaneously.

Uncle Ricky chimes in. "They kept it hush-hush because it wasn't too long after his first wife died. Also, his second wife's husband had just passed, too."

"Jesus, guys, just spit it out," Bash orders. He's been less patient than me.

"Cesare's second wife was Nina Liu. The late Peter Liu's wife," Dante states.

My body stills. We all do. You've got to be fucking kidding me. I look up from my glass, making direct eye contact with Dante, then Bash, then Uncle Ricky, and Enzo. All of us going back and forth. Peter Liu was one of the most dangerous, notorious, and infamous leaders the Triad had ever seen. A sick motherfucker. He was *the* dragon head. The underworld knew him as *The Mad Dragon*. It shocked everyone when he was murdered. He was found dead in his office. The killer was never caught, and he didn't have a shortage of enemies.

When none of us respond, Uncle Ricky continues. "When Peter died, Nina's brother ensued on a hostile takeover and assumed the role as dragon head of the Triad. Nina and Peter had a little girl, Anya Liu, making Anya Cesare's step-daughter. After Nina died of illness, Andrew ordered a hit, and Anya Liu was reported to have been murdered at six years old. Cover-up was a car accident."

"Okay, a child? That's sick. But, so what?" Enzo asks.

"Okay, so . . ." Uncle Ricky answers, annoyed that we haven't already connected the dots with story time. "That little girl would be twenty-five years old today. Don't you think it's a little weird that Dominic Violante has this nonsexual attachment to *that*," he says, pointing to the back room, "twenty-five year old woman?"

"And she just happens to be the same girl that the Triad is suddenly hunting," Dante finishes.

*Fuck me. She couldn't be. Anya Liu? The dead Triad princess.* We were all quiet for a moment. Thinking about what we had just learned, I finish my drink and pour another one before speaking up.

"That doesn't make any sense. We saw her file. She's not adopted. There's a record of her mother giving birth to her," I argue.

Dante's face lit up like a little kid on Christmas. "I'm so glad you brought that up. It's not a coincidence," he says as he pours himself another drink.

## Rise Of An Heiress

"Nineteen years ago, the Yang family received a large sum of money. I'm talkin' money you'd kill for. They then moved from Brooklyn to Manhattan—" Dante says.

"Dante was able to access some encrypted files. Turns out, the couple did have a little girl named Natalie. But she died at—you guessed it—the age of six from cancer. Her treatment and death were wiped from the system, and somehow, the little girl is still *technically* alive," Uncle Ricky says.

None of us say anything.

"We also found a photo of *Natalie* when she was four with her parents. We can't tell if it's the same woman in that back room or not because she's . . . well, four." Uncle Ricky places a tablet on the table with an old image on the screen.

*I know that little girl isn't the same one on our jet. The parents were holding the little girl in between them. The little girl was smiling, too, but I could tell her eyes were shaped differently, and she didn't have the slightest hint of a dimple.*

Not one of us speaks, swigging our drinks.

Swapping the girls out? It was a genius plan. Heartless. Twisted. But still genius. Cesare Violante is known to be a cunning, manipulative man. One of the smartest bosses. He put a lot of thought into keeping this girl hidden. Right in plain fucking sight. Could the girl laying in our back room right now be Anya Liu? Assuming the identity of a dead six-year-old? I almost couldn't believe it. But then I remember she killed three of my men. And she put up one hell of a fight tonight. She fucking held a gun to my head just a few hours ago. She's clearly trained. Suddenly, I'm reminded of the shiner on my face. I rub my left cheek.

"Did she give that to you?" Enzo asks with a shit-eating grin, then sips his drink.

"Fuck off." I shake my head, laughing.

I finish my drink, appreciating the warm liquid, before getting up and heading to the backroom. No one says anything to me. For some reason, I needed eyes on her to stay calm.

So, she isn't an assassin or spy, but that doesn't mean she's not an enemy. As I watch her sleep, I contemplate what to do with her. We could keep her as a hostage. We could use her as collateral against the Outfit or as a trade for some territory from the Triad. I wasn't actually considering any of that. I knew, in the back of my mind, what I wanted to do. Fate's decided that. And you don't mess with fate.

# Chapter Eleven

## NATALIE

Holy shit, my head hurts. What happened last night? I've never had a hangover like this. My head is actually throbbing. Did I do drugs? Or—*fuck*, was I drugged? I groan. I'm laying on my stomach as I feel around my bed. Why is it so hot? Feeling around some more with my hand, I freeze. *Is this a man's chest? Am I laying on a man's chest?*

Then the memories assault me. The explosion, Nico, the two men standing over me. Someone speaking Mandarin. *Fuck! They got me!* I have to get out of here. I try to get up, but my head and body say that's not an option. Strong arms wrap around me, and I'm pulled into his scent. Deep ocean and mahogany. It's him. I know it's him without even seeing him.

I'm calm for a second, then I panic again. Shit, *he* has me as a hostage, and I'm sharing a bed with him. I feel around to make sure I'm not hallucinating. Definitely him. His broad, muscular chest.

"Like what you feel?"

He finally speaks up, and I can hear his smile. I freeze, pull my hand back, and close my eyes.

I open one eye and take in the room. Then the other eye. I try to lift my head up, but the weight of the pain immediately takes me back down, my eyes close again.

"Hey, hey," he says gently, his voice devoid of emotion, "don't get up too fast. You took a pretty bad hit to the head."

"Oh god," I grumble as I try to lean back to get some distance between the two of us. Once I'm on my back and my head settles on a pillow, I open my eyes and look over beside me.

Two dark eyes stare back at me. One of them is swelling as bruising forms around it. I smile a little, knowing it's from me. My eyes can't help but wander down his tattooed neck and broad chest, which is, unfortunately, covered by a T-shirt.

"What happened? What am I doing here?" I get the words out in a whisper.

Everything hurts.

He doesn't answer right away. He just lays there like he's deep in thought, thinking about his next move or words.

I stare back, grimacing. "Am I a hostage?"

"No, you're not a hostage," he answers.

That doesn't reassure me in the slightest. I look down and notice I'm in a T-shirt and boxer shorts.

"Where are my clothes?" I ask, looking around to take in the large room.

## Rise Of An Heiress

A gorgeous fireplace sat in the room with lounge chairs and a coffee table in front of it.

"They were ruined," Nico says, like he's bored.

"You undressed me?"

*Seriously, what the fuck.*

"Relax, it wasn't like that. I like my women conscious and responsive. Like I said, your clothes were ruined. I had Valentina clean you up."

We're both quiet for another moment, staring back at each other, before he finally opens his mouth.

"Who's Valentina?"

"Who are you?" he asks, ignoring my question.

I look away, covering my eyes with my hands. My head throbbed. The light made it so much worse.

"The same year you showed up in New York." He pauses. "A little girl was killed in Chicago by the Triad. Or so they thought."

My body stills. I don't respond. Well, he certainly doesn't waste any time.

"Then, last night, it was the Triad trying to take *you*. So, who are you?"

I shake my head, which I immediately regret. It causes me to grimace again. I keep my palms over my face to soothe my headache.

"No one. Just Natalie," I whisper.

If I talk any louder, my head will explode.

"So, how do you know Cesare and Dominic Violante?" My heart skips as he mentions Papa and my brother. He grabs my arm, causing me to look at him. "Who are you?"

"*Natalie*," I insist, voice raised.

Desperate to get some distance from this man, I roll over slowly and force myself to sit up and stand. I walk over to the fireplace and press my palm into the wall, steadying myself. I have to get out of here. Wherever here is.

I can feel his warmth behind me.

"I think you're the dead princess." He waits for a moment, then turns me around. "And I think it'd be in your best interest if you didn't lie to me. Now"—he steps closer to me. I have to look up as I back up until I hit a wall—"tell me who you are." He places both hands on the wall on either side of my head.

"I can't." I whisper.

"*Do. Not.* Test me. Answer my question."

Shaking my head, I say, "I can't. I haven't been her in a long time."

## NICO

Fear is clouding her eyes. She is definitely her. The long-lost Triad princess, who we all thought was dead. The Mad Dragon's daughter. She was living right under our noses the whole time. And she's right in front of me now.

Smart move on Cesare's part. We'd never given a shit about the Triad. We never would've gone looking for her. *Why would the Outfit attack us, knowing she was living in our territory? Why's the Triad after her?* That doesn't sound like Cesare. He's cunning and calculating.

After I convinced her she wasn't a hostage and could roam freely—as long as she didn't leave the property—she calmed down. I don't think she believed me, but I couldn't have her doing anything stupid while she was still injured.

I left her alone so she could shower and have time to herself. I sent the doc to check on her one last time and Valentina, the housekeeper, to bring her food a few hours ago. I'm in the office with Bash, Enzo, and Dante. Cosima, Valentina's daughter, also a maid, brought us coffee. She looked like she smelled something nasty and was staring daggers into me. *What was her problem?*

"Cosima," I bark.

"Yes, Mr. Delucci," she says eagerly, the glare gone, accompanied by a smile.

My mind wanders to the dark-haired beauty, and images of her in the classroom resurface. *Yes, professor.* I shake my head to cut off my thoughts. The last thing I need is to sport a hard-on around my brothers and the fucking maid.

"I have a list of items for you to grab from the grocery store this afternoon, then I need you to buy a full wardrobe for our houseguest. Valentina will be coming down shortly with her sizes," I say curtly, and Cosima's face scrunches back to the snarl.

"Will do, sir," she says through gritted teeth before exiting.

My brothers and I look at each other. I know what they're thinking. Cosima's had her sight on me since we were kids. She doesn't like that Nat—*Anya* is in the house, and she especially doesn't like her sharing a bedroom with me. Tough shit. She's my staff and nothing more. She better not cause any problems. I don't have any issues killing her, but we're all really fond of her mother. Valentina has been with us since we were boys, as loyal as they come. We don't get a lot of that in our world.

Once the door is shut, Enzo is the first to speak. "So, the attacks on the harbor?"

"My theory? Had to have been the Triad. My hunch says they spoke Italian to throw us off their trail. It's the only thing that makes sense. If everything we just learned about Nat"—I pause—"*her* is true, there's no fucking way Cesare would risk her. I think that's why the Outfit's left us alone the last twenty years," I answer.

"I think you're right. But it still doesn't answer why. Why is the Triad attacking us and framing the Outfit?" Bash asks.

"I called around this morning. I got word that there have also been some strange attacks in Chicago, too. They lost five men in a shootout, they thought it was us," Dante says.

"So what? The Triad is attacking us both and blaming the other?" Enzo questions.

"It makes sense. If we start a war with the Outfit, The Triad is probably hoping we just take each other out and then they get New York, Chicago, and all our territories combined to themselves," I answer.

"Motherfuckers. And how does the girl fit into this?" Enzo asks.

"I think finding her was a lucky accident. The current dragon head, Andrew Li, is Anya's uncle. She's the only person standing in his way. He will stop at nothing to make sure she's dead. His ego is probably wounded to find out she's been alive this whole time. He failed," Bash explains.

"Well, what do we care what happens to her? I say we hand her over and stay out of it if we're not going to use her to bargain with." Enzo chuckles and gives Bash a cocky smile. "Or better yet, she's sexy as hell. Before we give her back, at least let me take her for a—"

I see nothing but red. Next thing I know, I'm grabbing Enzo by the throat, lifting him into the air. Then his ass is on the floor. I'm on top of him in seconds, with Bash and Dante trying to pull me off.

"What the hell was that?" Bash shouts over a coughing Enzo, face red as he's pushing me back, Dante behind me, restraining my arms.

"Oh, I think your little brother has a crush on the little princess," Dante taunts over my shoulder.

I elbow him, and his grip tightens. Enzo is looking at me furiously but doesn't say a word, picking himself off the floor.

"Well?" Bash presses.

"Nobody is going to fucking touch her. Nobody is going to take her anywhere," I try to say as calmly as possible, but my anger is seeping through every syllable.

The room was silent. Bash looks into my eyes, and I swear he can see right through my bullshit. Not that I made a huge effort to hide it.

"Fuck," Bash sighs as he runs his hand through his hair, taking a deep breath. "Have you fucked her?" He points at me.

I growl as I make a move toward him, trying to shake Dante off, but he pulls me back, so I let him. I can't hit our capo. I don't want him thinking about her or sex at the same time.

Dante laughs from behind me. "Bro, when did you have time to get into her panties? She was knocked out. Unless"—he pauses—"oh, you sick bastard! You took advantage of—"

I turn and punch him square in the jaw, gritting my teeth. "Never talk about her clothing again, you fucker."

Dante looks over at Bash. "Capo, your brother's unhinged," he teases, unfazed.

Bash wipes his hand over his face and turns his gaze back on me.

"I'm gonna ask you this once, and you better tell me the truth . . ." He says in the calm, but not I'm-anything-but-calm voice. "Have you been fucking her while you were supposed to be getting intel on her?"

Despite being a grown-ass man, I stay quiet.

"Looks like he was getting more than intel," Enzo says, laughing as he elbows Dante and bumps fists.

I was going to have to kill my best friend and my brothers if they wouldn't stop talking about her like this.

"Dante, Enzo. Out," Bash orders.

Dante lets go of his restraint, and they leave the room.

The door clicks, and he says, "What happened, Nico?" He walks behind his desk and adjusts his suit.

Why does he insist on always wearing a damn suit? We're at the safe house, for crying out loud.

I sigh. "I don't know. One second I was watching her, doing my job, and the next, I couldn't stay away."

# Rise Of An Heiress

I answer honestly, unable to look him in the eyes, feeling like I just got caught taking a bite out of the forbidden apple, which was fitting, since that's exactly what I did.

"Are you in love with her?"

"No," I answer quickly, looking up. "I don't know anything about her. Anything we have learned isn't even true. Her lies have lies." *At least that's what I'm telling myself.* "Plus, she's not ready to tell us anything."

Bash narrows his eyes and looks like he doesn't believe me. "Well, you better figure it out soon, because we can't stay here forever. She's a liability. So, if you don't intend on continuing anything serious with her, we don't have a choice. We have to let her go. This isn't our war."

*Let her go.*

"You can't be serious?" I yell.

"I'm deadly serious, Nico." He points at me, teeth gritted. "Violante knew you were at that gala. Hell, he probably thinks we ordered the attack and kidnapped her. We have to give her back to the Outfit before they attack us and let them know what we found out. They can deal with the Triad. This has nothing to do with us."

"Is that all?" I ask.

Bash nods.

I walk out and slam the door behind me.

\* \* \*

When I get back into the room, I see she's eaten. That makes me happy. At least that's one thing she isn't going to put up a fight on. I look over onto the bed where she's laying. She's freshly showered with another one of my shirts on. And fuck, if I didn't love the sight of that.

Her eyes are closed, but I can tell she isn't sleeping. Her head is probably killing her, though. As I walk closer to her, she opens them, blinking at me with those long lashes, and she catches me checking her out before looking down.

"I don't have any clothes," she says, adjusting to sit up straighter.

I'm well aware she has nothing else on. She must have seen the look on my face because she started blushing.

"I've sent Cosima to buy you a new wardrobe. That's why Valentina was in here earlier."

"Oh"—she perks her head up—"thanks, I'll pay you back of course. And she doesn't need to get much. I won't be here long." She pauses. "Right?"

"No need. Your money's no good to me. And that all depends," I answer back.

"On what?" she asks, suddenly angry.

"On what you tell us," I say.

"I don't know anything other than someone is trying to kill me. I need to get to the Outfit so we can find a way to take him out."

She's determined.

"Someone being your uncle?"

She pauses for a moment and straightens her posture. "Yes. It's either he goes, or I go."

"You want to take over the Triad?"

"No," she answers quietly. "But I don't have a choice. Like I said, it's either him or me. He won't stop until I'm dead, whether I want to take over or not. You know how this world works." Tremors lace her voice.

I nod, taking in her confession. It's really her. The Triad princess.

"Can you show me to my room, please?" She winces as she throws her legs over the edge of the bed.

"Is something wrong with this one?" I cross my arms.

She gulps. "No. It's just . . . Well, it's yours, isn't it?"

My eyes wander up her legs. I can see her nipples through my white shirt. "What's your point?"

"My point is, I'm not sharing a room with a total stranger."

I scoff, trying to hold back a laugh. "But you'd fuck one in a night club?" I raise an eyebrow, and she shoots me the look of death.

Damn, she's cute, even when she's ready to kill me.

"I'm sure you have a room to spare in this mansion," she replies with no effort to hold back any sass.

"No can do. They're all taken," I retort through a lie.

"That's a lie." She calls me out quickly.

I give her the "try me" look, and she rolls her eyes. "There're no other rooms, so you're stuck with me," I say, leaving no room for an argument.

She's quiet for a moment, but eventually, she sighs. "Fine. But you take the couch and no touching."

"No deal," I counter.

"Then, take the floor. I don't care."

"Afraid you won't be able to keep your hands off of me?" I smirk, teasing her.

"Please, we both know it's you who can't stay away from *me*."

*She isn't wrong.*

I laugh. "Fine, but I still sleep in the bed."

She thinks about it for a moment. "Fine."

"Fine," I repeat.

"Okay," she pipes back.

"For now." I pause. "But trust me when I tell you, you'll be begging for my cock again in no time."

She pushes me off of her with a grunt, and I can't help but laugh. I could get used to being around her. I move over to the fireplace, where the bar cart stands, to pour us both a drink.

"Where are we, anyway?" she asks, changing the subject, looking anywhere but at me.

"A safe house" is all I give her as I turn around.

"But, where?" she presses.

"Somewhere safe," I answer, handing her the glass. Her eyes widen like she just remembered something.

"I need to call Dom!"

She looks worried. "He's probably worried sick. This is going to be bad."

Shit, I forgot about her step-brother.

"You can't call him yet." I down the rest of my drink, and she slams her glass down on the table.

"And why the hell not?" she asks angrily. "They already think you're the ones who wanted to sell me out to my uncle. I'm sure they're furious. I need to get back home. And I have school.

I literally have less than a month left before I'm finished. I thought I wasn't a hostage?"

*Is she seriously thinking about school right now?*

"You're not. You need to meet my brothers first. We'll talk. Then we'll decide," I tell her, heading toward the door.

"Dinner is in two hours. Cosima will be back with clothes before then. Don't be late," I call back, not bothering to turn as I slam the door shut before she has time to argue.

# Chapter Twelve

## NATALIE

As promised, Cosima showed up about an hour later with an assortment of clothes. Valentina told me Cosima was her daughter. I saw it instantly. Cosima looked exactly like her mother but younger, and Valentina has some grays coming in. They were both medium built, and I couldn't help but notice how nice their breasts were and be a little envious of that. Both had light brown hair and gorgeous, smooth olive skin. Valentina went on about how her daughter was so sweet and docile. That was not the woman standing in front of me. If Cosima could shoot needles out of her eyes, I'd be a living voodoo doll right now. *What was her problem?* She throws the bags carelessly to the ground.

"You won't be here long, so I didn't go crazy," she says with a snarl.

As I walk over to pick them up, she crosses her arms, giving me the death glare. If she doesn't stop, I won't hesitate to put her on her ass. I didn't do anything to her.

"Thanks. I can take it from here." I muster up the kindest voice I can.

Another second with her attitude, and I was going to have to put her head through the glass coffee table. *Where did that come from?* I take a deep breath, trying to relax. Dom always had the anger issues, but the more and more I get sucked into this world, the less patience I have. I usually don't have violent thoughts. *Natalie didn't but maybe Anya does.*

I shake my thoughts and look into the bags she bought. The clothes were hideous, but I'd make do the best I can with them. Something told me she did it on purpose. Whatever. If Maya taught me anything, it was that "you rock the clothes, the clothes don't rock you." I don't plan on staying here for very long anyway, so it's just temporary. I'll be rocking the Little House on the Prairie wardrobe. Nothing a pair of scissors couldn't fix. The thought of my friend had me worried for her. I have a lot of explaining to do when I get home. If I ever get home.

I choose the blue dress with daisies on them. It's not a completely unfortunate-looking dress. *You'll have to do.* I rip off the puff sleeves and cut out the extra layers in the skirt. It was floor length, so I cut it to mid-thigh. It's actually cute now.

I brush my hair, and I don't have makeup, so that's the best I can do. Nico was wearing sweatpants, so I don't think the dinner was anything formal, but I was going to be meeting the capo of the Cosa Nostra for the first time, so I had to look somewhat pulled together.

After taking a good look at my handiwork, I make my way downstairs. I smile at the sight. The brothers are gathered around, laughing and teasing each other. They look almost normal. As I walk up to the table, the man sitting at the head of a table, who I assume is Bash, gestures to the seat next to him.

"Join me," he says kindly, with a warm smile on his face.

I can't tell if it's just an act.

I slowly make my way over, my body still sore. "Thank you." I look around the table.

"I am Sebastiano, but you can call me Bash. You already know *Nico*." He points at the man across from me.

I don't miss the way he said his brother's name with his teeth gritted. Shit, did he know? My cheeks feel hot.

"And to his right is our youngest brother, Lorenzo."

I smile at him, and he nods his head. "Call me Enzo," he replies with a sweet smile.

*Oh, this one was trouble.*

"Can we get you anything? Ice? My brother here tells me you took quite a hit," Bash says.

He sounds genuine.

I look directly at Nico, admiring the black eye and bruising on the side of this face, and smile.

"He looks worse. But not at the moment, thank you. Maybe after dinner," I say. Bash and Enzo chuckle, while Nico's gaze doesn't leave mine. Cosima saunters in and hovers over Nico.

"Can I get you anything?" she asks him, giving him her best puppy dog eyes, puffing out her chest, giving him a show of her perfect boobs.

She even ignores the capo. She's fixed her hair and put on makeup since earlier, too. It hits me why she was so hostile. She likes Nico. I wonder if they were ever a thing. I lick the top of my teeth, trying to rein in my . . . annoyance.

Nico looks over at me, and as if he can read my thoughts, he leans in, grabs Cosima's hand, and whispers something to her that makes her blush. I fake a smile at their interaction. I know he's only doing it to piss me off. Why the hell is it working? I won't show it, though.

As if my prayers were answered, a familiar, tall handsome force with dark hair, hazel eyes, and tan skin walks into the room. Casanova himself. He looks fresh off the runway. He was only in sweatpants and a T-shirt, but it was his attitude. All the brothers were in sweats or casual attire, except for Bash, who sported a navy three-piece suit.

"Party's here," he exclaims.

We make eye contact, and he gives me a wink. I push my hair behind my ear like a goddamn school girl and give him my sweetest smile.

He heads straight to me, grabs my hand, and kisses it. "Dante Borelli. But I believe we already met."

I see the look he gives Nico. He wants to mess with him, too. I think we're going to get along great.

"Dante, it's nice to meet you *again*." I pull the chair out to my left. I can see Nico's glare out of the corner of my eye. Two could play this game. "Why don't you sit next to me? You owe me a drink, after all."

Dante's eyebrows raise to the ceiling, and he gives me a shit-eating grin. "I'd love to, sweetheart." He plops down, and I swear I hear Nico growl from across the table. Dante leans close to my ear. "I know what you're doing." He's wearing a devious grin.

I lean back into him and whisper, "And I know what *you're* doing. I see right through you, Dante Borelli."

We both laugh, but Nico looks like he's going to flip the table over, his fist in such a tight grip, his knuckles turning white. Cosima is completely unaware, still trying to keep his attention. He dismisses her with a wave, not even bothering to look up at her. She gives me one last glare before exiting, and I make a mental note to keep an eye out for poison.

Dante leans back in his chair. "So, what should we call you, sweetheart? Actually, don't answer that. I like sweetheart." He winks.

Realizing the room is silent, I roll my eyes, and all four men stare at me. I don't know what to say. What should they call me?

Bash broke the silence. "You do have a name, don't you?" He stares me straight in the eyes. Right at that moment, Valentina and Cosima appear with large dishes of pasta, bruschetta, and bottles of wine, buying me some time. The men's shoulders relax, and I think about my answer while they're distracted.

Thinking back to what Nico asked me this morning, I ask myself, *Who are you, really*? I wasn't lying. I *hadn't* been her in a long time, but I could feel her breaking through the surface.

When I killed their men, when the Black Rose was bombed, and just now, when I'd imagined Cosima's head detached from her body. *She* was always there. I made the choice to own it. I am who I am, and whether I like it, the underworld is about to know about her. Once Valentina and Cosima head back to the kitchen, I sit up straight and take a deep breath. I hold my head up to address the men in front of me, but I don't make eye contact with any of them.

Four sets of eyes are still trained on me.

"Anya. My name is Anya."

# Chapter Thirteen

ANYA

The room is silent again. You could slice through the tension.

After a moment, I break the silence.

"I only just found out who I *really* am. I thought my name was Anya Cheng until I learned about my . . . parentage."

"Anya Liu, huh?" Nico replies, as if he's testing it out.

The first person to use my real name in twenty years.

I begin to tell them everything. It didn't matter—they already knew the truth, they just needed me to confirm all of it. They even fill in some of the gaps. The words poured out like they had been bottled up. I guess they had. Twenty years is a long time. I recall the conversation I had with Cesare—after their failed attempted kidnapping, I remind them. I explain to them about my mother's marriage to Cesare, how my adoptive parents came to be, and how I ended up in New York. The real Natalie Yang. They didn't even act surprised by any of it.

Bash explains that the Triad have been sanctioning attacks on the Cosa Nostra and Outfit and framing the other so that the Italians can take each other out without the Triad having to get too involved. We all sit in silence again, waiting for Bash to decide.

Dante stares at his phone but then cuts in. "I just got word that, after the attack at the Black Rose, Andrew Li went into hiding. Anya is definitely the target. No one knows how he found out about her, though. He thinks the Outfit is going to come after him."

"How do you know? Is there a rat?" I ask.

"Yeah, and where are you getting this information?" Nico asks.

"I made some connections. Don't worry about it. Dominic probably got caught visiting you—it's not hard to put two and two together," Dante says.

"Connections?" Bash asks, raising an eyebrow.

"Yep," Dante says, offering no further explanation.

"How do we know they're not setting us up?" Nico asks again. My head ping-pongs between them.

"It's not a trap. I need you to trust me. Let me do what I do best." Dante shoves another spoonful into his mouth.

I remember Papa saying Dante was the enforcer. A people hunter.

"If he's been attacking the Outfit and the Cosa Nostra the whole time, why is he just going into hiding now?" I ask.

"My guess is, because neither of us knew it was him. We thought it was the Outfit and vice versa. The men he sent to get you at the Black Rose failed, so their cover's blown. Now he doesn't want any smoke," Dante answers.

This is a lot to take in.

"But Dom knows you were at the gala," I say to Nico. "They still think you're behind the attacks, and now they probably think you're holding me against my will." I look at Bash. "I need to call Pa—Cesare to let them know what I just found out and so I can get home."

"We'll help you," Bash finally says.

What? I don't remember asking for help. I just want to go home.

Dante and Enzo look up at him with their eyebrows sky-high, looking surprised by his decision. Nico didn't take his eyes off me.

"You'll help me get home?"

I need him to be clear.

"No. You'll stay here under our protection, and we'll help the Outfit locate Andrew Li. Once we find him, you can return to your family."

"Does this mean I can call them?" I perk up.

Bash nods, picking up his fork. "Nico and I will be in the room. We need to make sure Cesare and Dominic understand the conditions."

I nod, and to lighten the mood, I hold my drink up in agreement. The rest of dinner held lighter conversation. Mostly Bash updating the guys on the legal side of their business.

After we finish eating, Bash, Nico, and I head into Bash's office so I can call my family. Bash doesn't go to his desk. He gestures to the love seat, sitting on a leather chair by a giant fireplace. I bet they have one in every room. I sit on the love seat, and Nico sits by me.

"Why are you helping me?" I ask as Bash pours three glasses of whiskey.

Bash shrugs. "The Triad has been a pain in my ass these last few months. We've lost millions because of them. If there's anything I can do to get Li out of my hair faster, I'll do it. He won't leave you alone—that's trouble for all of us."

Nico and Bash share a look I don't understand. For some reason, I don't believe him.

## NICO

Someone knocks on the door, and Uncle Ricky comes in with a burner phone, hands it to Bash, and leaves with a nod.

Bash hands Anya the phone before he says, "Keep it short."

She takes the phone and nods. She dials a number, and someone picks up almost immediately.

"Violante."

He sounds like he's trying to keep his voice calm. Anyone else would be fooled, but not me. He's panicking.

"Dom!"

"Nat! Where the fuck are you? Are you okay? I swear to God if those Delucci bastards lay a hand on you—"

I snort at his statement, and I can hear commotion in the background. "Dom, listen to me."

"Bambina?" another voice comes on the line.

"Papa," she whispers.

I can hear the love in her voice. A part of me imagined what it would be like to be on the receiving end of that. I shake my head out of my thoughts.

"We're both here. You're on speaker," Dom replies.

"Are you hurt? Where are you?" Cesare's voice comes through the phone.

"Listen, I don't have a lot of time, but I'm safe. It wasn't the Cosa Nostra behind everything. Andrew knows I'm still alive," she whispers.

Dom lets out a string of curses in Italian.

"Amore," Papa says, "are you sure you're all right?"

"Oui, quand on rougit, ça signifie 'oui,' n'est-ce pas?" *Yes, when someone blushes, it means 'yes,' doesn't it?* she replies back in French.

Where have I heard that? I wonder if she knows I'm fluent in French, too. That must be their code so she can signal to them she's safe. Smart girl. Or she just used the code to say that she is in danger.

"Tell me everything," Dom demands.

She explains to him how she ended up at our safe house. The two men that came after her. That the Cosa Nostra is willing to help.

"Where are you? We're coming to get you," Dom says.

She looks at Bash and me, and we nod. She knows what to say.

"Dom," she whispers, "their capo has agreed to let me stay here with them until Andrew is found."

"LIKE FUCKING HELL YOU ARE!" Dom screams so loud my eardrums could have busted.

"You don't have a choice," I say. "She is safer with us, and you know it. The Triad doesn't know she has any ties to us."

"Ties to you? The fuck do you mean? She still doesn't," Dom spits back, annoyed.

"He's right, Dom," she responds, probably not wanting him to ask any more questions on how we met. "Andrew won't think to check out the Cosa Nostra for my whereabouts."

"We'll help you find him. Then we'll hand her over, and he's all yours. Our only condition is that you take him out," Bash says to the phone.

Dom sighs. "Why do I feel like there's a catch?"

"There isn't one. We want Andrew off our asses. He cost us money, tried to manipulate us and almost sent us into a war. We'll help you find him, but you take him out. Consider this an act of goodwill," Bash answers.

Dom scoffs but is quiet for a moment as he thinks it over.

"If anything happens to her under your watch," Dom finally says, "I will hunt every single one of you down, kill your loved ones one day at a time until there's no one left, right before I kill you myself."

"I'd like to see you try," I pipe back, holding back a laugh.

She shoots me an exasperated look, and I can't help but smile. She's so damn cute.

"She'll be safe with us. We'll do the east, you guys take the west," I say before he can argue any further.

"Don't fucking tell me what to do," Dom barks.

"As soon as we locate him, you bring her to us," Cesare adds.

"Agreed," Bash says.

I feel something strange in my chest. The thought of taking her back doesn't sit well with me. I push it to the back of my mind.

"We'll keep you updated, and we expect the same courtesy," Bash says. He's just about to hang up when she swipes the phone out of his hand.

"Papa, Dom. We'll talk soon, I promise," she says to them.

"Good night, sorellina," Dom says.

"You get some rest now, amore." Cesare replies right after.

"Oh." She pauses. "You can call me Anya now."

"Welcome back," Cesare says.

You can hear the pride in his voice just before the line goes dead. It amazes me that even Cesare Violante is soft toward her. She definitely isn't as sweet or as innocent as she looks, but they both speak to her like she was the most delicate thing on the planet. I imagine that's why the conversation went so well. To outsiders, it might seem like there is a lot of hostility, but as made men, this was about as good a meeting could get. Anya heads off to bed—my bed—as Bash and I hang back in his office to discuss some business.

After a few hours, I'm ready to crash for the day. I walk into my room and find Anya has already snuggled up, reading, coincidentally, *The Art of War*. She doesn't even look up, as if me coming to *our bedroom* is an everyday occurrence. I can get used to this. She's in one of those white granny nightgowns. I shake my head and laugh as I make my way to the bathroom to take a shower. No doubt Cosima bought her hideous clothes out of spite. Her mission failed because this woman could pull off a trash bag. I shoot a text to Valentina to go buy a new wardrobe.

When I come back out, she's still reading but looks up at me with a smirk on her face. I look at the bed and see the reason for her expression. She's taken every single throw pillow within a fifty-mile radius and created a wall in the center of the Alaskan king bed.

She closes the book, turns off the lamp on her side of the bed, and lays down, turning her back toward my side as I eagerly get dressed and hop into bed with her. I pull back the sheets and turn off the lights.

"No funny business," she says to the dark.

I smile, laying with my hands behind my head.

"Wouldn't even dream of it, princess."

I'm lying. I will most definitely be dreaming about this goddess laying next to me.

# Chapter Fourteen

ANYA

It's been a couple of days, and I'm realizing Nico isn't anything like I'd thought he'd be. I heard about the Delucci's growing up; they were as ruthless as they come. No one was safe if you got in the way of their business. Which is why I'm skeptical of their help.

Bash told me at dinner what the Triad did at the docks, costing them twenty million. I can't believe any Triads are still breathing. Nico could've killed me himself—or worse, let me get taken by the Triad. But he brought me here instead. Something tells me there's more to that hard, inked exterior.

Needing to move and get my blood flowing, I opt for a walk in the back yard after breakfast. I was a little too sore to do much of anything else. Taking in the landscaping, I notice the property is quite gorgeous, spacious, and full of greenery. I'd like to explore it more, but there's a lot of forest surrounding the area, so it doesn't seem safe to wander off on my own. Finding a gorgeous clearing with the sun peaking through the trees, I plop myself down and take in the fresh spring smell. Birds chirp and leaves rustle. I take several deep breaths.

Am I really about to do this? Can I? Lead the Triad? Just because you don't have a choice doesn't mean you can't contemplate the matter. So many questions whirl through my mind. Yes, I'm tired of being Natalie. Bored, even. Yes, I've been craving excitement. Although, I should've specified with the wish-granting genies that I was thinking something along the lines of steamy nights in Greece during Yacht Week or following some popular DJ around on their world tour. I'm not entirely sure I can be Anya. Anya is the heir. Anya has had people gunning for her since she was six years old.

Then there was my tall, dark, and handsome roommate who came barreling into my life. Nico is . . . thrilling, sexy, intelligent, dangerous. Nico is everything. But I can't have him. I knew being Natalie was going to be a lonely path. I just didn't realize being Anya was going to be an even lonelier one. But if I choose one, my new life will have more perks. At a steep price, but there'd be no more hiding and no more pretending. I can't lie, the thought of taking my power back and having agency over my own life. The prideful part of me wants to make my siblings, and even Peter and Nina proud.

After wallowing in self pity for half an hour, I hike back up to the mansion. When I get back, Valentina is in the kitchen preparing dinner. I don't see any signs of Cosima. I was not in the mood for a throw down with her.

"Where's Cosima?" I ask Valentina, grabbing an apple off of the counter.

"I sent her home. She's been in a terrible mood these last few days, I don't know what's going on in that girl's head!" she responds, exasperated, kneading what I'm assuming is pasta dough.

*I can think of one thing.*

I'd really have to get back to the gym if she was cooking like this every day. I wasn't vain, but I trained really hard to be strong. People always look at me and see a petite girl, nothing that exudes strength.

"Is there anything I can help with?" I ask her.

"Oh, no. You relax, Miss Anya."

*Anya.* That is going to take some getting used to.

"No, seriously, I don't mind. I have no idea what to do with myself right now," I insist.

She looks at me hesitantly.

"Okay, you can peel and mince the garlic." I hustle over to the counter, and she shows me how to handle the knife.

I only lasted about fifteen minutes before she sent me off. I moved too slowly, and it didn't help that the garlic kept flying off of my cutting board and onto the floor.

"Dinner smells amazing!" Dante says as we gather around the dining table.

Cosima comes back. She's laying the last dish down as I walk to my seat, not bothering to hide her glare when she sees me.

"No thanks to Miss Anya," Valentina jokes, patting me on the back.

"I just need a little practice," I say to the table, laughing as I take my seat.

I don't miss Dante making his way to the chair next to me, only for Nico to growl and shoot him a look from across the table. Enzo sweeps in to take the seat.

## Chapter Fifteen

### NICO

Dante and I are sitting in our security room, working on finding any underground chatter about Li's whereabouts. I've hacked his and his known associates' bank accounts. He should know better than to use them. I try anyway, just in case. But, as expected, it was a dead-end.

"Man, she's something," Dante breathes out in awe as I look up to see what he's referring to.

His eyes are on one of the monitors, and I look to find Anya reading outside on the library balcony. She's in a crop top and what are supposed to be shorts. *Dammit, Valentina.*

"Focus, Dante, we're not here to meet women." I growl at him, not liking that his eyes glaze with hunger and lust every time he looks at her.

"Says the man who already fucked her *and* tricked her to sharing his bedroom. What did you tell her, anyway? You ran out of rooms? She has to know you're full of shit."

When I don't answer, his eyebrows shoot up to his hairline, and he shakes his head. "You did, didn't you? Fuck, man, you've got it bad."

"Fuck off. It's not like that."

I have no interest in divulging my sex life with my bastard of a best friend—or lack there of, since Anya enforced the unfortunate no-touching rule.

"So, you wouldn't mind, then, if I invited her to stay in my room instead?" He raises an eyebrow. I squeeze my fists so hard, whitening my knuckles and popping them through our silence. "Thought so."

Dante is finding this situation hilarious. I fail to see what he finds so funny.

"She obviously doesn't mind sharing a room with you, or I imagine she would've put up more of a fight."

I'm done with this conversation.

After a few hours of hitting one dead-end after the other, I give my eyes a break and head to our gym to release some tension. I work out every morning, but lately, I've been needing to do more these last couple of days.

As I'm heading down the hall to my room to change, I notice Anya has moved to the library's big oak desk, who's writing something as she reads. She's so entranced with her work she doesn't even notice I walk up to the opposite side of the desk. I

## Rise Of An Heiress

knock on the desk three times to grab her attention. She jumps as her head shoots up.

"I didn't see you there," she says, surprised.

"Yeah, you looked really into your work."

"I hope it's okay that I'm in here. You only had *The Art of War* and *Hacking for Dummies* in your room. I didn't have much else to do since you won't give me a phone."

I don't miss the sass in her tone at that last part.

"Bash got me that as a joke for Christmas," I tell her, recalling the funny memory. "You can use the library whenever you want."

I ignore the phone comment. She knows we don't trust her yet.

"Isn't it ironic that you guys keep this in your library?" She laughs and holds up a book. *Rico - How Politicians, Prosecutors, and the Mob Destroyed One of the FBI's Finest Special Agents.*

I fight back a smile, but I still let out a small chuckle. "Why are you reading it?"

"I found some helpful stuff in it. The plan was to be a criminal lawyer. That's if I even get to finish school. I only have a couple of weeks left. Not that it matters, I could be dead any day—"

"You're not going to die."

"Not even the all-powerful Deluccis can make a call like that," she sasses. "Besides, we agreed that you'd help us find my uncle, and that's it. I'll be out of your hair soon enough. At least until Bash hits me up one day to call in a favor. Probably to ask for my first-born child," she jokes.

I didn't like the unexpected feeling her comment gave me. I didn't want to think about her having someone's children. I shake my head to stop my thoughts immediately. Something I found myself doing more and more. She's right. We find the son of a bitch, Li, and I get back to the way my life was before this raven-haired, dimple-having pain in my ass came storming into my life.

"Bash would *never* take your child from you." I pause. "He'd send me to do it," I joke. That got a laugh out of her. A real laugh.

"Guess that means we'll get to see each other again someday," she says once she's calmed down.

*Get to.* Not have to.

I give her a small smile. "I suppose so. Good luck with that." I nod toward the open book.

I don't give her a chance to respond. I book it out of the library to get to the gym. I have even more tension to release than before. I never should have gone in there. The more time I spend with her, the more I need to know. Just as I'm whipping around the corner, my body collides with another. My arms instinctively go to grab it, and I notice it's Cosima.

Once she gets her footing, she adjusts her clothing and mutters, "Sorry, Nico," through gritted teeth. *What now?*

Cosima was always jealous. Sure, we flirted growing up, but she was never anything more than a social climber. She thought being a housekeeper like her mother was something to be ashamed of. I respect Valentina more than any other woman, aside from my own mother. She's respectful, works her ass off, and we make sure her paychecks reflect it.

"Do we have a problem, Cosima?" I ask her, trying not to lose my patience.

"Why did you have to bring *her* here?" She snickers and crosses her arms.

"Anya? Because she's valuable and needs our help. I don't owe you an explanation, but I am telling you this so you don't do anything to fuck this up."

"Valuable," she repeats the word like its poison, rolling her eyes.

I walk toward her slowly, and she backs into the wall. "Listen to me very carefully, Cosima." I whisper it, but I'm practically still yelling. "The only and I mean *only* reason my family hasn't kicked you out on your ass yet is because of your mother. But make no mistake, we have our limits. You don't get to question us, and you sure as fuck don't get an opinion on who we allow into our home and do business with. Do you understand me?"

I left her there with tears in her eyes and her jaw to the floor.

Ask me if I give two shits.

## ANYA

The next couple of days were uneventful. Nico and Dante pretty much spent all their time in the security room, hacking whatever they can to locate my uncle. Enzo is in charge of the soldiers staying nearby and running perimeter checks. Men are constantly coming and going. Not sure how a safe house works, but they didn't seem to be doing anything safe. Nico assured me they're being smart about it, so I suppose I just have to take his word for it. Bash pretty much stays in his office all day. After all, he still has legal businesses to run.

I miss Maya and Donna, so I've been distracting myself by spending my days in the library, reading. Bash caught me in there one time, and I woke up with a Kindle from him one day. He assured me no one could trace us from it. Bash has been very thoughtful. Come to think of it, they all had. I'm getting more and more comfortable with the men. We share almost every meal together.

Nico surprised me the most. He knows how I like my coffee. I overheard him telling Valentina to make sure we never run out of oat milk or honey. I'd never told any of them that out loud. I smile at the memory. He always makes sure my favorite snacks are in the library ever since he's found me there. I have a whole new wardrobe as well, one I definitely approve of, along with some skincare products I've requested. Men and their 9-in-1 products. Cosima has also steered clear of me. I have a feeling Nico had some words with her.

Thoughtful.

My body always comes to life whenever he was near. I can't explain it. I've never reacted this way to a person before. It's only been a week since I woke up here, and I never thought I'd say this in a million years, but I can see myself falling for him if I'm not careful. Which is why I'm hell-bent on sticking to my no-touching rule. A rule I regretted the same day I made it. Hence, the pillow wall to keep me in line.

I still don't know where we are, but I know we're up north. It's May, and the temperature stays pretty mild. I'd say the highs are in the 80s. So much green surrounds us, I don't ever want to leave. I explore the mansion and all its glory. It's massive and modern. It's either a new building or it's been highly renovated. Everything was cream and brown with hints of red. There were a number of paintings hanging around that I'm sure cost a fortune. Now I know for a fact Nico was lying. There are definitely more bedrooms, but it's not like I put up a huge fight.

This afternoon, I had grown tired of reading but have been feeling so much better physically. My body wasn't sore anymore. I still had some bruising but nothing too bad. I worked out and trained again. This is the longest I've gone without at least getting a workout in. Feeling restless and full of energy, I set my book down and head to the room to change my clothes.

The mansion had a huge state-of-the-art gym in the basement next to the security room. It had rows of machines, punching bags, and a ring to spar in. Music seeps from Dante's room. *Oh, what the hell*, I think, knocking on the door.

He answers the door, and it takes him a second to notice me. He has to look down. When he sees me, a smile lights up his face, and he looks at his watch.

"I knew this day would come." He leans against the doorway, letting his shirt rise. He makes a show of checking me out. "Midday quickie?" He winks, followed by a head tilt toward his bed. "Shirt. Off."

I roll my eyes. "Dream on. I was actually seeing if you wanted to train with me. I could use a partner right now."

"Oh, right," he says as he heads back into his room, stripping his clothes off in front of me. I'm too stunned to move. He starts to put workout clothes on. *Oh, thank God.* "I almost forgot you aren't just hot but deadly, too." He walks past me.

"You'd do well to remember that," I joke, following him down to the basement.

The gym is empty when we walk in, and I head over to the treadmill.

"I'm just gonna warm up for a bit."

We warm up in silence. Once I'm done with the treadmill, I stretch. It feels good to move again. My muscles have been so stiff from sitting in a chair, hunched over, reading all day. Eventually, I make my way to the punching bags. Running a series of combos, I feel Dante come up behind me.

"Pull back faster when you punch, like this"—he grabs my wrist—"squeeze your abs." We get in a few jabs. "You're tiny. Use speed as your advantage."

"You do remember the footage, right?" I say, rolling my eyes.

"I did, and you had a gun on you. That won't always be the case," he replies. "Get into the ring." He gestures with his head.

I step in, and I'm actually excited. Dante was right, though, I've always been on the defense when I fight, I know my opponents will always be bigger than me, so my job is to make sure they never get their arms around me or the upper hand in any way.

"Let's make a wager," he says with a smirk.

He really is handsome. Tall, muscular, dark hair with hazel eyes and olive skin. There was only one dark-haired man on my mind, though.

"Go on." I put my hands on my hips.

I had no intention of making one, but I was curious.

"If I win, you give me a kiss. If you win, I give you a kiss." He smirks.

"And how does this benefit me?" I say, crossing my arms.

He gestures down his body as if that alone held all the answers. I roll my eyes so hard I swear they almost got stuck.

"Okay, okay. If I win, you let me take you out when we get back to New York."

"You're serious?" I ask.

"Deadly," he replies, wiggling his eyebrows.

"Not a chance," I reply.

"Scared you're going to lose?" he goads.

"How about no wager, and we just train," I say.

"Your loss," he says, taking his fight stance.

We run through some drills and combinations. Dante's actually a good trainer. I knew he could fight, but training and coaching's a whole different ball game. I like learning from him. He hasn't said or done anything inappropriate since I shut down his wager, much to my surprise.

I'm really into it, and he's stopped going easy on me. We pant and sweat. This is the best I've felt in days. I kick him in the stomach, but he grabs my leg. I use the momentum to kick him off of me with my other leg, but we fall to the ground, grunting in pain. I let out a string of curses. So much for not being sore anymore. This'll do it. I'm flat on my stomach, breaking Dante's fall with my own body. Lucky for him. He lies on top of me, his stomach to my back as I practically eat the mat.

"What's going on here?" a loud voice echoes into the room.

I don't even have to look up to know it's Nico. Dante crawls off of me, groaning, before lying on his back, panting. We look over at Nico in the doorway with his arms crossed. He does not look happy. His eyes are glazed over; he looks almost possessive and jealous?

"Combat training," Dante says, catching his breath and hopping back on his feet. He holds his arm out to help me up, and I take it. "She's getting better, thanks to me." Dante smirks at Nico, who is still wearing the same expression.

I roll my eyes, but he's right. I've learned a lot in the last hour. I'm used to my old trainers. I know all their moves.

"She's fast," Dante continues, when Nico doesn't respond. "Which is good. Anyone can pick you up with one arm." He elbows me.

Nico uncrosses his arms and walks—no, struts—into the ring.

As he takes off his shirt, I can't help but admire the pure muscle that surrounds his arms, shoulders, and abs. Every hard inch is covered in ink. He stands directly in front of me. My eyes meet his, and he's wearing a smirk on his face. He totally just caught me checking him out.

"Let's see, then." He gestures with his arms to attack him. Is he serious? I'm tired, but I didn't want to back down. I narrow my eyes.

"Let's go." I give him a teasing smile.

We circle around for a moment. I notice soldiers are beginning to trickle into the gym as well as Enzo. He's looking at me like a hunter would stalk its prey. I won't make the first move. He takes a swing at me, and I duck quickly. I try to get him behind the knee, but he's too quick and grabs my leg. I'm able to twist out of it, but he swipes my other leg with his, and he knocks me on my ass. *Fuck.* He puts his arm out to help me back up, and I take it. The first time he's touched me since I woke up in his arms, and it's because we're fighting. He grabs my waist and turns me around.

"Next time, move your hips this way."

He's behind me now, and fuck if my body doesn't come to life. He grabs my waist with his big hands and repositions my hips into the right position.

"Take your supporting leg and pivot that heel so you don't lose balance and don't hurt your knee."

I nod. I don't have words. I'm not sure I'm even still breathing.

Just as I gather my thoughts, Nico points to a soldier and gestures for him to move into the ring. "You."

The soldier rubs his palms together, looking at me with a shit-eating grin on his face. I want to wipe the smile off his face. He comes at me, but I'm faster. He loses his balance from his momentum. He tries to grab me, but I use the weight to knock him to the ground and put him into an arm bar. He struggles as I hang on for dear life until he taps out.

Dante and Enzo clap proudly. The soldier stands, but he won't make eye contact with anyone and stalks away.

"You keep embarrassing my men. Good work, I guess." Nico looks like he's hiding a smile.

"Good? You mean great!" Dante says as he picks me up and spins me in a circle.

I can't help but laugh and throw my head back. How's this guy so laid back?

As he sets me down, Nico grabs Dante by his collar.

"Get your hands off of her," he demands through gritted teeth.

My eyes are wide as I watch the interaction. Enzo just shakes his head, laughing.

I could've sworn I heard him say, "This will be interesting," under his breath.

Bash comes in, and Nico releases Dante. I wipe my forehead with a towel and drink from a water bottle as Bash examines the room. Enzo runs up to him and pats him on the back.

"'Sup, boss?" he asks to Bash, making his way to the door.

"You need a pool," I say to Bash, only half joking. I love swimming after a good workout.

"Great idea," he replies. Enzo freezes and spins.

Nico and Dante throw their heads back in surprise, looking at him as if he'd grown another head.

"What?" Bash asks them.

"You wouldn't even let me get a pool *table*, and she gets a whole pool?" Enzo says.

Dante laughs. "Looks like Bash can't say no to the princess." He saunters out of the gym.

Bash is behind him, and he slaps the back of Dante's head as they exit.

"Looks like my brother is taking a liking to you," Enzo says as we both leave. Nico grunts like a caveman, not too far behind.

# Chapter Sixteen

NICO

I came down to the basement to get some work done in the security room. When I heard her and Dante in the gym, my mind went *there*.

To say I was relieved they were just fighting would be an understatement. I've never been jealous like this before. Ever. And we're not even hooking up. A part of me needed to find Andrew ASAP so she could be off on her way, but the other part of me wanted to stall to keep her close longer.

Fighting her was every bit exhilarating as I thought it'd be. It was quick but so worth it. I just wanted a reason to touch her. I can't wait to do it again.

After dinner, I ask Anya to take a walk around the property with me. She agrees tentatively, but I think she's been itching to take a look around. She hasn't strayed too far out. The property is several acres, though, and easy to get lost in, so she was wise to not go off on her own.

"The property is surrounded by smaller cabins the soldiers live in. There are eight total that make a circle around the mansion. Well, they're more like houses; each has four or five bedrooms, but we've always called them cabins."

"It's stunning," she says and stops to look around.

She closes her eyes and breathes in deeply. I can't help but admire her. We stop underneath a large tree centered in a clearing just outside of where all the cabins are. It fans out, looking like one of those picturesque ones you'd see in a pop-up book. Surrounded by tall trees, it allows for some privacy.

This is new for me. I never just talked to a girl. Ever. Hell, Anya and I barely spoke the first time I took her.

"We also have an area fenced off for target practice. You can shoot whenever you want, just not alone," I tell her, and she nods, eyes still closed.

"I don't want you to train with anyone else unless it's me, one of my brothers, or Dante."

She opens one eye. She looks at me and raises an eyebrow.

"You didn't look too happy today when I was training with Dante," she teases, opening her other eye.

"If it were up to me, I wouldn't let anyone touch you," I answer honestly. "But I'm compromising."

"It's cute that you think you get a say." She narrows her eyes at me.

# Rise Of An Heiress

"I'm only going to tell you this one time, princess. If anyone else touches you, I will chop off his fingers right before feeding them to his family and drowning him in acid," I promise.

She pauses, then crosses her arms.

"Fine. But just so you know I'm only agreeing because I don't want a bunch of random men touching me, not because you said so or because you threatened to kill someone. I couldn't care less if you take out your own men." She lifts her chin in defiance.

She is so damn cute.

I walk up to her, and she slowly backs up until her back hits the tree. Damn, she's tiny. Leaning down, I grab her waist, and I want to kiss her. I can tell she wants to kiss me, too, with the way she's breathing and staring back at me.

"I wasn't *just* talking about my men," I say, making it very clear the rules still apply when we leave here. What am I even saying?

"Are you really not mad I killed your men?" she asks, surprising me with the change of subject.

"They didn't disable the cameras. I would have had to kill them myself." I let out a sigh.

"Would you have enjoyed it?" she asks, eyebrows coming together.

"Yes," I say shamelessly. I'm a killer, and I don't need her approval.

"I think I enjoy it, too."

"You like killing people?"

"Only when they deserve it." She shrugs. "At least I think I do. When your men came after me, that was the first and only time I've killed anyone. My ears felt foggy, and all my other senses were heightened. It felt good. I know it shouldn't."

My hands are still on her waist. I could kiss her. Something about her confession makes me feel closer to her.

"It was either them or you. Don't feel bad."

I accept her. And she accepts me.

"When I found out who my real father was, it started to all make sense. Why I like it so much, why I get a rush from killing those men. Now I can't help but wonder if one day I'll be like him," she confesses.

Peter Liu was a sick son of a bitch. Everyone knew it.

"That's up to you, if you let it consume you or not."

She's quiet for a moment.

"Nico?" She's still whispering.

"Yeah?" I breathe out, still face-to-face with her.

"What happens after we find Andrew?"

*I have to send you back. You're not mine to keep.*

We both know the Cosa Nostra would never allow it, neither would the Triad. Hell, not even the Outfit. I am so fucked. Yet, just as the thoughts escape me, I know it's a lie. Again—fate. Not even the mafia could stand in the way of fate.

"I don't know," I answer honestly.

She nods as she breaks away and heads back to the house. *Fuck.*

*Rise Of An Heiress*

# NICO

A whole week since she asked me what was going to happen after we found her uncle. Lying in bed next to her every night without touching her was killing me. We spent our days training, going on walks and eating every meal together when I wasn't hunting Andrew. I had to train twice a day, and my cold showers lasted twice as long if I wanted to get a good night's sleep.

When I did perimeter checks, she'd join me. When she read in the library, sometimes I'd work in there with her in comfortable silence, or she'd join me in the security room, helping with the search.

She's been spending time with Valentina, trying to learn to cook to avoid boredom. She's the worst cook ever, and Valentina is about one more fire away from banning her from the kitchen all together. I didn't care if she knew how to cook. I love that she can fight and shoot and is easy to talk to.

We made a habit of going on walks after dinner. I wouldn't make a move on her, but I'd find reasons to touch her. I'd graze her hand when she passed me something at dinner, walk too close to her when trying to get past her, grab something from the fridge over her shoulder while she had it open. I want to get her hooked on my touch as much as I am to hers. We talk—a lot. I have never talked like this with a woman. Not only talked but laughed. I enjoy spending time with her.

I told her what it was like growing up with Bash and Enzo.

She told me Cesare would read *The Little Prince* to her every night when she spent summers with them. I had a hard time imagining him reading a children's book. He was a beast of a man.

She told me about the time she and Donna left a frog in Dom's bed.

I told her how we convinced Enzo to stick a marble up his nose when he was three and how Ma tanned mine and Bash's asses afterward.

Her middle name is Meilin.

My middle name is Amadeo.

I told her if I wasn't a Delucci, I'd probably still be a hacker but maybe for the government. She laughed at that. God, I love her laugh.

She thinks she'd still be a lawyer, just maybe not a criminal lawyer.

She's been teaching me Mandarin. I didn't think I was half bad; I speak Italian, French, and Russian, so I'm pretty good at picking up languages. Her face when I repeated after her told me she didn't agree with the sentiment, but she encouraged me anyway. She's brilliant.

"What was it like growing up apart from the Violantes?" I ask, still taking myself by surprise every time I show interest.

She thinks for a moment. "It was lonely, honestly. Being an outsider. They tried really hard to make sure I didn't feel isolated, but it didn't always work. But we'd spend the whole summer around parts of Italy every year. Papa has several properties out there. I always had the best time, but every year leaving got harder. I used to cry at the end of every summer. Eventually, I just stopped myself from feeling too much happiness, so I wouldn't feel so sad all the time. Our summers were more like boot camps, so that helped."

Tightness engorged my chest. I imagined a younger version of her feeling lost, craving affection, and feeling like she didn't belong.

"I would love to only be around my brothers part-time," I joke.

She laughs. "Yeah, I imagine it's different with three boys. Especially violent ones like yourselves." She sighs. "It wasn't all that bad, though. I love Manhattan, and I have friends. Have you ever been to Italy?"

"A few times. Don't remember the scenery much, though. I was more concerned with *other things*."

"Other things being *women*," she teases, bumping my shoulder.

"What can I say?" I shrug, teasing her back.

I like that she's jealous.

"I got my first kiss in Naples," she says, cutting me out of my thoughts. I knew what she was doing, and I was tempted to take the bait. "By one of the boys in the village we'd see every year."

"Yeah, we don't have to talk about Italy that much," I mumble, half joking but half serious. I knew she'd been with men before me, but still, I didn't want to hear about it. *Be cool, Nico.*

She laughs. "What about your brothers?"

"What about them?"

"Has Bash always been so . . . Broody? And Enzo, so charming? Classic older and younger child syndrome. You also have middle child syndrome," she says.

"First of all, Enzo isn't charming. He's spoiled rotten, never struggled a day in his life, and has always been a pain in the ass. Bash was always going to be capo, so he had to be more disciplined." She looks at me as if she's saying *point made*. "And I don't have middle child syndrome," I say, trying not to pout.

"Sure you don't," she says, smirking.

# Chapter Seventeen

ANYA

The clock ticks with each passing second. Staring at the ceiling, I can't sleep. I'm not even sure I'm breathing. If I breathe, I'll smell his erotic scent. I don't dare move, either. I know he's still awake. I can tell by the way he's breathing. I can tell he feels the tension, too. I want him. And there he is. Less than an inch away from me. If I even coughed, we'd be touching. I regret giving up on my pillow walls.

We're both lying on our backs, staring at the ceiling, our hands on our stomachs like two virgins at church camp. Not that I would know, but it's what I'd imagined they'd be like. He hasn't made a move, but I haven't missed how he's found ways to get close to me and touch me. He wants me. Right now, it's in the tension in his shoulders and the way he's breathing.

It's been two weeks since our almost-kiss, after my first day of training. Resisting him is getting so much harder. I think having sex with him would've been easier than talking and getting to know him. A part of me is hoping they never find Andrew, so we can stay here forever. I know this won't last, but I can't help but wonder. *Is it just sex? You can't ever be together.*

Fuck it. I want this. I not-so-subtlety drop my left arm, so now it's touching his. *Your move, Nico.* Before I can even finish my next thought, he grips my upper thigh. My body comes to life from the heat of his skin. It's not a soft hold, not rough, either. But firm and confident.

Neither of us dare move. We sit still for what feels like forever, but it was probably three minutes. We've had sex before, so why am I so nervous now?

I feel a rush of bravery run through me. I slowly move and pick up his hand that was still on my leg and gently move it over my now aching core. Painfully slow, I move, giving him a chance to pull his hand back if he wants to, but I was praying he wouldn't. I don't think my self-esteem could handle his rejection. Taking control of his hand, I graze his middle finger along my slit over my thin cotton panties, the touch light as a feather and torturously slow. I let out a sigh. He doesn't stop me, and I can hear his breathing becoming more ragged and desperate. My skin feels like it's on fire, and I start moving his finger in circles around my slit, still not applying any pressure.

My core is pleading—no, begging—for more. My panties are embarrassingly soaked, and his chest rises and falls with each labored breath. His eyes are closed. I stop the movement, wanting to see what he'll do next.

## NICO

I'm so hard right now I could hit a baseball. Right out of the park.

My hand is on her pussy. She fucking put it there. If that wasn't the hottest thing I'd ever witnessed. She's waiting for me to make the next move. I know if I take her now, I'll never be able to let her go. Do I want to let her go? Let another man touch her someday? *Fuck no.*

We sit, motionless, and next thing I know, I'm grunting a string of curses and taking the same hand she just used to touch herself with and pull her underwear to the side. I use two of my fingers into her wetness. And fuck is she wet. She gasps as I let out a moan, spreading her legs slightly for me. I move between her entrance and clit, working up her arousal.

Drenched. I already know. I could feel it over the fabric, but touching her skin directly sent a shock through my system. She lets out another moan and circles her hips. That encourages me more. I stroke her slit with my fingers, applying more pressure this time.

"Nico," she moans.

"Fuck" is all I could manage.

Her moans only make me want to take it further. I slip two fingers inside of her and fuck her with them, my palm massaging her clit. She's writhing beneath my hand, and all I can think about is how badly I want her under me. We're still laying side by side; she thrusts her hips into my hand, grabbing onto the sheets.

"I fucking love your cunt, Anya. It's so tight. I want it around my cock."

Taking me by surprise, she rubs her small hand gently down my stomach before stroking my cock over my briefs.

I had no control over my mouth. "I need you."

It was out before realizing I even said anything. Fuck, this woman is making me crazy. She reaches into my briefs, takes my cock in her hand, and strokes painfully slow, barely touching me. I am going to lose my mind; I need more. She pants as I work my fingers.

"Harder," I bark.

When I look over, she's biting her gorgeous bottom lip. But she doesn't listen. I grab her hand from my cock and stroke myself.

"Listen to me, or I won't let you come," I tell her.

She strokes me as she thrusts her pussy into my palm. Her eyes are closed. I couldn't take much more of it. I need to be inside her.

"Oh, fuck, Nico. Yes!"

Her moans grow louder. I could tell she was close, just on the edge, and that's when I take my hand away.

"Why did you stop?" she yells breathlessly, lifting her head and opening her eyes. I return a smirk, getting up to kneel over her. I take off my boxer briefs.

"Because if you're going to come, princess, you're going to do it on my cock, not my hands." I kiss her neck. "At least not this time."

## Rise Of An Heiress

"What makes you so sure there will be a next time?" she asks, as I climb on top of her, settling myself between her legs. A teasing smirk on her face.

I don't respond right away. I rub my erection against her slick core as her back arches, and I block her moans with a painful kiss. I don't stop; I keep teasing her, not letting go of her lips. I push my tongue into her mouth, and she takes everything I'm giving her. Her hands grab my ass, pulling me closer to her, and I grab behind her knees to wrap her legs around my waist. She needs this just as much as I do. She thrusts against me, begging to be fucked.

"This right here"—I palm her pussy, which is somehow wetter than before—"is what makes me certain we will fuck again."

She presses herself against me and kisses me again. I devour her mouth and pull her panties off.

I kiss a trail down her neck, inhaling her scent. As I exhale, I can't help but groan. "Mm, you always smell so good."

I lift her shirt and take one of her perfectly hard nipples into my mouth, taking my time on each one. I work my way down, kissing her belly and work my way back up to take the other nipple in before taking off her shirt. I kiss her again hard, and my hand works its way down her body.

"Fuck, Anya, you're so wet." I play with her pussy.

"Please," she begs, "I need you inside me."

I didn't need her to ask me twice. I line my cock up at her entrance, gauging her response. She tenses and places her palms on my chest. She looks up at me questioningly, and I just smile.

"I don't want anything between us when I fuck you."

"Are you clean?"

"Yes. I've never fucked a woman without a condom before. Are you?"

"Yes, I'm clean."

She was breathless.

"I'm going to fuck you now. Hard. You'll come when I tell you to. And I'm going to come inside you."

I know she has an IUD. I made damn sure to work that into a conversation.

Her consent channels through her actions as she grabs my head with her hands and slams my lips into hers. I thrust inside her. She broke our kiss to let out a scream, adjusting to my size, and fuck if that didn't turn me on more. I kiss down her neck as I fuck her hard and relentlessly.

"Fuck, Anya, your cunt is so tight." I pull back, worried that I'm actually hurting her.

What the fuck? I'd never checked on a woman before. I always fucked hard—the women knew that.

"Don't stop! Fuck," she cries.

I speed up. I fuck her so hard her head makes its way to the headboard.

"You take it so good," I grunt into her ear.

She lets out another string of curses as I take her, and I can feel how close she is. I grab her arms and place them above her head and press them against the headboard.

"Keep your hands there," I demand, looking into her eyes as they glaze over in pleasure.

## Rise Of An Heiress

Wrapping one arm behind her back, I take her waist to hold her in place. I thrust into her mercilessly, kissing her to block out her cries. She bites my lips. I bite hers back. She screams, and I bite into her neck to stop my own cries. Fuck, she felt so good.

"Ah, fuck! Oh, god! Fuck! Nico, please!" she screams over and over breathlessly.

Her pussy tightens around my cock, and I'm so fucking close, but I need her to come first. I move faster. I move my hand to circle two fingers over her clit.

"That's right. Let go, baby. Say my name as you come," I encourage.

She releases, screaming my name.

I continue to thrust inside her to find my release. Her moans don't stop as she rides out her orgasm.

"Nico—"

"You'll come again," I tell her as a pound relentlessly into her.

Her nails dig into my back as she lets out an unintelligible string of words.

"That's right, baby. You'll take it how I tell you to."

My balls are tightening. I can't think straight.

"You ready to come for me, baby?"

"Oh god, yes, please!" she cries, squeezing her eyes shut.

"Eyes on me when you come." Her eyes shoot open as she releases for a second time. I don't slow down.

"Come for me, Nico! Vieni dentro di me!" *Come inside me*! she cries.

Fuck. It was all too much. The Italian, the way she said my name, her begging, the sounds of our bodies meeting. I taste colors as I join her in ecstasy and explode into her. Her pussy tightens around my cock like a vise. I pump into her until there's nothing left.

There was no going back. I will never get enough of this. Of her.

# Chapter Eighteen

ANYA

The sunlight kisses my face as I wake. The delicious ache between my legs reminds me last night wasn't a dream. Strong arms hold me in place. Nico's spooning me from behind. His warmth surrounds me. His scent mixed with our sex. All I had to do was wiggle my ass against his cock. His erection grew almost immediately. He responds, letting out a sleepy groan, moving his hand from one of my boobs to in between my legs. He strokes my already wet core and circles my clit as a let out a pathetic whimper.

"Mm, does your pussy miss my cock so soon?" he says in the sexiest sleepy voice I've ever heard, his breath grazing the back of my neck and sending shivers up my spine.

"Yes," I whisper, rocking my hips into his palm.

"Are you sore?"

"I don't care. I want you."

I didn't need to say more. He lifts my leg up and pulls it behind me to wrap around him and fucks me. Twice. And another time in the shower—for good measure.

We're late to breakfast, and everyone seems to know what we were up to by the looks on their faces. Fuck. Did they hear us? We didn't exactly try to keep it down. I just assumed the walls were soundproof. I feel like I was a toddler who got caught with her hand in the cookie jar. I try not to walk straight, but I really am sore. His cock is huge. Nico looks at me with that stupid, smug face as he saunters over to the table.

Cosima looks like she's about to explode. Her face is so red, and her eyes are practically bulging out of her skull. Valentina makes the sign of the cross, like Lucifer and his whore are in her presence. I take my seat, and to my surprise, Nico sits next to me.

I lean over to him and whisper. "Your walls are soundproof, right?"

The sexiest and biggest smile flashes across his face. He brings his lips to my ears, "Yes, but when your face went beet-red and the fact that we were late, not to mention the way you walked in"—he nodded his head down toward my legs, smug bastard—"you all but screamed it from the rooftop." I roll my eyes.

"Much like you did last night and this morning," he added before taking a gulp of his coffee.

We eat in silence. A phone goes off, and Dante pulls one out of his pocket. He scans what I'm assuming is a message before he puts it back.

# Rise Of An Heiress

"I just got a lead that Andrew was spotted in Kansas City. Apparently, he has a secret warehouse out there. We should be getting confirmation in the next week or two."

*Of course, the day after I give into my sexual hunger, we find my uncle. Damn him.* I realize I've made a big mistake. I shouldn't have slept with Nico. Nothing could ever come from this. I'll be leaving soon. Back to New York and back to our lives. I did a Google search on him after I found out who he was, and he's always photographed with a different woman. All of them tall and blonde, much like the woman he was with at the Black Rose. He definitely had a type—not me. I didn't pay much attention to the tabloids before, but now, I'll actively avoid them. We cannot have sex again.

If there is one thing the Cosa Nostra and Outfit have in common, it's how adamant they are about tradition. Cosa Nostra would never let Nico marry an outsider. I was Triad-born. It wouldn't surprise me if all three of their wives have already been chosen. The thought of him already engaged made my blood boil. I don't even realize I'm gripping my knife until I hear someone speak.

"Is everything okay?" Bash asks me, breaking my train of thought. I look up and shake my head.

"Everything's fine. I just can't believe he wants me dead." I lie.

"We won't let anything happen to you," Bash says firmly, surprising everyone at the table.

Later this afternoon, in the library, I pick out a new book. Cosima walks in with a tray of food and slams it on the table. I don't flinch or turn. This isn't anything new with her.

"Thank you," I say, still not bothering to turn around as I pull a book out and inspect its cover. Usually, she can't get away from me faster, but I can feel her still standing in the room. I flip through the pages, pretending I have no idea.

"It's not going to last, you know," she finally says. I close the book, turn around, and cross my arms. I don't respond. I just stare at her.

She lifts her chin and opens her mouth to speak again. "You and Nico. He'll get tired of you soon. He always does this."

I stroll toward her, and she backs up slightly, her nose in the air.

I walk right past her when I call back, "Then, I guess you don't have anything to worry about."

I have a change of heart. Walking away silently is something Natalie would've done. But I'm not her. I'm Anya Liu, the Triad princess, soon-to-be queen—if I don't get myself killed first. No one should ever speak to me like that. I can't kill her, not that I was considering it. I'm not quite there yet, but I can still put her in her place. I'll probably never see her again, even if the Cosa Nostra continues to do business with the Triad. I have nothing to lose. Fuck it.

"Cosima"—I stop in the doorway and turn to look at her—"if you *ever* come at me like that again, I will smash your head into the concrete before I shoot it off that pretty little body. The Deluccis might hold back on behalf of your sweet mother, but I sure as hell won't. I'll take you apart and mail what's left of you to her." *There, that should do it. Or was that too much? Well, too late now.*

Her mouth falls open in shock, but I walk away before it escalates. I wanted to crack her skull open right then and there. I'm not sure where all this suppressed rage has come from, but she didn't seem like a bad choice to practice it on. However, I force myself to rein in my anger because the last thing I'm going to do is fight over a man.

## NICO

Anya's been different since Dante informed us about Andrew's whereabouts. She hasn't looked at me since breakfast, and when I found her in the gym, she made an excuse to leave and ran as if her ass was on fire. *She's freaking out.* Well, so am I, and she doesn't just get to run away. After dinner, relieved she didn't make an excuse, she agrees to go on our nightly walk. She was reluctant, though; I saw the hesitation, but I'll take what I can get.

"Something on your mind?" I ask as we sit under the tree that I've come to call Our Spot in my head.

"No," she says too quickly and looks like she's lost in thought.

I raise my eyebrows and tilt my head down, like I'm looking out of sunglasses, showing her I don't believe her.

"It's just happening so fast. Last month, I was a law student." She pauses, looking like she's deep in thought. "And now I have to kill my uncle and take over the Triad. *And* there's no guarantee I'll even survive either way."

She laughs, but there's no humor in it.

There's a pregnant pause as I don't reply, waiting for her to go on. I know that's not the only thing that's bothering her. As if she can read my mind, she opens her mouth.

"And then there's . . ." She pauses.

"What?" I press. I want her to say it. I want her to admit there's something going on between us.

"It's stupid," she answers, shaking her head.

"Tell me," I demand a little more harshly than I intended.

She lets out a sigh. "Look, I'm not trying to sound like some crazy girl just because we just slept with each other, but we *did* and I just thought . . ." She pauses again.

I'm beginning to see that opening up is not her forte.

"You just thought what?"

I'm not going to let this go.

She takes a deep breath. "I don't know. I thought we'd have more time," she says, looking down.

*Me, too.*

"We don't know anything yet. In the meantime, let's not worry about it yet. Not much we can do right now until we find him. Don't know how long it'll be, so might as well have fun while we're at it."

Her face falls at my words, but she recovers quickly, then she nods. Fuck. I made it sound like she was just a fuck until it was time to leave. I took her hands into mine. She won't look up at me, so I force her head up by nudging her chin with my finger.

"I didn't mean it like that. I want you, and I don't think we should stop what we're doing because Dante may or may not have a lead. If you want to stop, I'll respect that, but I want you to talk to me about it instead of pulling away. Two people who're having sex should be able to communicate."

She looks at me like I told her I'm from another planet.

"That was a very . . . mature and responsible response," she answers.

No doubt the question was on my face. I laugh at that.

"I have my moments." I kiss her forehead.

"I have one more thing I want to ask you," she says, looking up at me.

"Ask away."

"Has anything happened between you and Cosima? I think she's under the impression you two are supposed to be an item."

*Fucking Cosima.*

"No," I reply.

Now it's her turn to shoot me a look that tells me she doesn't believe me.

I sigh. "We used to flirt with each other growing up, but I never acted on it. I knew better than to cross that line. Her mother works for us, and we knew she would, too, once she turned eighteen. Cosima probably thought, if she batted her eyelashes enough, one of us would marry her. It's not about love for her, it's about rank," I tell her, hoping it's a satisfactory response. I didn't want to talk or think about Cosima. When she doesn't respond, I ask her, "Is she causing problems?"

A devilish smile takes over Anya's face as she looks to the side. "I took care of it."

"I'm not even going to ask." I chuckle.

"She's in the Cosa Nostra," Anya says matter-of-factly.

"She is," I say in the same tone.

"I'm not."

I know what she's thinking. She doesn't belong in our world.

"No, you're not."

She thinks for a moment. "You knew better to cross that line with her, but not with me?" she teases.

"Let me show you just how far I'm willing to cross that line," I say back to her, directing her back into the mansion.

I've been holding back on her but not anymore. If she knew how much mental real estate she took up. she'd stop doubting what this is. The want—no, need—to consume her grows every day I spent with her. Maybe it's selfish, unreasonable, demented even, but I want to ruin her for all other men.

## ANYA

Nico leads me back into the bedroom we're sharing but doesn't stop at the bed. Instead, he grabs something out of his dresser and takes me over to the French doors that lead to his balcony. The sunbed is my favorite place to read, but I think the reasons are about to change.

He picks me up, and I wrap my legs around his waist instinctively. He walks us over to the sunbed as predicted, throws me down. A yelp escapes my lips. I can already feel myself getting wet. I didn't think I could enjoy getting manhandled this much. I look up at him, biting my lip. All muscle and control.

"I'm going to fuck you," he says, his voice gravelly, tone firm. He crawls between my legs and tears off my clothes. "And there's not going to be anything gentle about it." Kneeling over me as I lay on my back, legs spread to him, he demands, "Say you understand."

"I understand," I reply breathlessly, feeling needy. I love that he was so different in bed than he was outside. He's always so calm and collected, but this man right now, this man was controlling, possessive, and hungry for me.

"Good girl. You will beg for your pleasure," he says as he grabs the ties he pulled from the dresser. "Give your body to me fully."

I nod. "Yes." My mind is blank. It was the best I could do.

My core was already throbbing. He gives me his sexy smirk that I've already grown attached to as he ties my wrists together to the bars of the sunbed. He climbs back over me and starts leaving gentle kisses over my body, working his way up. I'm panting with anticipation. He sucks on my neck, massaging my breast before he plants his mouth over my nipple. My chest rises as I whimper as his lips make their way to the other one.

His palm slowly works down my torso, and he gently rubs my slit. Not enough to give me any friction. I move against him in an attempt to get more.

"You're already so fucking wet. Your pussy is begging for me," he says against my neck.

"Please, Nico."

"Are you going to be a good girl?" he asks, teasing me as his lips still work around one of my nipples, his hand still teasing my slit.

"Yes."

"Say it."

"I'll be good. I want you inside me," I tell him as he works his lips down to my belly button and lower.

"Not yet. I want my dessert first."

Before I could reply, his tongue makes a dive for my entrance, and he slowly runs up to my clit. I'm already so close. Fuck.

As if he could read my mind, he asks, "Do you want my tongue?"

"Yes, Nico."

"You don't get to come until I tell you to."

And with that, he devours my pussy, and I cry out. I'm sure anyone outside right now can hear me. He slaps my ass as he moves his tongue around my slit, as if he's starving.

"Do not come yet. Or you will be punished."

"Fuck, Nico!" I cry. "Please, please. I'm so close."

I can't hold off anymore. Just as I'm about to release, he stops, and I let out a cry in frustration. My wrists are starting to sting from all the pulling.

"Good girl," he says, looking up at me with a smile. "And because you were such a good girl, I'm going to fuck you until you can't walk. Is that what you want?"

"Please," I cry. His mouth is back on my pussy, and he inserts two fingers inside of me. My wrists strain against the rope, my back arched. Working his fingers in and out of me, he attacks my pussy with his tongue. He looks up and makes eye contact with me.

"Such a good girl, not coming yet." He continues to fuck me with his fingers.

My whole body is writhing.

"Nico—" I'm about to release, and he stops again. "Fuck!" I yell back at him.

"You want to come now?" he asks, kissing his way up my body.

"Yes, please," I beg.

He grabs me by the throat. "I am in control of your pleasure. Not you."

The look in his eyes are of hunger and power. Before me is the made man, not the lover.

"Yes" is all I can get out as his lips leave trails down my body.

He strokes my clit with his fingers before his lips are back on me. I wrap my legs around his head, arching my back not wanting him to go anywhere. He puts two fingers back inside me and sucks. I cry out, writhing beneath him.

Just as I'm on the edge, he pulls back and looks directly at me before saying, "Come for me," as he slaps my clit with his palm before his lips are back on me.

I cry out my release, my legs shaking. I don't know how long it lasts, but I don't have time to recover.

He plunges himself inside of me, and we both cry out.

# NICO

"Fuck! Nico—" she says as her pussy greedily welcomes my cock.

I slam into her over and over. She cries out my name over and over again, wrapping her legs tighter around my waist. I love that I can make her like this. As stubborn as she is, even if she doesn't want to admit it, she loves being dominated when I fuck her.

"Oh my god, Nico!" she screams.

Anyone on the property can hear us, and that makes me even harder. I keep thrusting.

Her arms are pulling against the restraints, jet black hair fanning across the sunbed. Her skin is flushed as her mouth forms an O-shape. Fucking beautiful. And mine.

"You gonna come for me again like the good girl you are?" I thrust into her hard.

"Yes, Nico," she says breathlessly. "I'm so close."

Good because she's going to come again before I come inside of her. I keep pulsing into her, harder and harder. The sounds of our bodies and cries fill the air. Her body tenses as she searches for release. I place my palm and apply light pressure to her lower belly. The sight of her eyes widening makes my cock harder, if that's even possible.

"Nico, I—" She throws her head back.

"Come on my dick, princess." Adding more pressure, I feel her pussy tighten, and she lets out another release. But I don't stop slamming into her. Her legs are shaking—her whole body is shaking. It's the most beautiful thing I've ever seen.

"Nico!"

She's still coming as I quickly flip her over onto her stomach, so she's forced to cross her arms, and it tightens the ties even more and I plunge into her, not giving her recovery time. I wasn't done yet. I pick her up by her hips, so she's on her knees, and slam back into her.

"Fuck!" she screams into the bed as I have my way with her.

I keep slamming into her relentlessly, fast and hard.

"Nico," she breathes out, "It's too much, it's too much. I don't think I can—"

"Do you want me to stop?" I ask her.

"No!" she screams.

I smile as I slap her ass. "Then, take it."

"Yes," she says into the mattress.

Her dark hair a wild mess and contrast to the white sunbed, her perfect ass in the air, face down as my cock fucks her. I feel her shaking again.

"Talk to me, baby," I say to her, knowing full well she can't think right now.

"Don't stop, Nico," she says through gritted teeth.

"You like when I fuck you like this?" I'm hitting her so deep, our bodies slap with every thrust.

"Yes," she says.

"I want to hear you say it."

I love when she talks to me.

"Fuck, Nico. I love how your cock feels inside me. Fuck, I'm close. Please come, Nico. I want to feel you fill me as you fuck my pussy."

I lean forward and move my hand to her clit. Her body jumps at the sensation she's so sensitive right now.

"I'm gonna come in this sweet little pussy." I speed up as she lets out the sexiest moan. "Come for me. Do as you're told," I tell her.

Releasing, she yells out a string of words, probably not in English, her whole body jerking and quivering.

I bite down on her shoulder as I let out my release, filling her up. I keep pumping into her until the last drop of my come is inside of her. Her thighs are drenched with both our arousal dripping down.

Her body goes limp as her knees give out. I lay on top of her for a minute, careful not to put all my weight on her. I leave a trail of kisses down her spine before I get up to untie her. She whimpers as I pull out of her. Kissing the marks left on her wrists, she turns to lay on her back with a dazed look on her face blinking in disbelief, cheeks flushed, sexy as ever.

I grab my T-shirt to clean her off. When I get to her pussy, she winces, and I can't help but smile. She's so sensitive after what we did. After I get done wiping both of us off, I lay back down beside her on the bed and pull her into me.

We lay only for God knows how long. She tries to pull away from me, but I hang on tighter. I notice she is always quick to pull away, too. Now that I think about it, I'm usually the one that initiates any sort of contact.

"Do you not like being touched?" I ask her, which was a weird question after what we just did, but her walls are usually up outside of sex.

She's quiet for a moment but then turns around to face me, her eyes sleepy, looking gorgeous as ever. I keep one arm wrapped around her as I use my other hand to take her wrist that's on my chest and kiss the marks again.

"I guess I'm just not used to this much of it," she says.

"What do you mean?"

"Well, I'm not exactly the relationship type. And I didn't grow up receiving much affection, either," she answers, looking up at me.

Hell, I didn't date either or cuddle, but with her, it was different. I never want to let her go. I like feeling her body pressed against mine. No, I love it.

"Your parents didn't show you affection?" I ask her, and she takes a deep breath.

"I imagine your parents—despite your father being the don of one of the most powerful mafias in the country—love you very much, and they weren't afraid to show it," she replies.

I gave it some thought and realized she was right. My family's love language is definitely touching. When my father was capo, I'd see him rip his men a new asshole, only to embrace them and kiss them on both cheeks in the next second before parting ways after meetings. It's how we do things.

"Yeah, I suppose you're right."

"Well, my parents—my adoptive parents—were never like that with me. Cesare, Dom, and Donna are, but we only saw each other during the summers growing up. You know that."

"Did your adoptive parents abuse you?"

I try not to get heated, but she can hear it in my voice.

"No!" she says quickly. "Jet and Nora were always kind. But I was always just a job to them. They made sure I was warm, fed, and went to school, but that was the extent of our relationship. I didn't even call them mom and dad unless we were in public. Nannies are probably more affectionate."

It's as if she were telling me about something she had heard on the news. She doesn't seem beat up about it.

It all made sense. She had a softness and a warmth to her, but she didn't seem comfortable with it yet, like she didn't know what to make of it. I felt pride spread through me. I know, besides her family, I'm one of the few people that gets to see that side. But I could see why it was easier for her to be cold.

"That must've been hard," I tell her as I move a stray lock of hair behind her ear, thinking about earlier when she mentioned how lonely being an outsider can be.

This is new territory for me—personal shit. But I want to know everything about this woman.

"It was at times. When I was younger, I was confused when I'd see how other parents were with their kids. But I also didn't look at them as my parents. And I don't blame them for not wanting to replace their daughter, the real Natalie. I didn't even realize how twisted and sick it was until I was a teenager."

"No offense, but Cesare is a messed up motherf—"

She covers my mouth and slaps my chest, laughing.

"Don't call him that. Yes, it's fucked up. But there was nothing that could've been done for Natalie. His plan kept me alive."

I remove her hand from my mouth and kiss it as she rolls her eyes. We'd need to work on this touching thing because I plan on doing it to her any chance I can get. I lean in to kiss her, holding her head in place. We stay like that, and not too long after, we both fall asleep after staring at the night sky.

## Chapter Nineteen

ANYA

Nico's been everything. Does that even make sense? He leaves this overwhelming, powerful rush of emotions I'm not sure how to process. I've become engrossed by him. His smile, his smell, and his thoughtfulness.

Him telling me he wants me, being so firm about it, and going out of his way to show me. Things are easy with Nico, no lies or pretending. I feel liberated with him. Not to mention, the sex is mind-blowing—explosive, and they do say actions speak louder than words. There was no question this man wanted me.

He fucked me everywhere he could, in any way. And I let him.

In the library.

Under our tree.

On Bash's desk.

The kitchen pantry.

My belly is all in knots over this man. I was falling, hard and fast, and I needed to get a handle on it before it turns to something I'll never recover from. Could I love him? Could he love me? Could we be together?

Tense and anxious, I head to the gym to let out some steam and frustration. I'm warming up at the punching bags as Nico walks in. I stop to admire his physique, and he made no attempt to hide he also likes what he sees. *He's so handsome.* I purposely wore the tightest and tiniest spandex shorts and only a sports bra. You know, because it gets hot during a workout. Wouldn't want to have a heat stroke.

He smirks and nods toward the ring. As I walk over, he's jumping and doing a half-ass stretch. He really should warm up better.

"We're going to work on overpowering your opponent. You're fast, but you need to be prepared in case they get the upper hand."

We go through a couple of exercises that last for about three minutes. I can't fight him seriously right now. I'm too horny, so every time he makes a move, I melt into him like a teenager with her first crush. He doesn't seem upset about it. Not wanting him to think it'd be that easy, I lean into him as he tries to wrap his arms around me, causing him to relax, giving me the upper hand. This move always works. When will they learn?

Before he can figure out my plan, I'm able to flip him onto the ground. His back hits the mat with a thud, and I quickly straddle his neck, kneeling over him, holding him in place. I know he could easily flip me over, but he doesn't. He grins up at me proudly, grabbing onto my thighs. I squeeze them tighter around his neck as I bite my bottom lip, looking down at him.

"Tap out, Nico," I say panting.

He licks his lips. His hands move from my legs to my ass, and he squeezes. I lean forward, placing my hands on the mat, so my breasts are now on his face. "Come on, Nico. Just tap out, and it's yours," I whisper.

He lifts his head up into the valley between my breasts and inhales just before he lands two firm pats on my ass. Relaxing my body, I squeal as he quickly flips me onto my back. I wrap my legs around his waist and his lips land painfully on mine. His erection already pressing against my throbbing core as we explore each other's mouths. Not missing a beat, he moves his hands up to grab my breasts as he yanks my sports bra off like he's offended by it. Then he removes his own shirt and leans forward to suck on my nipple and bite down on it. I yelp as he moves on to the next one, giving it just as much attention.

"Nico, someone can walk in at any moment," I say breathlessly.

"You started this," he says as he pulls my workout shorts off and kisses down my stomach. God, I love the way he kisses me.

He kisses up my inner thigh, and as he gets to my center, he takes a deep inhale. It's so primal. Fuck, he's so hot. I'm so turned on.

"Mm. You smell as good as you taste, babe."

He licks my clit slowly as my back arches, and I brush my hands through his hair.

He alternates his tongue between fast and slow as I moan out in pleasure. He inserts two fingers in me, and I cry out at the intrusion.

"So fucking tight and so fucking wet."

"For you," I breathe out.

He fucks me with his fingers and sucks on my clit until I'm nothing but a trembling mess.

"Come on my lips. Fuck, you taste so good." I let out my release with a cry as he sucks harder.

Once I'm able to gain some sort of rationale, I push him onto his back, work his shorts down quickly, and take him in my hand.

"So eager for my cock," he smiles, looking down at me.

I smile back at him as I lick the tip of his cock, tasting the saltiness of his pre-cum.

"Mm." I can't help but moan.

I swirl my tongue around the tip, teasing it. I lick from the base to the tip. I don't take him into my mouth right away. I repeat this motion until he's panting. I want him at my mercy, begging for me to take him.

"Babe, I need to feel your lips around me."

"Do you?" I say, looking up at him as I work my tongue underneath his tip. This move always drives him wild.

"Yes. Fuck," he warns as he grabs my hair.

I chuckle. "Like this?"

Covering his cock with my mouth, I take him as deep as I can. Then I start sucking, pulling back slowly and continuing to repeat the motion.

"Fuck yes, Anya, just like that." He growls.

I release his cock, causing a popping sound as it leaves my lips.

"Or how about this?" I loosen the grip my mouth has on his cock and just barely surround my mouth over his cock as I move up and down his length, not applying any pressure or sucking as I take his length.

"Oh fuck, fuck, fuck, babe. I need more. Suck harder."

I listen to his command and suck down harder as my head bobs, and I use my hand to pump his cock. I look up at him, my breasts grazing his thighs, the sensations making me wetter. I speed up, and you can hear the sounds echoing around the gym. His hands are in my hair, guiding my head as we don't break eye contact. I'm so close just from sucking him off.

I release his cock with another popping sound, and he protests until he sees me climbing on top of him with my back to him before straddling his hips. He has a nice view of my ass.

He groans and smacks my ass. The impact causes me to cry out as I line his cock up to my entrance and slowly lower myself until my body tenses at his size. I love the way he stretches me. Just enough pain with my pleasure.

"Fuck," he growls through gritted teeth, grabbing my hips.

I let out a string of curses as my pussy tightens around him. I feel so full.

"Fuck, Nico, you're so big it hurts," I whisper, throwing my head back as he grabs my hips and guides me up and down. "But all I think about is you inside of me."

# NICO

My brain short circuits I'm so fucking hard. Her perfect, perky ass is on full display as she takes my cock and rides me in reverse. She's moving up and down slowly, so fucking wet I can feel her arousal dripping down her thighs.

"You like when my cock fills up your tight pussy."

"Yes," she answers breathlessly, throwing her head back, her silky black hair cascading down her back. She's still moving slowly on top of me.

"Show me how much you like it, baby. Fuck my cock like a good little girl."

"I don't think you want me to be a good girl," she says teasingly, keeping her tortuous pace.

I slap her ass. "Then, fuck me like a whore."

My vision goes blurry, but that is all the encouragement she needs. She leans forward, resting on her hands on the mat, and she pops her ass up and down on my cock, slowly upping her pace. I thrust my hips up to meet hers, and she cries out every time. I'm railing her fast and hard. The sounds of our bodies meeting made my dick harder, if that was even possible. The sight of her ass. God, her ass.

"Fuck, Anya. Keep going. Fuck, you feel amazing."

I watch as her pussy takes my cock, ass bouncing, making me lose any restraint I had left.

"Oh. My. God. Fuck. Ah. So. Deep. Fuck. Nico," she whimpers with every thrust.

I'm fucking her so hard and deep, I can't tell where one of us ends and the other begins. She turns her head back toward me, biting her lips, her eyes hooded and completely lost in ecstasy. She makes eye contact with me.

"Vieni dentro di me," *Come inside me*, she calls back to me.

I love when she speaks Italian as I fuck her.

"You first, baby," I say through gritted teeth. She's trembling, and her thrusts are getting more and more uncoordinated. She's fucking close.

"Oh god!" she screams out, her pussy clenching my cock tighter, and she rides out her orgasm as I slam into her.

"Fuck, Anya," I follow shortly after her, releasing inside of her.

It crosses my mind that I wouldn't be mad if I got her pregnant. She's on birth control, and call me a caveman, but the image of her carrying my baby turns me on again.

We're both a pile of panting messes. Once her breathing is under control, she leans forward, leaving just my tip in her pussy as she wiggles her ass letting me watch my semen drip out of her and down my cock. She turns back and looks at me with that smile. Fuck me. This is the hottest thing I've ever seen in my life.

"You look so sexy right now," I tell her, stroking myself, rubbing my semen in, then massaging her ass with it. She climbs off of me, and we lay on the mats for a moment.

I finally sit up, deciding I'm going to fuck her into oblivion but not when anyone could walk in. We'd risked it this time, but

I wasn't going to take any chances again. No one is seeing her naked.

"Get dressed," I say to her as I toss her sorry excuse for workout attire toward her. She was trying to kill me.

"I have more plans for you." I grin at her while I put my own clothes on.

We barely make it to the bedroom door when I take her again from behind on the floor. On the bathroom sink. One more time in the shower against the wall. When we're done with our sex marathon, we lay in bed in comfortable silence. She lies on my chest, stroking my tattoos with her finger, eyes hooded. I hear her breathing even. She passes out quickly, thoroughly and properly fucked.

## ANYA

Two weeks of bliss. Exploring each other's bodies and getting to know each other. Nico thinks he's this big scary-ass hacker and killer—I mean, he is, don't get me wrong—but that's not all he is. Underneath is a thoughtful, protective, loyal, sexy man. I love the way he interacts with his brothers and how he treats Valentina. The way a man treats his staff says a lot about him. Cosima's a different story. She's obsessed with him, but I still find it sexy when he tries not to lose his patience. He'd rub his hand over his face, taking in a deep breath, messing up his hair with his jaw flexed. Even angry Nico is still sexy.

Could you love someone after knowing them for a short period? We're in isolation with no outside factors. Back in New

## Rise Of An Heiress

York, Nico's family are public figures—I was the exact opposite. I avoided any and all attention.

We're in a bubble. A bubble I didn't ever want to leave.

We're having dinner when Dante strolls in late, looking excited as ever. He pauses, standing at the edge of the table while we all stare up at him.

"Come on! Is no one going to ask?" he taunts.

"Finally lose your virginity?" Enzo asks with his mouth full.

Nico and Enzo high five, laughing, while Bash rolls his eyes.

At that exact moment, Uncle Ricky walks in behind Dante. "We got his location."

*Pop goes that bubble.* Thanks, Dante and Uncle Ricky. *Come on. I thought we'd be great friends.*

My eyes immediately connect with Nico's. I can't read his expression. My heart takes a dive.

"Way to ruin the dramatic effect." Dante pretends to be offended as he sits.

Uncle Ricky hands Bash a folder.

"He's holed up at one of their facilities. It looks like a normal warehouse on the outside but there's two underground floors. Security is tight around the perimeter and the building itself. Blueprints and exact location are all in there. We still need to study them up," Uncle Ricky explains.

Bash looks through the folders while I eye them curiously.

"So, what happens next?" I ask.

I'm not sure if I want to hear the answer.

"We need the Outfit's cooperation," Bash replies.

I can't hide my shock. The brothers look equally as surprised.

"We?" Nico asks.

"Cooperation?" I follow.

"Yes. We. Cooperate," Bash says, sounding annoyed that we made him repeat himself.

"I thought once he's located, you're out and I go home."

I need to hear him say it; otherwise, I'd think I hallucinated this whole conversation. *Am I not going back?*

"Change of plans. I'll set up a video call with the Outfit," Bash says as he wipes his mouth with a napkin, indicating he's finished with his meal and this conversation.

Then a thought occurs to me. The Natalie part of me would hang back in the shadows, not because I was submissive but because I couldn't draw attention to myself. However, now, as Anya, I can't just sit around and let not only the Cosa Nostra and the Outfit call the shots for me but anyone for that matter.

Before he leaves, I call out to him. "I'll be there."

He stops and turns around to look at me as we silently communicate. I'm scared as shit, but I need to take agency over my own life, and the time is now. I can't keep letting these men run things. The Triad is mine. Mine to build and mine to rule.

Bash nods and leaves. I grab the folder from where Bash left them and look over at Dante. "I want these blueprints blown up so I can study them."

"You got it." He grins.

I couldn't help but smile to myself. I look over at Nico, who is smiling proudly at me, and my heart strings tug. I can't let him go.

## Rise Of An Heiress

This gives me time to consider my options. Whatever they may be, leaving Nico isn't one of them. I swear I'll call my uncle himself and leave an anonymous tip that his location has been uncovered, so he can find somewhere else to hide. Shit, I don't even know if Nico wants me long-term.

## Chapter Twenty

### NICO

She's smiling, her dimple appearing. I love that smile. Actually, I love so much more than that. I shake my head to cut off my thoughts, but it's no use. There's no getting Anya Liu out of my system. Was a man like me capable of love? Worthy of it?

Ten minutes after Bash leaves, I get a text from him saying our meeting is in an hour. We all sit in Bash's office. Anya, my brothers, Dante, Uncle Ricky, and a few of our captains. Cesare, Dominic, and a room full of men I'm assuming are also their captains appear on the screen. I spot the Matteo fucker to the left of Dominic. Anya jumps up like a firecracker with the biggest smile spread across her face. Fuck, it's kind of hard to hate the two men that can make her smile like that. Then again, I want to be the reason she smiles like that.

"Cesare! Dominic!"

She sounds more like a boss than she does family, but the warmth in her tone isn't missed.

"You look well, bambina." Cesare smiles, looking younger than his age.

He was still buff and just as scary looking as the stories we heard when we were little. Dom doesn't say anything, he knows better. He's not capo yet. Anya can get away with it because she is technically a boss, which is why no one says anything to her. We all recognize it. The shift that is happening. Although I'm convinced, even if she wasn't, Bash would never tell her otherwise. If my brother wasn't already a killer, he'd let that girl get away with murder. But hey, so would I.

"I am, Papa. The Deluccis are taking very good care of me."

I snicker, and she shoots me a death glare. I give her my cockiest grin.

"Thank you for looking after my daughter," Cesare says to my brother.

"She's been a pleasure to have. You raised quite a woman." Bash smiles at Cesare.

This isn't normal by any mafia standards. Two—or, in this case, three—bosses never hold a meeting like this with so much informality and pleasantries. It's usually tense and silent, and any sudden movement is a death wish. It's rare for someone to not make a bloody statement by the end of it. But I guess that's the effect Anya has. I have no doubt she'll be able to rein in the Triad.

"Of course I did. Now onto business." Cesare directs the conversation straight to the point.

## Rise Of An Heiress

Uncle Ricky and Dante retell the Outfit men their discoveries. We agreed to meet here at the safe house in two weeks. The Outfit isn't happy about waiting but tough shit. We can't have twenty Outfit soldiers traveling simultaneously to the same location. We finally reveal to the Outfit and Anya that we're in Poquoson, Virginia. It's a shame we're going to have to get rid of this place after we're done with the Triad. Too many people know about it now.

Anya will spearhead the mission's plans with Bash and soon-to-be capo Dominic. Both Cesare and Dominic try to argue, but she insists since this was her mission, it was essential for her to be involved. And the fact that she was to be the leader of the Triad is her right. She made a fair argument even the Violantes couldn't argue.

Anya's plan was brilliant. I don't think we could have planned it better ourselves. The Outfit will send the hackers and security experts here first to assist Dom, Uncle Ricky, and me to figure out how to break into Li's security measures. We'll need several men to break the firewalls and lock codes of the building.

The snipers and arms experts will come next to join ours, to plan our physical attack, and also to make sure our shipment of weapons arrives on time.

Lastly, Cesare, Dominic, and their higher-ranking soldiers will come out to solidify the plan. My father, mother, and some of his men will also be arriving at that time. This means I have two weeks to convince Anya to stay with me after we take down Li. I don't care if she's the Triad Queen or not. I want her by my side, and I need her to know that. I just pray she wants the same thing.

## ANYA

Nico and I had to postpone our post-dinner walk until after the meeting, but the sun was just setting, thanks to it being summer. We're making out under our usual tree, which Nico confessed he started calling it "Our Spot," with a blanket laid out under us. We have a delicious spread of charcuterie, jams, cheeses, fruit, bread, and white wine. Nico learned I didn't like red very much. I don't know why he insisted on bringing snacks. I'm still stuffed from dinner, but it was still sweet and thoughtful, so very like Nico.

The kiss is wild, passionate but not sexual, though his erection might disagree. He feels so good on top of me, my legs around him like he belonged with me. When he finally pulls away, allowing me to catch some air, I smile up at him.

"This is nice," I say. "I like just making out with you."

He chuckles into my neck, then looks into my eyes. "What do you mean?"

"Don't get me wrong, I like the other things, too, but sometimes a good make-out session is what a girl needs."

I hold his head in both my hands. I love running my fingers through his hair.

His eyes narrow. "And just how many guys have you *just made out with*? Actually, don't answer that." He brushes my hair out of my face and cups my chin. "I'll have to murder someone."

## Rise Of An Heiress

I laugh, even though I know he means it. He swallows it in a kiss but pulls away too soon. "Is Matteo coming?" he asks. He says his name like he just bit into something rotten.

I tilt my head at him. "How do you even know who Ma—"

My eyes are wide with shock. *He didn't!*

"Wait a minute." I punch his chest. "It was you who set off the fire alarms, wasn't it? Are you insane!"

His laugh is a low grumble that vibrates through my body and sets off all of my senses. He grabs my hands, kisses them, then pins them down beside my head.

"First of all," he says, kissing my mouth, "yes, I am fucking insane, Anya. You have no idea the lengths I'm willing to go for you. And second, I did you a favor."

"Nothing was going to happen, you know," I taunt.

"Obviously, I made sure of that," he says, wiggling his eyebrows.

I don't even hide my laugh. Before I can tell him I was sending Matteo home, he grabs the back of my neck, pulling me in as he claims my lips and deepens the kiss, robbing me of my thoughts. I know I should be, but I'm not even mad or fazed by what I just learned.

# Chapter Twenty-One

NICO

"Nico! Your hair's all wet!" my mother yells as I greet her with a hug and kiss on both cheeks, trying to hide my irritation.

Don't get me wrong—I love my parents, but they have the worst timing ever.

"Yeah, Ma. I just took a shower." I don't care to mention that it was a fucking cold shower, considering I was balls deep in Anya in the library when Enzo all but broke the door down to let us know about their arrival.

I look at Bash. He looks just as confused. It looks like my parents' arrival surprised us all.

Anya stands off to the side, smiling and looking cool as a cucumber, not a hair out of place, holding her hands in front of her.

"You weren't supposed to be here for another few days," I say as my mother brushes by, ignoring me.

"You must be Anya. I'm Marcella." Ma rushes up to Anya, pulling my girl into her arms. *My girl.* Anya doesn't flinch or stiffen. She hugs and kisses my mother back on both cheeks. My mother pulls back, still cupping Anya's face. "Oh my, you're as beautiful as my son says you are!"

*The fuck*? I never talk to my mother about women.

"Nico told you about me?" Anya asks, confused.

"No, Lorenzo did, but you just confirmed it," my mother replies with a wink.

Anya's eyes widened, but she was smiling like she was holding back a laugh. *My mother had a way with these things.*

"I didn't realize Dipshit is also a gossip queen. We really need to get you laid, bro," I say as my mother greets the gossip himself.

"Don't talk about your baby brother like that, Nico." My mother chastises.

"Jesus, Ma! I'm twenty-three!" He fights my mother off of him while she licks her finger and tries to rub lipstick off his cheek. He really is her baby.

"The Triad Princess in the flesh," a deep voice says from the doorway. My father walks over to Anya and pulls her in to greet her.

"Anya. Of course I know who you are, Mr.—"

"Call me Giuseppe," he says with a polite smile. He greets my brothers, saving me for last with a glare. "We'll talk about this." His eyes gesture to Anya.

She's talking to Ma, so she doesn't notice. Fuck, what did Enzo tell them?

"Is that why you showed up here unannounced? You aren't capo anymore," I joke, knowing it gets to him. Giuseppe Delucci is a controlling, micromanaging asshole. But we love him anyway.

"That, and I want to know what Anya's plan is for taking down Li. I know you're working with the Outfit. I've always liked Cesare," my father says as he pats Bash on the back and walks away, only to stop to kiss my mother on the cheek.

"Have Valentina set up antipasto and bruschetta on the back patio," he calls back without a glance, and my parents take their exit to the backyard.

"You're practically quadruplets," Anya says, stopping next to me.

My brothers and I look exactly like my dad. The only thing we got from Ma is her black hair, whereas my father's was a lighter brown, and Enzo has her eyes.

## NICO

For the next two weeks, Outfit men show up two or three at a time along with some of our men. They're all staying in the cabins surrounding the property. We can fit about six to eight men in each cabin, so there's plenty of room. I notice the more Outfit soldiers that turn up, the more tense and reserved Anya gets.

She's been spending time either in the library or in the security room with me, memorizing the blueprints, accounting for all the men and weapons and even timing the whole damn mission. She doesn't smile as much or joke with me during our fight training anymore. Hell, even sex feels different. I'm on high alert. I told her she needs to talk to me about this shit, but my girl's stubborn. I should've known better than to think it'd be that easy.

I watch her standing in front of the bathroom mirror rubbing creams and serums—the ones she requested after only two days of being here—on her face. Her eyebrows are pinched together like she's deep in thought. I know something's bothering her. Watching her get ready for bed feels so domestic. I smile at the thought of how far we've come in the several weeks.

After walking up behind her and grabbing her hips, I pull her in so she can feel my erection against her back. She's so much shorter than me, I tower over her more than a foot. I have to lean forward to kiss her neck. She tilts her head, giving me access, but her body's still tense. I kiss from her ear down to her shoulder.

"Are you going to tell me what's wrong, or do I have to coax it out of you?" I ask.

"That depends on what you have planned in your coaxing," she says in a seductive voice. *Fuck. Focus, Nico. Don't let her distract you.*

I spin her, lift her onto the bathroom counter, and place my hands on each side of her.

"Tell me," I demand in a low tone.

She sighs before she rubs the leftover moisturizer onto my face. She's been going on about how important it is to take care of your skin. For someone who's not good at talking about feelings or showing affection, she sure is good at finding other ways to nurture and show she cares. Her eyes finally make contact with mine, and my lips turn up.

"I don't want to let you go, Nico," she whispers.

Her confession takes me by surprise. I thought she was tense because of the mission. This whole time, she's been worried about us.

*Did she not get it by now?* Her body tenses when I don't answer right away. It also doesn't help that I'm looking at her, confused.

"Look, I know it hasn't been that long, but Papa and Dom are going to know—they're observant like that. And they're going to be here in a few days. People talk, they'll be furious. Not that they have a say in what I do, but I'd rather you all not fight. We're on the same side—at least for now. And I'd like to know what to say if they ask," she says.

Man, she was really sitting on this one. There's so much I want to say to her. I want to tell her I won't let her go, that she's better than any dream I could come up with, and that she's worked her way into this heart I never thought was capable of love. I love my family, but this is different. What I feel for her puts me so far out of my element to comprehend. I'll kill anyone who tries to take her from me. Hell, I've killed for a lot less.

"You're mine," I say with a smile.

# Chapter Twenty-Two

ANYA

"You're serious? Just like that?" I ask him, less than amused.

"What part of this sounds like a joke to you?" he asks in an easygoing manner, shrugging. He looks at me like *I'm* the one with two heads.

In this world, marriages or alliances could happen overnight. It's certainly not customary to date casually, especially for long periods of time. Fucking double standards. In this world, women didn't just sleep around. If you're sleeping together, the woman's labeled a whore or you marry. My heart sinks at the thought of Nico marrying someone else. It wasn't unusual for men to take on mistresses, but I sure as fuck would not be his. *I'm the damn Triad princess! Soon-to-be queen, dammit!* But that fact makes me an outsider to them. How could this work?

"I can hear you thinking, babe. Have I not shown you in these past few weeks how much I want you?"

"Well, you have," I say slowly, "but I wasn't sure if this was your way of making the *best of this while it lasted*."

He grabs the back of my neck with one of his hands.

"I'm not letting you go. I thought you realized that when we didn't send you home after we located your uncle."

"Nico, are you even thinking this through. Be realistic. Is there some plan I'm not in on?"

I don't expect him to have an answer on the spot, but I think we've spent a little too much time enjoying ourselves, and now it's time to face the consequences. A part of me is begging for him to fight for us.

"We'll figure it out. Together. But rest assured—you're mine."

His tone was almost threatening. As if the result will be catastrophic if anyone tries to say otherwise.

"This is too fast, isn't it?" I ask, testing him.

Surely, we're insane. It's only been a few weeks and part of that time we thought we were enemies.

"Do you want to slow down?" he asks.

I look into those dark eyes that completely suck me in. *No.* I know in my heart no one will ever compare to Nico. There's no one else. I grab his face, pulling his lips to mine before answering.

"No," I breathe.

He smiles against my mouth as our lips devour each other. He moves his hands beneath my ass and picks me up. I wrap my legs around his waist as he walks us into the bedroom.

He tosses me onto the bed as if I weigh nothing. I lay back on my elbows as he stands over me, lust glazing over his eyes. He climbs on top of me. I'm already wet with anticipation. He grabs my waist, pulls higher on the bed, and settles his hips between my legs. His erection pushes against my core.

I moan at the sensation. He works his way up my jaw to my earlobe, biting it, then working more kisses down my neck.

"Clearly, I haven't made it obvious enough how much I want to keep you. I better rectify that as soon as possible," he says before smacking my ass.

I let out a yelp, and he kisses me so passionately and so painfully I know he's going to leave my lips bruised. Though we haven't said the words, we make love to each other for the first time tonight.

*Oh my God, I'm in love with Nico.*

## NICO

Cesare and Dominic are the last to arrive. We're all lined up outside to greet Cesare's arrival as a sign of solidarity and respect. Everyone's tense but pretending they aren't. It's not unusual for meetings like this to turn into a bloodbath after a surprise attack. I doubted this was the case with Anya being in our custody and the Outfit being involved, but you really never know.

Anya's standing two feet from me, and I don't like it at all. I know she's keeping space between us on purpose. Enzo uses this opportunity to stand next to me and Dante on his other side, so he's now next to Anya. *Fucker.* I know he has a crush on her. Bash is to my right, and our parents are to his.

Uncle Ricky and the rest of the men are strategically placed around us. The Outfit soldiers that arrived earlier stand behind us on the steps waiting for their capo. In our world, you only face your back to people you either trust or don't see as a threat. In this case, it's both. It's a sign of peace but also an insult at the same time. I can tell Bash has the same thoughts as he turns his head briefly and nods.

Three black SUVs with tinted windows drive up. Everyone's shoulders straighten. I hear Anya take a deep breath. I hate not being able to see her. I hear Dante whisper something to her, and she giggles. *Bastard. I'll have to kick his ass later.*

Three men get out of the first vehicle. I recognize one to be the asshole, Matteo. His gaze falls directly on Anya, his eyes locked on hers, like a lion who just found his next meal. I fantasize about shooting him right between the eyes. I can't see her to gauge her reaction. *Fuck.* The dark-haired one, I know to be Franco, one of Dom's closest friends and their best hacker. He didn't know it was me at the time, but I'd gotten through most of their firewalls when I was collecting information on their family. The last one, I recognize, but I had forgotten his name. He's the shortest of the group, with brown hair and a lip ring.

The door to the second vehicle opens, and Dominic Violante struts out of the car in sunglasses, like he's about to walk the red carpet. He looks around and smiles when he spots Anya, giving her a once-over, making sure she's unharmed, no doubt.

He looks at my brother and nods, then at my parents as a sign of respect.

Cesare Violante steps out in all his gigantic glory. That bastard was even bigger in person. He's at least six-foot-six, and I don't doubt he has to turn sideways when walking through the doorway. A bright smile on his face.

"A welcome committee," he says with his arms open, palms in the air gesture. "How kind of you."

Dominic and their men move to stand by their capo. I see a small figure with dark hair sprint out, and I instinctively move to follow her. Bash and Enzo pull me back by each arm. Anya throws herself into Cesare's arms as he embraces her in a hug. He laughs, watching me from over her shoulder as he holds her while Dominic and the men are now staring daggers into me. Everyone's now watching me. They all saw what I just did.

Dominic breaks his gaze to turn back toward his sister. He picks her up and spins her around, kissing her on both cheeks. I don't care if he's her brother. I don't like his hands on her.

As if Bash can read my mind, he steps forward. We follow to greet Cesare and his men. I maneuver, so I'm behind Anya now and as Dominic sets her down. The nameless lip-ring guy and Franco nod at her, but Matteo stalks forward with his arms out as if he's going to give her a hug. I don't give a fuck. I reach for her and pull her back to me, giving him a warning with my eyes. She turns to me, eyes wide as she stares up at me. He's surprised but recovers quickly, smirking. Cesare and Dominic look over at me. Cesare curious, Dominic less than thrilled. *Well, they're going to find out sooner or later.*

Bash interrupts before things can escalate further.

"Cesare, pleasure to meet you." He shakes Cesare's hand, holding my brother's hand in both of his.

"Pleasure's all mine. Thank you for having us at your home. I know it's not ideal to reveal the location of one of your safe houses," Cesare replies as he shakes Enzo's hand, then mine.

"Cesare!" My father steps up, and they kiss each other on both cheeks.

Anya tries to get out of my grip on her arm. *Oh, no you don't.* I just hold on tighter.

"Giuseppe, it's been too long, my friend!" Cesare returns the warmth.

This is going better than planned.

"Marcella, a vision as always." Cesare kisses my mother's hand, then introduces the three gentlemen.

"Matteo, Tony, Franco," he says, pointing to each of them.

They nod. Matteo still has that smirk on his face.

We all take turns shaking hands with one another. When Matteo reaches out, I make sure to grip his hand just a little harder. He had the same idea.

Anya darts off as soon as everyone split up, who is now nowhere to be seen. Probably off studying the blueprints she's been obsessing over for weeks in Bash's office—another weird thing he lets her get away with. He never lets anyone except my father, myself, and Enzo in his office without him being present.

My father and Cesare head off like they're old high school buddies or some shit. Cosima shows the men to their cabins, while Valentina shows Dominic to his room and gives him a tour of the mansion. Cesare and Dominic stay in our home as a sign of respect as capo and heir. The glare Anya shot at me when Bash confirmed there were more rooms was priceless. I make my way to the security room, needing to wrap up some things before I can play host with my family.

After an hour, I head to the foyer and find Anya heading back to Bash's office, I assume. I sneak up on her from behind and grab her waist, which, apparently, isn't the right move. She screams, elbowing me in the face. Water flies everywhere.

"What the hell, babe!" I pinch my nose with one hand and rub my head that's now drenched in water.

"What's wrong with you?" she replies, trying to suppress her laugh. "You gave me a heart attack."

Just then, Dominic and Tony appear at the top of the staircase, staring at us intently.

"This conversation isn't over, double oh seven," I say to her quickly before I return my attention to Dominic and Tony. "We're going to talk about this relationship your elbow's established with my face."

She smiles.

Valentina tells him dinner is at seven as she speeds off, knowing that it's best to make herself scarce. Dominic takes his time making his way down the stairs. His eyes never leave mine. Out of the corner of my eye, I can see Anya looking around, as if she's searching for an escape route. He walks right up to me, eye-to-eye now. I'm just barely taller. It's coming, and I let him. It's his sister.

"You fucking bastard!" Dominic gets me good on my left cheek, right where Anya left her mark when we first got here.

These fucking two.

I recover quickly and punch him in the stomach, then the jaw when he hunches over. Bash races in from the kitchen. Before it can escalate, we're pulled apart. We glare at each other, nostrils flaring like wild animals at a watering hole.

"You guys are fucking children!" Anya yells, but he shoots her a look that keeps her in place.

*The fucker can't treat her like that.*

"Everyone clear out!" Bash yells.

The random soldiers hanging around the house leave, and Tony stays with Dominic. Bash stays with me and Anya and stands off to the side, watching all of us tentatively.

Dominic's staring directly at Anya, who's staring right back.

She recovers quickly, seeing as she's now pissed off, too, staring daggers into him with her arms crossed.

## Anya

I'm in a stand-off with my brother. We've never been in this position before. We rarely ever fight, and it's never about anything serious. Once the room clears out, Dom doesn't hold back.

"You fucking him?" he asks through clenched teeth, using his head to gesture in Nico's direction.

The look of disgust on his face, like it's the 1800s and I'm some common whore. Nico steps forward, but I shoot him a pleading look to not do anything.

"That's none of your fucking business, Dom," I tell my brother.

Who the hell is he to judge me?

"How could you be so STUPID!" He takes a step toward me, but at the same time, Nico stalks up and pushes him back, finger pointing in his face.

"Don't you fucking talk to her like that!" Nico's face is red with fury. Dom laughs menacingly. Nico takes a step back as I pull his arm, allowing me to see my brother. I've never seen Nico so angry.

"This why they're hell-bent on protecting you? You spread your little legs and—" He makes an opening gesture with his hands.

*My turn.* Before he can even get the rest of his words out, I charge at him and punch him so hard across the face it echoes, and my knuckles scream. His face has to feel the same, but I don't give him a chance to recover the second he looks back up at me, then I deck him again.

"Don't you *ever* fucking disrespect me like that!" I scream back at him.

Dom looks shocked for a moment, palming his face, but then he takes a deep breath. I can tell he's trying to rein in his anger before he does something he'll regret.

"They are using you, sorellina." He points to Nico and Bash. "Don't you see that? You can't trust them. Don't you think it's weird they're suddenly being nice to you when they find out you're about to be the queen of the goddam Triad! They tried to kidnap you!" His pitch increases, yelling by the end of the sentence.

Nico doesn't give me a chance to reply. He's back to swinging. Dom strikes him back, and they fall on the floor, taking a vase and a painting with them. Dom gets on top of him, getting a good hit in before Nico swings pounds into Dom's face. Bash and Tony pull Nico off of my brother.

"You're dead!" Dom screams, pointing at Nico as Tony pushes him back. "Fucking dead! Do you have any idea what the fuck you've just done? Of course you do!"

"What exactly do you think I did?" Nico taunts.

"You claimed her, you fucking idiot. She wasn't yours to take!" Dom screams, Tony still pushing him back.

"Are you fucking kidding me!" I yell, hearing enough of his sexist bullshit. "It's the twenty-first century! I'm an adult, I can do whatever I want—"

"That's not what I mean, and no, *you* can't, Anya! How do you not get it?" he asks me incredulously.

"Why don't you enlighten me, then?" I throw my arms up, exasperated by my idiot brother.

"When you decided you were going to take the Triad back, your life was no longer your own. You have a duty now. You're going to be the leader of the Triad, Anya. You can't just *be with whoever you want*. This isn't some fairy tale fantasy and"—Dom points at Nico, always with the pointing—"*he* knew that. He knew better!"

"What are you going on about?"

Now I'm confused.

"Where are your loyalties now, Anya? Where's your allegiance? To the Outfit? To the Triad? Or to the Cosa Nostra? To him? To the Triad, he's a fucking outsider," Dom asks.

I flinch back like he had just slapped me. I wasn't expecting that.

He had a point. I'd never even thought about how this might affect the Triad if I succeed in taking over. Or how it would affect my relationship with the Outfit. The Outfit and the Cosa Nostra are at peace at the moment, but that could change at the drop of a hat. Nico and I aren't married. Neither of us are obligated to choose the other. There is no alliance between any of our houses.

Dom thinks I've betrayed him.

## NICO

I could see the wheels spinning. She doesn't know the answer. Fuck, I can tell she's fighting back tears. We'd really have to work on that if she was going to become the next leader of the Triad. Don't get me wrong, she can cry to me all she wants, even if it breaks my heart, but she can't do this in public. Not as a boss. Not in our world. She didn't strike me as a crier, but I'm guessing it's different when it comes to her brother.

"That's what I thought," Dominic says, taking a breath before looking straight at me. "You had no right to take that from her."

"Don't you dare question my loyalty, Dom," she says firmly.

I can tell what he said hit a nerve.

"Think about it," Dominic utters as he storms off back upstairs.

After a few hours of cooling off, the last thing I wanted to do was sit in this office with Dominic fucking Violante. I'd just spent a majority of that time trying to rein Anya and her overthinking in, so there wasn't actually any calming down on my end.

I get it. She values her brother's opinion highly, much to my dismay, and she's never fought with him before. She doesn't want to have to choose. I don't want that for her, either. Selfishly, I hope she isn't second guessing us. I left her in our room once she tired herself out and fell asleep. I hear the door click, and it breaks my train of thought.

Dominic walks in, looking as annoying as ever. I want to gut the fucker, but I can't; that would just hurt her more. Damned if I do, damned if I don't.

I get up from Bash's chair and gesture to the seat in front of me for Dominic to sit. I walk over to the bar cart and pour us both a glass of whiskey. I walk back over, whiskey bottle in hand, and place our glasses on the desk before taking a seat. We sit in silence for a moment. Only when both of our glasses are empty Dominic opens his mouth.

"You can't have her," he says simply, as if his word was God.

Who does this fucker think he is? He's not capo yet, and he sure as fuck isn't *my* capo. I don't reply right away. I pour us both another glass and take a sip, savoring the taste.

"That's not up to you," I tell him.

"She's not your whore. Now you've gone and fucking ruined her." I roll my eyes at his statement. Fuck, it's going to be hard not to take another swing at him.

# Rise Of An Heiress

"I know she's not a whore. I respect and admire her greatly. The only person in this room that's degraded her today is you."

Dominic scoffs.

"If you respected her you would've left her alone. How's it look to the other families that the Triad princess is shacking up with the Cosa Nostra consigliere? You'll fuck her, but you won't marry her?"

"Fuck off," I grumble. I don't have to explain myself to him.

"That's how our world will see it, and you know it. And you're not going to marry her. I won't allow it. So, whatever this is, it ends now."

My blood is boiling.

"And if it doesn't?"

Is he really going to threaten me in my house?

"It will because she's getting married next week," Dominic says with a smug grin.

I don't want to take the bait, but I have to ask. "Who?"

He gives me a smile that tells me he's going to be satisfied by my reaction.

"One of our captains"—he pauses to pick fake lint off of his sleeve—"Matteo"—his smile widens—"they're . . . well acquainted, if you know what I mean. Should be an easy transition."

I can't hear over the blood boiling inside me. I slam my hand on the desk and stand. "You even think about marrying her off to someone else, I will drown you in acid!"

Dominic stands, unbothered as Bash enters.

"You don't get a say in this, Nico. It's a *family* matter." He heads toward the door.

"Is that all she's worth to you?" I call out. "She's about to be the head of her house, and you marry her off to a captain? He's a nobody."

"I'll be capo soon. And I'll be needing a consigliere." He slams the door shut, not waiting for my response.

He can't actually be serious. Not just about the marriage but making rocks-for-brains Matteo his second-in-command. Fucking hell. I'm going to lose it.

"He's right, you know." Bash stands across the office with his arms crossed. "You can't just have your way with her, take *our* men into battle for her, then leave her."

"Have my way with her?" I scoff, looking at him like he's lost it.

"I don't see it that way, but you know a lot of men in our world will and hers, too. If word gets out about you two, if it hasn't already, they'll label her as your whore. Is that the reputation you want to leave her with when she takes over the Triad?"

"You know it's not like that!"

Whose side is this fucker on?

"You'll ruin her more than you already have in the eyes of her own men. You have to let her go and pray word doesn't get out about the two of you."

Over my dead body will she marry that fucker, Matteo, or any other fucker for that matter. And then the idea hits me.

"Sure, brother." I nod and leave my brother standing in his office. *Married, she will be.*

I head back to my room, but before I walk in, I shoot out a series of texts to Dante, Valentina, and Uncle Ricky—all with a list of things to do. Let's get this show on the road.

When I enter the room, Anya's sitting up on the bed, watching TV. She's wearing my T-shirt, and I can't help but admire her. She looks away from the screen as I walk over to the bed and sit on the edge.

"He told you to end it, didn't he?" she asks quietly.

I turn and lay on the bed, pulling her into my lap, with her back to my chest, and kiss her temple before resting my chin on her shoulder.

"Here's the thing, babe. He can't tell me what to do. I'm not letting you go. I love you too much, and I'm a selfish bastard." She stills in my arms.

"You love me?" Her head perks up, turning to look at me.

I never said it out loud, especially to her. I hadn't even admitted it to myself. But there's no going back now.

"Isn't it obvious?"

"Isn't it too soon?" she asks, not making eye contact with me.

"I mean, I love you now, and I'll love you in six months, and I'll love you forever if you'll let me. I can wait to tell you, but what's the point?" I loop my fingers around her hair that's fallen onto the side of her face, and she looks at me with that damn smile.

"Say it again."

"I love you."

She kisses me deeply and pulls away, looking into my eyes. "I love you, too, Nico."

I grab her head and deepen the kiss. She maneuvers her body and straddles me. My cock is already at full mast, aching for her pussy.

I want her so much. Removing my shirt from her, I show her exactly how much.

After a long night of sex, she lies on my chest. I love that I can just be silent with her. I run my fingers through her hair as she rubs my chest. Fuck, if I want this forever.

"Your thoughts are practically bouncing off the walls," I joke.

She laughs before taking a deep breath.

"What if we can't kill him? What if we do but I'm a bad leader? I didn't grow up with them. What if they don't accept me? What if this ruins us?"

"That's a lot of what-ifs." I pause. "First of all"—I grab her by her shoulders and force her still, her tits in front of my eyes—"you and I are a done deal. We're solid and always will be. Second, we *will* kill him. And third, you won't be a bad leader because you'll have the support of the Outfit and the Cosa Nostra. But even without us, you're smart, strong, and despite your size, terrifying. I've seen it firsthand and have no doubt you'll turn things around for them. Plus, you can't be worse than Li."

I shouldn't have lifted her up, goddamnit. *Focus.*

"Dom was right, you know. My loyalties are all twisted," she says.

"Don't see why you have to pick, babe. There's family, business, and pleasure. Your duties are completely different. The Outfit is your family. So long as Cesare and Dom are alive,

# Rise Of An Heiress

they won't abandon you. Think of the Triad as business and me as pleasure," I say, wiggling my eyebrows, leaving out the part that I hope to also be included in the family part very soon. That gets her to laugh at least.

"Do you think the Triad will accept the Cosa Nostra *whore* as their new boss?"

"You're not a whore. Although, there's that one thing that you do that just makes me—"

She smacks me with a pillow. "Focus, Nico!"

I chuckle. "Do you trust me?"

She lays back down on my chest, and I wrap my arms around her.

"I do," she replies.

She has no idea how ironic her reply is.

"Okay, then. Get some sleep. I have a plan." We lay in silence until we both fall asleep.

# Chapter Twenty-Three

ANYA

I wake the next morning and look at the time: six thirty a.m. Nico is already dressed and walking back over to the bed.

"Where are you going?" I ask, yawning.

He leans forward to kiss me. "Got lots to do today."

And with that, he's out the door.

I don't see him for most of the day. He wasn't at breakfast or lunch. Dinner was awkward with my brother and Nico staring at each other, as if they were trying to set each other on fire with their minds. Cesare and Giuseppe act like they've been besties since they were in diapers. *At least someone's getting along.*

Nico won't even look at me and seems distracted, checking his phone every thirty seconds. It wouldn't piss me off so much, but he's paying extra special attention to Cosima tonight. He keeps getting up and whispering into her ear every so often.

She's enjoying it too much. I just might set her on fire myself. Not with my mind, either. *Okay, so the bloodlust is back. Stop.* He just told me he loved me. Did he change his mind already? To snap out of my thoughts, I shake my head.

Marcella and I make small talk. She's a sweet woman with a lot of patience. I guess you have to have it being the wife to a capo and mother to three boys all with tempers. We get along well. She can't cook, either, so we've spent a lot of time driving Valentina crazy in the kitchen, though I think she secretly likes having us around.

"So, tell me, mia dolce bambina, what have you been up to here?" Cesare asks me.

Before I can answer, Dom grunts, and Dante inserts himself into the conversation.

"Training. She can kick some serious ass. A natural," Dante says proudly.

I roll my eyes. Dom's gripping onto his knife so hard his knuckles are turning white. I'm afraid the utensil will turn to dust. He doesn't like the fact that I've grown so close to these men.

"Of course she can. Paid a lot of money to ensure that," Cesare says proudly, with a chuckle.

"Dom, you should spar with us sometime. I'd love to see you try and take on your sister," Dante says, and the table goes silent. *Why must he taunt him?*

"Sure thing," he says before taking a bite of his steak.

The rest of the evening goes by smoothly. Dom has considerably calmed down, but he doesn't say much.

## Rise Of An Heiress

I keep trying to make eye contact with Nico to get some reassurance, but he still won't look at me. When we all get up after dinner, Nico is already heading out the door without a second glance.

## Chapter Twenty-Four

NICO

"She's an outsider, Nico," Father expresses before sipping his whiskey.

We're in Bash's office, sitting on the leather armchairs by the fireplace. Bash is sitting on the couch across from us. I twirl the dark liquid in the glass before sipping it. He wasn't wrong. Traditionally, we almost never married outside of the Cosa Nostra. Alliances rarely lasted, so marrying outside of your syndicate was outdated.

"I love her," I tell him.

"I'm not saying you don't. It only took me a day to know your mother was the one. I'm saying she's an outsider," my father states.

"She's not some random nobody off the streets." *Although, if she was, I was certain we'd still be having this conversation.* "She might not be Cosa Nostra, but she's Triad, and high born at that. Hell, she outranks me."

"Exactly. She's *Triad*," my father says.

The "we can't trust them" is implied. A man of few words.

"You're right, Father. But this could be good for us if we take Li out," Bash interjects, to my surprise.

"And if we don't, and if this fails? You expect us to use our resources and possibly lose men because of some girl? What if they don't accept her?" my father asks, then downs the rest of the liquid before refilling his glass.

"We won't. Have some faith in our men. Her, too," Bash says.

"She's not just some girl, Pa," I say to my father.

"This marriage could benefit us," Bash pipes up again.

Wow, I really didn't expect him to back me up like this.

"The Triad's weak. They have nothing to offer us. She has nothing to offer us. She'll have to turn things around significantly. Otherwise, she *will* just be a nobody off the streets," Father retorts.

"I wasn't asking for permission," I finally say. My father looks up from his drink and has a sly smile on his face.

"So, it's safe to assume Cesare and Dominic have no idea?" Father asks.

## Anya

After getting ready for bed, Nico still hasn't returned. Where the hell has he been? It's not like him to not at least check in. I wouldn't consider myself clingy, but his strange behavior has me on edge. I try to read but can't concentrate, so I try to watch

TV instead. When that fails, I walk to Dom's room. We haven't had any time, just the two of us, and I really want us to talk.

I knock on his door, and shuffling comes from the other side. When he opens it, I hold up a bottle of whiskey and two glasses. He looks surprised to see me.

"I come in peace?" I say, looking at him, giving him my best angel eyes.

He smiles and rolls his eyes, but he steps aside to let me in. I climb onto his bed and lean back against the headboard, and he joins me. I pour each a glass, and we clink them before drinking.

"Where's your room?"

"Really? That's the first thing you're going to ask me when we're alone? I'm good, Dom. I've been learning how to cook, fight, and shoot better. How are you doing?" I answer sarcastically.

He smiles, but it doesn't reach his eyes, and he doesn't say anything back. He finishes his drink and pours another one.

"Don't ask questions you don't want to know the answer to, Dom. You know which room is mine."

"Yeah," he says, nodding, then takes a large gulp.

"He's not bad, Dom. None of them are," I tell him.

"We're all the bad guys, Anya. I just want to protect you from getting hurt, that's all. I don't trust him," Dom says.

"I know, but I don't need to be protected from him. I *do* trust him," I plead calmly, even though he's pissing me off. "And I've been the one spending time with him."

"This won't last, Anya. You can't be with him."

He's not angry, he's just stating it like it's a fact.

"He told me he loved me," I tell him, devoid of animosity.

"You don't see it now, but you will one day. I always knew I was going to be capo, so I had to look at things differently. You didn't know about the Triad, and that's not your fault. But you'll see. You have to make sacrifices as a leader."

He tries to mansplain to me like I don't understand the role I'm taking on.

I let out a sign, realizing we're just going to have to agree to disagree. I didn't have it in me to fight him right now. We're supposed to be working together. *Sempre.*

"I'm tired," I say, climbing off the bed and leaving the whiskey and my empty glass on his nightstand. "Good night, Brother." I kiss him on the cheek and head back to my room.

Nico still isn't in bed when I get to the room. It's only eleven p.m., but he's usually back by now.

I toss and turn for two more hours, and he still doesn't come back. *What the hell, Nico?*

## Chapter Twenty-Five
### Nico

I had everything in place. Timed to the exact minute. I woke up early again so Anya wouldn't ask me any questions. There's one more thing I need to take care of. The sun's barely rising as I walk over to one of the cabins, and I spot two of our men with three Outfit men sitting outside on the porch. I guess having a common enemy does bring people together. Scanning the men as I approach, I see just the man I'm looking for. I knew they'd be up. After all, I made the schedules. His eyes lock with mine as I take the steps up. He has a smug grin across his face.

"I take it you heard about the engagement," he taunts, not even bothering to stand as I stop in front of him. "Don't worry, though. I'll let you keep your little roommate situation with my betrothed until this mission is over. I don't mind sharing."

My fists clench, and I can hear my knuckles pop. I wanted to put a bullet in his head right then.

Bash'll kill me, though, if I start a war, and I can't put Anya in the position of having to pick a side. I promised myself I'd never do that to her.

"Engagement is off," I say calmly.

The two Outfit soldiers next to him still. One jerks his hand toward his jacket, ready to pull out a weapon if necessary.

Matteo finally stands. I'm a few inches taller than him, so he has to tilt his head up. "That's not your call to make."

"Sure it is," I reply. "Besides, it's already done." I shrug.

His nostrils flare. "The fuck makes you think you can get away with this?"

"The fact that I can do whatever the fuck I want."

"You're really going to fight over pussy I had first?"

Finally giving me a reason to do what I came here to do, I lift him by the throat and slam his head into the glass table. The table smashes in an instant. His men are about to jump on me but mine pull out their guns. Two Outfit barrels point at me, while one barrel from each of mine points back at them. I don't pause. I pick him up by his throat again and slam him to the floor face down as I kneel on the top of his back.

"You fucker!" He tries to fight back, but he can't move. "You're going to die for this."

I grab his arm, placing his palm flat. Using my other knee to hold his forearm in place, I pull a knife from the holster on my calf and stab it straight through his hand, pinning it to the porch.

*Rise Of An Heiress*

He whimpers, probably waking up everyone in the neighboring cabins.

I bring my head close to his ear. "I didn't come here to chat. I came to give you a warning. You blink in her direction, you even think about her, and I'll fire a bullet into each eye. The only reason I don't end your life right now is because Anya cares about Dominic. She is the reason I'm *letting* you live. So, instead of disrespecting her, you should be thanking her." I spit in his pathetic face, then straighten up and fix my shirt.

Without another word or glance, I head back into the mansion.

## ANYA

Soft kisses trail my jaw and neck as I gain consciousness. I take a deep inhale, smelling his signature fragrance. I open my eyes as he peppers more kisses on me. Nico came back to bed late last night. There's no way he's already up and dressed.

"I want to be woken up like this every morning." I blink, letting my eyes adjust to the light and taking in the sight of the man in front of me.

"Get dressed. I want to show you something. You have thirty minutes," he says with his devilish smile and darts out of the room before I can question him.

I get up to get ready. I choose a matcha-green minidress, put some light makeup on, and curl my hair loosely. Maybe we're going on a picnic? He's seen me at my worst, but I want to look nice for his surprise.

When I come downstairs, he's waiting for me at the bottom with the biggest smile on his face. *How could I have ever doubted him?* He's wearing black dress pants and a black dress shirt that shows off his muscular tattooed arms. My mouth just waters at the sight of him. Damn, my man is hot. He takes my hand, and he walks me to Our Spot, over by the giant tree in silence. I don't know why, but I'm nervous, and my palms are sweating. Is he about to dump me? He interrupts my thoughts when he begins to speak.

"Anya, from the moment I saw you, I was obsessed. The more I learned about you, the more I needed to know." He pauses to grab both of my hands into his. "When I saw you at the club, I had no idea if you were the enemy or not. But I knew then it didn't matter. Nothing else mattered. Fate had taken complete control the moment you came into my life. You were mine from the moment I saw you, and I was yours."

He gets down on one knee. *Wait, oh god.* My right hand shoots to my chest as he holds my left. I can't see him anymore. Tears flood my eyes. Just as I blink them away, he pulls out a small black Graff box.

Covering my mouth, I muffle my sobbing. *When did I turn into such mush?* He opens the box, but I can't concentrate on anything but him.

"Anya Liu, will you do me the honors and become my wi—"

"YES!" I yell breathlessly, launching myself into his arms, crying from excitement, smothering him in kisses.

I never thought I'd be that girl—hell, I never thought I'd get married let alone fall in love.

He catches me and chuckles before he picks me up, spinning me. I pull in his head and take his lips to mine. I don't know how long we kiss for, since I've completely lost the concept of time. The kiss quickly turns heated, and I wrap my legs around his waist.

In two strides, he pins my back against the tree. I quickly undo his pants as he lifts up my dress and moves my panties to the side. He thrusts inside me in one swift move, and I let out a cry. His pace picks up, and as he thrusts into me over and over, he takes my left hand and slides the engagement ring on my finger, his lips never leaving mine. He isn't just fucking me. He's claiming me, and I relish in the moment.

After the quickie, we walk toward the mansion hand-in-hand, but instead of going back, he pulls me into a different direction. As we walk, I finally take a moment to look at my engagement ring. *Oh my. He did well.* I would honestly marry him with a Ring Pop, but this ring is exquisite, with its huge oval-shaped diamond set in platinum with a pave band.

"I want to show you something else," he says, heading for the heavily wooded area. We'd never gone in there before.

"Is this the part where you kill me?" I joke.

"Why would I kill you when you're just about to be mine?" he asks with a wink.

We walk for some time, and my mind starts wandering again. I know I want to be with him, but are we rushing things? How will Papa and Dom react? I have to tell Donna and Maya.

"I can hear your thoughts, as usual, babe. Why don't you just share them?" he asks as we walk holding hands.

"Do you feel like we're rushing things?" I've asked him this before, but I need the reality check.

"You already said yes. There's no backing out now," he chuckles.

"Are you only marrying me because you feel obligated to?" I ask, wondering if he's just trying to save my reputation. These goddamn double standards suck.

"No, I asked you because I want to spend the rest of my life with you."

"How do you know that, though?" I ask him seriously.

"You said yes. I could ask you the same thing."

I took a moment to think about his words. I do love him, and I'll never love anyone else. He turned my lonely existence into something worth living for.

"You brought me back to life in more ways than one, Nico. Before I met you, I was living a half-life. Barely existing, just getting by. I've never had to be anyone other than myself with you. And you accept me in every form. The heir, the outsider, the orphan, the sister to a mafia don. Natalie. Anya. You've awakened something deep inside me I didn't know was possible and given me things I never thought I'd ever have."

I kiss him deeply, thinking about the kind of future I could have with this man. Love, family, children. I pull away, needing to have this conversation.

"I know I have a lot of baggage. We still have Andrew to deal with, and I still have to finish law school, and—"

He kisses me. "You asked me if we were rushing things. I told you before. I love you now, and I'll love you in six months, and I'll love you forever if you'll let me. Why wait?" He cups his hands around my head. "You can be married and go to law school. You can be married and kill your uncle. But we're solid. You're my forever."

The *kill my uncle* part was just as casual as he said law school. Jesus, we make one hell of a couple.

He has a point.

"You're everything I never knew I wanted, Anya. Everything I didn't think I could have. I always thought my fate was to marry someone who was groomed to be a homemaker and have my children because it's our duty—what's expected. I never thought a woman like you existed. One that's not only intelligent but driven and strong. But somehow, I found you. And I actually want all of that with you. Not out of duty but out of my love for you. I want to create things with our love. I never thought love was a part of my path."

I took in his words. I didn't know what to say.

The best I can come up with is "I'm not part of the Cosa Nostra."

I remind him like an idiot. He just poured his heart out, and that's my response?

"You will be."

"No. After the mission, if it's a success, I'll always be Triad."

"But you'll be mine no matter what happens with the mission." He cups my face in his hands. "Do you love me?"

"Of course."

"Don't think of anything else when I ask you this. Just think of the question. Do you want to marry me?" he asks.

*Yes.*

"Yes," I say firmly, with no hesitation.

"Good because nothing's keeping me from you." He plants a hard kiss on my lips. "Plus, you're at least Catholic, so Ma isn't upset in the slightest." He shrugs, like that settles it.

I shake my head, laughing at him as he takes my hand and walks me over a few more yards.

White tents and a white carpet lines an aisle, covered in pink flower petals.

"What's this?" I turn to look at him.

"Our wedding."

## Chapter Twenty-Six

### NICO

Her eyes grow wide, looking up at me.

"What do you mean? We're getting married right now?"

"Yes, right now. Well, in a few hours. We need to get ready," I say, pointing at one of the tents.

Before she can argue, I kiss her deeply. "I know this isn't the wedding you deserve. You deserve the big celebration, but I can't wait to make you mine. So, please, will you become Mrs. Delucci tonight, and we can plan a bigger and better wedding when the dust settles?"

I know I'm forcing her hand, but there's no guarantee we're all going to walk out alive after we face Andrew. Of course, I'm not going to tell her that. But there's no way I'm going to die without her being mine. Surprisingly, she kisses me, to my relief.

"Yes"—she smiles—"let's do it."

Just then, my mother grabs her and takes her into the tent where her lunch is waiting. I've been on the receiving end of her fury when she's hungry, and I wasn't going to have that on our wedding day. She still needs to get her hair and makeup done. We had a long day ahead. I didn't need her passing out.

I had Cosima pick out a selection of dresses. The crazy bitch thought I was asking her to pick out her own wedding dress, which, I guess, in turn, was a good thing. I could at least count on her picking out dresses Anya might like. Valentina is also an amazing tailor.

My father, brothers, and Dante wait inside my tent with whiskey in their hands. They hold their glasses up, welcoming me, hugging and kissing each other on both cheeks.

"It's my brother's wedding day! Who would've thought we'd see the day?" Bash says, pouring me a glass.

"You know," Dante interjects, "you're lucky Bash ended up calling me to take care of that Sanchez bastard at the club that night. Otherwise, this would be my wedding we'd be celebrating," he jokes, popping a grape in his mouth.

I know he wants her, and it's definitely more than mild attraction.

"Asshole," I laugh, pretending to punch him in the stomach as he blocks me. He pulls me into a hug and pats my back.

"What? Mrs. Anya Borelli has a nice ring to it," he taunts.

"Yeah right," Bash snorts. "From what I've gathered, Nico all but pissed on her the moment he saw her. You didn't stand a chance," he jokes.

I roll my eyes.

He's right, though. She was mine the moment I laid eyes on her. Never thought I'd see the day, either. Then I realized something.

"That why you decided to let her stay?" I ask my brother.

He smiles back. "I don't know what you're talking about," he says in a tone that tells me he knew exactly what he was doing.

"Okay, cupid." I tease back.

"Congrats, man," Enzo says, clinking his glass with mine.

My father's the last to approach me, big dark eyes like mine staring right back at me.

"This will probably bring on a shit storm, but I'm proud of you, Son. Now maybe you can make your mother's dreams come true by popping out some grandbabies." He laughs.

"No babies anytime soon. We just want to enjoy each other for now," I reply.

I can't deny it. I want to get Anya pregnant as soon as possible, but I know how that conversation will go if I even think about bringing it up at a time like this. She'll cut off my balls and work her way to other body parts. Then she's going to want to establish herself in the Triad, finish law school, and work to prove herself for a while. I could wait, but damn if I wasn't excited to see her pregnant with our child. Maybe it was feral and old-school, but I couldn't help it.

We're all standing at the end of the altar with both the officiate and the priest so we can declare our lives as one not only in front of God but the state of New York. Money can buy you anything. We paid a substantial amount of money for the late notice, to keep their mouths shut about our location, and to forge our marriage license into being filed in New York. We didn't want any Triad members getting our location through this. Anya's still technically dead, but one thing at a time.

My mother and father are seated, while Valentina and a very pissed off Cosima stand in the back. I'd rather not have them here, especially Cosima, but I needed someone to help Anya get ready and bring lunch over, and I didn't want to invite any more people onto the property that didn't need to be here.

Bash, Enzo, and Dante stand by my side.

A vision in white appears at the end of the aisle. She locks eyes with mine immediately and smiles. My vision's blurry, but I bring my hand up to cough and rub my eyes, recovering quickly.

"Saw that," Bash whispers.

"Shut the fuck up," I reply back, smiling.

She walks down in a simple strapless, white lace gown that hugs her waist and hips too perfectly. The bustier of the dress makes her tits pop up to her eyeballs. I have to think about kittens dying to prevent a hard-on. No veil. Simple and elegant. Fuck, she is beautiful.

As she makes her way to me, I can see she's looking around. She doesn't miss that I left Cesare and Dominic out on purpose, but she keeps a smile on her face. It only falters for a second. I'm a goddamn bastard. When she gets to me, my mother stands to take her bouquet, kisses her cheeks, and I take her hands into mine. I don't even hear what the priest says. I'm eager to make her mine, so I listen for when it's time for us to say our vows.

Bash pulls out our wedding bands and hands them over to me.

"Do you, Niccolo Amadeo Delucci, take Anya Meilin Liu to be your lawful wedded wife? To be true to her in good times and in bad, in sickness and in health? To love and honor her for all the days of your life?" the officiant asks.

"I do," I say firmly as she slips on my ring.

"Do you, Anya Meilin Liu, take Niccolo Amadeo Delucci to be your lawful wedded husband? To be true to him in good times and in bad, in sickness and in health? To love and honor him for all the days of your life?"

"I do!" she exclaims, bouncing on her toes as I slip on her wedding band.

"By the power vested in me, by the state of *New York*, I pronounce you husband and wife. You may now ki—"

I know what to do. I grab my *wife* and dip her back and take her mouth with mine. She tries to pull away, not liking the audience, but I don't care. That only makes me deepen the kiss more. She lets out a moan. When I let her go, she's flushed, and I can't help but laugh. You'd never guess she could kill grown men three times her size.

The family joins in to congratulate us. We sign the documents before we leave, and that's it. She's officially my wife. *Mine*.

I had a car waiting for us not wanting her to walk back to the mansion in her dress and heels. I'm not a total bastard after all. We drive back in silence as I look over at her sitting in the passenger seat. She's biting the inner corner of her mouth. I notice she does that when she's overthinking.

"Everything okay, Mrs. Delucci?" I ask proudly.

"Liu-Delucci," she corrects me quickly, catching me off guard.

Call me old-fashioned, but I never considered she might want to hyphenate her name.

"And yes . . . I just wish Cesare was able to walk me down the aisle. Donna and Dom should've been there, too," she says with a shrug, trying to conceal her sadness.

"I'm fucking selfish, Anya. I know they should be here, but I didn't want anyone trying to stop us or cause a scene. I wanted today to just be about you and me, no drama."

"You're not selfish, Nico. I understand why you went about it this way. And I agreed to it. I don't have any regrets. I just feel like I betrayed them."

I grab her hand and kiss her wrist. "You didn't betray them. And you will get your wedding, I promise."

"I don't need a big wedding, Nico. This is enough for me," she says earnestly.

"No, you deserve more than just enough. You're going to be a queen. And you deserve to have the memory of Cesare walking you down the aisle."

"I love you," she replies.

As we pull up to the front of the mansion, Dominic is outside, face red, chest puffed. Tony tries and fails to hold him back. This dude was a ticking time bomb with his damn temper. Dominic pushes Tony off and approaches the car as I pull up.

"So much for no drama," Anya says to me with a small smile on her face.

## Rise Of An Heiress

I don't even get the chance to open the door for my wife. As I get out of the driver's side. Anya's door is pried open by a very furious Dominic. He yanks her out of the car by the arm, and I'm on him in a heartbeat.

"Are you fucking kidding me, Anya? What the hell is wrong with you?" he screams at the top of his lungs in her face.

Well, if no one knew we were hiding out here, they sure do now. She looks him dead in the eye, but before she can say anything, I'm on him.

I push him off of her and grab him by the collar. "You don't ever get to yell at her, and you don't ever get to put your filthy hands on her again!"

"She's my sister, and I'll do as I damn well please!" he says through gritted teeth, shoving me. He quickly reaches behind to grab his gun and point it under my chin, but at the same time, I reach into my jacket, pull mine out, and bring it to his temple.

Out of my peripherals, I see Tony has his gun pointing toward me, while Enzo is pointing his gun at Tony, and Bash is now standing in front of Anya, who just looks annoyed. Dante has his gun in hand, but he's waiting to see if he'll need to use it.

"You're outnumbered, Dominic," I say to him as he pushes the barrel to my temple.

"What is going on here?" I hear a voice call from the door. From the corner of my eye, I spot Cesare walking down the front steps.

"Dominic, we do not point guns at our kind hosts," he says to his son calmly, as if he's not telling him to put his weapon away.

Dominic's nostrils flare, and he stands still for a moment, like he's seriously contemplating a shoot out. He backs away and pushes me off of him.

"Do you know what they've done! Did you see what he did to Matteo?" he yells at his capo.

I smile at the thought.

"Hush, boy, I'm still capo, and you will not disrespect me!" Cesare gets into his face and grabs his shirt with both hands. His usual calm demeanor disappears.

"It is done, Dominic. Nothing you can do," he says as he releases Dominic from his grip.

Sure, we might torture, kill, and bribe, but we have some honor. Marriages were held in high regard in our world. Once God witnesses two lives becoming one, the only way out is death.

Dominic looks at me. "You continue to take from her. She'll have nothing left because of you."

Then he looks at her. "He's only marrying you to solidify an alliance with you, Anya. He's trying to block us out so the Cosa Nostra has an in with the Triad's drugs and weapons supply."

*Oh, please. The Triad is bleeding money right now.*

"Dom—" she says.

"No. You've ruined yourself enough. I don't want to hear you explain your way out of it," he says through gritted teeth. And with that, he storms off.

Anya looks at her stepfather. She smiles at him tentatively. His face immediately relaxes, as if he weren't angry just a few seconds ago. I can see where Dominic gets his short fuse from.

"My daughter, you look beautiful. Congratulations." He kisses her cheeks.

My shoulders relax.

"You're not angry?" she asks.

"I had my suspicions the first time you called from here," he reveals.

Anya's eyes grow wide. "But—"

"I raised you. I know you. My daughter would've fought harder to get home." He pauses just before he looks at me. "Unless there was something stopping her."

Anya doesn't cower. In fact, she straightens her spine and lifts her chin proudly. I love watching her come into herself. I love that I get to be here witnessing it.

"I won't apologize, Papa. I love him, and whatever consequences there are, I'll face them."

"*We* will," I say as I put my arm around her.

"I'm not thrilled about the timing or the way you went about it," he says, staring directly at me. "But I'm happy if you're happy."

"I never meant any disrespect, Cesare," I say to her father. "I want her to be my wife. But she'll get a proper wedding for you to walk her down the aisle."

Cesare thinks for a moment, staring back at me like he's trying to solve a puzzle. Then he lets out a sigh and reaches out to shake my hand. "I'll hold you to it." He pulls me in for a hug. "And if you ever go back on your vows or harm her in any way, I won't hesitate to kill you," he whispers in my ear and smiles as he pulls away. "Congratulations, Son." Beaming, he pats my shoulder.

That's the Cesare the world knew.

## NICO

I take Anya to our room to collect ourselves while the staff sets up the reception. I had Valentina and some soldiers set up tables and decorations in the courtyard in the back so the household and all the soldiers could join us for a meal and lots of wine. We have three days after tonight to solidify our plan of attack, so Bash and I agreed this is a good opportunity for Anya and the rest of the men to enjoy themselves before we get into it.

"Did you marry me to prevent an alliance between the Outfit and Triad?" she asks me, breaking the silence as I pour myself a glass of whiskey.

Her eyes were empty, completely void of emotion. *Is she serious right now? After what she just said to Cesare.*

"No," I retort, failing to hide my irritation. "I already told you it has nothing to do with that." I try my hardest to keep my composure at my dear wife.

She crosses her arms. "That's the only reason our marriage would ever be accepted, right? If it was just an alliance between Triad and Cosa Nostra. Are you guys only helping me so you can align with the Triad and take over?"

"No!" I answer more harshly than intended, but I need her to get this through her head. "That's not how loyalty works, Anya. I know there's nothing I can do to sever your relationship with the Outfit, and I have no interest in doing so. I told you I won't make you choose a side. That's not how it works. Loyalty isn't a choice, Anya. The alliance is just a convenience, but it has never and will never affect what I feel for you!"

She doesn't say anything, but she nods, her gaze glued to the floor.

Releasing a sigh, I walk over to her. "Anya, I don't care if you take over the Triad or not. I'll stand by you and fight for it if that's what you want. But if you walk away from it all, I'll still be here. I just want you."

She plops down on the chaise by the fireplace and exhales.

"I'm sorry I doubted you. Fuck, we're only an hour into marriage, and I'm already a terrible wife," she says on the verge of tears.

"No, you've had some major life changes the past two months," I say, getting down on my haunches, wiping a tear off her cheek. She takes my head in both hands and pulls me into a kiss.

## Chapter Twenty-Seven

ANYA

If Nico were good at anything, it was talking me off the ledge. I shouldn't have questioned him. I knew the answer. I need to stop letting Dom's words get to me so much. After I fix my makeup, we head downstairs just in time for our reception to begin. It's a small gathering, and by small, I mean his family, Cesare, Dominic, forty soldiers from the Cosa Nostra, and the Outfit.

Everyone's already outside enjoying wine, champagne and other cocktails. Nico's looking off with a sly smirk on his face. Following his gaze, I spot Matteo sulking in the corner with his hand wrapped. My husband could be a real caveman sometimes. His eyes meet mine and I just roll them, not even bothering to fight him on this. We'll have plenty of arguments for the rest of our lives, and Matteo sure as fuck wasn't going to be one of them.

The sun on the horizon sets the mood, string lights dangling from above. Center pieces with candles adorn the round tables draped with white cloth. Classic love songs play in the background. It's gorgeous and tranquil. We walk up to our guests hand-in-hand and greet everyone. I made it a point to learn everyone's names during my time here, and I've grown quite close and fond of them.

"You have inside jokes with my men? When did that happen?" Nico asks, sounding equally amused as he was jealous.

"Some of us can hold a conversation outside of torturing and interrogating," I reply.

His eyebrows pinch, but before he can respond, we're struck with a flash of light as Giuseppe and Marcella approach us with the biggest smile on their faces. Marcella has her phone clutched in a tight grip. You'd think we just told them they were about to be grandparents. Marcella's crying, with tear-stained cheeks, taking pictures of everything on her phone, while Giuseppe holds her close.

Marcella pulls me in for a hug. "My dear, you look beautiful. I didn't have a chance to tell you earlier."

"Thank you." I pull her in, hugging her tighter. I wish my parents could be here for this. As if she could read my mind, she speaks up.

"I know I'll never replace your mother, but I look forward to you joining the family. I've always wanted a daughter, but, of course, I get stuck with three crazy boys." She nods toward Nico, who rolls his eyes as his mother kisses his cheek.

"I can't imagine three boys running around. Dominic was enough for Donna and me. He was so gross as a teenager."

"The teenage years are the worst. Nico's showers were so long I almost had to—"

"Ma, it's time to sit down for dinner," he tells her as he pulls me along, trying to escape the conversation. I couldn't stop laughing.

Deciding to mess with my husband, I yell back, "Hey, I wanted to hear why your showers were so long!"

Ignoring me, he directs me to our table that sits at the front with a loveseat at the end for us to share.

As we eat dinner, I calm down. Nico doesn't take his eyes off my chest, though I don't blame him. The corset practically pushes my boobs up to my chin. As I take a sip of champagne, Nico pulls me in to plant a kiss on my temple.

"Don't drink too much. Tonight, that pussy is mine," he growls into my ear and laughs as I cough up my drink.

## NICO

I thought the night would never end.

Anya and I shared a dance, then she shared one with Cesare and a reluctant Dominic. After that, I shared a dance with my mother, while Anya danced with my brothers and father. We skipped the garter and bouquet toss this time around, saving it for the real wedding. We cut the cake and feed each other. Take photo after photo. All I can think about is getting my wife alone and naked. As soon as I see an opening, I make up an excuse. I'm practically dragging my new wife up the stairs.

"Nico! Can you make it any more obvious?" she yells, giggling as we run down the hall.

"Do you think I care? It's our fucking wedding night." She yelps as I pick her up bridal-style and enter our bedroom. "You'll get a real honeymoon soon, too, I promise." I place her in the center of the room.

I take a moment to admire her. She's staring back at me with love and anticipation in her eyes. I slowly inch up toward her. I rub the back of my fingers down her bare arms. Her skin was so soft. I lean in, and she tilts her head to the side, giving me access to her neck. I inhale her sweet scent that I love so much.

Backing away and taking my suit jacket off, I pull my knife out. I hold it to her chest as it moves up and down with her breathing. I slice the fabric of her dress down the middle, and it falls to a puddle at her feet. My eyes work their way up, and my erection grows harder by the second.

She's standing there like a goddess in her white sparkly heels, lace thigh-highs, a white lace thong that doesn't hide a damn thing, and that white and tight corset. I don't know where to start. I want to devour her.

"I knew those heels were a good idea."

My mouth is salivating.

"Do you like them?" She looks down to admire them.

"I chose them."

"You did?" Her eyes shoot up at me.

"I did. I knew they'd look good on my shoulders as I fuck you dizzy."

# Rise Of An Heiress

She blushes and inches forward, taking my belt into her hand, undoing it. Her small hands unbutton my shirt slowly, and she tosses it to the ground. Her palms run over my abs, slowly working their way down. She works my zipper, pulls my pants down, and gets on her knees in one swift move. *Fuck, she looks so good on her knees.* I step out of my pants as she looks up at me. She takes her hand and rubs my erection over my briefs, and I close my eyes. She kisses my stomach, and just when I don't think I can take it anymore, she pulls my briefs down and takes my cock into her small hands, rubbing my tip with the pad of her thumb.

I rock my hips into her hands, as she teases my cock with her tongue. She feels so good. She's leaning forward, her back arched, giving me a perfect view of her ass, but I need to fuck her mouth. Now. I grab her head and look down at her, her eyes locking with mine.

"I want you to take all of me into your mouth." She nods, lips suctioning my cock. I back her up against the wall so her head is resting against it. "I'm gonna fuck your throat now." She obliges eagerly.

I waste no time thrusting. I let out a grunt as I feel the vibrations of her moans around my cock. I slowly work my hips into her mouth, the suctioning sound of her lips and moaning bringing me closer to the edge. I push back further, so her head is now against the wall, and she has nowhere to go. Her hands grip the backs of my thighs, eyes closed as she sucks me off.

"I want you to look into my eyes while you take my cock."

Her eyes open.

I thrust harder with her head in place. Her moans vibrate through my cock, nails digging into me, telling me to keep going. Fuck, her mouth feels so good. I work faster and faster, fucking her throat. She stares up at me, eyes watering, cheeks hollowing, and I can see she's fighting for air but won't stop. I love how she takes my cock.

"I'm gonna come in your mouth, baby. I want you to swallow every drop."

As if on cue, she sucks harder, and I explode into her mouth. I come so much that some of it starts to drip down her chin. Fuck me, she's so beautiful.

"Yes, baby, take my fucking cock."

She's still sucking as I finish, and I almost can't take the sensation anymore.

# Anya

"Fuck, baby, you're gonna kill me," he says, but I don't stop, even after I swallow the last drop of cum.

He quickly picks me up and kisses me, and I know he can taste himself. I instinctively wrap my legs around his waist as he walks over to the bed.

He sets me down next to the bed. I'm standing still in my heels and lingerie as he lets his gaze travel up and down my body. He takes his hand and rubs his thumb on my clit over my panties. I know he can feel how wet I am. I always get so wet from sucking his cock.

"Do you like my cock in your mouth?"

"Yes," I say breathlessly.

"Tell me how much you like it," he says as he teases my slit, kissing my neck and collarbone.

"I love your cock in my mouth." I bite my bottom lip. "I love it so much I can come just from sucking you off alone."

"Apri le gambe." *Spread your legs*, he demands.

I love when he uses his bossy voice in bed.

He drops to his knees, pulls one of my legs over his shoulder, and starts sucking my clit through the fabric of my thong, adding more friction. Instinctively, I cry out. My core was already throbbing before he touched me. I graze his head, pulling his hair. His lips don't leave my pussy as he pushes me back down onto the bed.

He wastes no time as he's crawling onto the bed, only breaking contact with my pussy to rip off my thong. It feels so good. I can't hear anything, but I know I'm screaming. Fuck, he knows how to use that tongue. He grabs my hips and swings me around. Suddenly, I'm straddling his head.

"Ride my face, baby," he demands, as he flicks his tongue over my core and inserts two fingers into me.

I'm leaning forward with my hands on the bed completely spread over his head, thrusting myself into his tongue.

"You like when I fuck you with my tongue?"

"Yes, Nico," I say, grinding into his face shamelessly. "Your tongue drives me crazy."

He claims my body with his mouth as I cry out my release. He grabs my hips to hold me into place. He doesn't give me much time to recover. He gets up, kneels with me, and rips off my corset, taking each nipple into his mouth as I tug on his hair.

"You smell so good. I want to lock you in my room and use you as my own personal sex doll. To fuck as I please," he says as he kisses down my neck and breasts.

"Fuck me, Nico, please. Puoi farmi quello che vuoi." *You can do whatever you want with me.* I dig my nails into his back.

"Sei mia." *You're mine,* he growls as he pushes me onto my back.

"Sono tutta per te." *I'm all yours,* I whisper back to him before he kisses me . . . so hard I think my lips are bleeding.

"These lips are mine," he says, working his way down.

"Yes," I tell him.

"These tits are mine." He bites down on my nipple, and I moan at the sensation. He pulls my ankles onto his shoulders, as promised, and he lines his cock up at my entrance.

"And this pussy"—he slams into me—"is mine."

His size, always taking me by surprise, makes me scream in pleasure and pull on the sheets. "Yes, Nico, it's yours," I cry out as he thrusts mercilessly into me.

"Fuck, baby, I feel like I'm gonna break you in half."

All I could get were inaudible syllables. I'm so full of him as he hits me deeper with every thrust.

"This tight cunt always takes my cock so good," he grunts.

"Nico, fuck, I'm gonna come."

"Come for me, wife," he says, putting pressure on my lower belly with his palm.

He knows how much I love this move. I let out my release. My whole body shakes, pussy clenching his cock as I scream his name.

He doesn't stop thrusting into me. God, he feels so good.

"Come for me, Nico."

He comes so hard, I'm so full from his length, I can feel his seed seeping out of me as he pumps into me.

When the high of the orgasm finally wears off, he doesn't pull out of me. He lowers himself on top of me and kisses me, like I was the only thing providing him oxygen, until I lose track of time.

We lay in bed, completely spent after the busy day we had. I'm getting better with the touching thing. In all honesty, it wasn't difficult with Nico. I want to touch him all the time. I lay on his chest as he runs his fingers through my hair.

"I can't believe we're married," I say to him with my eyes closed, listening to his heart beating.

"Really?" he asks, surprised.

"I never saw myself doing anything like this. Relationships. Marriage."

"Kids," he adds.

I smile at the thought. Looking up at him, I kiss his lips before I say, "I never thought kids were an option for me, either."

He looks at me for a beat, and my heart swells with how much I love this man. "I'll give you whatever you want, Anya. I don't think I have it in me to say no to you."

I laugh at his confession. "Dom was wrong, you know?"

Nico chuckles. "Of course I know, but what about this time?"

I lay my head back down on his chest. "About you taking. I don't think you've taken anything. I'm the one that doesn't have anything to give you."

He pushes me onto my back and adjusts himself between my legs. "You've given me a lot, princess." He kisses my neck, and his erection grows.

"You gave me these." He kisses my lips.

"And these." He sucks on one nipple before moving onto the next.

"More importantly, this." He kisses the place right over my heart and works his way down.

Before he gets to his destination, he looks back up at me. "You give me love and something to fight for. You're giving me a future I never imagined for myself."

I smile back down at him.

"And don't even get me started on this." He kisses my lips in between my legs, and I let out a moan. He takes his time with his mouth before he lines himself up at my entrance and pauses to look down at me with love in his eyes.

"I've been looking for you my whole life, Anya, and I didn't even know it." He makes love to me all night.

## Chapter Twenty-Eight

ANYA

"I CAN'T BELIEVE I HAD TO HEAR FROM SHIT-FOR-BRAINS THAT YOU GOT MARRIED!" Donna yells into the phone, referring to Dom.

Nico finally caved and gave me a phone, since I can be trusted, considering we are now married, and just about all of the Outfit knows our location, anyway.

"It happened so fast, Donna. He got down on one knee and next thing I know, I was walking down the aisle—literally," I plead to her.

Gazing out of the library's window, I tell her everything. I tell her about meeting Nico at the club, him coming to class. She found out about the safe house and where I was hiding from Dom. I told her about the time Nico and I have spent getting to know each other.

"Holy fuck, this has been going on since your birthday?" she shrieks into the phone.

"I really didn't think it'd turn out like this."

"You were just, what . . . going to sleep with him until he decided to kill you? My God, I knew you were twisted, but that's another level."

I laugh at her comment. "Honestly, that's exactly what was going through my mind at the time. I don't know what happened, but it's like my mind shuts off when he's around."

"Well, this could be good for you. You've always had to hide yourself. No more hiding, Anya!"

"Ugh, I miss you. It's been killing me not being able to talk to you," I confess.

"I miss you, too. So much. I know it was *your* wedding and all, but I don't even care, so I'm gonna say it. What about *ME*? You're being selfish. I was supposed to be your maid of honor! What about Maya?"

She's yelling, but I can tell she's not actually mad.

I laugh at her. "We're still going to have a wedding. You're still going to be my maid of honor, but you can't tell Maya any of this. At least not yet."

"Yeah, we told her you had a mental breakdown, so you needed a few weeks off at some cushy rehab," Donna responds nonchalantly. *Uh, thank you*? "If you're still planning a wedding, why couldn't you wait? You don't think he rushed into this for other reasons? Are you sure you want to be married to him? You've only just met!"

"Well, it's too late now, either way. But we didn't want to wait. It's definitely soon, but you know how things are in this world. You're either married or you're a whore. I can't start off in the Triad as the Italian's whore. They'd never respect me. Hell, they might still not, even if I'm married, but at least I'm not a harlot. Plus, I think *your* brother made things worse and accidentally sped up the process." I laugh.

"Yeah, trust the dumbass to only make things worse for himself. Ugh, and why's he only *my* brother when he's being an idiot?"

I laugh. "I really do love him. I can say it's for an alliance and use all of those other excuses to justify why we got married, but it's really not that complicated."

"Wow. I honestly didn't think you had feelings, so I can't help but take you seriously," Donna says, genuinely.

It wasn't that I didn't have feelings—I was just always trying to blend in. Getting too close to someone could put them in danger. I always knew there was a chance I'd be found. It didn't feel right dragging someone into this world full of monsters.

Nico, being the bigger monster, is perfect. He wouldn't go down without a fight and neither would I. He wouldn't judge me just as I wouldn't judge him. He knows this life. We're not good people, but it didn't make us any less of a match. He knows all of my baggage and chose me anyway.

"This isn't a good look for me, Anya," Donna continues. "Everyone is already calling me a spinster for still not being married and almost thirty!"

"You still have a couple of years. Besides, Dom's older, and no one gives him shit." I laugh, since Donna has drilled into us that she will never be getting married.

"Because he's a man," she says with so much attitude I can practically feel an eyeroll.

"Well, it's a good thing Papa will never force you to marry."

"True," she sighs.

Before I can respond any further, Nico appears at the door and nods, telling me it's time to go. We're all meeting in Bash's office to discuss the plans and everyone's roles to take down Andrew.

"Donna, I have to go. As soon as I'm home, I'll tell you everything else. You can help me with the wedding plans and come up with a cover story with Maya," I promise her before hanging up.

## NICO

Bash sits at his desk. Enzo and Dante sit in front of him. Cesare and Father each take a chair by the fireplace. They won't be a part of the mission, letting the next two capos take the lead, but they still sit in the meeting. No one will dare say anything out of respect and fear.

Dominic, Tony, and Franco take the seats in front of my wife and me on the couch. I smile, noticing Matteo isn't in attendance. Anya looks tense. She spent the morning going over the blueprints with Dominic, Bash, Franco, and Dante. Since she is head of her house, and all of this was for her, she needed to be present to come up with the plan. I'm curious to hear what else they've come up with now that everyone is here. This is her first mission, after all. I wanted to be there, but with Bash's morning consumed, I had to take care of other business.

"All right, let's get this plan straightened out. We've sat on it for too long," Bash says as we all get settled.

I can't wait to get this over with. I should be spending my days in marital bliss, fucking my wife until she can't walk. It must be on my face because she slaps my chest as if she can read my mind. I smile, take her hand, and kiss it. I hear Dom grunt, but I don't give a shit.

Franco and Dante then step up, and Dante clicks a button with the remote in his hand. The screen above the fireplace comes to life as my wife stands.

"I would first like to thank you all for being here. I am grateful to have your alliance as I claim my rightful place as the dragon head of the Triad. With that being said"—she nods at Franco—"let's begin."

"This is the blueprint of the grounds. There's a single level above and ground and two more below." Franco shines a red laser at the blueprint.

He continues. "Around the property, there's an electrical fence, as well, anywhere from twelve to fifteen guards surrounding the perimeter at all times. There's only one way in and one way out." He points the laser at what I assume is the entrance.

Dante chimes in. "The door is made of reinforced steel. Not only that, but there's four additional doors you have to go through, all with different access codes, before you can even enter the facility."

"Jesus Christ, what the hell is Li doing with a warehouse like that in Kansas City? The Triad has no business or alliances there," an Outfit soldiers asks.

"He'd only just attained it in the last couple of years. He's just using it as a hiding place for now, waiting to see if the Outfit will attack. We think that's where he planned on expanding west but had to put his master plan on hold because the Triad is losing more money than they're making. Not to mention, the sudden reappearance of a certain princess," Dante explains.

Everyone's gaze is now on my wife, who doesn't look away from the screen, looking calm and confident as ever. She's not my wife right now. She's the boss. She doesn't even realize we're looking at her.

"So, what plan and contingencies have you come up with?" Cesare asks.

Anya opens her mouth to speak, looking at me, which gives me reason to believe I'm not going to like what she has to say next.

"We'll need to also use jammers to block any signals so the soldiers on guard can't contact any soldiers inside. We'll have special earpieces so that our signals don't get crossed with the Triad's. Franco, Ricky, Dante, and Nico will stay back in a van so we can break through the security measures and get through the doors."

"Bullshit, like hell I'm staying back!" I yell.

"Nico—" Bash says.

"I'm not fucking sending Anya in there without me."

Now I know why she was tense. She had to have known I wouldn't agree to this.

"Nico, you don't have a choice. If we can't get through those doors, there's no point," she says to me, and I can't help but shoot her a glare.

She shoots one right back.

Is this what life with her by my side is going to be like? Plotting our battle strategies together and arguing over them? I can't say I'm mad about it, but I am mad about this plan.

"I don't fucking like this. At all," I argue, crossing my arms.

"She's right, Nico," Bash says. Fuck, I can't argue with the capo. "Uncle Ricky, Dante, and Franco are capable, but they need the extra hands between the signal blockers, breaking security codes, and keeping any alarms from sounding off. The Triad is known for explosives. We need to make sure they don't detonate anything."

I know they're right, but I have no desire for Anya to go in there without me.

"I'll be with her," Dominic replies, knowing exactly what I'm thinking. "Nothing will happen to her." I may hate the dumb fuck, but the one thing I can trust him with is Anya's life.

"First of all, let's not talk about me as if I'm not sitting right here. And second, I'm not some fucking damsel in distress, Dom. Don't you dare insult me by questioning my capabilities. We received the same training," Anya claps back.

She's probably the only person that can get away with speaking to him like that. He's in an even more difficult situation, trying not to argue since she is a queen in her own right. She outranks him until Cesare steps down.

"Moving on." She gestures with her hand for Dante to continue.

I shake my head, but I bite my tongue.

"Tony and Roger will stay back in the woods, since they're our best snipers. Enzo and his team will walk ahead, since they're the best at hand-to-hand combat. Dominic, Bash, and Anya will follow. We'll keep twenty soldiers outside, so they're outnumbered and send the rest of the men in with them. Franco said you have connections in Kansas," Dante says, looking at Dominic.

He nods. "Yes, I'll get clearance from the Civella family to enter their territory. They're longtime allies of the Outfit."

"It's best if we can just subdue them. We don't want to kill potential soldiers. They are still *my* men. Only kill if you absolutely have no choice. I want Andrew dead, not the entire Triad. You'll have your regular weapons, as well as tranq guns. They might not appreciate being tranquilized at first, but they'll be happy they aren't dead," Anya explains.

Of course, the Outfit is known for tranquilizing people rather than killing them outright. They really enjoyed the torture before the kill.

"And remember the most important part," Dante begins, "no one touches Li but Anya." His eyes dart to her. "You have to be the one to do it. If you want to earn any respect from your men, you have to kill Andrew yourself."

Anya stares at Dante blankly. "Done."

There's no emotion when she answers. She's in boss mode, and my cock jerks. I really need to get my shit together.

Bash addresses the room. "Some men will drive out tonight. Captains and higher ranks only will fly in that morning. The jet will drop you off fifty miles outside of the property, where vehicles will be waiting."

Everyone nods.

\* \* \*

Over the next few hours, we go over every single detail several times to make sure everyone is on the same page and no mistakes will happen. We can't let anything slip through the cracks. Soldiers will take our armed vehicles and weapons and start their drive tonight while Dante, Franco, Tony, my brothers, Anya, Dominic, and I lay low. We'll take the jet the following morning. Matteo had been sent back to Chicago, thank fuck. Can't do much with his hand, being injured and all.

The men are dismissed and take their leave. Anya, Dominic, and I stay back while Bash pours us all a glass of whiskey as we gather around Bash's desk.

Once the room is empty, Anya stands, planting her hands on her hips, shooting daggers into both me and Dominic. How am I suddenly in the dog house and with this asshole?

"Don't you guys ever do anything like that again." She starts pointing at each of us. "I don't need either of you making choices for me or declaring you're some knights in shining fucking armor, especially in front of an audience! If I'm going to be the boss of the Triad, I expect to be treated and spoken to as such. Do not insult me."

If we were actually dogs, our ears would be sagging. Feeling like we both just got sent to the principal's office, Dom and I share a glance at each other, then nod to her in silence, knowing better than to say anything.

"Good," she says with a sigh as she grabs a glass. "Now that we've cleared that up, it's not too late for you guys to change your minds."

"What are you talking about?" I question.

"There's a chance the fight won't be over, even with Andrew dead," she replies and takes a sip.

"You are family now, and we don't back down from anyone," Bash says, raising his glass.

"You've always been my family, sorellina. I'm not risking anything happening to you," Dominic follows up quickly, raising his glass as well.

Anya rolls her eyes.

# Chapter Twenty-Nine

NICO

*Jab. Cross. Jab. Cross. Kick. Block. Jab.*

"That's all you got?" Dominic says with a cocky smile on his face, bouncing from foot to foot.

We're sparring in the gym as to not get injured before we leave tomorrow, just enough exercise to release some of the tension we've all been feeling about our plans. Not to mention it feels good to knock Dominic around a bit, even though I have to hold back.

I'm having a hard time focusing because Anya's in the corner, on the stairs, in those fucking tiny shorts I love so much but currently hate because she's wearing them for the whole goddamn world to see. Dominic lands a good fist into my face, breaking me out of my thoughts.

"Stop staring at my sister, you pervert. You're making it too easy to kick your ass," he says, still smirking.

I look back at him and narrow my eyes. *Bring it on.* I charge at him and punch him repeatedly. He's able to dodge a few. The guy's actually a good fighter. He lands a kick to my ribs, but I duck from his next swing, and I'm able to turn and swing my leg up, connecting my foot with his face. He stumbles back. Blood is coming out of his mouth now, but he's still smiling. Anya is now looking at us slightly amused and nervous.

Dominic charges at me and lands a series of punches. He's fast, switching between my head and my torso. I'm able to block his hits. He'd be a serious contender if we ever had to fight seriously.

"Care to make a bet?" I ask, still in my fighter's stance, my hands blocking my face.

"What you thinkin'?" he asks, mirroring my stance.

"Best two out of three. Franco and Dante judge, so there's no favoritism," I say back.

"All right, and what are we betting on?"

"If I win, I get your Ferrari."

"Fine." Dominic agrees. "But if I win, Anya divorces your sorry ass."

I laugh. "Not a chance, asshole."

He chuckles. "Okay, okay, fine. If I win, we get full access to your New Jersey shipping docks."

"Deal." I stick my hand out to shake his.

## NICO

"Salute!" We all cheer as we clink our wine glasses. The Cosa Nostra has a rule about not drinking any hard liquor before a big . . . *event*. We're all praying for a successful mission tomorrow."

"That Ferrari is going to look so good in my garage," I say, taking a sip of my wine.

"You fuckin' cheated, asshole!" Dominic yells from across the table with a smile on his face.

Anya looks stunned that we were getting along. Her eyes dart back and forth between us during our exchange. The guy wasn't so bad when it came to anything that didn't have to do with his sister.

"I didn't fucking cheat. We didn't have any rules," I argue.

"Boys." Anya shakes her head to my mother as they both roll their eyes, smiling.

"This is all your fault, Franco!" Dominic says, slapping the back of his best friend's head.

"Ow! What did I do?" he asks as he stuffs his face.

"You had to give the last round to him," Dominic replies.

Franco laughs, shaking his head and returning to his dinner.

"Better luck next time, man," Dante says, patting Dominic on the back.

Anya is still speechless, eyes wide, watching us all bond, though I think her silence has less to do with her being stunned and more to do with her feelings about tomorrow. We'll have to discuss this later. I can't have her going in without me, with her mind all fucked.

"Listen, if you'll stop being a sore loser, we might still grant you access to *some* of our docks at a discounted rate," I say back.

"Like hell!" Bash laughs with us.

The rest of dinner went by quickly. Most of us just joke around and keep the conversation light. We end earlier than usual, so we can all get to bed early. Tomorrow is going to be a big day.

# Chapter Thirty

## ANYA

I'm lying in bed on Nico's chest while he plays with my hair. Normally, this would help calm me down, but I feel like I'm about to jump out of my own skin. It's our last night before we head out. I can't help but wonder what my life will look like twenty-four hours from now, assuming I live to even tell the tale. Will I survive this? Or worse, if any of our men die because of this, I'm not sure how I'll cope with that.

"I can hear your thoughts, wife. Do I need to fuck them out of your head?" Nico grumbles in a low, sexy voice.

Fuck, I'm wet from that statement alone. But I can't stop thinking about what can happen. I look up at him and admire him. His tattoos covering his torso, arms, and neck. He's let his dark facial hair grow out, and it's perfectly groomed. The sight of this man.

"I like when you call me wife," I say as I touch his face to mess with his scruff.

He grabs my hand and kisses my palm. "Don't change the subject."

"I'm not sure if I even want the Triad." I sigh. "I understand Andrew has to die or he won't leave me alone, but what if I do kill him, and—"

"You will."

I roll my eyes, though I love his confidence in me. "*When* I kill him, what happens if I don't want it?"

"Do you not want this because you think you'll fail, or do you truly not want to do this?" he asks me.

I pause before answering. "Failing. I'm going in blind, Nico. I know as much about them as any other outsider would. How am I supposed to lead people I don't know? Who do I trust? How can I expect them to trust me?"

"You don't have to know everything. Just think of it like a normal job. Not that you've ever had one—"

I smack him in the face with one of the throw pillows left on the bed.

He catches it as he chuckles but continues. "There's going to be a learning curve, but you'll pick up on how things work in no time."

He has a point, but I still wasn't convinced.

When I don't respond, he speaks up again. "You also don't have to do this. You're my wife now, which means I'll take care of you."

"No." I shake my head. *That's not an option.* "I'm afraid if I don't take over, something worse will happen. Like, what if the next person still wants me dead and is worse than Andrew? Plus, I feel like I'd be letting my parents down. Which I know is stupid, since I never knew my father and barely had my mother with me." A tear slips from my eye and lands on my husband's chest.

He pulls me in closer and sighs. "Babe, no one has the answer to that. I don't know what's going to happen when this is over, but the one thing I do know is that I'll still love you."

I know he's helpless right now, wishing he could put my mind at ease. *God, this man.*

I look up at and admire the man before me. His eyes start to glaze over with lust, and I lean forward to kiss him deeply. He wraps his arms tighter around me, pulling me up as I climb on top of him, straddling his lap. He hardens underneath me.

I pull away from his kiss and lean my forehead against his.

"Nico, I want you to know whatever happens tomorrow—whether I survive or not—I choose you. Maybe it makes me weak or naive to put a man first, but I don't care. It's you above all else. The Triad, the Cosa Nostra, the Outfit. And I know your duties, so you don't have to feel the same—"

His lips crash into mine.

"You will survive. And don't you get it? It'll always be you, Anya. You come first. I think a part of me knew that the moment I laid eyes on you," he confesses, his lips against me.

"I love you," I tell him before he pulls me back into a kiss, grinding his erection into me.

"Show me how much you love me," he demands.

And I do. All night.

Our bedroom is dim as the sun slowly starts to come up, barely peeking over the horizon. The alarm sounds, but I'm already awake. I have been for hours. I look over at my husband as he stirs; he reaches over to shut the sound off when he lays back down. His eyes meet mine. We lay there in silence, soaking in the calm.

Without a word, we rise out of bed to get ready for the day. In the bathroom, I stand in front of the mirror, doing my daily skin care before I pull my hair into a ponytail. I don't see the point of makeup for an occasion such as this one.

Nico keeps looking over at me with concern, but I don't give him any sort of reaction. I need to be able to remain focused. I have one job today, and failure isn't an option.

Nico stands behind me and looks at me through the mirror. He leans in to kiss the top of my head before moving into his walk-in closet.

*You are Anya Liu. Daughter of Peter Liu. The most feared and respected Triad leader in centuries.* I remind myself. A rush of calm-rage overpowers me. I wasn't going to let some entitled usurper get the better of me. This is what I've been training for.

"Babe," Nico says, cutting me out of my thoughts. I look into the mirror at him, and he's leaning against the doorway. "It's time."

I give him a tight smile and nod. He keeps his palm on my lower back as we exit the house into the SUVs that will take us to the airstrip. I look around at the men. A group of soldiers load weapons in several vans. Several vehicles are parked outside. Dom and his men are getting into two, Bash and Enzo another. Nico and I ride with Dante.

I look over to my left, and my eyes meet Dom's. We nod at the same time and pile into our vehicles. This is it. The second we leave this property, I leave my old life behind.

## Chapter Thirty-One

NICO

We're three hours into the five-hour flight, and Anya is strangely calm. She stares straight ahead, expression completely blank. That was her, though. My wife is sweet, warm, and emotional. The boss is cold, aloof, and calm. I love that she can be both. I squeeze her hand tightly. She finally looks at me, her expression softening, and kisses me.

"I love you, Nico."

I could tell by the way she says it and the look in her eyes that the *just in case anything happens to me* part was implied. I pull her back in and kiss her deeply.

"I love you. Nothing is going to happen to you. My brothers and yours won't allow it."

She doesn't respond, but she nods and looks ahead. That's how I know she's focused. She didn't even try to assert her independence. After some time, she leans her head on my shoulder. We don't talk the rest of the way.

When we're thirty minutes out, we gear up. She looks so sexy in her tight-as-sin black jeans. She's putting on a bulletproof vest, and my mouth practically waters as she straps on her weapons.

As we exit the plane, several armored SUVs and large vans wait for us. Franco points around, letting everyone know where they go. Franco points to Anya, directing her to an SUV. Then he points at me, directing me to one of the vans. I fucking hate that I have to stay in the van while she goes in. I think about fighting them again, but we can't change the plan, and we can't risk anything going wrong.

She doesn't move to the SUV right away. Instead, she stands there, looking at all our men. I grab her and give her one last kiss before we have to part ways.

## Anya

I pull Nico in closer to deepen the kiss, and he picks me up, so we're at eye level. I never want this moment to end. Our lives are about to change forever. It didn't help that he looks so damn good in his combat gear. It takes everything I have to stay in focus mode and not jump his bones. I'd have to survive, so I can get in on that later.

He pulls away and rests his forehead on mine. We don't need to say anything. I look into his eyes as he looks into mine.

"Let's go," Bash orders.

Nico and I nod at each other, put our earpieces in, and head our separate ways. It's about a forty-minute drive to the grounds where my uncle is hiding.

"We just turned on the signal jammers, and security cameras are now showing old footage. They shouldn't be able to contact each other now," Nico says through the earpiece.

The second we get within ten miles of the building, we hit gunfire, as expected. Our drivers had to memorize a specific route Franco had coordinated for them. We knew there were bombs hiding beneath, surrounding the property, and he somehow came up with an algorithm that predicted the best route so we wouldn't hit any of them. I stay calm as the soldiers shoot back at the Triad men.

We break through their gates, and our men immediately jump out of the cars to get the Triad men down. Not killing them seems impossible. The SUVs that Dom, Bash, and I are in stop right at the doors. Enzo and his men are already waiting for us.

"Open the door," Dom says into his earpiece.

The first door swings up, and Enzo knocks out two guards with his tranq gun.

"We're good. Next," Bash orders, and the next door opens with some more soldiers. We all tranq them before they have time to react.

"Third door!" Dom orders. The third door opens, and we manage to knock a couple out but several come swinging at us. One guy tries to tackle me at the waist, but I duck and slide into his legs, knocking him down. I pull a dart from one of the components on my belt and stab him in the shoulder. Just as

I'm turning around, a fist comes at my face, slamming into me hard.

"Fuck!" I cry.

Before I can react, I hear a gunshot and see Dom's hand at the end of the gun. Okay, he actually lasted longer without killing someone than I thought he would.

"Babe, talk to me!" Nico yells.

"I'm fine!" I yell back, looking at Dom to assure him I mean what I say.

"I'm done playing nice," Dom says.

"You barely started." I roll my eyes as he chuckles and helps me up.

I scramble up, and we enter the last door, but it's silent.

"Go straight down the hall and make the third left. There should be a staircase. We made a lot of noise so they know we're here. So, just make sure you're careful when heading down," Franco says.

Men shoot at us. Two soldiers stand in front of me as we make our way through the door to the stairs. Several men are heading up toward us, but between Bash and Dom, they're able to either shoot or tranq them. How many, I don't know. I'll have to find out how many survive later.

"There's only one room that's set up as a bomb shelter. That's the room he'll be in. Head to the very bottom floor," Nico commands. We make our way down the next flight of stairs and get to the entryway.

"We're here," Bash says, breathing heavily.

The lock clicks and releases. Dom grabs the door, and as he pulls it open, he points his gun and blindly shoots three times. I look into the doorway, and three men are dead.

"Fuck, Dominic. You can at least *try* to use your tranq first," Enzo says, exasperated.

"It's either their life or hers," Dom says, nodding at me.

We enter a corridor, and there's one giant door at the end. That must be where my uncle is hiding.

"The door at the end of the hall is the bomb shelter. There's at least six men in there, including Andrew. It can only be opened from the inside," Franco says.

"You're fucking telling us this now?" Dom yells at him.

"You didn't let me finish. It can only be opened from the inside—unless you're me," Franco says. I can hear his grin in his voice.

"Cocky bastard," Dom laughs and the door swings open. Two men come out with semi-automatic rifles. Fuck.

We duck where we can, which is really nowhere. The corridor is empty, except for some pillars. Dom sprints toward one of the guys and grabs his gun with Bash not far behind him. The second guy aims his gun at Enzo, and I shoot him in the head.

"Anya!" I hear Nico yell. Dom is able to get the rifle away from the first guy, and he knocks him out with the butt of it.

"Oh, so you keep *him* alive?" I look at Dom exasperated, and he just shrugs.

"Jesus Christ, we're never doing anything like this again!" Nico yells into the earpiece, and I can't help but laugh at how stressed he is.

I sprint into the bomb shelter and freeze. The first thing I notice is the size of the room. It's way bigger than the blueprint showed. It must've been expanded recently. The next is a long line of soldiers with various handguns, semi-automatic rifles, and knives pointed directly at me. The last thing my eyes catch is a man standing behind the soldiers on a slightly elevated platform, like a stage.

Andrew. My uncle.

I can hear the men behind me. We're at a standstill.

"Shit. So much for six men," Enzo mutters.

"How many?" Franco asks.

"Twelve," I say.

"If you can, get down here now," Bash says to whoever is listening.

"You all must know who I am," I address the men.

I can see a mixture of emotions between them. Some look unsure, as if they can't help but be loyal to me but can't seem to defy Andrew. Others look filled with hatred, and some have their bodies angled slightly to the side, like they'd rather slit the throat of the man next to them than hurt me.

"For those of you who don't, I'm Anya Liu."

I scan the men again, conflict in all their gazes at my admission.

"The choice you make right now will determine your future. Choose wisely," I tell the men.

We stand for what feels like an eternity. Then someone from behind the wall of men starts clapping. He walks forward between his men, and we're now less than four feet apart. He looks aged and tired. He may have been handsome at some point, but the greed and evilness had started to eat at him. His eyes were cold and dead, his mouth in a permanent sneer. Andrew.

"Wǒ de zhí nǚ. Nǐ ràng wǒ yìn xiàng shēn kè." *My niece. You impress me,* he says with his arms crossed.

"Wǒ lái zhè lǐ bù shì wèi le shuō huà." *I didn't come here to talk,* I say as I bring my Beretta up to his face.

"Bāng huì zhòng shì róng yù hé lì liàng. Bǎ qiāng fang xià. Xiàng zhēn zhèng dí shìbīng yīyàng zhàn dòu." *The Triad values honor and strength. Put the gun down and fight me like a real soldier,* he says.

"Anya, what are you waiting for? Shoot the guy!" Nico yells into my ear. I put my gun down, but I hear several others click behind me, who are ready to shoot if I need them to.

"Zuò ba." *Let's do this,* I say, charging for him. I notice, at the same time, only some of his men go after mine. There's chaos everywhere, but I'm focused on one man.

"*Anya, what the hell are you doing?*" I hear Nico yell back, but I tune him out.

Andrew dodges me and quickly retreats back. I can't let him get the upper hand. He's older, but I don't want to underestimate him. Cesare is a prime example that age doesn't determine strength. That man is a tank, even well into his fifties. He comes at me, kicking at me fast, but I'm able to bob and weave around him. He pulls out two knives, one in each hand.

"What happened to honor?" I yell back at him.

He laughs menacingly. "You stupid brat. You think you can just come in here and take everything from me!" he screams.

"You're insane!" I yell as I land a series of punches. I land a solid kick to his chest that has him stumbling. "*You* took everything from *me*!" I scream back as I charge at him, avoiding his knives.

"I should have suffocated you when you were an infant," he yells, swinging at me with both knives. I dodge him, pulling out my own. "Killing your father was easy enough. A baby would've been so much easier!"

The fog I've learned to welcome settles in. All my senses are alert.

My rage blinds me. I charge him, and he swings his right arm at my face. I lean back, avoiding it, and when I come back up, I'm able to swipe his arm. This takes him off guard, and I'm able to land a kick to his face. He recovers immediately and charges at me full force. I duck and kick him in the stomach. But he throws himself forward and lands one of his knives into my left shoulder blade.

"AHH! Fuck!" I cry out.

"Anya, what happened? Babe, fuck. Talk to me!" Nico is still yelling. I have no idea how long he's been going off for.

"Bastard stabbed me," I get out through gritted teeth.

Nico lets out a string of curses.

"Shit, the security protocols have been activated! There are bombs set to self destruct. You guys need to hurry and get the fuck out of there!" Uncle Ricky yells into my ear.

I'm furious this bastard was able to stab me. I see red, charging him putting all my strength behind me. He was able to block me at first, but I can tell he's getting tired. I'm not even close to being done. He tries to use his forearms to cover himself, but I slice both wrists and his forearms with my blades. Not enough to kill him, but if I weaken his arms, I get the advantage.

I don't stop. I keep charging him. I'm punching him and kicking him. He backs up and trips over the platform, so he's now on his back. I must've gotten his face a couple of times. I'm just now noticing it's sliced up, and his eyes are starting to swell.

I punch him one more time, and as I'm about to swipe my knife across his neck, an explosion knocks me off my balance, and I hear Dom cry out. I look over to find he's stuck underneath some rubble.

"You better be getting the fuck out of there!" I hear Nico cry out.

Next thing I know, legs are swiping under me, and I'm looking at the ceiling. Before I can get up, my uncle stands over me and puts his boot on my neck. He presses down, and I can't breathe. *Fuck, this is it.* I try to pry his leg off with my hands, but I can't.

I look around, but everyone is fighting someone. Bash notices and tries to make his way over, but a Triad soldier wraps a wire around his neck. Dom is screaming. I try to reach for a knife, but it's just out of my reach. I'm starting to see spots. Another bang throws Andrew several feet back.

I inhale, coughing and choking. Is this what a crushed windpipe feels like? I don't know, but I can't seem to get enough oxygen. I look over to the source of the explosion and see—

"MING?" I try to scream out, but my body fights for air. He somehow hears me, though, and looks over, smiling. He starts shooting, and behind him are some of the men we fought earlier. *Fuck, Ming is Triad?* He rushes straight for me, and just when I think he's about to kill me, he pulls me in for a hug. I look at him in confusion when he releases me.

"I'll explain it all later. Now, go kill that son of a bitch," Ming says.

I look around and find a machete. *That'll do.* I crawl over and grab it. I stand slowly and look around for Andrew. He's just gaining consciousness and trying to get up.

Enough is enough.

Andrew looks up at me, then looks over at Ming. Fury takes over his face.

"Traitor!" Andrew yells, struggling to get up.

"You're the traitor," Ming replies back calmly.

I don't waste anymore time. I walk over to the two-faced, backstabbing, greedy asshole, and swing the machete back. He's on his knees now. Perfect.

I'm able to find my voice. "Go to hell." I swing my arms across his torso, disemboweling him.

His eyes grow wide for a moment as he gazes down, watching himself pour from the inside out, before he convulses for a moment. He looks back up at me in disbelief and rage before he falls forward on his face. The fighting ceases almost immediately when they notice Andrew is nothing but a pile of organs on the floor.

"We have to get out of here before the building self-destructs!" Ming yells.

Everyone starts moving to get out, and I look over, and Dom is still stuck. I rush over to him and remove the rubble pile. A couple of soldiers run to help, and we're able to get it off, but his leg is crushed.

"We have to carry him!" I yell to two soldiers.

"You have to go!" Dom yells back, swinging his arms, gesturing for me to leave.

"Don't be ridiculous!" I look over at the two men. "Grab him. We have to carry him out." The two soldiers lift him up, but he cries out in pain.

"Sorellina," he whispers. My heart constricts before I even turn to him. Once I do, I follow his gaze, and I see the timer counting down: eight minutes. When I look back at him, I can see in his eyes what he's asking me to do. "I'm not going to make it. These men shouldn't die trying to save me."

*No.*

"Dom"—my voice cracks, and I fall to my knees. I can barely get the words out—"we have time. I'm not leaving you."

"You have to," he says.

I shake my head. "Stop arguing with me. We're only wasting time." My eyes fill up with tears. "Grab him."

They make a move toward him, but before they could touch him, he commands, "Stand down, and that's an order."

The men stop moving, eyes filled with confusion and fear about losing their future capo.

"Anya, go," he pleads.

"Get the fuck out of there now, Anya!" Nico yells.

"No," I whisper.

"We're running out of time," Ming says.

"Grab her and go," Dom says to Ming.

"No, no, no," I sob, grabbing onto this shirt. "Please, Dom. You have to come."

"Go live your life," he says with a soft smile.

"I can't leave you!" I scream.

"You have to. You have a husband now, you have a family."

"You're my family, too!"

I can't breathe. I grab his shirt.

"Sorellina—"

"No! Don't say it."

"I love you." *Goodbye.*

"Please don't make me, please," I beg again, desperately trying to get air into my lungs.

"Sempre. I'm always with you," he tells me and kisses the top of my head.

"Dom, no. Please, don't do this."

"Take her," he says to Ming as he grabs my wrists and pries my grip from his shirt. Before I can protest, Ming grabs me and throws me over his shoulder.

"Nooooo!" I let out an ear-piercing shriek.

Blood rushes to my ears. I can't hear anything, my throat protesting after being nearly crushed. I'm reaching out for my brother, but the distance keeps getting greater and greater. I fight as hard as I can, ignoring the pain in my shoulder from where my uncle stabbed me. It's no use. I can't get out of Ming's grip. Dom is farther and farther away.

"No, no, no, no, no!" I beat into Ming's back, crying and screaming at the top of my lungs until I have no voice left.

The air has completely been sucked out of my lungs.

# Chapter Thirty-Two

### NICO

"Anya!" I yell into my headset. "Anya, are you moving?" I run my hands over my hair and face like I have for the last hour since she's been in there. All I could hear was her yelling. Then it stopped. I hope someone grabbed her. Fuck.

I hop out of the van, and just as I'm about to run in, I see some soldiers make it out of the building, sprinting to the vehicles. Enzo and a few others are next. When I see Bash come out next without Anya, I charge them up and push against Bash's chest.

"WHERE THE FUCK IS SHE? TELL ME YOU DIDN'T LEAVE HER!" I feel like I'm going to lose my mind.

"Calm the fuck down, Nico. We wouldn't leave her! She's right behind us!" Bash yells, pushing me right back.

I look over his shoulder, and I see . . . the restaurant owner? He's carrying her, and she's fighting for dear life. I relax for only about a second, then I look around. She was arguing with her brother a minute ago.

"Dominic?" I ask.

Enzo locks eyes with mine, face stone, and shakes his head cautiously.

*Fuck.*

*Fuck. Fuck. Fuck.* Anya loves her brother. I heard her say that she was staying over the earpiece. I didn't know what she meant. Fuck. She was going to die with him.

Ming heads straight to me and hands her over as if she weighs nothing. She wraps her arms and legs around me. I pull her close, and she lets out a gut-wrenching sob. Her entire body shakes as she screams and fights for air.

"We need to move. Now!" Bash commands.

I sprint back into the van as she sobs into my shoulder. I notice she has a stab wound in her left shoulder that will need to be treated.

The ground shakes. Anya looks up, but I turn around, so her back is to the scene and push her head back down to my shoulder, not wanting her to see the building cave into itself. She lets out another cry. I can't help her. I don't know what I'd do if one of my brothers was still down there.

We all load into the vehicles. Just as we're about to drive off, I notice three more soldiers making their way.

"Everyone head out. There's a few more coming, but we'll get them," Franco says into his headpiece.

I notice two of them are carrying a blond man on what looks like a large piece of metal. My heart lifts for a second, but I keep

Anya's head down. I don't want to say anything to give her hope. She's still crying into my shoulder as I hold her. They get closer, and I see it's Dominic, face ashen, his leg fucked up. But he's alive. Hell, I never thought I'd live to see the day, but I thanked God for Dominic Violante being alive.

## ANYA

It's been two days since killing my uncle. I don't feel any remorse. The sick, greedy bastard deserved a much slower death than the one I gave him.

I try not to dwell on it. I'm grateful we all survived. Dom survived. I thought I lost a part of my soul that day when Dom didn't come out of the building with me. When Nico said his name, I lifted my head, and I almost didn't believe it. At least not until I ran over to him and touched his face myself.

Dom's currently healing in one of the guest bedrooms. The doctors say his leg is crushed, and he had to undergo a very long surgery, but he'll make a full recovery. We're back in New York, at Nico's—*our* two-story penthouse. My arm is in a sling from when the bastard stabbed me. He didn't hit anything vital. I readjust to get more comfortable and let out a small groan of discomfort.

"Are you okay?" Nico asks, sitting up straight. He hasn't let me out of his sight and is treating me like I'm made of glass. I swear he ages by the minute with worry.

"Babe, my injuries aren't life-threatening. I'm just trying to get comfortable."

"Do you need water? Painkillers?"

He's been hovering, and as much as it drives me crazy, I let him. I know it makes him feel better, and I love watching him care for me. But I need to calm him down before he gives himself a stroke.

"Babe, for the millionth time, I'm fine. I was just moving around. I can't sit like a statue all day."

"I was not cut out for this marriage shit," he says, pinching the bridge of his nose, leaning back against the headboard.

He's so damn dramatic.

"Why do you say that?" I ask him, trying not to laugh.

"It's too damn stressful. Especially when your wife is a magnet for trouble," he says as he moves on to rub his temples. I can't help but laugh at him.

"Oh, sure, laugh at my misery."

I lean over to kiss him. "I want to go see Dom."

"It's too soon," he replies, but I'm already getting out of bed, putting my slippers on.

My body is aching, I have bruises everywhere. My neck is the worst from where my uncle stood on it. Every time I catch Nico staring at it, he growls, and I swear he's imagining bringing my uncle back just to kill him again. I might've gotten up too fast, but I don't let him see it, or he's seriously going to have to get on medication to lower his blood pressure. I wonder if I can hit Max up for her special calming drugs. She was always experimenting with shit. She makes the best stuff.

"I wasn't asking. And I'm fine. Nothing is broken. It's just a sling until my shoulder is healed," I say, walking to the door.

He follows me. "The doctor said you need to rest."

"Getting up and walking downstairs is hardly doing too much. Plus, I'm sure moving helps with blood flow and healing. Let me see Dom for ten minutes, then I'll crawl my ass back to bed."

"You need to learn to follow instructions better"—he follows me down the hall—"and when you're healed, I'm going to teach you exactly how," he whispers into my ear with a grin.

"I can't wait." I tilt my head up and stand on my tiptoes to kiss him.

He leans down to meet my lips. I open the door to Dom's room. He's awake and alert but looks tired.

"Dom!" I say, rushing toward his bed and sitting on the chair while taking his hand.

Nico doesn't follow but shuts the door behind me. I didn't have to tell him, but he knew I needed time alone with Dom. He looks up and smiles back at me.

"I'm not going to pretend. I was ready to die but holy shit. It's good to be alive."

"Yeah, no kidding," I say, smiling, but my eyes are filled with tears.

"Don't cry, Anya. You know I hate it when you cry."

He shakes his head and wipes a tear off my cheek.

"I almost lost you, Dom. There were minutes when I actually believed you were gone. I never want to feel like that again," I say through my tears.

"This is the life we live in." He shrugs. "I'm so proud of you, you know. I knew you could do it."

"Really?"

"Never had a doubt in my mind, Little Sister."

I smile proudly, and he smiles back at me.

"Speaking of little sister, Donna's on the way. Her flight gets in tonight."

He groans, running his hands through his hair, "Oh, great. Now I'll have both of you around to terrorize me."

I wipe my tears and laugh. "Oh, shut up. You love us."

"Not when you gang up on me!"

"Don't tell me the big bad capo can't handle two small girls," I tease in an annoying baby voice.

"You two are anything but harmless," he defends, unconsciously rubbing his shoulder where I shot him all those years ago, and I can't help but smile.

We laugh and make small talk for a little. I can tell he's exhausted, and I'm about to excuse myself when he speaks up again.

"I'm sorry about how I acted when I first got to Virginia. I just saw you with the consigliere to the Cosa Nostra and lost it. I shouldn't have said those things or insulted you like that."

"Hold on. Is Dominic Violante, future capo of the Chicago Outfit, apologizing?" I say to him sarcastically, wide-eyed.

"Don't fucking get used to it." He waves his arm at me to go away. I laugh. "But I've been a goddamn asshole especially to you. You don't deserve that disrespect, and if any man says shit to you, you better put a bullet in his skull."

I squeeze his hand. "I understand where you were coming from."

"A part of me thought they could be using you, and I didn't want to see you get hurt. And the other thought is, if he really did love you, and if you married into the Cosa Nostra, you'd leave us behind. I thought he was going to ruin things between us."

I sigh. "Dom, he would never come between us. He's made that very clear. He would never try to, and if he was the type to, I would've never fallen in love with or married him. Whether you like it or not, he accepts you. You need to learn to accept him, too."

"I know. I'm working on it, as you've probably seen."

"Yeah, you lost a Ferrari in exchange for friendship," I joke.

"Once I'm better, I'm getting that rematch," he replies. "Plus, it couldn't hurt to have their support. It'd sure make life easier organizing trade routes."

"See! And you called me stupid," I say smugly.

His face is racked with guilt. "I really am sorry."

"Stop apologizing. I forgive you. Now, if you're really sorry, you'll do everything in your power to heal as quickly as possible. And don't act like you're too good for physical therapy. This was a serious injury, and you just had major surgery."

"Deal," he says.

I kiss his cheek and leave.

## Chapter Thirty-Three

### NICO

A week's gone by, and Anya's healing like magic. I took the week off just to be around for her, but she won't stop working. She's constantly making calls to either Donna, her friend, Max, or the university to figure out what credits she needs to make up. I suggested she not finish school since she was going to be the boss anyway, but she argued she needed to have a leg up on her men. She's going to do so good as their new leader. She talks about her ideas with me all the time.

We also needed to legally declare her alive and Natalie dead; otherwise, our marriage is invalid. Which is why we have a bunch of people from the social security office coming to our penthouse tomorrow. Luckily, my family's influence and money got us around most of the protocols, so we're able to expedite the process.

I also paid extra to make sure she took my last name and had our marriage license validated, effective immediately. She was going to be Mrs. Delucci—well, Mrs. Liu-Delucci to the world as soon as fucking possible.

I wanted to just hack into the systems to change it, but she made a good argument. *We can't just hack into people's memories and change them.* She was always arguing with me. I loved it. Mostly because it was followed by really great make-up sex.

Then there was the wedding, but luckily, Donna decided to become the self-appointed wedding planner. We also needed to brief Anya and get her some media training. We can't have her caught off guard. While we can keep most of our dealings private, my family doesn't have a low-profile lifestyle. Page Six and dozens of others have already reached out about our relationship. We came up with a good cover-up story on how and why she's suddenly called Anya. When you tell people you were in witness protection, they'll literally eat up anything you say after. Anya is used to an extremely private lifestyle, having been in hiding most of her life, and all of that is about to change, as if she wasn't dealing with enough already. In truth, we have a lot of work we need to do.

Dom's also healing. The doctor said he should be able to return to Chicago next week. Anya tried to convince him to stay longer, but I shut that down. I don't want to be a dick, but it's not like he wants to stay here longer than he needs to, either. Plus, I plan on having my way with my wife, without holding back, once she's fully healed and doubt he wants to be around for that.

Anya and I relax on the couch, watching television, very domestic. We aren't good people, but damn what a match we make. Life in the Cosa Nostra and Triad is going to be interesting with her by my side. As she leans into me, I can't help but note that she's initiating affection more and more. I kiss her forehead.

"Just say what's on your mind," I say to her.

I could always tell when something was on the tip of her tongue.

"I'm just thinking about what comes next."

My wife had a real problem with living in the moment. Life was going to pass her by if she didn't have me but, luckily, she does.

"Are you telling me you want to add more stuff onto our never-ending to-do list?" I chuckle.

"Well, we still need to figure out which publication the publicist is reaching out to—your mother won't stop asking me about it—how big this wedding is going to be, and our living situation."

"We're living here," I say like she's gone mad.

"You can't just decide that for the both of us. I love my penthouse."

"So, keep it, but we'll live here."

We stopped by when we first got back to the city to grab some of her things, and thinking about how many times Matteo had probably been over before we met, I about lost my shit. Maybe I'll buy the building and demolish it.

"Don't think I don't know your real reason for not wanting to live in my penthouse," she sasses back.

I love that she can see right through me. She rolls her eyes, knowing exactly what I'm thinking, giving me thoughts on how I'd like to punish her later. I adjust my position. My pants are getting tight.

"Well, your place is only a two bedroom. We'll have to move anyway, as soon as I start knockin' you up." I wink at her, and she glares.

"I have a lot of stuff." Was this really her argument?

"We have plenty of space here," I retort.

"It's a lot to pack."

"We'll hire people."

"We should do it ourselves so we can bond more as a couple." She looks at me seriously.

I can't help but chuckle. "I think we bond enough." I wiggle my eyebrows and pull her into a kiss.

She pulls away too soon. "We can't always pay people to do things for us. Manual labor will do us some good."

"Are you trying to tell me what we did last night in the shower or this morning in your closet and this afternoon in my office wasn't manual labor?" I kiss her neck, inhaling the intoxicating scent I'm addicted to.

She gives me that smirk that tells me she's ready for a repeat. Thank God. My cock was so hard it was about to rip through my pants. I climb on top of her so fast she lets out a yelp.

"Fuck, did I hurt you?"

"No. Don't stop." She wraps her legs around my waist.

## Rise Of An Heiress

Who am I to deny my wife? I tried to resist her so she could heal, but by the second day, she's pummeled through my resolve.

# Chapter Thirty-Four

ANYA

After a couple weeks of rest, I was feeling so much better. Ming had called and asked to come over so we could talk. I'm sitting in the library, pretending to read, when there's a knock at the door. Gabriella, our housekeeper, walks in smiling, as usual.

"Mrs. Delucci." I try not to roll my eyes. I've asked her a million times to just call me Anya. "Bo Xiao is here to see you."

Before I could question it, the buff man I've always known as Ming walks in and sits on the couch opposite of me.

"Bo," I say, testing the name out.

Then I remember the man Cesare was arguing with right before I moved to New York.

He nods as if he could hear my thoughts. "Yes, *Anya*." He says my name like he used to say Natalie, only this time, there's a different meaning. "I didn't tell you before because I wanted to have this conversation in person."

"Of course." I nod and gesture for him to take the seat across from me.

"I grew up with both your parents. We were all very close. I was Peter's best friend and"—he pauses—"your godfather."

I tilt my head in surprise. "Godfather? So, all this time, you knew who I was?"

He nods again. "When your father was murdered, I had to go into hiding. I was able to keep in touch with your mother, but when she died, I made Cesare promise to allow me to still see you. So, I moved to New York after you were relocated, and every Thursday, I'd pretend to run the restaurant you always came to, so I could keep an eye on you. Your uncle never bothered coming after me. He didn't think I was worth it."

"My adoptive parents were in on it, too? And you moved your whole life to New York to be close to me?"

I am stunned. I knew I felt a deeper connection to this man, but it was all making sense now. He was family. He nods. I straighten, it's like the light bulb went off.

"You were Dante's informant."

"Yes, ma'am."

"What was your role when my father was alive?"

"I was his second-in-command. The best assassin the Triad had," he says proudly. "Though, that was a long time ago, I've aged much since."

We share a laugh.

"So, what now?" I ask.

"Well, first, I'd just like to get to know you as my goddaughter, if you'll let me. I know I've lied to you for a long time, but—"

I hold my hand up to stop him. "I didn't know who you were, so it's not like I was entirely honest, either. I'd love to get to know you. Plus, I think you're the only person I know that has stories about my dad."

He smiles and looks off like he's remembering something. "Yes, that's true."

We sit in silence for a moment, but Bo speaks up again.

"I'd also like to help you transition with the Triad. I know these men, grew up with a lot of them. I know who's loyal and who to keep a lookout for. It's been years, but I think I can help get you up to speed. That is, if you still want to take over."

I'm so touched by Bo's offer.

"I'd like that," I answer. "Are they just going to accept you back after so long?"

"I was always loyal to the Triad, your father and you—the true heir. Anyone who's honorable will stand by me," he answers as he stands. "I should be going, then. I've got a lot to do to get you set up. We'll start with a formal meeting with the Triad, so they know you intend to take over. But we can sort out the details once you've rested and healed."

"I really appreciate this, Bo. I wasn't sure how I was going to do this," I say, getting up and giving him a hug.

He squeezes me back tightly, and we stand still for a moment. "Oh, one more thing," he says as we pull apart. He reaches into his jacket pocket. "I've been hanging onto this for a long time. I'm glad it's finally in your possession." He hands me an envelope addressed to me.

I immediately know who it's from.

"Thank you, Bo. We'll talk soon," I tell him as I walk him to the door of the library. Once he leaves, I take a minute to process the information Bo just gave me and also to gather up courage to open this letter.

I sit and take a deep breath as I open the aged envelope.

*My daughter,*

*If you're reading this it means two things:*
*You've taken your rightful place as my heir.*
*I am not alive to share this moment with you.*

*I want you to know that if you're having any doubts, you are to banish them from your mind immediately. I only ever saw myself with a son, if I'm being honest. It sure would be easier to have a male heir take my place. A woman has never led the Triad before.*

*But the second you were born and I laid eyes on you—I knew you'd be different. Strong and wise, and your smile can bring men to your mercy. Maybe I'm biased. But I do know this—you were meant to do this. To lead. To rule. I know in my heart you are going to bring men who are used to being in power to their knees and the Triad will be in a much better place because of you.*

## Rise Of An Heiress

*The dragon has always symbolized strength and power to the Triad. Live every day and let your strengths guide you. My sweet Anya, you are the new dragon head. I wish you nothing but luck and prosperity.*

*I'll love you always and forever,*

*Your father.*

I cry into my hands as the letter falls to the ground. Nico wraps his arms around me, enveloping me in his scent. He kisses the top of my head and holds me.

# Epilogue

## ANYA—ONE MONTH LATER

Bo and I pull up to an abandoned warehouse just outside of the city. Everything is either covered in graffiti or rust. Not a soul lingers. We walk around the corner of the old building, and Bo knocks on the scrap metal. The sheet moves open, and I can see there's a hidden door behind it as it opens. An older gentleman answers the door, and his eyes grow wide immediately as he tries to bow and open the door. Bo nods at me and gestures for me to enter before him.

As I walk in, my hand instinctively reaches behind my back for my Beretta. I look around, and there are three men guarding another door; they look young, no older than thirty-five, maybe. When they spot me, they immediately bow. I wasn't sure what to do, so I just nodded at them. They stand back up straighter than before.

"Ma'am," the all say in unison.

That's going to take some getting used to. I look over at Bo, and he gives me a reassuring look.

"Names?" I ask.

They each take turns speaking.

"Jimmy," says the shorter one with tattoos on his face.

"Kai," says the second one. He's tall, handsome, perfect skin, and long dark lashes.

"Tao," the last one finally says. He's tall, buff, definitely someone I want on my side.

I look at them and make a mental note on what their roles might be: bad-cop, brains, muscle. Bo reaches for the door, and they all nod at him with respect as well.

*You got this.* I take a deep breath before I descend the stairs and enter a larger room underground. Tables and chairs are set up, and men are gathered around, standing and seated from Illinois to New York. That's why it took a month for this meeting to take place. There had to be at least two hundred and fifty men in here. When they see me enter, most bow and stand straight right away, while a few others look angry and stay seated.

I memorize their faces in my mind. I don't have time for disrespect or the possibility of there being a rat or traitor in our midst.

When I reach the only leather chair that's placed in the front of the room facing the men, I assume it's the chair reserved for the dragon head. I turn, survey the room, and face my men. That still feels weird to say. *My men.* Taking one more look at the assholes who refused to stand and bow, I finally take my seat. The rest of the men follow. Bo stays standing next to me. We're all silent for a moment.

"We are gathered here today to introduce to you our true leader, the rightful heir, daughter of the late Peter Liu. Anya Meilin Liu-Delucci," Bo announces proudly.

I scan the room to see their reaction to not only a new leader, but a young female.

"Italian whore," someone coughs in the back, and I narrow my eyes.

"Tā zhǐ shì yī gè nǚ hái zi!" *She's only a girl*! a pudgy, short man yells.

"Tā tài nián qīng le!" *She's too young*! Pudgy number two next to him yells.

"Zhè shì tā de quán lì." *It is her right*, Bo says.

"Tā yīn ggāi jiāo gěi xià yī gè yǒu nán xìng jì chéng rén de zuì qiáng dà de jiā zú!" *It should go to the next strongest family with a male heir*! Pudgy number one cries out, and the room fills with voices of men chattering.

"Bié zài shuō le." *Stop talking*, I say flatly, and the room silences immediately. "Nín méi yǒu xuǎn zé." *You don't have a choice*. "I am Anya Liu, daughter of Peter, *The Mad Dragon* and *Nina Liu*. But I promise you haven't seen crazy yet."

It's not a threat, it's a promise.

"And what do you have to offer? You're a child," another man in the back yells, lips snarled and nostrils flared.

"You don't know any of us, our traditions, or what the Triad stands for."

I scan the room again, noting the hierarchy. They're right, I don't know, but I'm a quick study. I can already tell who the men are gathered in the three front tables; the ones brave and stupid enough to open their mouths are the captains of their respected regions.

"As far as I can tell, the Triad has been bleeding cash faster than you've been making. You won't last the next five years without me. I have the chemist who will be making all of our drugs moving forward, I have access to all of the shipping docks on the East Coast, *and* I have the firepower of not only the Triad but the Chicago Outfit and the Cosa Nostra. Does anyone have anything further to offer? Or would you all rather be homeless than let the one person who can turn things around do their job?"

Maya was right. Max made the best shit. Stuff I'd never even seen or heard of. We were still working on the names, but I'd hire her to be my pharmaceutical chemist for one of my shell companies I'd just opened up. It comes with a killer salary, multiple underground labs, a team for her to boss around, and the visa she needs to stay in the states. We are going to make a lot of money with her.

The Triad used to be a force. The name itself would instill fear. I learned we ran the largest black-market weapons ring and produced the best assassins in the world. That was until my idiot uncle apparently drove the business into the ground and threw us off the map. While all mafias hated each other, they had to work together. If you wanted anything shipped, you needed to go through the Cosa Nostra. If you wanted an official

## Rise Of An Heiress

elected or a bill passed, the Outfit was the answer, and if you wanted banned weapons of war or a contract killer, you came to the Triad. At least, that's how it used to be.

I was furious when Bo told me we used to have tens of thousands of men across the states when my grandfather and father ruled, but they all slowly jumped ship because my uncle was losing the business so much money and getting sloppy. A lot of them were useful, too—politicians, doctors, lawyers. So many left at once that Andrew couldn't keep up, so he let them go. It's not like he could kill thousands of men.

The original Chinese Triad wanted nothing to do with us anymore, either. Even though we'd split off seventy years earlier, we still did business with them. At least until the moron took over. Now, they deemed us irrelevant and like hell would that remain the case. I will restore the Triad and Liu name back to its former glory. Failure isn't an option.

Step one: make us profitable again and get us back on the radar. That's why I hired Max, The Chemist, as I call her, to protect her identity. Step two: take control over the weapons trade. Step three: Get our men back. Step four: whip said men into shape and turn them into assassins that would make the devil cower.

We have a few thousand men left across the U.S. but not nearly enough. If I'm anything, it's a woman with a plan.

I'm grateful for Bo. I could have all the ideas and plans I wanted, but without him, executing my plan would be a lot more difficult, if not impossible. I wasn't arrogant enough to think I could do it all by myself.

"Ó, méi cuò, nǐ xiàn zài shì yì dà lì rén de jì nǚ le." *Oh, that's right. You're now the Italian's whore,* Pudgy number two spits out, saliva shooting from his mouth.

Enough. I pull my Beretta from out of my jeans, aim it at the asshole, and fire a warning shot in between his eyes. The room is silent, with only the sound of his body hitting the concrete. And here I am, trying to avoid a bloody statement. That flew out the window fast.

"Hái yǒu rén xiǎng jiào wǒ jì nǚ ma?" *Does anyone else want to call me a whore*? I ask, raising my gun up and resting my elbow on my hip.

Silent.

"All right, so if you enjoy living in your homes, driving your expensive cars, and paying your bills, you'll do as you're told. You will respect our alliance with both the Outfit and Cosa Nostra."

This is new to all of us. An alliance with the Outfit based on trust and no marriage alliance, I can understand why the men are hesitant. Even so, marriage alliances have never worked in the past, but I'm determined to make this work. Luckily, Bash and I are on the same page.

"I want to know who specializes in what," I say, turning my attention to Bo. "Have meetings scheduled out with each specialty. Hackers, enforcers, legal, medical, arms experts, soldiers, and captains," I state, directing my attention back to the men. "Things are going to change around here."

I head toward the exit, and Bo follows. Once I get to the door, I turn to look back at the men.

## Rise Of An Heiress

"I look forward to turning the Triad back into a force to be reckoned with. I know there's a lot to do, but I have full faith we can do this. And, someone, take care of that body," I say in my professional voice.

I have a lot to prove. I also dread the official initiation.

Just as I make my exit, an older gentleman approaches me. Bo nods, indicating he's good.

"Boss." He reaches his hand out, and I shake it. "Dr. Ethan Zhao, this is my daughter, Liling." He gestures behind him to a beautiful young woman. She's taller, curvy but has a nervous demeanor.

"Lili," she replies quietly and bows her head, shyly smiling.

"Hi, Lili." I look back at Ethan. "Can I help you with something, Dr. Zhao?"

"My daughter is here to serve you."

I look at Lili, who is smiling back at me, but I can tell she's nervous.

"That's very kind of you, but I don't think I'll need her."

We have enough housekeepers.

"Please. It would be an honor. I was the assistant and advisor to your father, and my daughter would be an excellent asset. You have all these meetings to get scheduled, and I'm sure you keep Bo busy. My daughter is organized, smart, and she is fluent in Mandarin, Russian, and Italian."

*Impressive.* Smart guy in getting her to learn those languages. She does know the men, so she'd be better suited to set up our meetings. I also do have a wedding to plan and a lot on my plate on top of school. Speaking of—

"What about school? How old is she?"

"She just turned twenty-three and graduated summa cum laude from NYU," he replies proudly. His chest puffs out, and his eyes light up.

"You're from New York? I think she's a little over qualified to be an assistant."

"No." She finally speaks up, her eyes widened as if she's surprised she said anything at all. "My family is loyal to the Triad."

I take another minute to mull over it. Finding someone to work this closely with me was going to be difficult. I knew it would be difficult to trust them just as much as they'd need time to adjust to me. I could hire her on a trial basis. I nod, and her face lights up.

"I need an Executive Assistant. You'll assist me with anything from the business side—legal and not-so-legal—errands, meetings, travel arrangements, wedding-related tasks, and anything else that should come up." She nods excitedly. "This will be a trial basis for ninety days. Then we'll decide if it's a permanent position."

Hopping on her toes, she exclaims, "Of course!"

I notice a notebook and pen in her hand and nod at them. She hands them to me.

"Here is my phone number. We can work out a time, so we can discuss your complete list of roles and responsibilities, benefits, and salary." I hand the notebook back to her.

"Thank you." She reaches out for a handshake.

I shake her father's hand before heading to the car.

"That was a good call," Bo says, walking next to me, looking proud.

"I have a good feeling about Lili," I reply.

"Her father is a good man. Dedicated but not greedy or too ambitious. Nice work."

I wink at him before getting into the back seat of the SUV with one of the Cosa Nostra soldiers in the driver seat. Nico insisted I take some of his men with me in case something went wrong. While I argued it would make me look weak, he wouldn't budge, so we compromised, and they agreed to wait outside. Marriage.

I let out a breath as we drive off. I can't believe it. Just a few months ago, I was just a college student, barely living and pretending to be somebody else. Now I'm the Triad leader, wife to the Cosa Nostra consigliere, and Anya again.

# Grayson

Bacon sizzles. The aroma fills my kitchen as I pour myself a large cup of coffee. Between my odd hours at the bar, and all the time I spend training for my illegal underground fight matches, I bleed caffeine. I can't stop working, though. I need the money the bar and my fights get me. Taking odd jobs as a P.I. or security guard to make ends meet, my body is going to shut down before I turn forty. You'd think after ten years of serving one's country, you'd be afforded some sort of luxuries, but that's not the case.

I've been waiting to hear about my application status with the Federal Bureau of Investigation. I'm more than qualified, but they can be assholes sometimes. Once I get in, I'll have a stable job with benefits.

Pulling the bacon off the griddle, I place them on my plate that already has eggs and toast on it and make my way to the dining table. I take a deep breath and open my laptop after avoiding it for weeks. I knew they weren't going to answer my application right away, so I set it out of mind instead of obsessing over it. But now's a good time to look, just in case. If they happen to email me, I don't want to be a jackass and respond too late. That would just look bad.

I'm about to take a sip of my coffee when my hand stops midair as soon as I read the two pop-ups on my screen. I go to set my cup down, but I'm so out of it I miss the table entirely, and the glass shatters, coffee spilling everywhere. I'm in too much shock to care. I can't believe what I'm seeing.

Two alerts I'd never thought I'd see in my life. One time-stamped two weeks ago, the day after I decided I'd boycott my laptop, and the second came in yesterday morning.

It didn't matter how much I scoured the internet—there was nothing on them. For almost two decades, it was dead-end after dead-end. It was as if they never existed. I do remember *her* name, though. I grew up hearing it all over the place. Working in the military and as a private investigator, you learn a few tricks. I was obsessed with learning about my roots. I set up alerts for certain keywords and names, but nothing ever came through, so I had forgotten that I'd even had those alerts enabled. Until now.

I didn't know much, just her name, and she's been dead for two decades. Or so I thought. Blinking my eyes, I make sure what I was seeing wasn't a trick, but the subject lines remained:

*SUBJECT: Anya Meilin Liu - Change of Status*
*SUBJECT: Anya Liu Mentioned Page Six Article*

## Rise Of An Heiress

I click the first pop-up and there it was, blinking in big green letters:

*Anya Meilin Liu Status: Alive*

*Anya Meilin Liu Name Change: Anya Meilin Liu-Delucci*

Alive. This can't be right. I open up the old database my old buddy from the military taught me how to hack. I'm not a genius hacker or anything, I just know the basics. A simple virus or firewall could lock me out, but it helps me with my P.I. cases, and it's how I have access to the status change alerts. It wasn't always legal, but I don't get paid if I don't get results, and I'm in no position to pass up funds.

I look her up in the database, and there she is. Everything that wasn't there before. Where she grew up and went to school. It's like I imagined her death and made it up in my head somehow. I scan the information they had on her. Born on October 17, 1997 in Chicago, Illinois. Private school. NYU *and* Columbia Law. Manhattan. Jesus. I definitely got the short end of the stick as far as lives go. No death certificate, truly as if it never happened. I notice one other thing, though. Her parents' names are not listed as if they never existed, either, and she was born out of thin air. *Interesting.*

I remember there's a second pop-up. I close out of the tab and open up the next one. There's a link to an article from some gossip column. How did she go from nothing to being mentioned in a gossip column? Before I could analyze further, the headline and photo loads:

"New York's Most Eligible Bachelor and Notorious Bad Boy Engaged"

*Sorry, ladies. Nico Delucci, second-born son of global logistics, magnate Giuseppe Delucci is officially off the market. If you live under a rock, the Delucci's are one of the most influential and wealthiest families in the world. Boasting a combined familial net worth of $42.3 Billion, Nico doesn't do too badly for himself, either, quickly becoming one of the hottest nightclub and restaurant chain owners in the country as well. We won't mention their rumored ties to organized crime (oops!).*

*He's been tight-lipped about his dating history though he's rarely photographed with the same woman twice, so it's safe to say this one played the field for some time. However, all of that is about to change. The happy couple just announced upcoming nuptials but aren't sharing venue details or even a wedding date, though rumor has it the two eloped in secret months ago! According to a source close to the family, Mr. and Mrs. Delucci freaked out when they found out, so they're holding what we can only assume will be the hottest event of the decade. Isn't that romantic?*

*Who's the lucky lady that stole the heart of our wet dreams and turned him into a one-woman man? Here is everything we know:*

## Rise Of An Heiress

*Her name is Anya Liu—though like we said before she might already be the newest Mrs. Delucci, isn't she stunning?*

*She graduated from NYU and will be graduating from Columbia Law—we love a smart queen!*

*Speaking of queen, if the photo hasn't already blinded you, she, of course, is wearing Graff's stunning and rare five carat oval—a ring fit for royalty.*

*Her coffee order is a large cold brew, extra ice with oat milk and honey—warning all coffee shops to stock up now.*

*No—she is not pregnant, their team confirms.*

*The couple made their announcement through the family publicist and could not be contacted for further comment and do not plan on scheduling any interviews. Don't worry, though, not all hope is gone. There are still two very available Delucci brothers still on the market.*

*Congratulations to the beautiful couple!*

I can't believe what I'm seeing. My past haunted me for years, and there she is. Breathing. Alive and well. Very well, actually—rich from what I can tell and marrying into even more money. I shake my head in disbelief. For a second, I considered the woman in front of me an imposter but quickly shut that theory down. I remember her face, though. She was a child the last time I saw her. Bright smile on her face. The same dimple on her left cheek she'd been known for. Manicured hand with the engagement ring strategically resting on her fiancé's chest. Long dark hair, even darker eyes, staring right back at me.

*My sister.*

Did you love Nico and Anya's story? Well, their journey's not over yet. They're still learning how to navigate life as a married couple while Anya finds her footing as the new dragon head of the Triad! There are quite a bit of consequences when you come back from the dead. Part Two of the duet is coming soon! Thank you for reading! xx

# Connect With Me

Instagram: @paulina.writes

TikTok: @paulina.writes

Email: paulinap.author@gmail.com

Website: www.paulinapanyauthor.com

# Acknowledgments

This journey would not have been possible without the entire army of support and mentorship I'm so lucky to have.

To my family, for being so supportive—no questions asked. To my brothers and cousins, who were onboard despite having no clue what the book is about—that's a bold stance.

My friends for their unconditional guidance and inspiration, always.

I was so blessed to have found the best beta readers a new author could ask for. Thank you for your candor and time.

To my incredible editor, Samantha, my grammar queen, for saving my ass. Editing can be a thankless job, but I am so grateful for you. Ashton, my talented cover designer who completely understood me and my vision. And my Mandarin and Italian translators for helping me make this work as authentic as possible and educating me.

And to my readers for giving this new indie author a chance.

Made in the USA
Coppell, TX
19 July 2023

# WRITING
## SINCE THE REVOLUTION

# WRITING IN CUBA
# SINCE THE REVOLUTION

*An Anthology*
*of*
*Poems, Short Stories and Essays*

*Edited*
*and*
*Introduced*
*by*
ANDREW SALKEY

Published by
Bogle-L'Ouverture Publications
Limited

First published by Bogle-L'Ouverture Publications Limited
141 Coldershaw Road, Ealing, London W13 9DU

copyright © Andrew Salkey 1977
all rights reserved

distributed by Bogle-L'Ouverture Publications Limited
141 Coldershaw Road, Ealing, London W13 9DU

Third World Books and Crafts
748 Bay Street, Toronto, Canada

ISBN 0 904 521 04 4 (paper)
ISBN 0 904 521 05 2 (cloth)

Printed at the Press of Villiers Publications Ltd
Ingestre Road, London, NW5

For
Nancy Morejón
Olga Ojeda Díaz
Roberto Fernández Retamar
Marcos Díaz Mastellari
Pedro Pérez Sarduy
Margaret Randall
(*in Cuba*)

Audvil King
Lucille Mathurin-Mair
Olive Lewin
(*in Jamaica*)

Sam Greenlee
Robert Márquez
(*in America*)

Gus John
Darcus Howe
Errol Lloyd
Jessica Huntley
Leila Hassan
John La Rose
(*in England*)

and
in memory of
Karl Parboosingh
and
Sarita Gómez

No,
not always,
do men
know
where they go
when they return.

They keep quiet, though they shout,
the quiet people;
they shout, though seeming quiet,
the loud-mouthed;
no matter.

It matters, only, that they all know
where they set out to reach
when they leave,
and where they go
when they return.

**POEM**     Marcos Díaz Mastellari
(Translated by John La Rose)

# CONTENTS

| | | |
|---|---|---|
| Introductions | | 11 |
| | Poems | |
| NICOLÁS GUILLÉN | Land in the Sierra and Below | 17 |
| | Che Comandante | 19 |
| NANCY MOREJÓN | Poem | 22 |
| | Central Park, Some People, 3:00 p.m. | 23 |
| DOMINGO ALFONSO | Madrigal written in the Year of the space rocket, Mariner IV | 25 |
| | A Little Biography | 26 |
| | People like me | 27 |
| | Señor Julio Osorio | 28 |
| | Poem | 29 |
| PEDRO PÉREZ SARDUY | Che | 30 |
| | The Rebellion of the Warrior | 32 |
| ROBERTO FERNÁNDEZ RETAMAR | How lucky they are, the normal people | 33 |
| | The Last Station of the Ruins | 34 |
| | No word does you justice | 36 |
| | For an instant | 37 |
| | To whom it may concern | 38 |
| FAYAD JAMÍS | For this liberty | 41 |
| | Poem in Minas del Frío | 43 |
| | The Victory of Playa Girón | 46 |
| MIGUEL BARNET | My Country | 48 |
| | Che | 49 |
| | Revolution | 50 |
| GUILLERMO RODRÍGUEZ RIVERA | Working Hours | 51 |
| BELKIS CUZA MALÉ | I haven't forgotten you | 52 |
| | Photogenic People | 53 |
| FÉLIX PITA RODRÍGUEZ | The Guerrillas arrive | 54 |
| | Rifle Number 5767 | 55 |
| | Poetry with a Purpose | 57 |

| | | |
|---|---|---|
| ALBERTO ROCASOLANO | *Revolution is not simply a word* | 58 |
| VÍCTOR CASAÚS | *Moon-9* | 59 |
| | *We are* | 60 |
| EDUARDO LOLO | *Anna* | 61 |
| | *If you get up some morning* | 63 |
| CÉSAR LÓPEZ | *Who can be certain?* | 65 |
| ORLANDO ALOMÁ | *The Militant Angel* | 67 |
| LUIS SUARDÍAZ | *Witness for the Prosecution* | 68 |
| ANTÓN ARRUFAT | *Playa Girón* | 70 |
| MANUEL DÍAZ MARTÍNEZ | *Bread* | 71 |

### Short Stories

| | | |
|---|---|---|
| FÉLIX PITA RODRÍGUEZ | *The Seed* | 75 |
| VIRGILIO PIÑERA | *The Philanthropist* | 82 |
| SAMUEL FEIJÓO | *Soldier Eloy* | 91 |
| VÍCTOR AGOSTINI | *Pepe* | 102 |
| LUIS AGÜERO | *A certain Friday 13th* | 112 |
| ARNALDO CORREA | *The Chief* | 118 |

### Essays

| | | |
|---|---|---|
| EDMUNDO DESNOES | *The Secret Weapons* | 125 |
| AMBROSIO FORNET | *The Intellectual in the Revolution* | 131 |
| ERNESTO CHE GUEVARA | *The Cultural Vanguard* | 137 |
| ERNESTO CHE GUEVARA | *"El Patojo"* | 141 |
| FIDEL CASTRO | *On Che's Assassination* | 145 |
| FIDEL CASTRO | *On Intellectual Property* | 148 |
| Biographical Notes | | 155 |
| Acknowledgements | | 161 |

# INTRODUCTION

One of the facts of Caribbean cultural history is that the Area was first *written about* by its European discoverers and conquerors rather than by either its aboriginal inhabitants or later by its 'settled' natives; this is only natural and logical, as there hasn't been any evidence of primordial records or traces of story-telling unearthed from the sites of the first peoples of the Caribbean, the Caribs, Arawaks, Siboneys, Mayaris and Tainans. Spanish, Portuguese, French, Dutch and British colonialists were the 'first acknowledged describers' of the New World in the Caribbean, and ironically, their histories and chronicles, although intended to be statistical travel documents and straightforward reports of European conquest and 'property settlement and development', read, nevertheless, like narrative literature, replete with highly personal observations, vivid descriptions of landscape and even wry anecdotes.

Cuba showed its vanguard spirit early by being the first of the conquered Caribbean territories to produce poets and prose writers who attempted to tell their own Island tales from a native rather than a colonialist viewpoint. The beginnings of the Cuban national literature were marked by the very early nineteenth century contributions from a poet like José María de Heredia, and from novelists like Anselmo Suárez Romero and Cirilo Villaverde.

Both the Spanish and French Caribbean writers, in time, turned away from their Island- and territorial-centred writing, and embraced broader themes and more sophisticated styles, which, they hoped, would add a coveted modernity to their work, and make them into 'professionals' and 'internationals', which were the expressions used then. But the historical background exerted its influence on most of the Cuban writers of the late nineteenth and early twentieth centuries; their finest poems, plays, novels and essays continued to reflect the urgency of their extremely dramatic past: European discovery and settlement, slavery, the African and Asian infusions, colonialism, exploitation, independence struggles and the resistance to neo-colonialism.

The literature and the practice of the other arts were imbued with social and political realities. One distinguished Cuban literary critic tells us that Cuban writing, like much of Spanish American prose and poetry, would seem, originally, to have been placed at the disposal of the native and Imperial historical processes, social affairs and the later struggle against alienation. He implies that, for example, the Cuban novel, short story and narrative poem were used as literary instruments of accusation and near-polemic; most of the writers were certainly aware of nature and the world of the individual imagination and aesthetic excellence, but they were more occupied in putting their writing at the service of ideological propaganda and the issues arising out of community problems, and in bolstering the causes and aspirations of the endemic Revolutionary Movements, spread over the years, beginning around the middle of the nineteenth century. It could be said that a conspicuous proportion of the writing of pre-Revolutionary Cuba was a literature of historical themes, political subjects, and social consciousness. There was the introduction of Modernism, a period of very nearly twenty-five years, during which stylistic competence, universality and the eschewing of social and political content held sway; but after that pause, the poets, playwrights, novelists and belletrists reverted to the kind of writing which projected their concerns with localism, social interpretation and national identity, albeit with great care about style and technique.

But then, as the European Imperialist domination was shaken off, there came the seemingly attractive cultural influences of North America; New York shared, and in some respects, took over, the position of leadership in the metropolitan approval and confirmation which some Cuban intellectuals had previously sought from Paris and Madrid. Yet, certain Cuban poets fought back by asserting the counter-influences of *criollismo* and Afro-Cubanism and won through, in part. But the spirit of the literature, as a whole, was not entirely victorious; the Cuban short story, in particular, suffered the casualty of the North American penetration. The educated Cuban middle class produced poets, novelists and essayists whose work revealed the contacts they had made with the best models in contemporary American and European writing, and which they were prepared to nurture, and continued to imitate.

Later, however, the attractiveness of the Revolutionary cultural values began to assert itself in the society, especially among its younger writers. What has remained, after many years of cultural invasions and counter-actions, nationalist visions and reverses, is the essential Cuban genius for adaptation, assimilation, innovation and consequent development.

In this selection of poems, short stories and essays, I have tried to show the new evidence of those elements at work, and I have also attempted to indicate the Revolutionary purpose of creative writing in Cuba, today: to rid the individual and the society of alienation, through inventiveness and experimentation and conflict, and to attain the uphill road towards a better cultural life. Ernesto Che Guevara, writing in *Man and Socialism in Cuba*, reminds us that artistic experimentation must be invented and taken implicitly as the definition of creative freedom; but even this, he warns us, has its limiting factors, which are imperceptible, until they clash with the new society's demands, when, in other words, they are thrown up against the backdrop of the real problems of alienation among the people. He also urges the intellectual and the artist to fight to make art into a weapon of denunciation and accusation.

And, in a way, this is precisely what Cuban art and culture and history would seem to have been preparing the new intellectuals and artists to undertake, when one recalls a much earlier statement by the critic José Antonio Portuondo: 'The novel, in particular, has been, for us, an accusatory document, a display of doctrinal propaganda, a calling of attention to serious and urgent social problems, so that the mass of readers may take immediate action.' That was written six years before the Revolution.

In the Revolution, today, a younger critic, Ambrosio Fornet, is able to say (after admitting that the first thing the intellectual discovers, in his transformed society, is his own ignorance) that it is important for the artist 'to invent the road that leads directly to his objective; and in this fascinating and risky task, the concrete responsibility of the intellectual is . . . to address himself and his work to the soul of the people, to conquer nature and create new highways and visions of reality; and that cannot be achieved in isolation from the concrete responsibility to the other sectors of the Revolution.'

And yet another young critic, Julio Martínez Páez, has pointed, too, that 'Cuba's *new man* will be achieved through artistic, cultural, political and ideological education; and as such, art and literature are fundamental activities in the formation of the whole personality of the new Cuban.'

The poet, Roberto Fernández Retamar, states his commitment this way:

> *Now I understand*
> *that our history is History itself,*
> *and that the fire that has burned my hand . . .*
> *I can't put out.*

During my visit to Cuba, in 1968, my friends in Havana assured me that their cultural life-style, like their revolutionary politics and their new ideology, is steering clear of dogmatism. It is being recreated constantly. It is Cuban in every detail of its ever-changing and restless course. A young playwright, Rogelio Martínez Furé, told me that he took it for granted that all his fellow intellectuals, writers and artists are free. He said, in an hour-long conversation, with a group of visiting delegates, at the first Cultural Congress of Havana, 'To be free in Cuba is not our only freedom; we're achieving the larger freedom of being faithfully responsible for the future of our society, and of Mankind. We write as we like; but we think, always, of the years ahead and of the best of us yet to come. That's why we invent as we go along. We avoid straight, set, inflexible paths. We make our future as we go towards it. We have the freedom for the journey.'

This anthology is an attempt to take the reader along the very early path, just beyond the starting point of that journey.

ANDREW SALKEY.

# POEMS

# NICOLÁS GUILLÉN

### *Land in the Sierra and Below*

(On the announcement of the
Agrarian Reform Law, 1959)

You're the lord of my land,
of the trees and the rivers, and
you'll have to reckon with me.

You're the master of my life,
my life, which, is nobody's but mine,
not even my parents', just mine, and
you'll have to reckon with me.

In fact, from the sugar cane to the rose bush,
and from the rose bush to the sugar cane,
you've staked your claim, and
you'll have to reckon with me;
Lord, how you're going to reckon with me!

Yesterday, I sent you a letter,
written in my blood,
to tell you that I want back
the mountains and the plains
and the rivers you stole from me,
the ones that run between the trees,
swaying in the wind,
full of birds
and my life
which is nobody's but mine.

Lord, you'll have to reckon with me!
From the sugar cane to the rose bush,
and from the rose bush to the sugar cane,
you've staked your claim, and
you'll have to reckon with me;
Lord, how you're going to reckon with me!

I live without land,
in my land,
and have always lived without land;
I haven't a yard of ground
to lie down and die on, and
you'll have to reckon with me.

Together with olive-green Fidel,
flourishing Fidel,
I'm coming to crack your fangs,
to take back what's mine, and
you'll have to reckon with me.

Sierra and more land,
mountain and plain : and
you'll have to reckon with me.

And the rivers that run between the trees,
swaying in the wind,
full of birds
and my life
which is nobody's but mine : and
you'll have to reckon with me.

(Translated by Anita Whitney Romeo
 and adapted by the Editor)

# NICOLÁS GUILLÉN

### *Che Comandante*

In spite of your fall,
your light is undiminished.
A horse of fire
celebrates your glory as a guerrilla,
between the wind and the clouds, in the Sierra.
Even though they've silenced you, you speak,
and even though they burned you
and let you rot in the earth,
and lost you in the cemetery,
in the forest,
in the swamp,
they can't stop us from finding you,
*Che Comandante,*
*Amigo.*

With her filed teeth,
North America chuckles,
squirming, at this very moment,
in her bed of dollars.
And yet, her chuckling becomes a mask,
as your noble body of steel rises
and swarms everywhere in other guerrillas, like flies,
and your universality, bruised by merc soldiers,
lights up the American night, like a sudden star,
dropped in the middle of an orgy.
You knew all about it, Guevara,
but you said nothing,
in order not to draw attention to yourself,
*Che Comandante,*
*Amigo.*

You're everywhere. In the Indian,
made of copper and dreams. In the black man,
covered in the spittle of the white backlash.
In the oil refineries, in saltpetre,
and in the terrible helplessness of the banana,
and in the magnificent animal *pampa*,
and in sugar, salt and coffee,
you, a moving frieze of your own blood,
as they cut you down, breathing,
because they couldn't love you,
*Che Comandante,*
*Amigo.*

Cuba knows you, in her heart.
Your bearded face instructs us.
Like a young Saint, your body is ivory and olive.
Your voice is firm,
without the edge of command in it,
as you command *compañera,* friend,
affectionate and responsible,
leader, comrade.
We remember you, each day, at the Ministry,
each day, in the Army,
each day, as an easy companion,
each day, as an uncompromising man,
pure, as a child and as a man,
*Che Comandante,*
*Amigo.*

And so, you pass our way in your fading battle fatigues,
lived-in and torn, you,
in the jungle, just as you were, before,
in the Sierra,
half-naked,
secure in weaponry and the word,
churning the wind
and prising the slow-opening rose.
There's no peace.
*Salud,* Guevara!

Or better still, from the very depths of America,
wait for us. We will leave with you.
We want to die and to live,
as you have died,
and to live,
as you live on,
*Che Comandante,*
*Amigo.*

(Translated by Margaret Randall
 and adapted by the Editor)

# NANCY MOREJÓN

*Poem*

(A fragment of a poem, taken from
the Poet's book, *Amor, Ciudad
Atribuida*)

The morning is sullen.
The water forgets to flow.
The street trembles in the rain.
It has crossed centuries of stone.
It has marked the installation of a new god,
a just reward.

I see the clean fall of the drops.
I come across the flaccid skin of Old Havana,
and I'm drenched, though I'm dry,
hoping for some kind of incontrovertible kiss.

I walk on the skin
and the rain runs and takes communion
with the unsuspecting people.

I embrace the street
and the large echoing houses
and the bricks, bread and broken crusts.

(Translated by Tim Reynolds
and adapted by the Editor)

# NANCY MOREJÓN

### *Central Park, Some People, 3:00 p.m.*

If you cross a park, in heroic Havana,
in splendid Havana,
in a flood of afternoon light,
white and blinding,
blazing enough to drive that Van Gogh sunflower mad,
and completely filling the eyes of Chinese street-photographers;

if you cross a park and misjudge
that blinding, white light,
very nearly repeating itself, everywhere in the city;

if you're at a loss, at that time of day,
and you take those unnecessary trips of yours
round Havana's Central Park;

if you cross the Park, strewn with sacred trees,
and walk, seeing everything
and noticing nothing,
loving the Revolution's impact on the eyes,
then, you will know it, like the sensation of rum in the night,
because, in our parks, and in this one,
so central, in Havana,
very old men sit on the benches
and light large cigars
and look at one another
and talk about the Revolution and Fidel.

The old men are pieces of warm toast,
on the benches. It's no secret:
there go two men and a tired brief-case,
a vein-bloated hand,
a shout, wearing a grey felt hat.

The old men meet under the statue
of the Apostle Martí, in 1966,
in December, 1966;
the year is nearly over,
and they wait for 'the anniversary of freedom
to pay tribute to the Martyrs',
to the men of the people
who died, and whose blood is drying,
in the afternoon sun,
in Havana, Cuba, free territory of America.

So, if you cross the Park, the world,
the womb of the Revolution,
you must hesitate,
walk slowly, breathe self-consciously,
step lightly,
hesitate,
breathe self-consciously,
walk slowly,
and give your whole life,
violently,
*Compañeros.*

(Translated by Sylvia Carranza
and adapted by the Editor)

# DOMINGO ALFONSO

*Madrigal written in the Year of the Space Rocket, Mariner IV*

    In spite of your broad nose
    and the strong smell of your armpits,
    you have the Queen of Sheba's cunt.

    Your hard body was made
    to win all the games
    in the people's gymnasium,
    throughout the world.

    I am writing this
    in the year of Mariner IV,
    and I will call it a Madrigal.

    (Translated by Stephen Schwartz)

# DOMINGO ALFONSO

### *A Little Biography*

When she died, she left behind
her clothes, school books,
her confidential diary,
a boy friend in the fifth grade
and her love for Che and Fidel.

The dead fifteen year old,
with whom I used to chat
about everyday things, while,
now and then, her small breasts would heave
and swell,
left other things behind, as well,
which I try to ignore : her dreams of motherhood,
a kitchen full of gleaming pots and pans,
an occasional bunch of common flowers
and a request for no more than a little freedom.

(Translated by Rogelio Llopis)

# DOMINGO ALFONSO

### *People like me*

People like me
walk the streets, every day,
drink coffee, breathe
and admire the Sputniks.

People like me,
with a nose, with eyes,
with marital troubles,
who take buses,
one day, quite suddenly,
slip underground,
unnoticed.

(Translated by Sylvia Carranza)

# DOMINGO ALFONSO

### *Señor Julio Osorio*

I suppose, quite frequently, these days,
Señor Julio Osorio remembers the time,
before the Revolution, when, not a year passed,
without his flying up to New York.
Those were the years, when my father was out of work
and my sister, Rita, was the victim
of Doctor Beato's sons,
while my mother sewed trousers and things,
on a Singer, for private tailors
with a meagre clientele.

These days, I work,
and my sister is about to graduate,
and we care, very little,
whether Señor Osorio makes his yearly trip
up to New York
or not.

(Translated by Rogelio Llopis)

# DOMINGO ALFONSO

*Poem*

(A poem, taken from the Poet's
book, *Poemas del hombre común*)

I'm an ordinary man.
During the usual hours of a working day,
like the world's millions,
I go up and down stairs,
then I have lunch, like some people,
talk with one or two students
(I carry no cross on my back);
day in, day out,
I run into many people,
some who're bored
and some who sing;
next to them, my insignificant figure
flits past;
I meet the working man
and I pass the bureaucrat;
the militiaman suffers;
the secretary stoops.

I'm simply describing the things felt
by an ordinary man.

(Translated by Sylvia Carranza
and adapted by the Editor)

# PEDRO PÉREZ SARDUY

## *Che*

just as if you were walking in the American jungle
and swollen with powder
just as if an urgent longing for the fatherland had interrupted
six rebel tears in the open street one night
just as if your mother proud woman had touched your shoulder
your guerrilla olive fatigues and told you
again about your next unknown journey
there is in the exactness of continents a whirlwind
as with wars
just as if a deep tumour were sucking a dying blind buffer
there are detonations of heroic words which shoot
the curve of the foetus
which hits back and returns to strike again
our shoulder of battles of bulky wounds is joined
and you are gone
there is an incredible myth like a sea like a chunk
of the Sierra around you
an agitated multitude a millenium of lore
immense like the morning which is waiting for you
in some place a presentiment
and you are gone with the sober drunkenness and you are gone
to live under the roof of the world
there was never any fear in the air that you sweated
in any of the circumstances
in my narrow streets of Santa Clara or among the thick beards
in December
your presence was low-keyed as it caressed the rough edge
the warmth of smallshot
and your brown steely glance penetrated like a mischievous child
the thunderous barracks of dead heroes who were robbed
and so the crisp new days came and January crossed leaving
in a corner of the sky clots of blood
and nobody stayed behind in the morning
and least of all you who in your suicidal fever knew how to
wound

the most prepared heart by your departure
nevertheless and like yesterday today we begin again
the new guerrillas
and rejoice like the flapping seabirds in the legend
of the soul
all this touches us in our most simple essence
and you are gone
just like that
just as if your mother proud woman had touched your shoulder
your guerrilla olive fatigues and told you
again about your next unknown journey
so we fix you firmly as our presage in the core of humanity

(Translated by John La Rose)

# PEDRO PÉREZ SARDUY

## *The Rebellion of the Warrior*

the rebellion of the warrior
my woman dressed proudly in her skin
rolls the black tobacco leaf my curly hair her warm voice
accustomed to the solitude of the nights in the summer
hurls herself into the sixth dimension
the intestines of roast chickens for the feast
for the return of the stranger yet again to the blue house
all the roads except one were open
and the tall totem was washed with the sperm of ramgoats
the surprise doesn't dissolve the happy embrace
accustomed to the tin eye on the wall
with the blood of all the stars
including those that were late in shining at birth
then the old inlaid church where we never dared fuck
really surprised
how suddenly the friend dies in the superstructure
of the fiesta which assumes such alarming proportions
the dawn in the fire
quiet please quiet
you make me afraid
that the lilies may have the taste of marble
a form for ever lost
your kindness informs your irrepressible frankness
and inscribes it indelibly

(Translated by John La Rose)

# ROBERTO FERNÁNDEZ RETAMAR

*How lucky they are, the normal people*

(For Antonia Eiriz)

How lucky they are, the normal people,
those peculiar ones: those without a mad mother,
a drunkard for a father, a delinquent son,
a house, nowhere at all,
an unknown disease: those who've worn
all their seventeen smiling faces and more: the ones
stuffed with shoes, the archangels with *sombreros*,
the satisfied, the plump, the cigar-Indians,
the Rin-tin-tins and their sectaries,
the one who 'Sure, why not. This way',
those who make money and are loved up to the hilt,
the flautists accompanied by mice,
the hucksters and their customers,
the gentlemen just a touch superhuman,
the men dressed in thunder and the women in lightning,
the delicate ones, the wise, the ones of refined tastes,
the courteous, the sweet, the edible and the drinkable:
how lucky they are, the birds, manure and the stones.

Just let them keep out of the way of the others:
the ones who create whole new worlds
and dream dreams
and cause illusions
and compose symphonies
and utter words that tear us down and build us up again:
the ones madder than their mothers,
more of a set of drunkards than their fathers,
far worse delinquents than their sons,
more eaten into by corrosive love:
let them leave their position in hell
and drop the whole thing.

(Translated by Tim Reynolds
and adapted by the Editor)

# ROBERTO FERNÁNDEZ RETAMAR

## *The Last Station of the Ruins*

Some time ago, I spoke of ruins. It was, I think,
among highflown, young verses, and I headed them,
rather like the crowning of a paltry king,
with Eluard's words:
*Regardez travailler les bâtisseurs de ruines.*
But I hadn't really seen the ruins. Those I named
were of paper, letters, allusions,
and gradually, even they, tenuous echoes,
were being forgotten.

Then, one morning, walking in London,
the ruins came crashing down on me.
Turning a corner,
living ruins, dead ruins: the solitary staircase,
rearing up like a huge bird,
spreading dissonant wings: the painted wall
of an obliterated house, the crude map in the dust,
giving on to the corridor, leading nowhere,
and the immense sky, circulating through the vacant eyes
of a smoking skull.
Mesmerized, I wandered through the shell of the city.
But they were European ruins,
ruins of a world being torn to shreds by electric shocks,
between cups of tea and futile circumspection.
Back in the light of the Island,
I was forgetting those ruins.

Then, the ruins reared up from the letters
and overflowed the European graveyards.
The builders of ruins were born, here, too.
And the fragile city of grassy plots,
and the city of a thousand red roofs
became the horrified table-talk of the world.

The powder-strewn streets saw long processions,
bundled under the rumble and thunderclap.
Nobody knew where it all came from, harsh and indecisive.

Later, I saw the ruins. Not those I spoke of earlier,
not the far-off ruins,
but the familiar ones,
the ones at home : the gaping holes in the peasants' huts,
the vaporized storehouse, like a disembowelled body.
(*We had,* the grave old man said,
*ninety-one deaths in the city.*)

This time, the exaggerated light of the Island
hardly clothed the dead and the stones.

And yet, it's of no consequence
that the froth of living, the joy, rushes in
to rehinge the doors,
to replaster the cracks.
Inconceivable ruins, suddenly wrought in the soft season,
scattered bricks,
set, dead eyes
look on ceaselessly;
they demand their place in our memory,
a fate denied the ruins in books : the English
or Italian ruins.
(That happened somewhere else.)

There is nowhere else. This is the somewhere else :
the somewhere that knew horror
so that hope might draw sustenance.

(Translated by Angela Boyer
and adapted by the Editor)

# ROBERTO FERNÁNDEZ RETAMAR

*No word does you justice*

Tremor stronger than coupling,
Company intenser than solitude,
Conversation richer than silence,
Reality stranger than dream,
Truth pervading day and night,
Song without stop-note,
Sky flushed with banners,
Reason for being here :
You see that no word does you justice,
Revolution.

(Translated by Angela Boyer)

# ROBERTO FERNÁNDEZ RETAMAR

*For an instant*

That glow in the night:
Is it one of *our* reflectors?
Is it one of *their* weapons?

(For an instant,
 I'd forgotten
 that there's a moon
 in the sky,
 and that there are stars.)

(Translated by Angela Boyer)

# ROBERTO FERNÁNDEZ RETAMAR

### *To Whom it may Concern*

(A fragment from a poem
of the same name)

From one end to the other of the Island,
we're far fewer, in number, than those
who daily pass through the streets of a large city.
We're fewer: a mere handful of men
on a ribbon of earth, pounded by the sea.
But we've recaptured a forgotten joy.

The dawning of the finest Sundays sees us,
setting off, singing for the tilled fields,
and for the stones that are to become schools.

One morning, on the coast of Pinar del Rio,
by the sea, already beginning to be spiked
by the sun, a sensation seized us
and made us know that we were the owners of everything
spread out before our eyes: the factories, the land,
the trucks slipping past, the music and the flags,
the light hovering over us, the rainstorm
implacable as a lover.

There we were, black with the dirt of the fields,
having just finished cutting
the last burnt sugar cane stalks.
('This is for you.'
    'No! It's for you.')

We were on the hill,
our hands outstretched.
('Mario García. I'm a carpenter.'
    'Roberto Fernández. I'm a teacher.')

And earlier, there was the shadow of my house
in France, still hanging over me,
my first rifle in my hand,
as I kept watch by night,
blinking against my closing eyes,
watching over the broad coastline
which must be protected,
knowing that, there, behind us,
stretches an Island it's up to us to guard,
our woman, a flower.

They come back,
exuberant,
with lighted lamps
and laughter.
They had penetrated the back country,
to learn more than to teach,
to learn about the real suffering
of the men and women, there,
while giving the Alphabet
to the fertile earth;
later, the men and women sent papers to the cities,
papers with laboured, raw handwriting, for the first time
reminding us of the quality of a tilled field.

My lost years, the misspent hours,
between childhood and long after,
will never recur;
they're, here, all of them, rescued years,
in our young brigade that returns
announced by the chorus of lighted lamps.

What's your part like
in the weapon preparing to destroy all this?
In the register of what ship of death
is your name entered?

What unknown voice spits it out?
You know, of course, you won't be able
to turn your face on the pillow
without being stained
by the blood you've spilled.
You won't see the leaves
for the dead bodies
falling from our trees.
You won't be wet by the rain
but rather by our tears.

Now, I understand
that our history is History itself,
and that the fire that has burned my hand
(and, here, I'm not referring to my writing hand,
but to my real hand; and I'm naming the reality
of fire)
I can't put out.

Your identity
and the deep wound you've inflicted
are scored in my heart.
We're surrounded by fire and water.

While tossing my old papers
on to the fire
to feed it,
I feel my life growing,
fanned like the flame,
and I sense my usefulness;
I'm no longer unnecessary.

The singers take my arm
and together we sing the same song,
as we move on.

(Translated by Angela Boyer
 and adapted by the Editor)

# FAYAD JAMÍS

### *For this Liberty*

(For Manuel Navarro Luna)

For this liberty, we enjoy,
to sing in the rain,
we must give everything.

For this liberty
to be so finally welded together,
all the people, weak and strong,
we must offer our total sacrifice.

For this liberty,
so like an open sunflower, at dawn,
for the light in our schools and factories,
for the startling earth
and for our alert children,
we must give everything.

There's no alternative of liberty,
no other high road,
no true home,
and there'll be little verse
without its violent music.

For this liberty,
we must withstand the terror
that dares violate its sanctity
and would bring back our poverty of spirit.

For this liberty,
we achieved the eclipse of our oppressors
and the full restoration of the people.

For this liberty,
the scales dropped away,
barefoot men looked up,
patched roofs were sealed securely
and the glance of the children
showed a glint of the sun
in the corner of their eyes,
as they wandered in the dust.

For this liberty,
the kingdom of the young.

For this liberty,
beautiful as Island life itself,
we must give everything;
and, if we have to,
even the very cool of the evening;
and yet,
that will never be enough.

(Translated by R. Frank Hardy
and adapted by the Editor)

# FAYAD JAMÍS

### *Poem in Minas del Frío*

The rain beats out a song
on the corrugated zinc roof.
The fragrance of the land
leaps up to our window.

The soldiers talk about war,
about the death of Ciro Redondo
and Camilo's smile,
about the long marches,
pricked by hunger and rocks,
and they talk about Fidel
and Che,
Juan Almeida,
Raúl
and about the other sons of our people,
and about those
who were mere names under fire,
in the ooze of blood
and in the bramble,
and about those
who fell very early in the dust.

A soldier, with a book by John Reed,
borrowed only recently,
and moving about on his bunk,
and the barking dogs, outside,
make the rain and the wind and the night
even more marvellous
than they naturally are.
Nobody speaks. Everybody speaks.
I'm too much of a good listener.

The voices converge
and pelt me,
but the speakers say so little
about the life they lived in the Sierra,
as they listened
to the song of the streams
and the bullets,
while breathing in the scent
of the fruits
drooping down from the *jobo* trees;
these are the things
they never talk about;
they're the earth,
the trees,
vague memories,
bridges,
schools,
an old man who chuckles,
a path that leads to the depths
of the Sierra darkness.

(When it rains,
we often sing,
while marching,
without a thought for our wounds
or our hunger.
We're united.
We're brothers.)

Quite suddenly,
a clump of clouds
passed over us
and seemed to touch our bunks,
and then disappeared, like smoke,
across the corrugated zinc roof,
like the sound of rain.

My poem thickened
and took form.

(If we must fight again,
I would do so
a thousand times, again,
and give my blood
a thousand times, again,
and expel our enemies
from our home
and abroad.)

The rain beats out a song
on the corrugated zinc roof.
The fragrance of the land
leaps up to our window.

We sleep
where there's the smoke
of our Revolution.

(Translated by R. Frank Hardy
 and adapted by the Editor)

# FAYAD JAMÍS

### The Victory of Playa Girón
(A Sketch for a Cantata)

(In memory of José Alvarez
Baragaño)

Treason strikes.

Our cities sleep in the smoke of our factories.
The countryside sleeps in the dew.
Our children sleep in the dark.
The windows of our houses are stained
with the warmth of the night
and our breathing.

Many of us are awake,
in the lamplight,
forging new ideas,
resolute as granite,
forging a life of hardship and joy.

Many of us shoulder our weapons
at whispering outposts
or in the dark corner of a workshop,
behind a sturdy tree,
beside the throbbing waves,
under tree-limbs and the stars,
and everywhere love flourishes,
as wide and as blue as the night,
the love a man feels for his woman,
the love of being, here,
our love of Cuba.

And even while the quality
and meaning of our love
circulated through our blood,
and in our work-tools,

in the dew,
the sky was being sliced
by gunsmoke and the traitors' markings,
and deafening blasts were replacing
the fever in our factories
and the silence of our guards.

A splintered frame replaced
the open window on the street,
and death called in
on little-known communities,
all along our southern coast and sky,
piercing its way
with heavy wagons,
death dressed in battle-dress,
alien and soiled,
death, at a distance,
rattling ancient blood-stained fetters,
forged in the inferno of terror.

(Translated by R. Frank Hardy
and adapted by the Editor)

# MIGUEL BARNET

### *My Country*

I can hardly wait to speak,
and to speak, again,
because, with each day that passes,
my love grows stronger
for the Island winds
under the leaves.

I'll know, soon, how to cherish
the house I live in, every day,
and the shade thrown by the *jagüey* trees
and the land.

But that's not enough.
They'll hear my voice,
tempered in fire,
because they're calling for me.

And I feel
as though the Island were someone close,
a personal friend,
and my heart comes to understand me,
because I know that, at my side,
and in distant country places,
there's a force,
like all the Island winds,
defending our Cuban life, itself.

(Translated by R. Frank Hardy
and adapted by the Editor)

# MIGUEL BARNET

### *Che*

Che, you know
the secrets of the Sierra,
asthma over the damp grass,
the speaker's platform,
the tides at night,
and even how the fruits grow
and how the oxen are yoked.

I wouldn't, for anything, give you
my pen for your pistol,
for it's you
who are the poet.

(Translated by R. Frank Hardy
 and adapted by the Editor)

# MIGUEL BARNET

### *Revolution*

You and I are separated
by a mass of paradoxes
which come together
and mobilise my spirit.

Sweat pours out of me
now that I'm building you.

(Translated by R. Frank Hardy
and adapted by the Editor)

# GUILLERMO RODRÍGUEZ RIVERA

### *Working Hours*

And, now, that the dust has settled
and we're able to move
towards our new destiny,
the image we grieve
will take on another form.

We'll not hear that voice, again.
The presumably right way of doing things, then,
won't be mentioned, ever, again.

We'll pick ourselves up
from the handful of dust,
from the terror of the dark stairs,
from the rain that made him shudder
in the afternoon,
and we'll utter the word made flesh, now,
and we'll find that it suffices.

(Translated by Claudia Beck
 and adapted by the Editor)

# BELKIS CUZA MALÉ

*I haven't forgotten you*

(For Major Luis Augusto Turcios Lima)

There's an eye of rain over Havana, today.
A very definite hurricane threatens to devour
the fish in the inkwell.
There's no cloud at the window. No voice. No dust.
Night's a habit in the bowels of the houses.

Though your body is lost, for ever,
and your spurs have been chucked aside
with the rooster;
though your hands no longer detonate the pistol,
and your back has become a length of bare bones;
I'm looking at death and its Havana reality.
But I refuse to accept you, as a visitor.
I refuse to set up a cross, in your name,
and keep watch over it,
and allow the news agencies to forget about you.

(Translated by Sylvia Carranza
and adapted by the Editor)

# BELKIS CUZA MALÉ

### *Photogenic People*

You can see them walking
over the yellowing corners
of the sheet of paper,
and disappearing at the turn of the page.
They people an island in the tropic of war,
an island where all the traditional vessels are shattered,
an island on horseback.
They enter the suburbs of the evening
and the stop-over hotels.
They navigate on a bed of white sails,
while he sings
and she, simply, makes noises,
a wave under the bed.
Better be quiet and let them sleep
          and let them live
          and let them die.

At the corner of the photograph,
a few lines bear witness to the fact:
neither is sure of the other,
but they both navigate;
they find their way on the Island
across all the oceans of the world.

(Translated by Rogelio Llopis
 and adapted by the Editor)

# FÉLIX PITA RODRÍGUEZ

## *The Guerrillas arrive*

When the great doors of the day don't open
                the guerrillas arrive
When our dreams suddenly lose their steering-wheels
                the guerrillas arrive
When at the birth of the infants death is carried in
under the arm instead of lengths of fresh bread
                the guerrillas arrive
When freedom can only be written in secret codes
                the guerrillas arrive
When blood is spilled and forgotten, dropped from the memory
with the weight of quarry stones
                the guerrillas arrive
When a joker assures us that men can't reach up
and touch the stars with their hands
                the guerrillas arrive
When our small delights must be kept in dungeons
under lock and key until later in the evening when
there are no witnesses and we can sit down in a corner
and savour them
                the guerrillas arrive
When the mornings are dark and we open our eyes in fear
                the guerrillas arrive
When bread and laughter and salt and hope can no longer
be shared
                the guerrillas arrive
When the ghosts of heroes wander troubled and alone
in the gloom shouting their protest again and again
When we begin to feel ashamed of being men
                the guerrillas arrive
with their heavy boots and their old guns
and with the bright morning of the world in their hands
                the guerrillas arrive
                the guerrillas arrive
                and it's dawn everywhere

(Translated by Lionel Kearns)

# FÉLIX PITA RODRÍGUEZ

### *Rifle Number 5767*

This is the story of Félix Faustino Ferrán
and his national militiaman's rifle.
On the cold night of January 19th,
in the trenches of the Revolution,
somewhere in Cuba,
Félix Faustino Ferrán recited
a short, powerful poem
about his rifle, Number 5767,
the most telling, rhythmical,
touching poem
of the Revolution.

Our militiaman spoke it
in the profound voice
of a black man, Revolutionary fighter, Number 1061,
trapping the essence of Cuba
in his words,
as plain as flowers of steel.

I've forgotten
how the first words began
but I still hear the hoarse voice
and I recall his velvet grasp
on the barrel of his rifle
which he held like a precious stone,
as he said :
        Antonio, the barrel,
        Viviana, the trigger guard,
        Caruca, the bolt,
        Filiberto, the bullet,
        Irene, the recoil chamber,
        Lucía, the trigger,
        Fabián, the safety catch,
        and I'm the stock of the rifle.

In the naming of the parts,
each, a child of his,
a rose of his blood,
a castle of his skin.

For the fighter's children,
for all the children of Cuba
whose names are parts of militiamen's rifles,
we offer the hoarse voice
of a black man, Revolutionary fighter,
Félix Faustino Ferrán,
worker for the national glory,
on the cold night of January 19th,
in the trenches of the Revolution,
and I accept, gratefully,
the lesson he taught me
about the quintessence of poetry.

(Translated by R. Frank Hardy
 and adapted by the Editor)

# FÉLIX PITA RODRÍGUEZ

### *Poetry with a Purpose*

(A fragment from 'Chronicles of a
New Dawn', a long poem, taken from
the Poet's book, Las Crónicas)

Now's the time
to slam our cards down on the table,
certainly no longer the season for petty traps
or for turning the lamp low
to write out, in the dim light,
the entries of contraband stuff,
hoarded for trifling personal gain.

Having first agreed what it will be,
we must act from a principled *focus*.

Here, life starts from the vein of the rose,
for there's been a Revolution
of metaphysical anxieties
into bustling craftsmen.

Here, we play hard
for all our tomorrows,
and the cards we hold say
that all's treason
which isn't poetry with a purpose.

(Translated by Claudia Beck
and adapted by the Editor)

# ALBERTO ROCASOLANO

*Revolution is not simply a word*

(A fragment from the Poet's unpublished poem, 'One Cigarette after another and still not enough')

One cigarette after another
and still not enough.
Hard ash is the memory
lit by the lamp.
Outside, a car passes
and someone says,
'The family gave up that house
 to go abroad, because, you see,
 not everybody understands, with
 the same clarity, when dealing
 with the future, that . . .'

In reality, that's true :
Revolution is not simply a word
which sprouts slogans and banners
or digs up dead papers
to have them read out cold
as they were written
or smashes our identity
across an Island mirror,
but rather, the only way of trampling
cactus memories
until the future thrusts up a pattern,
one day squeezed into another.

(Translated by David Ossman and Carlos Hagen and adapted by the Editor)

# VÍCTOR CASAÚS

### *Moon-9*

Last evening
the metaphysical poets
drafted a formal protest
to the Soviet authorities
against the sending
of a scientific instrument
to the moon

I believe the main idea
of the document
is that they have no right
yes
that they have no right
to deface their last icon

(Translated by Stephan Schwartz)

# VÍCTOR CASAÚS

### *We are*

Unquestionably, we are.

We are amused by the *yellow* messages
of the cablegrams
flitting across
our lighthouse Island
built only the day before yesterday.

We are,
even with the corners of our eyes,
raw from the dawn,
with the fist
and the shortcoming
and the mistake
and the man who doesn't know
and the man who does
but has slipped up.

We are,
even beneath the weak smiles
of the bland
and the defeated,
and in spite of the butterflies.

We are, for ever,
in this small ethos
we live in.

(To be,
simply to be,
is, at this point in time
and in this latitude,
a noble achievement.)

(Translated by Stasia Stolkowska
and adapted by the Editor)

# EDUARDO LOLO

## *Anna*

(A fragment from a long
poem of the same name)

Anna
born
and clean down each thigh
a declaration of war

born
with a dirty postcard
across your arse
and counting down rockets
in your head

born
June 22nd 1966
with a hole
ready
in the middle of your back
for the bullet

I will you a scream
a terrible longing
a book by Kafka
this poem

with these
you may do what you must
burn past transactions

where I died
crushed
by an avalanche of aspirins
you'll die
closer yet

where I was poisoned
by the mass media
you'll feel
the seasickness
of the *Reader's Digest*

I will you one death a day
a love you can see through
a distant desire not to be
a mother drowned
by force
in a puddle of Coca Cola

You may
if you wish
be my enemy
discarding me
when a Sierra of codified petitions
raises its head

and if you choose
to have it
like that
share death
with some father
gone three hundred million years
when God was just a kid
wandering naked along the beach
singing songs
we've long forgotten

(Translated by Tim Reynolds
 and adapted by the Editor)

# EDUARDO LOLO

### *If you get up some morning*

If you get up
some morning
and hear
on the radio
of more children's deaths in Vietnam
or in Venezuela
or in whatever country
and hear
as well
of more fighter-pilots' deaths
by error
a worn out part
a screw perhaps
and the dead bodies
checked
in the air raid
a mistake
that wasn't a war zone
at all
and hear
of the ship that went down
with five hundred passengers
crew included
because its radar blinked out
and it rammed an iceberg
and why not
and of the infants
deformed by one drug
or another
and you hear
and understand
and see
war in thirty countries
where one man kills another
where people are afraid

to go into the streets
and to stay in their houses
afraid for their sons overseas
and the sons for their mothers at home
and if you get up
some morning
and hear
on the radio
and understand
that at any moment
the bombs might fall
don't be frightened
go to breakfast
as usual
just as it was
for us
some years ago
and know that
it's nothing
but the end of a grotesque
and pathetic world
an end
in which
you yourself
have had
a hand

(Translated by Stephan Schwartz)

# CÉSAR LÓPEZ

## *Who can be certain?*

The sun's almost the same at this end of the city.
It shines everywhere, here, but it seems suspended,
in shadows, over the confused faces of the children.
What's the sun's challenge like
and what's the fire
and what's the laughter like
for those others who point out and persistently adulate
the colour of the skin of the chosen people of the city?
But where are the chosen people of the city?
Here, there are only men.
Here, we've purged the magic of Slavery
and killed the creak of the surreys
and the slow sailing ships
and the mannered strolls along the promenade, the esplanade,
and the city has set its history straight
and discovered a heap of truths in the dusty corners,
dreams beyond the myths of local colour and hallowed artifacts.
Words can be profound. Adjectives are subject to great suffering
in the grip of compulsive hero-worship.
There's an obligation, more than a mere gesture, something real,
owed to the future, which we're groping towards,
as we explore the tangled void behind us.

Agripina Estrada's more than a name on my grandmother's lips;
she lived, entwined in the threads, between the swish of the
                                              scissors
and the slice of the fabric.
Agripina's face is gone but her black countenance persists
and presides on certain street corners.
True, we don't run into the rhetoric of her statue
but she's around, all right, camouflaged and dynamic,
in the clandestine exultation of the drums.
From the smooth hill, levelled off like an open balcony,
she had to go down to the Villa's black quarter.

Only on holidays does the city bring out its dungeon rhythms.
In the meantime, the proud young people painstakingly conceal
all the possible revealing traces of their black blood,
and shy away from the doors that might not open to them;
a few of the desperate ones even put the golden touch
to their black mestizo hair.

Adelina Landrián, earth mother, an image of the Island,
has been struck down and is waiting to be rescued.

(Translated by Claudia Beck
 and adapted by the Editor)

# ORLANDO ALOMÁ

### *The Militant Angel*

The angel came down to that country,
in strict angelic dress, white buttons,
and with his wings in a violin case.
He was, what you might call,
a pre-pubescent angel,
with not even peach fuzz
in the two or three required places.

The angel wasn't superstitious,
and the very first thing he did
was throw handfuls of salt
from the top of the stairs.
The second day,
he received a threat of expulsion
because of his declaration to the press
of his solidarity with the chauffeurs' strike.

Naturally, since he was a hot-tempered angel
and allergic to police and seafood,
he broke the emperor's mirror
in a thousand pieces
and asked to join a political party of the left.

(Translated by Margaret Randall
and adapted by the Editor)

# LUIS SUARDÍAZ

### *Witness for the Prosecution*

(For Jorge and Noel Navarro)

Every day, at about a quarter to three,
she would walk into the Dime Store cafeteria,
place her elbows, delicately, down
on the shiny formica counter,
just as though it were a precious piece of crystal,
order her ice cream, vanilla,
an ice cold Coca Cola, with a straw,
syrup, and an enormous slice of chocolate cake.
She ate slowly.
Then, after she had tucked it all away,
she descended from the revolving chair,
like a twentieth century goddess.

She did this every week-day.
I never knew what she did on Saturday afternoons.
But, at night, she rode around
in her cousin's convertible,
sat near the dance floor
in the most exclusive night club
and drank *extra seco* with soda.

I used to watch her in the afternoons
behind my dark glasses.
I knew her name, once, but I've forgotten it.
She worked in the office of a foreign concern,
lived in a two-storey house, without a garden,
and had studied to be a teacher;
then, she was probably about twenty-three.

I believe she left about 1961,
though I can't prove it.
She never interested me personally.
(She did interest George, but I imagine
he's forgotten all about it now.)

I liked to observe her.
She was a symbol of a straightforward,
mechanical way of life,
a certain social type,
who consumed an expensive snack
at about a quarter to three every afternoon.

It's hard for me to believe
that she's still here.
Would she be likely to put up
with voluntary work, queues,
ration books
and the possible shortage
of chocolate cake?

(Translated by Claudia Beck)

# ANTÓN ARRUFAT

### *Playa Girón*

With my useless hands,
whose only weapon is a pen,
I'd gather up all your heads,
my brother countrymen,
those of you who've died
staring at another sun,
your heads blown off
and scattered.

For a countrywoman's breast,
defiled by a machine gun,
leaving behind its innermost secrets
like a victim in an open field
(and because there was an ordinary
brave heart beating there);
and for the splattered flesh
and the bullets
and the blood-soaked handkerchiefs,
no one can imagine my shame,
my impotence,
and how I long to make
another eternal life for you.

I work at a shabby little trade,
hanging around,
waiting for other people
to do my living for me,
even with their sacred breath.
I wish humbly that my veins
would suck up your blood.
I need you for a dignified death.
And now, I don't fear the words
justice, liberty and bread.

(Translated by Claudia Beck)

# MANUEL DÍAZ MARTÍNEZ

### *Bread*

Bread searches out the hands
of the common man;
it seeks the callus
from his work-tools;
it hunts the blister
from the household bucket;
it tracks the scratch
from the schoolboy's pencil;
in short, life,
in its basic energies,
rubs shoulders
with a simple crust
of bread.

The Island sun is plain,
taut and powerful,
as dawn,
held, in our hands,
first thing, in the new day.
The spike of wheat is erect,
a noble presence,
opening its heart to our table;
and yet it's surrounded
by certainty and doubt.

Bread is such a compassionate banner.
It's sweet in the hands of the worker.
It's so ordinary throughout the world.
Its music enriches our rooms.

(Translated by Angela Boyer)

# SHORT STORIES

# FÉLIX PITA RODRÍGUEZ

*The Seed*

*There's a peach tree in the old Son-La prison in Vietnam. Its fruits are delicious. The tree was planted in a condemned cell, during the heroic period of the people's struggle against French Colonialism. The seed was put into the ground by To Hieu, one of the leaders of the Communist Party of Indo-China, a few weeks before he was executed. The tree flourishes, today.*

F.P.R.

When Dieudonné saw him scraping away with the twig in the hard soil of the cell, his very first reaction was as curious as the explanation the prisoner offered. But Dieudonné would later claim that there was good reason for his bafflement; he was merely one of the average dutiful warders at the Son-La prison. And, of course, an average warder's constant preoccupation is that every prisoner is waiting for the right moment to escape.

This was precisely what he thought when he saw To Hieu squatting on the ground and digging with a twig in the dry earth which had been worn as compact as concrete by the millions of footsteps of all the prisoners who had occupied the cell. Because his mind worked painfully slowly, Dieudonné, much later on, laughed at his own early notion which seemed utterly ridiculous to him, after the fact. How could anyone escape from Son-La by scratching in the dirt floor of his cell with a twig?

He gazed intently at the cell for a few minutes. From the narrow passage-way, he was able to see To Hieu in profile, seated, in a devotional attitude, on his heels, and poking at the earth with the twig. The prisoner's movements were deliberate, graceful and so typical of the everyday movements of his people. What was it that Sergeant Aveline had said that time, about them, and about how they moved? Something to the effect that 'all these people in Indo-China always seem to be rehearsing a ballet'. And, it was true. Their gestures, movements and attitudes usually gave the impression that they were following the complex rhythm of a delicate musical composition which only they could hear.

Intrigued by To Hieu's balletic grace, Dieudonné asked him, 'So, what're you supposed to be doing down there?' It was then that Dieudonné heard the prisoner's absurd explanation which he found as illogical as his own suspicion of attempted escape.

'I'm going to plant this seed.' To Hieu stood and held out his left hand. Dieudonné saw a peach seed, all right, but its irrelevance disturbed him.

'You're going to plant that?' he asked.

'Yes.'

The situation was very strange. Dieudonné did not understand it then or later; in fact, he never came to understand it. He looked at To Hieu, with surprise, half suspecting that he had been made the butt of a private joke.

To Hieu smiled and nodded to re-affirm his reply.

'But,' Dieudonné said, 'you're going to plant it, here, in your cell?'

'Yes.'

It was senseless. The soil was rock-hard. Dieudonné also thought of the other factor that made the whole thing positively unfathomable: To Hieu was going to be executed, in a few weeks, and what was more, he knew it.

'This earth isn't bad, you know,' To Hieu was saying, still smiling politely. 'It's not bad, at all. All the land in this area is good, fertile land. Come to think of it, it's just right for peaches. I know the land well. I was born near by.'

To Hieu's words were convincing. He was a local. Dieudonné knew that to the Vietnamese peasants the land was a trusted friend. Perhaps, it was possible for the seed to grow and become a flourishing tree. But what about the other aspect of the exercise? What sense was there in planting a peach seed, if the act implied waiting, as it no doubt did? A man plants a seed. He waits. And then he harvests the fruits. Hasn't it always been like that?

To Hieu said, 'It isn't the land that decisively says this or that; it's man who does the deciding.'

'And, if the land's not fertile?'

'That doesn't matter,' To Hieu said. 'It's man's will and determination and physical strength that get things done in his lifetime, and sometimes, after he has gone. That's true of the land just as it's true of everything else. The soil of this cell has not forgotten its genius of working with the seeds which may be planted in it. It can still produce grass and plants and flowers. If a man comes along and helps the earth to remember its function, the earth will turn the seed into a peach tree. You'll see.'

Dieudonné took the last two words to mean: 'I won't see it, but you Dieudonné, will.'

To Hieu pointed the twig towards the spot where he had been scratching away in the ground. 'Do you know why I'm going to plant it right there?'

Dieudonné said, 'Well, you know what you're about. I don't.'

And To Hieu said, 'Because of the sun'.

Again, Dieudonné looked at him and suspected that he was making a joke at his expense. But he remembered that every morning a sliver of sunlight entered the cell through the barred skylight.

To Hieu said, 'Look, Dieudonné, when the sun comes in, it goes from here to about there.' He moved back a little way to indicate with his right foot the exact area which the sun hit every morning. 'Then it comes this way. Do you see? I've made a mark, here, so that I won't make a mistake. Then it comes a little closer towards the centre of the cell and begins to dwindle away, leaving the cell in shadow and gloom. I've calculated the whole thing, and I'm going to plant the seed, here, where the sun shines the longest.' He patted the spot and smiled.

Dieudonné felt uneasy. To Hieu's confidence annoyed him. He said, 'That may be so, but what are you going to get out of it. Do you believe that because you have figured it out so well you'll have enough time to see the tree grow and be able to eat the first peach it bears?'

To Hieu was surprised by the violence of Dieudonné's words. 'You must forgive me,' he told the Frenchman. 'I've been concerned with one thing, and you another. I thought that you were asking about the difficulties with the land, and the seed I'm about to plant.'

'To hell with the land and your seed,' Dieudonné said. 'What kind of people are you? Have you got cold water running through your veins, or what? Or do you have some sort of traditional magic to make yourselves forget what you don't want to remember?'

As if he wanted to allow sufficient time to elapse for the warder's irritation to fade in silence, To Hieu looked away from him and waited a few seconds before replying to Dieudonné's question. At the end of the pause, he said, 'No, Dieudonné, that's not it. The situation is that I was thinking of the seed I'm going to plant, while you were thinking about the fact that the authorities are going to execute me in a few weeks. Obviously, these are two very different things. The confusion is understandable. Forgive me, again; it's my fault for not trying to see your point of view.'

Dieudonné was astounded. He had to make a great effort to realign his thoughts and hang on to To Hieu's statement which was so strange as to be mesmeric in its effect on him. He said, 'I honestly don't understand you people, and I never will. I've lived in Indo-China for fourteen years, and it's been like fourteen days! I don't know what to say, really. It's like day and night; you're one thing and we're another, each a totally different species. Anyone who says anything else doesn't know what he's talking about. I tell you we're like night and day! The Vietnamese and the French. Like oil and water. Understand, To Hieu? That's the position, as I see it.'

To Hieu stared at him.

'Of course, you can't understand me,' Dieudonné said, 'and I can't get you either. No Frenchman would be able to understand the idea of planting a peach tree when he is going to be shot in a few weeks. That's what I wanted to say to you earlier. That's what I was thinking about from the start.'

To Hieu said, 'That's all right, Dieudonné. But look, I don't think that that has anything to do with the fact that you're French and I'm Vietnamese.' He paused. He seemed to be trying to recall a half-remembered thought. He smiled. 'I know a number of Frenchmen who would have thought immediately of a tree when they saw the seed, just as I did. The possession of a seed acts on all people like that, Dieudonné.'

'Frenchmen? And in your position?' Dieudonné curled his upper lip in defiant disbelief.

To Hieu nodded. 'Yes, Frenchmen born in France, like you. And some of them have been here, living with us, well-known people.'

'Prisoners?' Dieudonné asked.

'Yes.'

'Now, wait a minute, To Hieu. I know what you're up to. You're talking about French Communists. Communists, like you.' He shrugged, as if the mere fact of saying what he had were enough to invalidate To Hieu's argument.

To Hieu's smile was distant, subtle, inexplicably melancholy. Then he smiled deeply. His distress hadn't lasted long. He said, 'You shrug your shoulders as if you were shutting a door, Dieudonné. We can't understand each other like that, you know, because it's only through an open door that you are able to see the right view of the picture you hope to find.'

Dieudonné was exasperated. 'What door? What the hell are you on to, now? I didn't say anything about a door.'

'You shrugged as though you were erasing the statement of a truth you had heard,' To Hieu told him, in the tone he would have used to a child who needs convincing about a simple matter.

The Frenchman said, 'No one can understand the nonsense you're talking. What does it all have to do with that stupid seed of yours? After listening to you, I still think that only an idiot could have got the notion to plant a peach seed when he knows that he's going to die shortly afterwards.' He bit into his words, as if trying to make them sharper and more cutting and insulting, as if he wanted to demolish To Hieu's strength and intolerable composure. His only wish, now, was to taunt him with that very certain death that was approaching a step closer every day, and that To Hieu, himself, knew to be inexorably advancing towards him.

To Hieu smiled.

Dieudonné said, 'Perhaps, you think that they're not going to shoot you after all, eh? That's it, isn't it, To Hieu? That's why you're so calm. Right?"

'No, Dieudonné,' To Hieu said. He made Dieudonné feel even more irritated, for it seemed to him, at that moment, that the prisoner's smile was more open and positively friendly than it was before. "I do know that they are going to kill me. I know there's no hope of anything else happening to prevent it.'

Dieudonné was relieved. His face showed it. He waved at To Hieu. 'Well, at last! Common sense from the common man. What you've just said is the only thing that matters. Now, if you know it, and if you haven't got some other mad idea up your sleeve, what's so sensible about planting the peach seed? Why are you going to do it, if you know that when the first peach comes out you'll be rotting underground? Tell me that.'

Dieudonné was surprised to see the expression of abject sadness that crept into To Hieu's eyes. It didn't last for more than a few seconds. Quite suddenly, the former serenity and the sweet smile were there again. To Hieu said, 'What happens to me isn't really important. Don't you see? One of the greatest mistakes, indeed, evils, in this world, is to put one's own fate in the balance. If I think of the peach tree, I should think of the tree and not myself. In this way, everyone will know that the important thing is for the tree to grow and bear good fruit.'

Dieudonné was fascinated. And yet, he felt irritated again. His reply was brutal. 'It doesn't matter how good the peaches are, you won't know about it, because you won't be here to eat them.'

'Others will eat them, Dieudonné,' To Hieu said, 'and when they do, they'll think with love of those who planted the tree, knowing that the fruits would not be for them.'

To Hieu's confidence made Dieudonné blind with rage. He said, 'That's a lie! There aren't any men like that. No man is born merely to spend his life thinking about others, planting peach seeds for them, and thinking about it the way you do. Or are you going to tell me that you Communists are like that?'

To Hieu nodded. 'Yes, we are like that, Dieudonné, and what you said is quite true: we weren't born that way. We learned to be, which is far better, for it makes us new people, stronger than we were. Do you understand? And that's why we never think of our death as being more important than the other things that may happen in the world. That's why we act always with others in mind, those who are here now and those who are not yet born and who will take our place in the society.'

Dieudonné didn't reply. He felt drained and alienated from himself. He turned, without looking at the prisoner, and walked slowly down the passage.

The door was open and Dieudonné stopped and looked inside the empty cell. There was the rectangle of sunlight which entered every morning through the barred skylight. Divided into six squares by the bars, it was there, bathing the small plant. The delicate stalk and the eight leaves seemed to be radiating a small light of its own, mottled with soft green. Dieudonné recalled how To Hieu had calculated the movement and duration of the sunlight in the cell. Then he remembered the first tender leaves, treasures, trembling on the tip of the pale stalk.

He walked into the cell. He stared down at the plant. He was fascinated by it. He squatted, as To Hieu had always done, and it seemed to Dieudonné that the plant had grown since the last time, the previous day, that To Hieu had looked at it, before he left the cell flanked by the special escort of soldiers.

Dieudonné thought of To Hieu. He recalled the original conversation they had about the planting of the seed. Suddenly, he noticed that the soil around the plant was dry. He looked at the bench in a far corner of the cell. On it were To Hieu's food bowl, spoon and clay water bottle. Dieudonné got up and went to see if there was any water left in the bottle. Sparkling in the bottom was the water that To Hieu hadn't had time to drink before he was taken away. Dieudonné held the bottle firmly and walked back to the plant and began to sprinkle it and the dry earth around it, with care. To Hieu had always done it that way.

(Translated by the Book Institute in Havana
and adapted by the Editor)

# VIRGILIO PIÑERA

### *The Philanthropist*

(An Extract)

'So, you want a thousand pesos?' Coco asked. He was a banker.

'One thousand,' Eduardo said. He was in love and wanted to get married as soon as possible.

'I demand that you borrow a million,' Coco said.

Eduardo felt faint. Had he heard right? The figure was so unfamiliar. He said, 'Excuse me, sir. I said one thousand pesos.'

The banker said, 'And I said a million.'

Eduardo was visibly going to pieces. No doubt, Coco was trying to trap him. Why should he? Eduardo admitted to being a nobody. It was a mean-spirited joke on the part of the terrible plutocrat, a very cruel way of refusing to lend an ordinary man a thousand pesos. Eduardo felt tempted to tell him to go to hell. The banker deserved to be insulted.

Eduardo said, 'I can't borrow that sum, sir. I could never pay it back.'

'All you have to do is ask for it,' Coco said.

'Ask for it?' Eduardo said. 'That I can't do.'

Coco made a paternal gesture. Then he patted him on his back. 'You can request the amount in writing. You know that. Just ask for a million in writing.'

'I can't. How could I ever pay it back?'

'Who's talking about paying it back?' Coco said. 'I want to give away a million pesos. I want to give it to you, son.'

'You're a charitable soul,' Eduardo said.

Coco nearly died laughing. The word 'soul' made him hold his sides. Then he said cryptically, 'I say strengthen your hand, not your soul.'

Eduardo was confused. What was Coco driving at? The situation was both comic and tragic. He looked at his hands. Why should he have to strengthen them? He thought it would be wise to leave the banker's office at that moment. One more step and he would land head first into Coco's stomach. He had already been swallowed whole during the first moments of the interview. Coco had had him in his mouth all this time. It was an extremely uncomfortable position to be in. Coco ate people.

'I can't understand a thing,' Eduardo said. He was on the verge of tears.

'You'll understand everything,' Coco assured him, sinking well back into his swivel chair. 'I'm a man of very few words, but this occasion demands that I explain in detail exactly what the situation is like. I'm seventy. We say what? Seventy. Eighty. One hundred years, maybe? What's time? Smoke, really. There was hardly time to catch a bus in the first few years.'

Eduardo felt inclined to pay homage to the old man. He said, 'Be that as it may, there still remains the satisfaction of having done one's duty.'

Coco looked at him as though he were a rat. He wanted to kick him. Instead, he said, 'I certainly worked hard. Morning to evening. Later on, I indulged in the pleasures of life. People hate me because of my yacht, my villa at the beach, my hunting lodge, the women I have had fun with, but they should also feel sorry for me. I am ready to give away the last penny I have, not as a saint, but as Coco, the banker. What does society expect from a seventy year old banker who has one hundred million? Society expects the banker to become a philanthropist. That is my situation now, and I can't be an exception to the rules of society. I must not postpone my philanthropy for a single minute longer. I'm sinning now. I'm not married. I haven't any children. I lead a clean life because I have to. I don't want my money to go to an institution when I die. The thought keeps me awake for months on end. Fortunately, Eduardo, you have given me the solution to my problem. I shall be grateful to you.'

Eduardo felt as if he had been catapulted out of his chair, straight into the air, so happy that the old man's closing remark had put matters on a normal basis. He said, 'We will be mutually grateful, in that case.'

'Don't be silly,' Coco said coldly. 'Only I will be grateful, as a result of all this. As for you, I think you'll probably curse me.'

'I don't understand.'

'You will. Write the following: *Coco, I want one million.*'

'Is that all?' Eduardo asked him. 'Are you satisfied with just that on a scrap of paper? Should I sign it?'

'You're to sign it when you finish.'

'But, sir, I have already finished. It didn't take me a second.'

'True,' Coco said, 'but the money will be yours only if you copy what you've just written down one million times.'

Eduardo felt the sting of moral humiliation and greed, all at the same time. The outward effect of the collision was localised in his skin and in the pupils of his eyes. He said adamantly, 'Madness!'

'The only kind I'm interested in,' Coco said. "Philanthropy for philanthropy's sake is senseless. No variety in it. Endowments to one hundred servants, protection of painters and poets, founding of asylums. I loathe charitable organisations. I was to be an original philanthropist. Classical philanthropists earn the affection of the persons they help. I wish to earn their hatred. Wouldn't you say that's a happy combination of philanthropy and cruelty?'

Eduardo hadn't been listening. Coco didn't mind. He knew that Eduardo was multiplying and dividing. A human being's highest degree of excitement is represented by the thought of possessing money. The thought was enough.

Eduardo managed to say, 'My life expectancy would not be sufficient to enable me to finish the writing job for the million pesos.'

'Time can be overcome through work,' Coco told him. 'The years will grow fewer and fewer, if you'll write the phrase an increasing number of times every day. Anyway, let the figures speak for themselves. I'll only explain four of the infinite number of possible combinations of time and number-sequences. How old are you?'

'Just turned thirty.' Eduardo was sad.

'Fine. My four combinations are feasible, though the first mightn't really be as wholly so, as the other three will be, when you hear what they are.' He smiled. 'If you write fifty times a day, *Coco, I want one million,* you'll need twenty thousand days to reach the million. Now, then, twenty thousand days is another way of saying fifty-five years, six months and twenty days. I don't think this would tempt you at all. Besides being my prisoner for many years (we'll discuss this at the right time), you'd be seeing your strength diminish progressively. Helplessness, frustration, hatred and disgust would claim you. That's not for you.'

Eduardo said dismally, 'No.'

'The second solution,' Coco continued, 'though problematic, would afford you pleasures of a modest kind, in your old age. Sad pleasures, mind you. So, for that, you simply double your daily task. You write the phrase one hundred times a day, and you end up needing ten thousand days to reach the million. How many years, Eduardo?'

'Never!' Eduardo was very nearly hysterical. 'I won't accept that. It's as cruel as the first choice.'

'Almost as bad. You'd need twenty-seven years, nine months and ten days.'

'Please, sir,' Eduardo implored. 'Would you like to spend years and years copying a stupid phrase?'

'Frankly, I wouldn't.'

'Well, then?' He clenched his fists. 'Remember the axiom, "Do unto others . . .".'

Coco reminded him, 'A man who has one hundred million can afford to forget the Bible. I wish to do unto others what I do not wish for myself. I wish, for example, to have you spend many years copying a stupid phrase.'

'I still have the choice of refusing to do it,' Eduardo pointed out. 'Then, you won't be able to see your scheme through.'

Coco was unimpressed. 'I don't like to waste time with useless remarks. Do you want to hear the third combination?'

Eduardo was curious. He nodded.

Coco said, 'Get a hold of yourself. We're going into high gear. You'll soon see how we leave decades behind at a fantastic speed. And remember, work, blessed thing that it is, makes it ultimately possible for all of us to conquer time. Well, now, you can reach your destination in only two thousand days, just two thousand days of writing *Coco, I want one million.* Don't think I'm trying to deceive you. You must be aware that the emotion produced by so intense a pleasure can cause you to calculate inaccurately. Be careful. Anyway, figures never lie.

If you write the phrase five hundred times a day, you'll only need two thousand days. Have courage and faith, Eduardo. Five short years, plus six months and twenty days. That's all.'

Eduardo's spirits rose. He had visions of possessing a million pesos just like that. He said, 'Didn't you say that there was a fourth possibility? It must be the most advantageous of the lot for the borrower.'

'You're right,' Coco said. 'The idea is to shorten the time required for the job. If you'll write one thousand times a day *Coco, I want one million,* in two years, nine months and ten days the money will be yours.'

'What's the catch?' Eduardo wanted to know, surprised at the apparently short time necessary to do the task.

'There's no catch in it. I play fair, as always. You should watch out for your courage, Eduardo. After you get used to hell, it's far too easy to live in it.'

'You can have your hell and your millions. I'll find somebody who'll lend me the original thousand I came to you for.'

'No doubt about it, Eduardo. Some people will lend a thousand, and others, one million. I, for example.'

Eduardo pretended not to hear. He thought: With one thousand pesos, borrowed on the usual loan-terms in town, I will be able to get married and my money worry will be under control.

'I'm at your disposal,' Coco said.

Eduardo said, 'This is our first and last meeting. I'll see myself out. As a first move, I will get up, right now, and this will prove that I'm a free man.'

But Eduardo thought again. He chose the quickest method of repayment. It would take him over four hours a day. At a rate of five a minute, he could write the phrase one thousand times in exactly three hours and twenty minutes. Since Coco had placed no limit on the number of times he could copy the phrase in one day, Eduardo was at liberty to double and even treble his daily stint if he felt so inclined. And that's precisely what he did from the very beginning. He plunged vigorously into the business of proving himself. At midnight, he had finished three thousand phrases. He was tired but very happy. He had divided the time into three periods: the first thousand, from

9.00 a.m. until 12.20 p.m.; the second thousand, from 3.00 p.m. to 6.20 p.m.; and the third thousand, from 9.00 p.m. until 12.20 a.m.

There were very good reasons for Eduardo's astute approach. The first and most important one was that, under the terms of the agreement, he had to remain confined to a cell. Coco was firm about this. The second was that he had to bear the extra burden of humiliation to prove that he was taking his work seriously. And finally, distractions of any kind were not allowed. Coco was convinced that Eduardo should tackle his job with wholehearted devotion.

Eduardo mused: I'll be his prisoner for about a year. I'll show the old goat that I have more guts than he had when he was making his one hundred million. And, after all, my situation isn't all that bad. I'm no common prisoner. I'm not a criminal whose crime is known throughout the society. Nobody, except Coco and my girl friend, Maria, knows where I am. In the meantime, I'll keep on writing and soon I'll surprise that multi-millionaire dictator.

He wrote to his girl friend:

*Dear Maria,*

*I feel at home. Your loving Eduardo has written* Coco, I want one million *ninety thousand times already. Aren't you proud of me? Just think, in a little over a year, we'll have that fine sum of money. Think what we could do with a million: jewellery, exquisite clothes, and what's even more important, not having to see Coco ever again. That, in itself, is worth a million.*

*I must tell you that I've made two hundred and twenty-four errors up to now, and that adds up to approximately ten hours' work. I'll have to be careful. The worst thing I can do is to take an adventurous course. This could lead to disaster.*

*A thousand kisses from your Eduardo.*

He was now nearing the half-million mark. And yet, something deep inside him told him that he was approaching the limit of his strength. The very first symptom was registered in his stomach. After five months of confinement, he had great difficulty in swallowing hard foods. He felt full all the time. Indeed, he felt as if a cancer was gradually invading his vital organs. He dreaded his three meals a day. Sometimes he vomited, sometimes he gagged terribly. During his daily visits, Coco never failed to suggest an all-round slower pace, but Eduardo wouldn't listen to anything as subversive as that. His motto was: Do or die!

Slowly he came to realise that Coco was not his worst enemy. At most, he was the symbol of the humiliation imposed by one man on another, and the humilitated man could always resist by choosing the right weapon. Eduardo's would be contempt. But how could he engage his energy in that, when he had so much writing to do?

His thoughts became gloomier every day. He climbed the steps leading to the roof of his cell where he took his usual afternoon stroll. He barely answered the guard's warm greeting as he rushed up to the landing. He flung himself down like a dog and started to fight off a bombardment of imaginary flies. After a while, he stopped beating the air with his hands and allowed a feeling of torpor to creep through his body. He was surprised to hear a child's voice nearby. There was another, too, mature and rather authoritative. Eduardo opened his eyes and saw a handsome boy of about twelve, and a young woman, who seemed to be his mother. Pointing to the man lying on the floor, she whispered something in the child's right ear. The boy looked at Eduardo and burst out laughing. Eduardo was about to say something, anything, to the woman, when the child put his arms around Eduardo's legs and said, 'I write the same thing as you do.'

Eduardo felt as though the world were coming to an end. He held the child against his chest, but he tore himself away and shouted, *'Coco, I want one million.'*

Things became clear later. The woman (the child's mother, as it turned out) was one of the many persons who had asked Coco for money. She had wanted only one hundred pesos, an amount not in keeping with Coco's fine sensibility. Instead, she was forced to accept the traditional million.

Eduardo wrote to Maria:

*My dearest,*

Yesterday, it was one year since the beginning of my confinement. Coco taunts me with the fact that a few more phrases will land me on Easy Street.

About a week ago, he came to my cell to torture me about the possibilities of my being a success or a failure. Then he said, 'At my age, it would be childish to go beyond the one hundred million mark. On the other hand, to reduce it would be catastrophic. Do you understand how ridiculous my position would be if I were to reduce my fortune to ninety-nine million?'

My darling, I felt desolated. I felt choked. I thought he meant that my case was lost, that the million I had fought so hard for had vanished like a dream. I begged. I implored. I explained that, even though my writing had lately become very slow, I hadn't given up yet. He smiled, patted my shoulder affectionately and said that I shouldn't be alarmed, that I hadn't lost yet and that his little speech had nothing to do with my own case, as such, but rather with somebody called José something or other.

This was an astutely calculated blow. I wasn't surprised by the existence of a José, who, like myself, was also in solitary confinement. Nothing could surprise me any more after my meeting with the child prisoner. Besides, it's only logical that Coco should have many voluntary prisoners. The shock didn't register because he told me that one of his prisoners had failed in his writing job. What floored me was his comparing José's case with mine. José had been almost within grasp of the prize. He had managed to write Coco, I want one million *eight hundred thousand times*, but that is as far as he got. His brain had become completely befogged. Coco told me about it. José's first slump was marked by a feeling of mental physiological fullness, not being able to contain his own thoughts or to swallow any kind of food at all. The second slump was characterised by a complete incapacity for writing. Something like an unconditional surrender to the phrase. Coco said that, like a lunatic, utterly obsessed with the dictates of his derangement, José would spend his remaining days monotonously humming Coco,

I want one million.

As it was to be expected, Eduardo did not make it. Now, after five years, the bitter taste left in his mouth by the celebrated phrase will remain with him to his dying day. After having 'earned' thousands of hypothetical pesos, he has had to accept the one hundred real pesos which Coco has allotted him each month. This means that Eduardo is merely one among many humble employees of the powerful banking firm, Coco & Co. He was given the job of a modest assistant cashier, thanks to his dear Maria. She was wise enough to get on her knees and beg the philanthropist to be merciful.

In fact, Eduardo handles millions which have to be correctly balanced every day by closing time, that is, by six in the evening. Nothing could be easier for Eduardo. Naturally, he never fails to stop the machine. Otherwise, it would continue adding tens of millions quite unconcernedly.

(Translated by the Book Institute in Havana
and adapted by the Editor).

# SAMUEL FEIJÓO

## *Soldier Eloy*

Eloy was born in the traditional peasant community of Vega Vieja Valley. His mother was a hard-working, pleasant mulatto; his father was a burly Galician whose constant boast was that he had laid more tiles on the San Juan-Potrerillo railroad than any other man.

Eloy was the fifth of nine children. From very early childhood, he was fully exposed to the usual drudgery of life on his parents' small holding. He was up at two o'clock in the mornings, during the Island 'winter' months of December and January, milking cows, wrestling with calves, weeding and plowing the fields, and afterwards selling the milk in the town.

He had had very little time to go to the Valley school. His mother taught him to read, but she was just barely literate herself. His father, who had never been to school, always spoke of his own illiteracy and complained bitterly of the pathetic lack of educational facilities in the Valley. Often he would say to his wife, 'If the children could study a little, they would shake off the slavery of the farm. As it is, they'll die working and never get anywhere.'

No teacher ever came to the Valley. However, two Rural Guards came, from time to time, on their sleek horses. They would be greeted like dignitaries and presented with turkeys and chickens by the frightened small farmers, who, once the presentation was over, would stand and stare at them with fear and suspicion. And, of course, the politician came, smiling patronisingly, flattering everybody, seeking votes for himself and promising a variety of jobs that never materialised.

Eloy was tall and well built, like his father. As the years went on, one of the Rural Guards was shrewd enough to notice the fact. The politician was told about it, and he made a proposal to Eloy's parents. 'I'll get the boy into the Army,' he promised. 'It'll have to be give and take the whole way, though. You bring me a hundred *cédulas* and I'll fix things for Eloy with the Colonel.'

The offer was very attractive to Eloy. Knowing the politician's habit of lying, Eloy's family put up a show of concern and doubt, but after a very short private consultation, the politician was told to go ahead with his plan. Eloy's mother said, 'If the boy becomes a recruit, he's definitely on Easy Street. Little work and a pay-cheque. Free food and clothing and enough money to help us a little.'

But Eloy's father, nobody's foolish Galician, didn't really like the looks of the thing, the politician or the future that lay ahead for Eloy outside the Valley. He said, 'A recruit is the least thing anyone would want to be. From Corporal to Lieutenant, everyone gives him the boot in his backside. In the Army, he won't learn a thing; he won't get anywhere. No education or anything, and possibly he will turn out to be like the other shiftless soldiers.'

But no one paid any attention to him. The family called on their neighbours, rounded up as many votes as they were able to and secured very firm promises from the slightly uncertain ones. The result was remarkable: more than one hundred *cédulas*. The politician came round, collected them and returned later with Eloy's appointment papers.

He embraced Eloy stylishly, handed him the official envelope and said, 'It's give and take. Here's your job. Take this envelope and report to the Army Headquarters in Las Villas.'

They embraced again and set off together for the town and a new life for Eloy. He carried a small bag with a change of underwear, a pair of socks, a shirt and a pair of work trousers. He was wearing his off-white drill *guayabera* which he wore only on Sundays, and extra thick trousers which were shiny and worn at the knees. At Army Headquarters, he was assigned to the Santa Clara barracks. There he made friends with the soldiers who were themselves of peasant origin, and easily adapted himself to the discipline of the strange military life. He was happy and proud of his khaki uniform and of the weapons he had to handle and care for, which made him feel curiously responsible and put him within reach of the seat of real authority. He felt very important and he enjoyed the distance which his new position had put between him and the poverty of the farm and the *bohío* and the futile struggle with the land.

At first, he helped his parents a little with a few pesos every month. One day, he appeared at the farm in his uniform, and dazzled his family and the neighbours with his rifle and military kit. His face seemed bleached by the city.

His father asked, 'Are you studying, boy?' His voice sounded as though he knew what Eloy would say.

He said, 'Not yet.'

'That's bad, Eloy. You'll be a nobody. Well-dressed and clean on the outside, but an idiot inside.'

They laughed and embraced, and shortly afterwards, Eloy left for the barracks.

He liked being a soldier. He owned up to the truth that he wasn't studying because he didn't care much for reading, and besides, life was easy. Of course, knowing the value of money, he didn't squander it, and he continued to help his parents, until he met Eulalia. After that, what little he earned, he spent on presents for her.

Then he asked her to live with him. He rented a room, furnished it modestly and soon began to get into a tangle of financial difficulties. He told himself that he loved his Eulalia, and he went on trying to give her whatever she wanted.

One evening, as he was about to go on leave, he was stopped by Lieutenant Valladares. He said, 'You can't go now. Tomorrow, we're going to Río Chiquito to perform an eviction ceremony.'

Eloy didn't understand what the Lieutenant meant but he obeyed as usual. He had been taught to obey his superiors blindly. He sent a message to Eulalia, and resigned himself to his bad luck.

They left on horseback at dawn. Soon they reached the open country with its deserted plains and lonely fields. The morning sun was already up, and the birds were singing and the buzzards were circling overhead. The subtle scent of the green grass hung everywhere over the landscape. Eloy felt the exhilaration of his childhood returning to him. He was going back to where he belonged. The sun made him feel free, as he rode along, humming a *décima*.

After riding for about six hours, they reached Río Chiquito. There, in a clearing, Eloy saw the people who lived in a shabby *bohío*: their tattered clothes, the thinness of their faces, their bare feet, the naked children in the women's arms, their faded eyes and silent, mucous-sealed lips.

The Lieutenant said, 'You've got to go. You're evicted.'

The head of the family replied humbly, 'We don't know where to go.'

'We're sorry,' the Lieutenant said. 'We're really very sorry, but the law is the law. You must go.'

An old man said, 'The law is unjust. We've always paid our rent.'

The Lieutenant frowned. 'I've got the eviction order here. That's what counts. The land isn't yours. Out you go. Pick up your things, put them on the ox cart and leave now. I want no arguments.'

Eloy watched the terrible scene. He was silent and upset. He saw the bony arms of the people making desperate efforts to lift the shaky iron beds and the rickety wardrobe with two boards missing, the pine table rotted by termites, the wooden plow, the stone water-filter, the large earthen jar, and he thought of his own family. This could happen to them too. He felt miserable.

They escorted the family as far as a coconut grove and watched them disappear around a distant bend in the road. Then the eviction squad went back to the *bohío* and set it on fire, as the Lieutenant had ordered. Eloy stood perplexed, with a fire brand in his hand and his skin shining in the glow of the blaze from the squashed hut.

On his way back to Headquarters, galloping through the fields, the landscape seemed to threaten Eloy. Nothing was beautiful any more. He felt guilty. He kept on seeing the evicted farmers, their faces, and the awful fate awaiting their family in the countryside, where there was no employment and where they would be exposed to the hardships and uncertainty of the 'dead season'.

When Eloy arrived at the barracks, he didn't feel inclined to stay there talking with the small group of men among the peasant recruits with whom he had become particularly friendly. Later that night, he found no consolation in the affection and companionship which Eulalia offered him.

He had to go on another unpleasant mission during the sugar harvest. The workers at the local Mill went on strike, after demanding a revision of their wage-scale and having had it turned down. When the soldiers marched up to the *batey*, they dragged many of the workers out of their houses and arrested them. Eloy looked at their faces. They were peasants like himself. One worker contended that he and his fellow cane cutters were acting lawfully. He said, 'We're on strike because the Mill owners won't give us a fair deal, and never will, unless we show them that we mean business.'

The Lieutenant was extremely brutal in his supervision of the arrests. 'Get on the truck if you know what's good for all of you,' he roared, glaring at the workers around him. None of them disobeyed. The soldiers aimed their rifles directly at their heads. The workers climbed silently into the back of the truck and squatted together.

Eloy watched the truck as it drove off, and he felt a twinge of remorse. That same day, he patrolled the cane fields. With his rifle at the ready, he strolled along the cane rows, dutifully prepared to shoot any striker attempting to set fire to the plantation.

The following day, while he was on guard duty at the deserted *batey*, a small boy came up to him and said, 'My mother is sick and I have to take her to the doctor. Please help me lift her. There's nobody around. They're all gone away somewhere.' Eloy went into the hut and lifted the emaciated woman from the dirt floor.

'She has very bad attacks,' the boy said.

'Where's your father?' Eloy asked.

'He's gone.'

Eloy looked at the boy compassionately. The woman was breathing faintly. She opened her eyes.

'Where's your husband?' he asked her.

'He's a striker. He's in prison.'

Eloy stared at the walls of the hut and saw the signs of poverty which he had lived with in his family *bohío*. He recognised the broken makeshift stove, the chipped earthenware pot, the bottomless chairs and the ragged bedclothes.

'He's in prison,' the boy said.

Eloy had put on a fair amount of weight. His life was easy. He couldn't ask for more. His work was undemanding, straightforward and completely different from the rough and continuous chores on his family's small holding. He closed his eyes, often, and recalled his dirty clothes and mud-caked shoes. He remembered how poverty-stricken he was. He swore to himself that he wouldn't change his position, now, for anything or anybody. He had known squalour and destitution. Nothing would be able to persuade him to give up his uniform and his regular pay-cheque, not even a loving command from Eulalia, nor their two year old son. He was protected in the Army. His job was steady. He cashed his cheque and did his routine military duties and he lived. Nothing worried him much, politics or abuses or the so called crimes of those in power. He was safe. The world was like that, and he had a position to maintain; he was a soldier. That was enough. Only now and again did he think of the evicted peasants and of the striker's small son.

In the Island world in which Eloy lived, the Government was not faring well. There had been many uprisings in the mountains. Tyranny was reaping a curious harvest, and already the soldiers had had to leave the barracks, frequently, and march into the hills to fight the rebels. The days were no longer quiet. War was bitter in its reality and Eloy knew that he would have to face up to it. He was no coward. He knew how to obey. Before he was sent off to the front, Eulalia hung the customary religious medals round his neck. She made him wear a special image of the Sacred Heart which she had embroidered to protect him against death, and she gave him a copy of *The Prayer of the Just Judge* to read and carry along in his kit. Eloy accepted everything she pressed on him. He kissed his son and embraced Eulalia. She cried as she stood and waved to him.

Eloy knew that the rebels were fighting against a Government they considered bad for the Island. But he confided to himself the fact that most, if not all, governments are bad, and that he would have to serve under one of them in his present position as a soldier. He resigned himself to his fate. The world seemed complex. What was Eloy to do? He wondered.

His Lieutenant went along with him and led the detachment. After a very hard journey of six days, they reached their objective.

'I hope this is over quickly,' Eloy told his friend, Julián, a fellow peasant recruit.

'So do I,' Julián said. 'This one is going to take time, though. Still, they can't beat us. There's no resisting the Army, not with what we have on our side.'

Eloy smiled. He was grateful for the comforting words. A cool breeze blew through the trees which sheltered them. He stared up at the Sierra. He saw the buzzards flying high, like small black moving specks dotting the dark blue sky. Up there, he said to himself doubtfully. There they are.

The detachment started climbing at dawn. They moved slowly behind a small reconnaissance patrol which had set off a few minutes earlier. The rest of the soldiers marched in single file at a distance of some yards from each other so as not to offer themselves as easy targets for the snipers hidden in the trees up on the side of the hill. Eloy sensed that death was waiting behind most of the tree trunks in the area, and he felt that his tired friends realised it only too well.

After a particularly long and cautious march, which lasted for about five hours, they camped at the foot of a hill and Eloy stood guard over the detachment. He positioned himself behind a massive rock overlooking the deep valley which was studded with royal palms and blanketed with heavy mist. And yet, he could see the sea which looked like a pale blue streak in the distance. He admired the view and waited.

Julián, his fellow guard, said, 'I hate being stuck in here with all this bush and stuff around us.'

'Same here,' Eloy said.

They stared at the horizon and tried to find some possible trace of the rebels.

The shooting broke out at sunset. No one knew where the shots came from. The sentries lost their nerve under the cumulative stress of the situation, and fired wild into the surrounding bushland.

Very early next day, they were climbing from one low hill

to another, covering each ridge carefully and passing through the ravines quickly. It was cold and wet. Fog cloaked the tree tops. Rain dripped from the leaves. Mud everywhere.

'Can't see a thing,' Julián complained.

'Why don't we turn back?' Eloy asked.

At a little after mid-morning, a group of rebels ambushed the detachment and fired on the soldiers in the vanguard. They fell, as they were accurately mowed down by the rebels' rifle fire which was very difficult to trace. Eloy saw his friends stumble and fall, pale and moaning. The Lieutenant rallied Eloy's platoon, waving his pistol and shouting, 'Our turn to attack, now. Move up, everybody!'

Eloy placed himself at the head of the column. The encounter lasted only a few minutes. The rebels withdrew into the thicket of the bushland and a baffling silence fell over everything.

The following day, the detachment went into action, having walked straight up to a spray of bullets coming from a sheltered pine grove. Three soldiers were killed in the first few seconds. Julián was cut down shortly afterwards. Eloy aimed his rifle at the trees in the direction of the entrance of a wood near by. The Lieutenant ordered the detachment to attack by instinct. 'That's where they are,' he screamed, and pointed to a wide arc in front of the men. 'The guerrillas are there, all right. Move in and flush them out!'

The soldiers advanced, running as fast as they could under the crossfire between the vanguard and the guerrillas. A few men fell before they could reach the wood. Eloy leapt over their bodies, doing his job, instinctively, as the Lieutenant expected of him, searching the immediate area and advancing well ahead of the rest of the detachment. He found nobody among the cluster of trees. Again, the ghost fighters had disappeared before they could be spotted. On his way back to the detachment, he stumbled on a bearded young man who was lying still against the lower part of the trunk of a tree which had been splattered by machine gun fire. Eloy approached him very quietly, thinking that he would seize him without a struggle and take him back to the Lieutenant. He saw the guerrilla's blood splashed on the tree and the fresh trickles staining the ground around him. Eloy lifted him gently and swung his limp body over his shoulders and prepared to carry him to the detachment position on the other side of the wood. The guerrilla weighed very little. He was thin. His uniform was dirty and torn. After walking for a while, Eloy felt tired. He eased the man down on to the grass. Eloy rested and listened. The action had stopped completely.

'Thirsty,' the guerrilla said. 'Water.'

Eloy raised his rifle and aimed it at the man's face. He looked into the sunken sockets of his eyes and couldn't help noticing the obvious signs of helplessness and fever.

'Water,' the guerrilla said again. His voice was low.

Eloy assisted him to drink from his own Army canteen and continued to watch his face. It was like his, a peasant's face, telling the usual story of anguish and poverty.

'Thanks.'

'That's all right,' Eloy said. He didn't know what to do next.

'I'm badly wounded.'

'No, you're not, I don't think,' Eloy told him.

'I'm dying.'

Eloy thought about the guerrilla's future as a prisoner. As soon as he was handed over to the Lieutenant, he would be executed. The Lieutenant would do it himself. He had already killed two guerrillas because they couldn't tell him where the others were hidden in the Sierra.

'How old are you?' Eloy asked.

'Nineteen.'

Eloy looked away. If he's taken in, the Lieutenant will kill him. He should be left right here for his own safety. He might make it back to the guerrillas. Yet, he mightn't live much longer. He's very badly wounded.

The young man knew that Eloy was trying to decide what to do with him. He pleaded with his eyes. 'Come with us, soldier,' he told Eloy. 'Join us.'

Eloy hesitated. He didn't know what to say. He was sure that he didn't like his detachment duties. He disliked the Lieutenant and he didn't really approve of the Government. He was confused.

'Come with us,' the guerrilla repeated. 'Carry me and I'll guide you.'

Eloy decided. He got up and said, 'I'm going to spare your

life. You're a peasant like me. Get out of the area as soon as you can.'

'I can't. I can't escape. If you're going to leave, kill me first. I don't want to die here alone. Carry me to my people and join the Revolution.'

Eloy said nothing. He turned his back on the man and walked out of the wood.

'We thought you were dead,' a soldier said, when he saw Eloy walking through the detachment clearing. 'They ambushed us, you know. Two of our men were killed on the spot. Others got into the wood and didn't come back.'

That night, the soldiers couldn't sleep. They were waiting for a surprise attack. Eloy was thinking about the wounded guerrilla's offer. He felt that he would go, but for Eulalia and their son. Indeed, starting all over again, from the bottom, would be tough, and besides, the Army was all right, in its own way. And there was all that suffering in the open, in the wood and in the Sierra. The wounded man was likeable. Will he live, though?

Eloy felt that he would like to put the whole miserable business right by wishing it all away. Then he wondered whether he should have granted the guerrilla's request and killed him. It would have been merciful. He was convinced that he couldn't have done it. Not just like that.

The detachment had a very early breakfast. Eloy hid two bananas, a tin of condensed milk and some crackers in the front of his shirt, and, at the first clear opportunity, he disappeared into the wood. The guerrilla was very pale. He was raving. His fever had soared.

'I've brought you something to eat,' Eloy whispered.

The man didn't recognise him. Eloy put the food down on the grass and wondered what course of action he should take. If I carry him, now, he argued with himself, I won't know where to go. Even if I decided to take the chance and go with him, I wouldn't know where his band of guerrillas had moved on to.

Suddenly, Eloy and the wounded man were surrounded by rifles. The Lieutenant was hysterical with rage. He said, 'We've got to hang you both. You, Eloy, you're a traitor. You must hang!'

Eloy saw the rope. He saw the noose. He didn't put up a struggle. When the column left the wood, the Lieutenant's aide looked back to see whether the two bodies were still moving, and he saw that the strong winds, blowing straight down from the Sierra, were making them swing back and forth.

The Lieutenant tried to work out the meaning of the expression on his aide's face, as he caught him staring at the dangling bodies. 'I never liked Eloy,' he said, scratching his eyebrows and squeezing the bridge of his nose. "I never trusted him. He wasn't a safe person. There was something strange about him.'

The aide didn't reply. He was puzzled.

They crossed a shallow stream. The surface of the water rippled under the force of the strong Sierra winds. There was a fine overlay of grey sand on both banks.

The Lieutenant knelt down and washed the skin just above his eyebrows where a mosquito had stung him and raised a small itchy bump.

(Translated by the Book Institute in Havana
and adapted by the Editor)

# VÍCTOR AGOSTINI

## *Pepe*

(A Monologue: a fragment from a long short story, *Rebirth*)

If you don't work, you don't get paid, and since now we don't have a trade union to fight our fights for us, we'll see what's paid and with what, because as far as I'm concerned, I'm not going out of here, not in a pig's eye. It's fine in here, knowing what's going on, and we're safe in here, watching television for the last day and a half, and everything's happening out there and we're in here with plenty of tinned milk, coffee, crackers, rice and beans, candles, matches, soap, and with the lights out four days, so that they can't cut off the electricity, and we can continue watching television and keep up with everything that's going on out there, while we sit comfortably in here. And we've heard some shots. It's true. Especially Eneida. She has become most frightened, when there are continuous shots, like from a machine gun, but that isn't often, and it has to be that way, as I explained to her, when people go on a stampede after having been repressed for a long time and everything is seen in a different light. The noises are funny and different. Everything's different. Things change. But fast! Not slowly, as they used to change, slowly, in the barracks, in the prisons, in the training camps, and at the fine mansions. Many things were done to the people. People, nearly all the people, weren't happy about the situation, but many things were done and big money was made by a few and they could be seen driving tremendous cars with large fishtails, two-tone cars that were a sight for sore eyes. And they were all over the place. And there were the people with real power who threw their weight around and who built marvellous houses in the new developments and raised welts on other people's backs. Of course, it wasn't the same people who built the big houses who raised the welts on the people's skin; we're talking about those who could really handle, not the cars, but the whips and the sticks and the rubber hoses; they also drove cars but their cars were all alike with large painted numbers on them and special radios that brought information to them like the numbers of reported cars; some were dressed as civilians and they gave the orders and lived high, and their cars weren't equipped with special equipment except maybe air conditioning to be able to roll up the bullet-proof windows and be cool inside; the others, dressed alike in blue or yellow clothes, were strong and fleshy, with eyes like hawks, and sat comfortably as they rode always listening for information coming through their equipment; they also had those long and sharp-pointed black things, some of which were used to raise welts and the brighter ones to make holes. All this went on and on. People got to the point where they saw them and shrugged; everybody kept his mouth shut and lowered his eyes and busied himself. Working people were careful of what they said, and they worked hard; there was nothing else to do. Eneida would tell me to watch my step, keep my mouth shut, not to let anybody get anything out of me, be careful. Eneida loves me; she didn't want anything to happen to me like those who rode in the numbered cars; she didn't want anything to happen. Wherever anything happened, they were there, with their long shiny machines, but it would be the same. Eneida would always tell me, going to work and coming back, to mind my own business and hold my tongue; she always told me things like that; she would never tell me, for example, that we must change things, that something must be done; she never would tell me it was necessary to do away with this mess, to get together with the others who feel the same and do something; she never thought of telling me not to shave any more, not to have my hair cut any more, grow a beard, so that you can show your opposition to this mess all over the place. She loves me and wouldn't tell me that there are other women who perhaps were telling their men, their husbands, their brothers, to do just that; they probably loved them very much when they told them to do that, but they told them to do it; they loved their men folk very much and at the same time they loved other things very much, so they advised their men not to shave and not to have their hair cut and to take to the hills, to the highest hills, and to wear olive green clothes, and endure the cold and hunger and torment, and to carry the long shiny instruments like the other ones the men in the numbered cars always carried; and those women loved their men when they advised them to do that. But Eneida loves me very much; she feeds me when I'm not working at the cafe, because when I work, Pierre, the chef, feeds me. Eneida does my laundry and tends to the house, our one-room thing, divided into two by a curtain. She sews buttons on my clothes and wakes me up in time to go straight to work, minding my own business. But the other women who must have loved their men still told them to go to the hills where they'll be given a rifle or a machete, anything, maybe, a home-made shotgun, anything. You should really go to the hills where you'll be able to breathe clean fresh air, and with a home-made shotgun, you'll be able to get better things, even if you have to fight for them. Very often, the best things have to be fought for, tooth and nail, taking them away from somebody who isn't the rightful owner of those things, and who will not turn them loose, until they are wrenched by force from him. But Eneida loves me very much. She has been good to me. She sits, now, next to me, and we both watch on television the things that have taken place from the hills to the plains, the men who have travelled from the hills to the plains and now come in carrying their long black shiny instruments which they won't turn loose when they meet the people; they come riding in metal vehicles which also roll along the streets like those long fish-tailed ones which used to be seen on the streets with their windows rolled up and the air-conditioning blowing inside; those cars that used to roll along and didn't allow their passengers to breathe fresh air but a special brand of canned air that was different from the outside air that the people had to breathe. These vehicles, now, are bulkier and ugly. They make more noise and they don't glide along like the others. They come to be seen and to force open the way with their guns which don't fire any more. They come to be welcomed and loved. Riding on them are the men who had been told by their women to go to the hills and get some kind of shotgun there and breathe the fresh air and capture one of those bulky noisy ugly vehicles that shoot large sharp-pointed bullets, one after the other, when it's absolutely necessary to do so. Now, it isn't necessary to shoot, and those men are here among us, those men who haven't shaved or had a hair-cut in months; they are wrinkled and they wear torn shoes and they are dirty but they hold their heads up when they're greeted. You can see their eyes. They shine brightly through a maze of uncombed hair. The bearded men look around them, smile and raise their arms while still holding their rifles tightly in their hands; sometimes, they wouldn't be holding them but rather wearing them crisscross on their backs. They are at ease. Later, they are like a lioness when she has her cubs next to her and the master lion is sleeping in a corner and the meat ration has been thrown into the cage. Eneida looks at the bearded men, smiles and touches my hand. She's now just a little like a lioness; but no, she's more like a woolly puppy who's no longer in need of scrounging around in the city's garbage bins or begging for meat scraps. She chuckles, looks at me and tells me to notice how the nice, well-dressed television announcer is so pleased to introduce the three bearded rebel fighters whom he asks to say something to their folks in Havana and in the Provinces, and how he embraces them even though they're filthy dirty and their clothes are so ragged. The fighters look at him without knowing what to say. They manage to mumble a few words. You can hardly understand them. They seem to be in a hurry to leave the studio, but the announcer insists that they stay a while longer. The announcer is very nice and expresses himself well. His clothes are very clean and nice. He must have always lived in Havana. He's a well-educated man. He has to be well-educated to be a good television announcer. But when he's introducing the bearded men, with their long hair, which sticks out from under their large hats, which they never take off, you can see that the announcer feels like a priest giving communion, but not so seriously as a real priest. That's what Eneida tells me. And when he smiles, his eyes also shine. Eneida tells me to notice the fighter on the left of the screen, the one without a beard, but with his hair down to his shoulders. What a sweet face he's got, Eneida says. Women can't resist those boyish faces, at all. This fighter has scars on both arms. When he got too close to a grenade, maybe. Or something like that. Many others must have remained up there in the hills, where they breathed the fresh air, but this one made it all the way here, and you can plainly see him smiling and not knowing what to say. When I was his age, I was already installing gambling machines in the bars in Havana and taking tourists to whore houses, where they would pay me a commission; and surely, I knew how to talk, even in English, a little. Three other bearded fighters and five others and a woman fighter, with a rifle in her hand. Eneida tells me that she was in the battle of Santa Clara. All of them hold their rifles and lean on them as you would lean on a friend's arm. I look at Eneida whose eyes are damp, and her lips quiver. I start to say something to her, but I wait a little; I feel something in my throat, just as if I might be catching a cold, or something like that. I know that if I speak, now, my voice will sound funny, all because those five bearded men and the woman and the young boy with the pretty face and the scars on his arms can hardly speak, and the nice, well-dressed announcer has to speak for them. He talks all the time but much more meaning gets across to me from the silence of the fighters. But Eneida reaches for my hand. Her hand is warm, and she holds mine tenderly and firmly, while, with the other hand, she wipes her eyes, and then she calls my attention to a bearded fighter who recites poetry well. Another group of shabbily dressed, silent men appears on the screen. These men stand first on one leg, then on the other, nervously scratching the backs of their necks, and coughing, and again, they stand on the other leg, like cranes, sort of; but one of them speaks for all of them; he wears a broad-brimmed hat with the front part folded over and pinned to the crown with a Cuban shield, like the *Mambí* fighters used to wear in the War of Independence we had against Spain in '95. This bearded fighter talks and laughs with the announcer. He says that he's a poet and he recites a pretty poem about his country and the War and freedom. He recites with such a lack of self that his comrades become very serious and they move about changing their weapons from one hand to the other. We particularly like the end, because, then, everybody applauds, and I can swallow, more easily, and blow my nose. I start thinking whether these men, I see now on the screen, had ever been able to go to the docks, as I did, when I was their age, and ride in a car with American tourists and take them down to Sloppy

Joe's, and make five and ten bucks' commission, and take them, men and even women tourists, to the raw burlesque shows, and later, to the whore houses. I just wonder. No. You have to wear nicer clothes and be able to talk smooth. These men must have had a rough time of it to take up the business of not shaving or having a haircut. You can tell by the way they grab their machine guns and bite on their words when they speak, just ordinary, that they never had to take any rough talk from professional tourist cab drivers or had to demand from barkeepers their rightful percentage of what the Yankees spent in their establishments, but you can bet that they never knew what it was like to fuck a high-class Havana broad after having procured her eight or ten well-paying Yankee clients, and stay with her the rest of the night, and all for free; maybe, though, they knew how to count the furrows in a ploughed field, weigh seed, saddle a horse, handle a team of oxen, and on Sundays, in the afternoon time, if the weather was good, stroll around in the park of a nearby town and look at the country girls. These men, with their steady eyes, who stand in front of the television camera, as if they were going to take root there, who can stand there, next to their comrades, for a whole half an hour, without saying a word, dead still, silent, as they were out there, where they lived, in the hills, or on the plains, where they worked the land, and in the woods they cleared to be able to grow something, where when they finished their work and sat at the door of their *bohío* and sighed, they quietly stared and waited for nightfall, are, here, now, and they speak very little, just as they did out there on their lonely land, when they worked it, like heroes. But they have a great deal to tell us. I know that. They could tell us about the mountain country where they have stayed many months, and, some, even for years. They could tell of what made them go there and what drove them to climb higher than they had ever climbed before, where, instead of watching over their crops, they had to watch out for those fellow countrymen of theirs who wear clothes the colour of the bad soil of Cuba. I can see them watching those men and playing a game of hide and seek with them. And the men who were good at watching and at hiding themselves were the better men. And these men, who have come from playing that game and winning it in every way and who were able to come back after playing it, now, stand before the camera as silent as the losers in that game, those who have remained up there in the hills where the fresh fragrant breeze blows but doesn't touch them because of the earth covering their bodies. But, before these bearded men left them there, in the cool earth, they plowed the land and planted strange seeds in it. And besides, there was the matter of the crosses of wood which were put over the losers. But these bearded men and these women who're dressed like men weren't talking, now, about anything like what I've mentioned. They were only giving their names in a very low tone of voice that sometimes couldn't even be heard, and they were giving their hometown addresses, and when the announcer insisted that they should send a greeting to their folks, adding that they should say that they would soon see them, these bearded men and the women with them went along with the announcer and asked if Nico had been able to keep his barber shop open, or if Joaquín was still holding down his job as secretary at the city clerk's office, or if Aunt Ubalda had been able to save her twins; that's the sort of thing that these fighters were asking on television; that's all they asked. That's the sort of people they are, really. Eneida gets up and says that we are too cooped up in the room with the television going, and it's true. We have everything we need in here, but we haven't opened the door or the window in a day and a half. We've been living through the television. We've been seeing the city and the people and everything on television, and not living as we used to, in the street, with everything going on round us. It's hard for me to take my eyes off the television screen lately. In fact, it's a strange thing, but I've been seeing so many quiet eyes and tanned faces and tough weather-beaten, bearded faces, and all of them faces with tender eyes, and smiles that are so still and deep, that I seem to have got that way myself. I smile and say nothing. I don't know whether Eneida notices it, but I feel it about myself. When I try to speak, my throat refuses to let the words through, and it hurts at times, and I ask myself what's happening, and I know that I have to swallow, but I can't swallow at all as I used to before Eneida and I locked ourselves in with the television. My nose runs, too, with the same stuff that comes out of my eyes, but I'm not sad about anything.

I even feel warm inside. I feel like grabbing Eneida and taking her out somewhere to a dance or to some party, but I hold back because she would notice that there's a different something in my eyes and in my mouth, like it was something new I'm feeling moving deep down inside myself which I had never felt before, and I don't want my Eneida to notice it. I don't want anybody to notice it, because I don't know what it is, and if somebody, anybody, should come and ask me, I wouldn't know what to say at all. And perhaps, if I go outside, the people might look at me and they might see something about me which I cannot see about myself but which I, now, feel has definitely taken place inside myself, something like when I get drunk, like the first time I got drunk and felt so good, as if I had changed into somebody else totally different from the person who had taken the first drink at the beginning of the session. I remember how I got rid of all my fears and all my second thoughts that usually hold me back, and I felt like giving away everything to anybody who would take it from me. It was the feeling of a child. As a matter of fact, when I was a child, they say that I used to give away my toys to the other children in our street, just like that, for nothing, at all. Perhaps, if I could get Eneida to dance with me, now, she would look at me and tell me that I am not Pepe, the Pepe, she has lived with for fourteen years; no, I seem like a mad man; I may not be mad, but Eneida would think so anyway. What she's actually trying to tell me is that there are people shouting in the streets, that she can hear shots outside somewhere and that there are people running and shouting all over the place. She looks through the half-opened shutters and she says that she would like to know how those men, those soldiers of the SIM, Batista's men from the Military Intelligence Service, are faring, especially those who were around here the other night, and the policeman down the street and the other policemen who work in this part of the town. She would like to know about Lencho. She would like to know if he's still hiding in that back room and if he has a bed to sleep in, if he has been able to sleep at all, what with all the terrible searching going on for those names on the very special list. I keep on watching television. I don't answer any of Eneida's questions. I can't talk. At this very moment, just as I said what I said to myself, a bearded fighter is embracing a long-haired young man whom he thought had died in the War, and the bearded fighter pats his comrade's back and ruffles his hair and really squeezes him, as if he were trying to kill him. All the others in the studio, the fighters, the men and the women ones, and the television announcer, are watching the scene and not saying anything at all. Everybody is quiet, even the two comrades who are hustling each other with joy and hugging each other. They are quiet. And I am quiet too. But inside, I feel as if I had talked a great deal, as if I had said everything and had nothing else to say. The bearded man finally tells his friend that he had thought he was dead. Then he squeezed the long-haired young man and repeated what he had just said. Dead, I say to myself, but he's very much alive, in front of me, on the television screen; dead, but he's a clean-faced boy with handsome eyes; dead, but he's a fighter with a long black shiny rifle. I think that he could surely have hunted with that righteous rifle, out there, in the country, where he lives. Many things are alive and running around in the country, where he lives, many things, with wide-open eyes like himself, like the new born baby everybody speaks about, down his street, at some time or other. And he's almost a baby, this one, so very young he looks on the television screen, like a baby not because of his age, which is the age of a grown man, but because of the way he looks at the fellow who is embracing him and squeezing him. He's looking at him, as if he's the first thing he ever saw in the world. And the bearded fighter says to him that he thought he was dead. But the baby is alive, dead, alive, dead, alive, dead, alive. A big roaring noise is going on about a block and a half down the street, and Eneida who can no longer hold back her curiosity opens the window a little and takes a look and says that it must be at the house of an informer. It seems, she says, that they're emptying the whole house; yes, they're throwing the furniture out on the street, and the people are shouting and several shots have rung out during the uproar, also a few bursts of machine gun fire. There are some small machine guns called 'babies' or something like that, I believe. You can hold them against your waist, and when you pull the trigger, just once, they spit out twenty or thirty bullets. All I know is that they are very handy for certain jobs, like opening a locked door, or maybe curving and cutting through a trash bin in the middle of an empty lot that might hold dynamite, or maybe in spraying a car full of people. These 'babies' can do the work of a whole platoon equipped with rifles and they can hold back a dozen men and keep them from advancing along a street. These 'babies' start raising hell as soon as they're born. But perhaps . . .

(Translated by the Book Institute in Havana)

# LUIS AGÜERO

### *A certain Friday 13th*

> (For Luis and Sergio Saíz,
> killed on a certain Friday
> 13th)

When Margarito got to San Juan y Martínez, all he could think of was what the Captain had told him that morning. 'Hey, Margarito, I've got a li'l job f'ya!' That's what the Captain had said. Margarito shuddered when he recalled the Captain's words. There and then, he had thought of pointing out the date to him and of leaving it for another day.

'It's a bad day, Cap'n,' he thought of explaining to the Captain, on the spot. He still doesn't know why he kept his mouth shut.

Now, all he could say to himself was, 'I never liked no Friday thirteenth.' He kept his voice down and chewed his words as if he expected to swallow them afterwards. And, now, that he was there, his own late excuse obsessed him.

The same thing had happened on other occasions. However, this time, it was different from the others. 'No, buddy boy, this here thing annoys me,' he had said once. But after that, when it was all over, he was in high spirits again.

'This is life, partner, goin' round with the Cap'n in the jeep, the whole day, raisin' hell everywheres,' he had said then.

Things had been like that, ever since he began to wear his uniform, which, incidentally, his family just couldn't stop praising, and daily appreciating, as though it were some sort of special vestment or other.

Only thing, what happened later hadn't yet happened when his family had been so bemused. After it had, nobody praised or appreciated his uniform any more.

'I don't like your uniform no more,' his Uncle Nicasio had declared openly for everybody to hear.

But the man in the uniform smiled, even though he succeeded in getting an ugly grimace across his face, and said, 'What can I do? I've got a trade, an' that's how it is. An', as the Cap'n says, "You're good at it, Margarito." '

An oppressive silence filled the small room, and hung over the two boys. The younger leant forward and said, 'Our contact promised to send the dynamite this week.'

The older boy nodded. They were Sergio and Luis, brothers. A syringe, a ping pong ball, a few bottles of acid, and we burn the tobacco store house down to the ground, Luis thought. He also thought of what a friend of his, who had nothing to do with this particular meeting, had told him: 'You know how things are in a small village.'

'How does it look to you?' Sergio said.

'What?' Luis asked.

Sergio repeated his question. Luis nodded his approval and thought of something else his friend had told him: 'Sure, you're both the sons of a judge.' Luis remembered having said: 'Yeah, Batista is a law-abiding citizen.'

'I must go,' Luis said to his brother.

He left the room. Outside, a warm breeze brushed his face. He liked the feeling of joy and exhilaration it gave him. He walked slowly, and his unintentional choice of route reminded him of the suspense he had lived through on those nights, not so long ago . . .

And Sergio, who had climbed to the top of Martí's statue. And an old man, who smiled, and whose laughter afterwards was so raw. And the group of boys, who ran down the street. And Sergio, still at the top of the statue. And the siren, shrill and piercing. And Sergio, talking and talking and talking. And a green jacket, talking and talking and talking. And a boy, lying in the middle of the street, with his mouth full of blood. And another boy, hiding behind a column. And a package, wrapped in a newspaper. And some men, wearing yellow uniforms. And an old lady, who screamed. And a dark room. And Sergio, screaming, in the other room. And a man, with a brown jacket in his hand. And another man, saying that all this was very funny. And Sergio, still at the top of Martí's statue. And a brown jacket, who was getting down from Martí's statue. And a little girl, playing ring-a-ring-a-roses in the park. And the blow that got him in the stomach. And another blow that got him in the head. And yet another blow, double this time, in the stomach and the head. And Sergio, still screaming, in the other room. And a package, wrapped in a newspaper, blowing up, on a street corner. And a broken mimeograph. And a boy, who said that he could fix it. And a small magazine, which he was hiding, in his pocket. And a blow, in the stomach and head. And another, in the head and stomach. And a man, with a brown and a green jacket in his hand. And another man, saying that all this was very funny. And a green and a brown and a red jacket. And Sergio, screaming, in the other room. And a dark room. And a blow in the head. And another blow in the stomach. And another blow that got him on his testicles. And another, in the head and in the stomach and on his testicles.

Quite suddenly, without the benefit of a hint of transition or any lapse of time, he felt the morning sunlight and the fresh morning breeze and the morning birdsong rang in his ears. He was perspiring. The sweat was sticky. A smarting, relentless pain shot from his stomach to his throat.

Margarito shuddered when the Captain told him that. It was just like the time when he was ordered to beat the hell out of some students who were holding a meeting in the park.

Now, it was worse than that. It was far worse than beating some students to pulp.

At this point, he thought of pointing out the date to the Captain and asking him to leave it for another day. If only it weren't Friday thirteenth, he told himself, despite his unwillingness to say it out loud.

The storekeeper's glance was a mixture of surprise and mockery. Margarito ignored him and suffered his presence while he cleaned the table and placed the bottle and the glass in their usual positions before him.

'Friday thirteenths're bad luck,' Margarito said.

The storekeeper stopped looking at him altogether. Margarito filled his glass and drank up in one gulp. He filled it again.

Three times. Many more times. He drank until his throat was hot. And then he filled his glass, but this time, he didn't raise it to his lips. He toyed with the glass, aimlessly, trying to recall something else that the Captain had said that morning. Margarito remembered: 'It's easy to say who'll do it, but you need a tough guy to do it, like Margarito.' Margarito smiled for a second. Then he tightened his hold on the glass.

He said to himself, 'Nobody's goin' to say that a black man, like me, chickened out on the deal.'

Darkness claimed the area. An old black woman came down the street. She looked worn out. She had been stripping tobacco leaves all day.

Two seperate groups of children were playing hide and seek near the grocery store. Two lovers were standing at a dimly lit corner. It was fairly quiet everywhere. The setting was very nearly to order.

After dinner, the two boys approached the stand on the corner to get some coffee. The younger put six centavos on the counter and said, 'Look, I'll wait for you, at the movies. Right?'

The older boy nodded and continued drinking his coffee.

On his way, the younger boy took out a small slip of paper from his pocket and read:
> *To kill: a short, abrupt*
> *impulse, a void,*
> *which fills the body,*
> *a running backwards,*
> *in pursuit.*

He liked his poem, and pleased with himself, he kept walking and turning over a few statements of concern in his mind: 'There's no better time for establishing clearly the ideas that lead us to the struggle than the time when the moment of turning ideas into action approaches us.'

The black man stood up. His legs were shaking slightly. He watched the boy as he put the slip of paper back into his pocket and walked on down the street. He left two pesos on the table, tapped his right side and walked away slowly.

The boy was saying: 'The Cuban Revolution, which will

erupt triumphantly, will not permit such evils, and it will sweep away all the promoters of hate and the self-appointed aristocrats.'

The boy stood motionless when he heard the voice behind him. The black man staggered, as he walked, and his speech was slurred and thick with saliva. He was very drunk.

The boy tried to avoid him, but the man swung blindly and knocked him down. It took only one blow. A few people, near the spot, actually saw when the boy fell against the rock-hard surface of the pavement, and when the man pulled out his forty-five pistol. It was at that point that the witnesses thought it best to clear off the scene.

'The essential function of education cannot be ignored.'

The other boy saw it, too. He started to run towards his brother. He screamed out to attract attention, as he ran, but no one came out to help. A bullet sliced into his chest and he fell backwards.

'A just solution for the military problem is fundamental.'

The boy lying on the pavement raised his head slightly and saw the people scuttling away everywhere, and he noticed a curious bystander peeping at him from behind a wooden post nearby, and he saw, too, a trickle of blood sliding towards him. Then he tried desperately to get up from the pavement.

'The Agrarian Reform must be the first step taken by the Revolution.'

An old black woman had the courage to beg the man not to kill the boy on the pavement. Her voice was rasping and loud, as she begged for the boy's life to be spared. The man heard her. He smiled and shot the boy.

The boy heard the noise of the bullet and felt it lash his cheek. Then he felt nothing more. He died.

'Public utilities, owned, today, by foreign and absentee monopolies, will be the first to be nationalised by the Revolution.'

The two boys lay completely still. One was sprawled face downwards. The other was facing the night sky. A pool of blood drenched their white shirts.

The black man knew that his job was done. Just two bullets, he thought. He so felt his pride in his job that all he could do was simper. Then he ran towards a car that was waiting for him on the corner.

'The Revolution cannot ignore the current evil of gambling and organised crime.'

The man had left a stunned silence behind him. Though it's difficult to say, it comes easy to describe the silence as something engendered by the guilt of the black murderer and the abject cowardice of the people in the street. It hovered over the dead boys irreverently. It mocked them. 'Maybe,' someone said, rather knowingly, 'when their mother finds out, she'll die, too, from shock.' No one else spoke.

'The bureaucracy will be organised according to the individual's technical qualifications, training and ability, thus eradicating the usual pre-Revolution meddling in the State's affairs by self-seeking politicians, and banishing, for good, the employee's belief that he owes a divine loyalty to a given political boss and not to the Republic.'

The murderer threw his body backwards and leant his head on the back of the upholstery. He felt relieved. He looked at his friend beside him and said, 'Chicken? Me? Friday thirteenth's jus' like any other day. What people say about it an' what we believe is nothin' but superstition.'

'The struggle awaits all of us. The work of the Revolution, which, one day, will be the pride of the people, is, today, the pain and the thought and the aim of all of us in Cuba.'

Thus ended the Manifesto written by the older boy.

(Translated by the Book Institute in Havana)

# ARNALDO CORREA

## *The Chief*

'We've been here two days, now, and not a soul has passed by, except for those mule drivers.'

'Ah, shut up, will you! All you do is talk, talk, talk. If you want to go, go.'

The first speaker was a young boy, barely fifteen years old. He had large, dark brown eyes, fringed with unusually long lashes which gave his frail body a look of doll-like delicateness.

The other was the Chief. In order to soften the impact of his reply, he patted the boy's shoulder, and in a conciliatory tone, said, 'That's how this business is. We must have patience, at all cost. Look, the very first time I fixed an ambush, I had to wait only half an hour, but there are times, and they are often, when you must wait.'

I looked at him and the young boy. We were all quiet. The silence was broken, now and then, by the high-pitched songs of the birds, ringing out over our heads. From where we crouched, I could see about two hundred clear yards of the roadway. We were posted at a point where a mountain range overhung the highway for many miles. There was a small forest of trees to one side of us, and following the slope of the hillside, against the mountain, for a distance of about a quarter of a mile, I was able to see the entrance to the deep part of the large forest. Once we were able to get there, the danger of being spotted would not be so immediate, partly because of the very thick vegetation and partly because of the fear the place inspired in the soldiers. Again, on the other side of the highway, there was a protective growth of Guinea grass which ran the length of the visible section of the hillside and beyond. Then the hill ended abruptly and the treacherous flat land began, deprived of all trees or mounds or high grass. We had studied all these topographical details with great care, simply because we knew that they would be decisive factors, later on, in our customary guerrilla retreat. Apart from that, it had been our only landscape for two days, and we could not help knowing it by heart. We had decided to lay an ambush so that we might get some working weapons for ourselves and set up our section as regular fighters. The Chief was the only one of us with a good rifle. 'El Niño', our very young, complaining guerrilla, had a one-shot twenty-two calibre rifle. I had a sixteen gauge automatic shotgun, the best weapon for the type of ambush we had planned, for each shot actually carried a vast amount of lead-fragments which had a deadly short-range effectiveness. The other man who had come along with us had no weapons, except for a small knife and two bottles of petrol which he prized. We had sent him the night before to see what he could round up for us to eat. We had exhausted the meagre supplies we had brought, and the long wait and the nagging hunger were beginning to tell, particularly on 'El Niño'. Of course, the hope of getting a few functioning weapons managed to keep us alert and divert us from the anxiety we were all feeling about our lack of food and the danger of the ambush not coming off successfully. Added to that was the fact that the highway, once so full of traffic and bustling military activity, was, now, dead still; only three months before, interminably long army patrols came and went frequently, and according to the Chief, ambushes were generally very fruitful.

The Chief was an unusual man. He appeared to have no nerves whatsoever. He seemed absolutely immune to pain, exhaustion, hunger, fatigue and even to joy, and to all the emotions we fondly give in to under stress. He didn't like the idea of fighting with the regular troops, where, in fact, he would have soon reached an important position as a high-ranking officer. He was more interested in roaming the hill country with a small consistently changing guerrilla band; he liked the practice which made it possible for his men to obtain fairly reliable weapons, in ambushes, share them around, voluntarily disband and go off in different directions, without him.

The rather small incident with 'El Niño' was the first time that I had heard him say anything approaching a harsh remark to anyone. I liked the Chief. He had taught me a lot. But I wanted to get my hands on a good weapon and leave for the mountains. I planned to speak to him about our future and to see if I could talk him into leaving with me. Naturally, I was very proud to fight by his side.

Suddenly, we heard the distant roar of a motor, muffled, at first, then becoming louder, as the vehicle started climbing up the hill. We crouched together and held our breath, keeping our eyes fixed to the point where the front wheels would appear. Although we were definitely expecting some form of military transport to pass by, we were nevertheless quite surprised when a jeep, with three Batista soldiers, showed itself round the bend on the slope.

The moments which followed were full of the usual suspense of most ambush operations. We glanced alternately at the jeep and at the mark on the farther side of the road which the jeep was to reach before we started firing.

I must confess that it all happened almost without our being aware of what was really going on. Even the devastating clatter of our own guns caught us unaware. We realised, certainly, that the jeep had skidded to one side, after our initial assault. Then it jerked to a stop. 'El Niño' and I pounced on it, as previously agreed, and grabbed the weapons, while the Chief covered the roadway. We both had a moment of hesitation when we arrived at the side of the jeep where the three wretched men lay dying. But we quickly seized two rifles and a pistol. The other weapon was lodged under the body of the driver, who was twisting and trying to speak. Something, possibly a mixture of repulsion, conscience and good sense, stopped us from moving him to take his gun. We were absorbed in our work, when the Chief began firing his Garand. Bullets rained down on us, ricocheting on the jeep and putting an end to the agony of the last soldier as he sprawled backward on the driver's seat. We discovered that instead of attacking a single jeep, we had drawn a whole company into ambush.

We doubted our chances of escape. Anyway, we dived into a ditch. The Chief joined us, and we scrambled over a fence and ran into the forest. Twice, the Chief remained behind to fire at the soldiers who had taken cover and were still pelting the place where we had been crouching by the jeep. We noticed that they weren't inclined to advance, even a short distance away from their position, down on to the edge of the roadway which led into the forest. In our haste, we had chosen the less advantageous retreat. We ought to have gone into the deep forest.

The Chief said, 'We can't stay here for long, and it isn't possible, right now, to get to the deep one, without being seen.' He paused and touched his Garand. 'Judging by the number of vehicles and the amount of dust they've kicked up, there must be more than five hundred soldiers out there.' He paused again. 'They'll certainly catch us, here, but I've got an idea.'

He marched ahead of us. We went down the hill, a little way, and retreated again to the road. We crossed it, once more, using the path above an old sewer pipe running through a dry stream. We watched every step we took. We hid ourselves in the Guinea grass, and after an hour or so of crawling, we stopped and saw the guards circling the forest. They had been drawn into the wrong one. We had fooled them. They had chosen the forest we had vacated earlier. Now, it was necessary for us to wait where we were until the soldiers finished their search. In time, they would begin to think that we had escaped into the deep forest, and they would abandon the hunt.

The time passed slowly, tediously. The heat was suffocating. In next to no time at all, the presence of the enemy column, which was nervously combing the area in front of the Guinea grass, ceased to bother us.

We were satisfied with the mere touch of the captured weapons: one rifle for 'El Niño', and the other for me. The Chief kept the pistol. I had held on to the shotgun for the fourth man in our group. 'El Niño' had lost his twenty-two rifle; he just didn't know how he had.

The Chief was angry. 'A gun's a gun,' he rasped. 'It doesn't matter how bad it is, a gun in your hand is better than none.'

'El Niño' became restless. He looked at his new rifle and played with the telescopic sight. The Chief looked at him, on and off, and it was more than obvious that he could hardly control himself any longer. Suddenly, 'El Niño' was quiet. Then he started up again, this time, removing the clip from the rifle and fitting it into place, several times. The Chief looked away. I relaxed.

The sun was now hitting our backs. At lunch time, our hunger became intolerable. We were also extremely thirsty.

'Why don't we go slowly through the flat land and cross the

highway on the far end?' 'El Niño' asked.

I thought it was a good idea. The long wait was getting on our nerves.

'No,' the Chief said, 'we stay right here.'

'El Niño' slapped his rifle.

The Chief said, 'Get this into your thick heads: wandering around in broad daylight is suicide. Staying put in one place is the best possible protection. If you don't learn this, you won't live long in the forest.'

Some of the soldiers were still circling the area, and others were bringing down a batch of machine guns and mortars from the stock truck. They were straining under the effort.

'El Niño' graduated the telescopic sight and pointed the rifle at the soldiers. 'How do we adjust this thing to shoot from here?' he asked the Chief.

The Chief didn't reply. He merely reached for the rifle and adjusted the sight.

'El Niño' continued to ask about the rifle, and the Chief replied in grunts and monosyllables.

I suppose I became a little drowsy with the heat, even though the hottest time of the day was over and darkness was only two or three hours away. I heard a shot, and I still vividly remember 'El Niño's' face, and will always be able to recall his very strange, hollow voice, shouting, 'I didn't mean to. It's an accident.'

Then everything happened quickly. His face changed from a panic-stricken grimace to a countenance of astonishing serenity, and his voice was low-keyed, when he said, 'You get out, and I'll cover you.'

He jumped up and disappeared in the direction of the roadway. We heard his new rifle being shot sparingly, just as the Chief had advised. We looked at each other, and the Chief said, 'Let's go. If we stay, we'll make his sacrifice useless.'

Night surprised us in the deep forest, and we sat down to rest.

'He was a real man,' the Chief said.

It was the finest compliment I'd ever heard him pay anyone.

(Translated by the Book Institute in Havana
and adapted by the Editor)

*ESSAYS*

# EDMUNDO DESNOES

## The Secret Weapons

We are and we aren't. It's been estimated that we are about two billion people. We cover the earth and we are treated as though we are invisible. Yet, we are a substantial presence, in spite of the fact that we have tried to convince ourselves that it's really Coca Cola which covers the surface of the planet. We occupy the wide tropical belt of the world. We work under the ground in the big cities, and in the mines in the rural areas, and we sweat in our green latitudes.

We are a majority of Mankind, and we scarcely have a voice or any real power. Iron and fire have kept us working as slaves without much hope of breaking out of our bondage, ignorance and poverty. Together with the evident pillage of our natural and human resources, the maniacal agents of the developed countries want to take away our souls with the help of their secret weapons, the mass communication *media,* spread over the world in a series of enticing myths and egoistical values, which, in most cases, clash with the authentic interests of our underdeveloped societies. Certain of our Greco-Latin ancestors have been denounced by José Martí: 'Our Greece is preferable to the one which is not ours. Let the world be grafted on to our Republics, but the core should be that of our Republics.'

Even white beauty, the unsuspecting blonde, sharpens the inferiority complex of the colonised blacks, orientals and metizos, in the most absurd and unintentional ways. Perhaps, the darkskinned Bolivian, who threw a stone at the Gioconda, in the Louvre, was rebelling against that curious situation which seems ironically locked fast in the smile of the Mona Lisa, sempiternally. The press published the news everywhere in the middle of the last decade: a lunatic, a barbarian, actually dared to attack a masterpiece of the Italian Renaissance. He left a scratch on her arm. I like to think of it is a quiet yet unconscious protest of the Third World against the First World which pretends the same eternity feigned by the hard masses which back the inane smile of the Florentine lady.

But it's not only the Mona Lisa, or Marilyn Monroe, or *bourgeois* freedom, or even the Cadillac (they could be converted easily into objects of simple pleasure and entertainment), but it's also our own image which appears deformed by the press, radio, television and the cinema, in the highly industrialised countries. Or is it that we are mere parts of landscape, cash-register fodder, or perhaps, submissive servants, and in our native territories? And if we rebel, our critics and exploiters say that we're primitive, ungrateful and violent. Gungha Din, the former British Empire's water-boy, became an informer against his brothers, because he had fallen desperately in love with his colonisers; Tonto is the clumsy, shuffling Mexican who speaks bad English but serves John Wayne faithfully. This sort of humiliation became absurd during Stokely Carmichael's childhood: 'I remember I used to go to the movies on Saturday to see Tarzan. The white Tarzan always defeated the black tribesmen. And I would shout, 'Kill those beasts, Tarzan! Kill those savages!' And, really, I was saying, "Kill me!"'

The Western powers, with their myths and war machines, have tried to obliterate the humanity of the colonised and neo-colonised peoples. Ralph Ellison, the black American novelist, justifiably complains: 'I am a man of flesh and blood, of vital fibre and substance, and it could even be said that I think and I am. Please understand me: I am invisible, simply because certain people do not want to see me. Like the bodiless head which appeared under a glass dome in the old-fashioned circuses, I'm surrounded by passers-by, who, when they come close to me, merely see, in the hard distorting mirror of the dome, whatever is around me, and themselves, as creations of their own imaginations. They see everything but me.'

The effect of the mass-media on *all* of us, on the whole human superstructure, becomes greater every day. C. Wright Mills points out: 'Neither conscience nor existence is determined within is own separate essence. There's an interaction between each, as Marx knew in a more or less inconsistent way. The supervising variables also operate: the mass-media, the entertainment machinery, the cultural apparatus: that is, the elements of the ideological superstructure. These variables mediate in the relationship between existence and conscience; they affect each, and they influence the resulting interaction. They can, and frequently do play an autonomous role in the development of class consciousness or in its phenomenal absence.'

And, of course, the class struggle manifests itself with accompanying violence between the highly sensitive and autocratic First World and the Third World; and, indeed, we may say that, nowadays, history is evolved, there, with greater speed than it appears to do in any other sector of our lives.

'Here are some black men, standing before us, looking at us! I invite you all to feel the sensation of being looked at. Yes, because the white man has had a privileged position, lasting some three thousand years, of having been able to look without being looked at: hence, my invitation. And, it was a pure glance; the light in their eyes brought each and every detail out from the natal shadows.' Jean-Paul Sartre made that discovery in 1948. And, here, may I make it quite clear that it isn't possible for us to become properly visible, unless through the delineating process of armed Revolutionary struggle. And where the guerrilla does not exist, there is a secret form of violence, sometimes in gestation, sometimes on the verge.

In the meantime, we face the secret weapons of the alien and alienating cultural penetration, coming at us from all sides. Fortunately, the mass-media have not penetrated, too deeply, into the psyche of the Third World man. There are some underdeveloped regions where they are totally unknown. During Jacobo Arbenz's government in Guatemala, the Ministry of Education began a campaign of building schools in the remote Indian hamlets. After that, the Ministry published, in the Quiché language, the *Popol Vuh,* one of the very early surviving Mayan books on the origins of the world and of man. The Indians were stupified, when they heard the teacher, from the distant capital city, reading it in their own language. They showed their appreciation by making extra demands and even by uttering threats: they told him that the *Popol Vuh* was their book, and forced the teacher to leave it in the hamlet, because, they said, they had, at long last, found their sacred text; some went to the extent of saying that the teacher's copy was the only one which existed.

In many parts of the underdeveloped world, things like that will also occur, real signs, danger signals for those who would penetrate with their secret weapons. There, men do not even know the principles or the gloss of mass reproduction, and for them, books, as well as, printing presses, are disconcerting mysteries. Thirty-five per cent of the Latin American population has never owned a book. Forty per cent has never been in a library or in a simple reading-room. Millions of families have never had a bookcase in their homes. We have no reason not to trust those telling quotations from the available UNESCO statistics.

Certain truths are self-evident. Imperialism, in the colonised world, kept the colonial in historic clandestinity, apart from lashing him to the consumer economy. The situation is changing. The Third World is stirring, in its own self-interest, and getting acquainted with its native literatures, radio broadcasting and television. The illiterate farmers of Columbia are being given, for example, free radio sets tuned only to one station which broadcasts technical and ideological information. In Africa, there are tests being carried out with the aim of mounting a series of literacy campaigns, using television in the inaccessible country districts. If formerly, the tri-continental man were a cheap economic tool, now, he has been turned into a machine which is becoming increasingly sensitive to the influences of the mass-media. The world of electronics, as the Canadian sociologist, Marshall McLuhan, has suggested, is closer to the oral community of the underdeveloped peoples than the formal structure and discipline of the printed page can ever hope to be in the near future; in other words, television will crash through the colonial aftermath of backwardness, far faster, and with more immediacy and with greater effect, than the traditional literary primer.

Generations of intellectuals have and no doubt will continue to discuss the quality of the power of the mass-media to change the appetites and opinions of all societies. McLuhan is convinced that we're looking at a world automatically controlled, to such an extent, that we're able to say that approximately six hours less of radio transmission in Indonesia, in any given week, and there'll be a fairly noticeable drop in the attention-rate usually marked up for ordinary reading in that society, or that the authorities can transmit twenty more hours of radio, in, let's say, South Africa, this week, in order to cool the tribal temperature created by the previous week's television output (and, we certainly know why that country hasn't yet run the risk of introducing television); and so on. Complete cultures can be programmed, today, so that a stable temperature may be maintained, in the very same way, that North America has been able, with the use of other *media,* to maintain, in its own interest, the *equilibria,* in the commercial economies of the world.

But, of course, this seems only possible, to me, in a world impelled by crass 'automatistation', where the mass-media form an integral part of the common society, where the press, radio and television services coincide with a population of passive consumers. The mass-media promote the necessary passivity to place the Third World man and his "better-off neighbour" within a precise, technocratic and trap-like situation. And yet, in the Third World, the mass-media could even be used to throw coals on the fires of the Revolution, and there's the remote possibility that they can be converted into the blaze which will spread the fire throughout the waste lands of Africa, Asia and Latin America.

The awesome power of the mass-media is not yet universal and much less unlimited. It is conditioned by the social structure within which it operates. It strengthens or weakens conditions and attitudes already existing in the environment. And, here, allow me to remind myself that we can't actually create emotions which are not there aboriginally : the propagandist should evoke or stimulate only those attitudes adequate to his intentions within the wide natural spectrum which natively exist in his audience. These attitudes may be innate, but sometimes they are socially acquired, we know; but even this is not urgently useful to the Third World. If we seriously consider the inevitability of a Revolution in Latin America, then the role of the mass-media, in rousing the continental conscience and destroying the colonial and neo-colonial belief that human degradation is an honourable Third World burden to bear, is positively crucial. In Cuba, a country, devastatingly pentrated, before our War of Liberation, by the North American presence (tourists, investors, absentee landlords and their resident agents, consumer goods, aid, diplomacy and cultural detritus) and by the values of a society of rabid profiteers and racists, the very dynamic Socialist Revolution in the Americas was created successfully. Our memory of the depth of the penetration and of the glitter of the rewards is painful; everything was possible, easily realisable, for the *bourgeois* minority: trips to Paris and New York, tropical lovemaking sweetened with French perfume, and an air-conditioned limousine: so very much in contrast and in violent contradiction with our "underdeveloped" reality.

Those years encouraged our spirit of rebellion, which, in turn, separated us from the usual Third World fatalistic response to jackboot misery and dispossession. The insolent *bourgeois* benefits helped to foster the Revolution within the mass of the people. The contrasts and contradictions between our reality and the fantasy of the North American penetration triggered our impatience. The conflict, which was engendered, could only have been solved by violence. Ernesto Che Guevara's dictum, in this regard, is strictly relevant to our awareness and understanding of the potency of the secret weapons, and not only of our own but also of those in the hands of the enemy. Che said, in effect, that, for us, the solution of the question is quite clear; we must, at all times, struggle to intensify the conflict between our reality and the invading fantasy, but we must not harbour any illusions (or have we any right to do so) of attaining our liberation without fighting for it; it all depends, in the final analysis, on our armed propaganda, in matters of culture, politics and Revolution, which we must develop with the sole intention of launching it directly at the secret weapons of the enemy.

(Translated by the Press Office of the Cultural Congress of Havana, 1968, and adapted by the Editor)

# AMBROSIO FORNET

## *The Intellectual in the Revolution*

Most of us have heard of the feelings of frustration, uselessness and rootlessness, experienced by the writers and artists in the underdeveloped and colonised countries. And, of course, we know something of their self-protection: the defence-mechanisms and the alibis. When one has mastered a foreign language, read *Ulysses,* and is able to discuss Surrealism, or *Guernica,* for hours, one knows he belongs to a select international community, which is, by all means, reassuring of one's position of privilege; and, even today, one may be deprived and be suffering certain humiliations without necessarily becoming a Revolutionary; and although neglected by the bourgeoisie, the intellectual shares, to some extent, its domination of the world, so to speak, and, at the same time, can allow himself the luxury of scorning it. The pretexts are plentiful and comforting. For example, the correct pronunciation of Goethe's name or Baudelaire's becomes a sign of spiritual superiority, a savage pleasure frequently enjoyed by the intellectual in the Third World.

But there are less innocent alibis. You may be committed to the Left, even reconciled to die of old age in it, without experiencing the need of joining the masses, or of compromising yourself with Revolutionary action. After all, a writer or an artist is not a man of action, and in regard to moral support, we know that it is possible to assume all the world's sufferings without forgetting to use an umbrella when it rains. Furthermore, history today is so similar to certain fables that it is hard not to be a Manichean: we recognise, at first sight, those who are good, because they struggle for their most elementary rights, and those who are bad, we recognise, because they have proven themselves to be unpardonably wicked. (The first fight for the soil they till; education for their children; and the dignity that enables them to regain their humanity. The second commit atrocious Imperialistic crimes in the Congo, Algeria, Cuba, the Dominican Republic and Vietnam.) Thus, to take sides with the former is not predictably an act of political maturity, but merely proof of a type of sentiment similar to the indignation of the boy who senses that kindness and beauty are threatened by the marauding manoeuvres of a wolf.

At any rate, we take for granted, today, the writer's political responsibility as soon as we recognise his artistic responsibility, which seems to us like the two sides of the same coin. The reason that permits us to despise and condemn the artist who becomes an accomplice of Imperialism, however indirectly, is the same reason that makes us reject academic art and prevents us from ever imagining counter-Revolutionary art.

It's because we have assumed our responsibilities and we are ready to answer for our actions, that the intellectuals of a country in Revolution demand concrete, responsibile co-operation from the other members of the society. I am not only referring to our civic responsibilities. To teach someone how to read and write; to learn how to handle a gun; and to cut cane, voluntarily; these, too, are component parts of our essential duties as intellectuals in an underdeveloped country, and since we lack the vital assistance of the intermediate cadres, we are, in addition, obliged to serve as links between our work and our public. The poet understands that he must become, among other things, a master-communicator and a cultural duty officer, so that the poem he writes in silence, today, will be repeated by the people in the streets tomorrow. This splendid process of mass education is, in a way, incestuous. But there is more to it than my statement allows. When we call ourselves heirs of a universal culture, we are not coining an idle phrase but establishing a fact; we are really ready to claim what belongs to us. We consider man's effort to interpret reality and create a world, in his own image, a very definite Revolutionary praxis; and let us not forget that the evolutionary stages, from the appearance of the Altamira bisons to Vasarely, from Homer and the Yoruba legends to Kafka, constitute our inalienable heritage.

Because that is how we genuinely feel, we have incorporated the spirit of our inheritance into our intellectual life. The evidence is easily seen in our cultural tastes and output. But the basic reason for this freedom is not always apparent to the outsiders who hardly see us as the inheritors of the kind I've described. They do not expect to find abstract and 'pop' art paintings in our galleries, editions of Proust, Joyce and Robbe-Grillet in our bookshops, Antonioni's and Bergman's films in our cinemas. Our friends from abroad usually slap us on the back when they visit us in Havana, perhaps, because they did not expect to see these things. Perhaps, they did not expect to hear the serial music of our young composers and those passionate discussions about aesthetics at the art seminars and coffee tables. 'Remarkable Revolution,' they say. 'Let nothing spoil it.' I must confess that this remark, which used to flatter our pride, has, lately, become irritating. Not only is there a mixture of paternalism and distrust present in the visitors' eagerness to see us preserve the untouched image of an immaculate Revolution, but it also transforms us into mere vestals, guardians of an already burning fire, when what we are, actually, are incendiaries, creators of a new fire.

Cuba has achieved the reconciliation of supposed cultural opposites, social justice with freedom of artistic creativity within Socialism, underdevelopment with vanguard art, and doing so, at a distance of, only ninety miles from this century's most watchful Imperialist power. This fact reveals that our Revolution is an authentic one, willing to forge, within the tensions of the modern world, a new man, finally liberated from his historical degradation. For the time being, this climate of experimentation and creative permissiveness has saved us many a useless discussion, and has delivered us from that troubled wake of frustration and discouragement which Revolutionary justice leaves behind, when it degenerates into an abstract passion.

But can we be satisfied with the situation, as I've outlined it? If we limited ourselves only to avoid our errors, to fulfil, punctually, our duties, and wait for our merits to be recognised, in what sense would we be different from a revenue officer in Brussels or a district commissioner from Buenos Aires? Responsibility presupposes liberty, but, at the same time, liberty for the intellectual of a country in Revolution presupposes the duty of creating new responsibilities. It is, here, that the intellectual finds his specific function and the support of his Revolutionary vocation.

In fact, the first thing that the intellectual in the Revolution discovers is his own ignorance. He has been so accustomed to pose foreign problems to himself and to talk only to hear himself talk that he does understand that he is not prepared to accept the intellectual challenge of the Revolution. As he looks around, he feels a kind of dizziness. Reality has exploded before his eyes and its power of transforming his life is incalculable. He then begins to grope between his old scepticism and the new enthusiasm; he is as lacerated as that man of the transition period whom Roberto Fernández Retamar, the poet, describes, splayed 'between the certainty that everything is a trap, a colossal jest, and the hope that things can be different, must be different, will be different.'

So, we take that one step farther, and the old metaphysical concerns become buried by the dramatic demands of the everyday combat in the Revolution. There are enormous risks, ranging from dissertation to extremism, from insolence to a mechanical repetition of *formulae* and slogans, but there is no innocent action, along the way; even enthusiasm becomes a mixture of good sense and madness. Besides, when we, at last, make a pause, we detect certain new ideas of our own which fit our reality perfectly. Even though our aesthetic tastes are almost the same, our vision has been totally transformed. A friend told me that if we wrote an essay, today, dealing with the theme of isolation with special references to our burdensome Cuban transport problems, we would make Samuel Beckett look like a contemporary Perrault.

So, our eyes are open, and we are seeing ourselves as we haven't done before in our history. Obviously, cultural decolonisation is an unavoidable product of this growing awareness. We understand what we are not, what we do not share with the intellectuals of the industrialised world, when we discover our reality and with it the inefficacy of the theoretical instruments which we had hastily made use of through our reading and foreign trips. 'We are not Europeans,' Mario Benedetti, the Uruguayan novelist, has said, 'and therefore, we have not yet reached the stage of contemplating the world through an intellectual tiredness of heart and eye. We are Latin American, and consequently certain typically European artistic phenomena, such as the "new novel" and the "new criticism", tend to appear as remarkable waste lands of talent, exhibits in a premature museum of new rhetoric.'

Again, if we have rejected dogmatisms and worn-out *formulae* in politics, then we must test the new concepts which come to us with vanguard labels in art. And it is not a matter of suppressing these, but of incorporating them with critical judgement and natural egoism, and ignoring those which simply cannot be assimilated. That is precisely what a healthy, developing organism does. If we open ourselves passionately to the conquests of contemporary art, we do so, not to stop there, but to stand above them. We must insist on this: we are not trying to attain a known goal; it would be like falling into the same pre-Revolutionary cultural pit but at a different level of consciousness; we are, instead, involved in creating a new society with new human relations, and an art and thought capable of anticipating and reflecting them. As far as there is not such a thing as a "great old Cuban art", when we come to talk about a new art, perhaps, we do nothing more than clumsily define a new form of producing and appropriating it; that is to say, a new form of conceiving life, a new culture which is essentially of our own making, within the Revolution. It was enough to open our eyes to find out what we were not, but in order to foresee what we want to be, it is necessary to close them, now and again, and imagine a city of the future, inhabited by men for whom history will have ceased to be a nightmare, and freedom, equality and fraternity mere words; it is no less than to imagine the life of men whom we shall not know and whose sole image nevertheless justifies this gigantic and fruitful effort which is what the Socialist Revolution in an underdeveloped country is really all about. This is where I think I can locate the specific responsibility of the intellectual, the technician or the writer, the political leader or the artisan, in a Revolutionary society. It is absolutely important to invent the road that leads directly to his objective, and in this fascinating and risky task, the concrete responsibility of the intellectual is to lead the way, to address himself and his work to the soul of the people, to conquer nature and create new highways and visions of reality; and that cannot be achieved in isolation from the concrete responsibility to the other sectors of the Revolution. And, as far as it is impossible to stop (and each step is decisive), and as far as there is no other *formula* but the one of boldness and dissatisfaction, the intellectual is compelled to be his own critic and the critical conscience of his new nation. He must go forward, measuring the distance that separates the means from the ends, always assessing what he is, in the light and hope of what he must be and of what he will be. It is his responsibility that, at the end of the Revolutionary road, he will not have created a domesticated and satisfied puppet, but a new man, finally liberated from his alienation, that new man whom Che Guevara described, shortly before he died fighting for him, as "the ultimate and most vital Revolutionary ambition."

(Translated by the Press Office of the Cultural Congress of Havana, 1968, and adapted by the Editor).

# ERNESTO CHE GUEVARA

## *The Cultural Vanguard*

For a long time, man has been trying to free himself from alienation through culture and art. While he dies every day during the eight or more hours that he sells his labour, he comes to life afterwards in his spiritual activities.

But this remedy bears the germs of the same sickness; it is as a solitary individual that he seeks communion with his environment. He defends his oppressed individuality through the artistic medium and reacts to aesthetic ideas as a unique being whose aspiration is to remain untarnished.

All that he is doing, however, is attempting to escape. The law of value is not simply a naked reflection of productive relations. The monopoly capitalists, even while employing purely empirical methods, weave around art a complicated web which converts it into a willing tool. The superstructure of society ordains the type of art in which the artist has to be educated. Rebels are subdued by its machinery and only rare talents may create their own work. The rest become shameless hacks or are crushed.

A school of artistic "freedom" is created, but its values also have limits even if they are imperceptible until we come into conflict with them; that is to say, until the real problem of man and his alienation arises. Meaningless anguish and vulgar amusement thus become convenient safety valves for human anxiety. The idea of using art as a weapon of protest is opposed.

If one plays by the rules, he gets all the honours, such honours as a monkey might get for performing pirouettes. The condition that has been imposed is that one cannot try to escape from the invisible cage.

When the revolution took power there was an exodus of those who had been completely housebroken; the rest, whether they were revolutionaries or not, saw a new road open to them. Artistic inquiry experienced a new impulse. The paths, however, had already been more or less laid out and the escapist concept hid itself behind the word "freedom". This attitude was often found even among the revolutionaries themselves, reflecting the *bourgeois* idealism still in their consciousness.

In those countries which had gone through a similar process they tried to combat such tendencies by an exaggerated dogmatism. General culture was virtually tabooed, and it was declared that the acme of cultural aspiration was the formally exact representation of nature. This was later transformed into a mechanical representation of the social reality they wanted to show: the ideal society almost without conflicts or contradictions which they sought to create.

Socialism is young and has made errors. Many times revolutionaries lack the knowledge and intellectual courage needed to meet the task of developing the new man with methods different from the conventional ones, and the conventional methods suffer from the influences of the society which created them. (*Again, we raise the theme of the relationship between form and content.*)

Disorientation is widespread, and the problems of material construction preoccupy us. There are no artists of great authority who at the same time have great revolutionary authority. The men of the party must take this task to hand and seek attainment of the main goal, the education of the people.

But then they sought simplification. They sought an art that would be understood by everyone, the kind of "art" *functionaries* understand. True artistic values were disregarded, and the problem of general culture was reduced to taking some things from the socialist present and some from the dead past (since dead, not dangerous). Thus Socialist Realism arose upon the foundations of the art of the last century.

But the realistic art of the nineteenth century is also a class art, more purely capitalist perhaps than this decadent art of the twentieth century which reveals the anguish of alienated man. In the field of culture, capitalism has given all that it had to give, and nothing of it remains but the offensive stench of a decaying corpse, today's decadence in art.

Why then should we try to find the only valid prescription for art in the frozen forms of Socialist Realism? We cannot counterpose the concept of Socialist Realism to that of freedom because the later does not yet exist and will not exist until the complete development of the new society. Let us not attempt, from the pontifical throne of realism-at-any-cost, to condemn all the art forms which have evolved since the first half of the nineteenth century for we would then fall into the Proudhonian mistake of returning to the past, of putting a strait-jacket on the artistic expression of the man who is being born and is in the process of making himself.

What is needed is the development of an ideological-cultural mechanism which permits both free inquiry and the uprooting of the weeds which multiply so easily in the fertile soil of State subsidies.

In our country, we don't find the error of mechanical realism, but rather its opposite, and that is so because the need for the creation of a new man has not been understood, a new man who would represent neither the ideas of the nineteenth century nor those of our own decadent and morbid century.

What we must create is the man of the twenty-first century, although this is still a subjective and not a realised aspiration. It is precisely this man of the next century who is one of the fundamental objectives of our work; and to the extent that we achieve concrete successes on a theoretical plane (or, *vice versa,* to the extent we draw theoretical conclusions of a broad character on the basis of our concrete research), we shall have made an important contribution to Marxism-Leninism, to the cause of humanity.

Reaction against the man of the nineteenth century has bought us a relapse into the decadence of the twentieth century; it is not a fatal error, but we must overcome it lest we open a breach for revisionism.

The great multitudes continue to develop; the new ideas continue to attain their proper force within society; the material possibilities for the full development of all members of society make the task much more fruitful. The present is a time for struggle; the future is ours.

To sum up, the fault of our artists and intellectuals lies in their original sin: they are not truly revolutionary. We can try to graft the elm tree so that it will bear pears, but at the same time we must plant pear trees. New generations will come who will be free of the original sin.

The probabilities that great artists will appear will be greater to the degree that the field of culture and the possibilities for expression are broadened.

Our task is to prevent the present generation, torn asunder by its conflicts, from becoming perverted and from perverting new generations.

We must not bring into being either docile servants of official thought, or scholarship students who live at the expense of the State: merely people who pursue "freedom".

Already, there are revolutionaries coming who will sing the song of the new man in the true voice of the people. This is a process which takes time.

(Translated by Gerald Paul, and excerpted from the Author's *Man and Socialism in Cuba*)

# ERNESTO CHE GUEVARA

## *"El Patojo"*

A few days ago we heard the news of the death of some Guatemalan patriots, among them Julio Roberto Cáceres Valle.

In our demanding responsibility as Revolutionaries, in the midst of the class struggles rumbling throughout the continent, death is a frequent accident. But the death of a friend, who was our comrade during all difficult periods, as well as during the moments when we dreamed of better times, is always painful. Julio Roberto was a great friend. He was short and physically rather frail, so we called him "El Patojo" which in Guatemalan slang means "Little One" or "Child".

While we were all in Mexico together, El Patojo had witnessed the birth of the idea of our Cuban Revolution. He offered to join us as a volunteer, but Fidel did not want to involve any more foreigners in the planned struggle for Cuba's liberation in which I had the honour to participate.

Very shortly after the Revolution triumphed, El Patojo sold his few belongings, left Mexico and came to me in Havana. He worked in various offices of public administration, and he became the first Chief of Personnel of the Department of Industrialisation in INRA (the National Institute of Agrarian Reform), but he was never really happy with his work. It was obvious that he was looking for something different to do; he was more concerned with the liberation of his own country. Our Revolution had changed him a great deal, in the same way that it had affected all of us. The bewildered boy who had left Guatemala without fully grasping the meaning of the defeat, there, had now been transformed into a wholly conscious Revolutionary.

The first time I saw El Patojo we were on a train, fleeing Guatemala, some time after the fall of the Jacobo Arbenz' government. We were headed for Tapachula. Then on to Mexico City. He was much younger than I, but we soon became very close friends. Together, we made the trip from Chiapas to Mexico City. We were both penniless and defeated, and we were forced to earn a living in an indifferent, if not openly hostile situation.

El Patojo had no money and I had only a very few pesos. I bought a camera, and we became photographers, without the necessary permission, as foreigners, going around the city parks and soliciting for jobs. Our partner was a Mexican who had a darkroom where we developed and printed our photographs. We became thoroughly familiar with the streets of Mexico City, as we walked from one end to another, delivering our miserable-looking prints and struggling with our unbelieving customers in an effort to convince them that, for example, the little boy in the picture was really very cute and that at the price of one Mexican peso, it was actually a great bargain to obtain such a work of art. We continued our photography for several months and we ate regularly. Gradually the pressing responsibility of my own Revolutionary life separated us. I have already mentioned that Fidel had discouraged El Patojo from joining the party bound for Cuba, mainly because he was reluctant to turn our small number into an international force.

El Patojo did a little journalism, while studying Physics at the University of Mexico. Then he stopped going to lectures for some time, and returned to the University, without ever getting very far ahead. He earned his living haphazardly at various jobs, but never asked for any assistance. I still really don't know whether that sensitive boy was too timid or whether he was too proud to bother to recognise his weaknesses and personal problems to approach a friend for help. El Patojo was an introvert, highly intelligent, cultured and, as I said before, sensitive. All these qualities he later used in the Revolutionary cause in Guatemala. He belonged to the Guatemalan Workers' Party. He benefited from the discipline, and was soon developing into a very fine Revolutionary. By then, little was left of his earlier over-sensitive temperament. Revolutionary work purifies the spirit and improves and matures those involved in the struggle, just as the good farmer corrects the imbalance in his developing yield and brings out its best qualities.

In Cuba, El Patojo and I shared the same house, as was proper for two old friends, but we no longer seemed able to revive the close friendship and confidence of the months we had spent together in Mexico. I suspected what his plan was, when I saw him, occasionally, studying one of his Guatemalan Indian languages. Then, one day, he came to me and said that he was leaving, that the time had come for him to go and do his duty by his countrymen.

El Patojo had had no military training. He simply felt that it was his duty to return to his country to fight, and in doing so, to repeat our own guerrilla struggle. We talked for an unusually long time. I asked him to observe three points only: constant movement, firm mistrust and strict vigilance. Movement: that is, never stay put for long; never spend two nights in the same place; never stop moving from one place to another. Mistrust: at the beginning, mistrust even your own shadow, friendly peasants, informants, guides, contacts; mistrust everything until you hold a liberated zone. Vigilance: constant guard duty, constant scouting of the area; setting up camp in a safe place and, above all, never sleep with a roof over your head and never sleep in a house where you can be surrounded. That was the synthesis of our guerrilla experience, the only thing I could give my friend. Could I advise him not to do it? What right would I have had? We had undertaken something at a time when it was believed impossible, and now he was convinced that it was possible.

El Patojo left, and a short time afterwards, we heard about his death. At first, we hoped that there had been a confusion of names, that there might have been some mistake, but unfortunately, there was no doubt that he was dead; his body had been identified by his mother. Others, too, had been killed. They were his comrades, all of them as brave and as intelligent, perhaps, as he was, but not personally known to us.

Yet again, we know the bitterness of defeat and we ask the unanswered question: why did he not learn from our experience? Why didn't those men follow the simple advice which they had been given? We don't know really what happened, but we do know that the terrain had been badly chosen, that the men were not physically strong enough for the action, that they were not mistrustful as they should have been and, of course, that they were not vigilant enough. The repressive army surprised them, killed a few, caused the rest to disperse, then came back at them and wiped them out. One or two prisoners were taken, while most of the others, like El Patojo, died fighting back. After losing their group solidarity, the guerrillas were probably tracked down, as we had been when we were set upon by Batista's troops in Alegría de Pío.

Once more, young blood had been spilled on the battle fields in America, to make freedom possible. Another stage in the struggle had been marked by defeat. We must make time to mourn our fallen comrades, even while we sharpen our machetes. From the valuable and tragic experience of the honourable dead, we must solemnly promise not to repeat their mistakes, to avenge all their deaths with as many victories, and to bring about total liberation.

When El Patojo left Cuba, he did not leave anything behind, not even any messages: his clothes and personal belongings were few. However, old friends of ours in Mexico brought me some of his poems which he had written in a notebook. They are the last verses of a Revolutionary; they are, too, a love song to the Revolution, his homeland, and to a woman. To that woman whom El Patojo knew and loved in Cuba, these final lines, an injunction of a kind, are dedicated:

*Take it, it's only my heart.*
*Hold it in your hand,*
*And when the dawn breaks,*
*Open your hand*
*And let the sun warm it . . .*

El Patojo's heart has remained among us, in the hands of the woman he loved and in the loving hands of the Cuban people, waiting to be warmed in the sun of a new day which will surely shine for Guatemala and for all America. Today, in the Ministry of Industry, where he left many friends, there is a small school of statistics, bearing the memory of his name "Julio Roberto Cáceres Valle". Later, when Guatemala has been liberated, his beloved name will certainly be given to a school, a factory, or a hospital, or to any place where people fight and work towards the building of a new society.

(Translated by Eduardo Bernat, and taken from the Author's *Episodes of the Revolutionary War* and adapted by the Editor.)

# FIDEL CASTRO

## *On Che's Assassination*

The fact that Che was wounded while advancing on the Bolivian and allied soldiers was a very natural thing for him to have done. Also characteristic of him was the fact that he continued to fight, even though he had been seriously wounded. I am sure that, only if he had been unconscious or if his rifle were useless or if he were unable to move because of his wound, they would have been lucky to capture him. It's been reported that while they were questioning him, he stared at them with cold indifference, even with loathing; that is also an essential part of his personality, as was his having died in active combat.

What is vitally important is not whether he died in battle or whether he was gravely injured before he was captured, but that he was later killed. Also important to remember is the certainty that he had been fatally wounded and that, in one way or another, that may have led to his death. And yet, a deeply interesting controversy has arisen about this, and partly explains, but only partly, what the Bolivians did with his body afterwards.

We remember those dispatches which indicated that he had been buried or that his body had been exhumed or that it had been cremated; we also remember the reports which mentioned that his hand had been cut off, and later, a finger.

It's logical to suppose, among other things, that the Bolivian authorities would be interested in preventing the release of the confirmation of the fatal bullet; they would, no doubt, be worried that a close examination of all the details might expose the incriminating bullet wound. But, in my opinion, there is something else that they must have given even more importance and that would be their fear of Che, even after his death. In fact, that is precisely the presentiment that they, themselves, gave prominence, when they removed his body, so that the grave could be converted into a shrine. It's quite reasonable to think that the Bolivians, knowing instinctively that they are condemned by history, and having eliminated Che by a mere stroke of luck, became afraid that his body and the ground in which it would be buried would become a shrine, today, tomorrow or some time later on. It was their intention to deprive the Revolutionary Movement of its memorial symbol, site and focal point in Latin America; in short, they are afraid of Che, even after his death.

We considered it our duty to speak out about this matter in order to express our conviction on the subject of whether the present state of uncertainty might be useful to the Revolutionary Movement or not; indeed, we think of it as a moral question, one of great principle, a duty to the people and to Revolutionaries everywhere. We firmly believe that the only sector of the world to benefit from the indefinite perpetuation of doubt and from the resulting unfounded illusions among the masses would be Imperialism. We refuse to believe that the Imperialist puppets in Bolivia, eager as they are to appear as the vanguard lackeys of their continental bosses, want us to doubt their news of Che's assassination. But the Imperialists are much more subtle. We haven't the slightest reason for doubting that, after having got rid of Che physically, they would like to dispel the image and impact of his heroic, Revolutionary example, and destroy it all with a surrounding vulgarity of speculation and illusion.

And, of course, because Che's life has had the power of impressing even his worst ideological enemies, it is logical that Imperialism should feel worried. His virtue, as a good man, is a unique example of how the individual is capable of gaining the recognition and respect of the very opponents he may choose to face and defeat. It is indeed logical that this should worry the Imperialists. Not a few people, including many political figures, all over the world, have said how astounded they were at the tragic universality of the news of Che's death. For us, in Cuba, it has been like the kind of brutal awakening to the reality of our position as a Revolutionary nation in a hostile hemisphere. We sincerely know and believe that the Revolutionaries throughout the world will continue to show their confidence in the truth and beauty of the Cuban Revolution. And we have come, here, before you, today, to make good that faith, to make that faith real in the finest spirit of the Revolution.

What good would it do for Revolutionaries to hold on to false hopes? Aren't we supposed always to be ready for surprises, prepared for all trials of our faith, for all reverses? Aren't the true Revolutionaries those of us who came through in the end, in spite of the overwhelming opposition to our struggles?

It's always been like that for us in Cuba. The death of José Martí and of Antonio Maceo were two of the hardest blows we've sustained in our Revolutionary history. But we have overcome those tragic losses.

Who could deny the significance of Che's death? Its significance to us? And to the Revolution? We know how we're going to feel without being able to count on Che's living experience, his vital inspiration, his exemplary life and prestige.

But let's not forget that he, himself, placed very little importance on the mere physical life of men and all on their conduct. That is the only way to explain his absolute scorn for danger, and that, too, fits his personality, as we know it, his actions, and tells us what we want to know about his death.

We must not allow the detractors of our faith, the enemies of our Revolution, to take the ideological offensive or to assume the psychological stand which could dishearten the Revolutionary Movement. Instead, we must begin from the truth we know and turn Che's example into our own invincible strength, and push the Revolution forward.

Now is the time to be firmer than ever, in our new life, more prepared and determined to keep going straight ahead.

(Translated by a member of the Department of Stenography in the Revolutionary Government of Cuba, and excerpted from the full text of Dr. Fidel Castro's television broadcast, on October 15th, 1967, during which he informed the Cuban people of the death of Major Ernesto Che Guevara in Bolivia. The translated excerpt was adapted by the Editor.)

# FIDEL CASTRO

## On Intellectual Property

Radio, television, movies, the press, magazines: apparently, we do not know how to use them as efficiently as we could, just as we previously didn't know how to utilise practically anything else as efficiently as we could.

But, fortunately, we have been learning in these years, and therefore, we are beginning to understand how to do things better. And we also hope that in the area of providing information to the people we are also learning and are going to improve.

So many things! Speaking of any one of these deficiencies recalls something we were able to prove in the mountains of Oriente not long ago: with all the publishing houses we have in this country, with all the workers who work in these publishing houses, with all the paper that they use, not one single book had been published in this country for the farmers. And you went into a store in the mountains and found books on philosophy. This does not in any way mean that philosophy is something to be underestimated, but those farmers were not about to study matters of deep philosophy. They were interested in books on agriculture, books on mechanisation, books on a whole series of subjects. One day I asked a man in charge of a store what kind of books he had and which ones were sold. The answer was: 'Well, we have a lot of books by Marx and Angel.'

'Marx and *Angel*?' I asked him. 'Ah! I see. Marx and *Engels*.'

So there were books on political philosophy, books of every kind, and we asked ourselves: 'What are these books doing here?' And the problem was simply that no books were printed in this country for our farmers. Nor for our students either, for that matter.

Fortunately, this is now practically a thing of the past, and for quite some time now, all the books our students needed have been printed and a Book Institute has been organised that is doing a great deal of printing, taking full advantage of the abundant human resources and machinery we have at hand in the printing field. And perhaps, we shall also learn to make better use of our paper.

At times, millions of copies of certain works were printed only to be submitted, as Marx would say, to the devastating criticisms of moths and mice, since there was no demand for them and they were simply stored.

Should it surprise us then that many of these things accomplished by our people, today, are not publicised, when not even many of the great accomplishments of humanity were publicised, when even elementary matters of agricultural technology were not made available to our agricultural workers and farmers, and technical matters were not brought before our students, nor did our students have textbooks?

Of course, the solution was not an easy one. It became necessary to make a decision that we considered revolutionary. There exists a thing known as "intellectual property". In these matters of property, we are increasingly less experienced. In the past, everything was "property, property and more property". No other concept was better known, more publicised, or more sacred than that of private property. Everything was private. Possibly, the ground on which you are now sitting was once very "private". The houses, the land, the mountains, the sky, the sea, everything was private; even the sea, the seas surrounding Cuba; because every vessel that crossed those seas was a private vessel.

Well, these are all becoming things of the past. Our entire new generation is becoming more and more familiar with a different concept of property and is beginning to look upon those things as goods of general use and as goods that belong to the whole of society. The air, it is true, could not be said to be private, for the simple reason that there was no way to get hold of all of it and enclose it in a carafe. Had it been feasible, the air would have been taken over in the same way that the landgrabbers took over the land. But better the air in their control than food. Air was available to everyone, because it could not be bottled up, but food was not available to all because the land that produced it was not in the hands of the people.

Among all of the things that were appropriated, there was

one, very *sui generis,* called intellectual property. You will say: but that is abstract property. Yes, it is abstract property. And strangely enough, air could not be bottled up, yet, nevertheless, something as abstract as intellectual property could be shut up in a kind of bottle.

What do we mean by intellectual property? It is well enough understood. But, in case anyone is not familiar with it, it is, simply, the property of anything that emanates from the intelligence of individuals, of a group of individuals: a book, for example, any book of a technical nature, or a novel.

I want to make it quite clear, because I do not want to earn the enmity of the intellectuals; in the first place, because it would be unjustified enmity; that this should by no means be taken as disregard for the merit, the value, even the right to survive of those who produce this type of spiritual goods. Very well! But, what happens? Those property rights over intellectual possessions (following custom, following a system that prevailed in the world until very recently, following the influence of the whole capitalist concept of society), those intellectual possessions were subject to purchase and sale.

And, naturally, some (and, in general, many) of the creative intellects were badly paid; many have gone hungry. Anyone who reads, for example, the biography of Balzac, who was one of the great novelists of the last century, must be moved by the poverty in which that good man lived. In general, many of the great creative minds have gone hungry, because they had no backing. Many products of the intellect have been highly valued years after the death of their authors. Many men whose works have gained fame and immortality, later, were completely ignored while they lived.

Persons producing works of the intellect have generally lived in poverty. They have lacked the support of society, and have often had to sell their intellectual productions at any price.

And, in what circumstances, in what conditions, did we find ourselves? We were an underdeveloped country, completely lacking in technical knowledge, a country lacking technology and technicians; a country that had to begin by taking on the task of teaching one million citizens to read and write; a country that had to begin establishing technical schools, technological institutes, schools of all kinds, from primary to university level; a country that had to undertake the training of tens of thousands, of hundreds of thousands of skilled workers and technicians in order to emerge from poverty and underdevelopment; a country that had to make up the centuries of backwardness that burdened us. When a country like ours sets itself the task of recovering all that lost time, when it proposes to create better living conditions for the people, when it proposes to overcome poverty and underdevelopment, it must, then, invest every cent, a large part of its limited resources, in construction, in purchasing means of production, factories, equipment. At the same time that we had to make countless investments, we were faced with the difficulties in educating the people.

Why? Because as our citizens learned to read and write, as all children began to attend school, as the number of sixth-grade graduates topped the 50,000 mark and reached 60,000, 70,000 and 80,000, as more students entered the technological institutes and the universities, and as we aspired to defeat underdevelopment and ignorance, we needed an ever-increasing number of books. And books were (and are) very costly.

Because of the existing copyright concepts, we found that, in order to satisfy the demand for books, we had to spend tens of millions of pesos on their purchases, often paying for them most dearly. But, in practice, it is very difficult to determine exactly what is copyright; copyright belonged no longer to the authors but to those who had paid hard cash on the market for these products of the intellect, at any price, generally a low one. Those who exercised a monopoly over books had the right to sell them at the price they deemed suitable. We had to arrive at a decision, a defiant one, indeed, but a fair one. Our country, in fact, decided to disallow copyrights.

What does this mean? We feel that technical knowledge ought to be the patrimony of all mankind. To our way of thinking, whatever is created by man's intelligence ought to be the patrimony of all men.

Who pays royalties to Cervantes and to Shakespeare? Who pays the inventors of the alphabet; who pays the inventors of numbers, arithmetic, mathematics? In one way or another, all of mankind has benefited from, and made use of, those creations of the intellect that man has forged throughout history. When the first primitive man took a stick in his hands to knock down a piece of fruit from a tree, mankind began to benefit from a creation of the intelligence; when the first human being emitted a grunt that was the precursor of a future language, mankind began to make use of that product of man's intelligence.

That is, all, or rather the vast majority of man's creations have been amassed throughout thousands of years. And all mankind feels entitled to enjoy those creations of the intellect; everyone feels entitled to enjoy all that past generations have produced in other periods of history. How is it possible, today, to deny man, hundreds of thousands of human beings (no, not hundreds of thousands, but hundreds of millions and thousands of millions of human beings, who live in poverty, in underdevelopment), to deny access to technology to those thousands of millions of human beings who need it for something as elemental as feeding themselves, something as elemental as living?

Naturally, to adopt such a decision generally involves incurring the enmity of those whose interests are affected. Often copyrights are ignored, and it is done secretly, surreptitiously, without admitting it. We are not going to adopt that procedure. We state that we consider all technical knowledge the heritage of all mankind and especially of those peoples that have been exploited. Because where is there hunger, underdevelopment, ignorance, a lack of technical knowledge? Right there, in all those regions of the world where men were criminally exploited for centuries by colonialism and imperialism.

Technical books are generally printed in developed countries. And then, the poor countries, the countries that have been exploited for centuries, have virtually no access to that technical knowledge, when for centuries they have been stripped of many of the resources with which, equipped with modern technology, they could have been developed.

In the United States, there are many thousands of technical books. We have begun by announcing an end to intellectual copyrights on all technical books from the United States. And we state our unequivocal right to reprint *all* U.S. technical books that we feel will be useful to us.

It is clear that we don't have to offer any excuses to justify this. We feel justified in printing U.S. technical books, entitled to this, at least in compensation for the harm they have tried to do this country. Well, then, we will bypass copyright in relation to the United States; but we, independent of those circumstances, consider as a right of our people (of all the underdeveloped peoples) the use of all technical knowledge that is available throughout the world, and we therefore consider ourselves entitled to print any book of a technical nature that we need for our development, that we need in the training of our technicians.

And what will we give in exchange? We feel it a duty of society to help, to stimulate. We feel it a duty of society to protect all intellectual creators. I don't mean protect them; perhaps that is not the correct concept. We feel that our intellectual creators must take their place in society with all the rights of outstanding workers.

Cuba can and is willing to compensate all its intellectual creators; but, at the same time, it renounces (renounces internationally) all the copyrights that it is entitled to.

Not many technical books are published in this country, but, for example, we have produced a great deal of music that is enjoyed all over the world.

And, in the future, in all intellectual fields, our people will produce more and more. As of now, we announce our renunciation of all copyrights relating to our intellectual property, and, with Cuban intellectual producers protected by the Cuban government, our country renounces all its copyrights relating to intellectual property. That is, our books may be reprinted freely in any part of the world, while we, on the other hand, assume the right to do the same. If all countries did the same, humanity would be the beneficiary.

However, this is utopian. It is impossible to think that a capitalist country would do this. But if all countries did exactly the same, in exchange for the books that each country created, for the books published, or rather written in a given country, that country, by renouncing its copyrights to those books, could acquire the rights to the books written in every other country of the world.

Naturally, we cannot assume that this will happen. But, for our part, we can state that this will be our stand on the problem of copyrights. And we believe that it is correct to state this frankly, no matter who may be discomfited.

We can, of course, come to mutually convenient agreements with any country: they sending us their books published in large editions, and we sending them our books published in large editions. Any type of exchange of already published books, any type of agreement of this sort, we can do perfectly well, meeting the convenience of any country. But this will be the policy that we shall follow. We shall do the same with what are called "patents". We, for our part, it is true, have not yet invented great things or many things, and it is not a matter of our planning to become inventors, but any gadget that we do invent will be at the disposal of all humanity, as well as any success in the technical field, any success in the agricultural field.

(Translated by a member of the Department of Stenography in the Revolutionary Government of Cuba, and excerpted from the full text of Dr. Fidel Castro's speech delivered on April 29th, 1967. The translated excerpt was adapted by Martin Glass.)

# BIOGRAPHICAL NOTES

VÍCTOR AGOSTINI: (b. 1908) A leading short story writer and belletrist, well known for his second book of short stories, *Bibijaguas,* published (1963) by the Union of Cuban Writers and Artists.

LUIS AGÜERO: (b. 1937) Short story writer, journalist and literary critic. Published his first book of short stories (1962), *De Aqui para Allá,* and quickly established his reputation among the Revolutionary writers of his generation.

DOMINGO ALFONSO: (b. 1936) Poet and Architect. One of the young vanguard intellectuals in the Union of Cuban Writers and Artists. His books of poems include *Sueños en el papel, Poemas del hombre común* and *Historia de una persona.*

ORLANDO ALOMÁ: (b. 1942) Poet, journalist and former lecturer in Spanish Literature at the University of Oriente. Managing Editor of the *Casa de las Américas* magazine in Havana.

ANTÓN ARRUFAT: (b. 1935) Poet, critic, playwright, short story writer and former Chief Editor of the *Casa de las Américas* magazine. Has published *Mi antagonista y otras observaciones,* a book of short stories; *Teatro,* a collection of five plays; and

MIGUEL BARNET: (b. 1940) Poet, Sociologist, critic and Biographer of Esteban Montejo, the one hundred and eight year old former runaway slave (b. 1860). Barnet's books of poems include *La Piedra Fina y Pavo Real* and *Isla de Güijes*.

VÍCTOR CASAÚS: (b. 1944) Poet, journalist and television documentary film director. His first book of poems, *Todos los días del Mundo,* was published in 1966.

FIDEL CASTRO: (b. 1926) The First Secretary of the Communist Party of Cuba, and Prime Minister of the Revolutionary Government.

ARNALDO CORREA: (b. 1935) Short story writer. His first book, *Asesinato por Anticipado,* was published in 1966.

EDMUNDO DESNOES: (b. 1930) Novelist and critic. He is the international literature Editor at the Book Institute in Havana. His best known novel, *Memorias del Subdesarrollo,* was published in Britain in 1968, with the title, *Inconsolable Memories.*

SAMUEL FEIJÓO: (b. 1914) Director of the University of Las Villas Press and Editor of *Islas,* the University magazine. He has written more than forty books, including poetry, critical essays, plays, short stories and novels.

*En claro* and *Repaso final,* two books of poems.

AMBROSIO FORNET: (b. 1932) Literary critic and the Author of two important Revolutionary works of criticism, *En tres y dos* and *En blanco y negro*.

ERNESTO CHE GUEVARA: (b. 1928 – d. 1967) Argentinian Revolutionary mystic, vanguard Marxist intellectual, Cuban guerrilla liberator and, for some years after the Revolution, a citizen of Cuba. His books include *El Socialismo y el hombre en Cuba* and *Pasajes de la guerra Revoluciónaria*.

NICOLÁS GUILLÉN: (b. 1902) The acknowledged father of modern Cuban poetry. Former diplomat and Revolutionary civil servant. Author of very many books of poems, and at present, since 1961, the President of the Union of Cuban Writers and Artists. Large folded roughpaper copies of *Che Comandante,* his most recent public poem, were handed out in the streets of Havana, when the Editor was there, in January 1968.

FAYAD JAMÍS: (b. 1930) Poet and former Professor of Painting at the National School of Arts in Havana. Winner of the *Casa de las Américas* poetry prize, in 1962, for his book, *Por esta Libertad*. Director of Publications of the Union of Cuban Writers and Artists, and Editor of the Union's official magazine.

EDUARDO LOLO: (b. 1926) Poet and unofficial cultural group leader in the City of Matanzas, where he is a great stimulating influence on the young poets throughout the Province.

CÉSAR LÓPEZ: (b. 1933) Poet, short story writer and critic. Studied medicine at the University of Salamanca, and philosophy at Madrid. Former diplomat (Revolutionary Cuban Consul in Scotland) and theatrical director in Havana. His best known books of poems are *Primer Libro de la Ciudad* and *Silencio en Voz de Muerte*.

BELKIS CUZA MALÉ: (b. 1942) Poet and literary journalist on *Granma* newspaper in Havana. Studied Spanish Literature at Havana University. Her published books include *El viento en la pared* and *Cartas a Ana Frank*.

MANUEL DÍAZ MARTÍNEZ: (b. 1936) Poet, short story writer and former literary journalist and cultural attache in Bulgaria. Now works as a Senior Research Fellow in the Institute of Literature and Linguistics at Havana University. His most recent books are *Palabra abierta, La tierra de Saúd* and *En el país de Ofelia*.

NANCY MOREJÓN: (b. 1944) Poet and one of the literary Editors of *La Gaceta de Cuba*. She studied French

VIRGILIO PINERA:

ROBERTO FERNÁNDEZ RETAMAR:

GUILLERMON RODRÍGUEZ RIVERA:

Language and Literature at Havana University, and has published three books of poems *Mutismos, Amor Ciudad Atribuida* and *Richard trajo su flauta y otros argumentos.*
(b. 1912) Short story writer, novelist, playwright and poet. His many published books include *Pequeñas maniobras,* a novel (1963); *Cuentos Completos,* a collection of short stories (1964); *Presiones y diamantes* (1967); and *Dos viejos panicos,* a play, for which he was awarded the 1968 *Casa de las Américas* top drama prize.
(b. 1930) Poet, literary critic, Professor of Spanish Literature at Havana University, and the Editor of the *Casa de las Américas* magazine. Former cultural attaché in Paris. Among his many books, the most important are *Historia antigua* (1964) and *Poesía reunida* (1966), both collections of poems.
(b. 1943) Poet and journalist. Educated at Havana University where he read Spanish Literature and obtained his Master's degree. Editor of Cuba's satirical magazine, *El Caimán Barbudo,* and Secretary of *Revolución y Cultura,* an Arts review, and the Author of *Cambio de impresiones,* his

ALBERTO ROCASOLANO: first book of poems, published in 1966.
(b. 1935) Poet and adult education specialist in Havana. *Diestro en soledades y esperanzas* (1967) is his first book of poems.

FÉLIX PITA RODRÍGUEZ: (b. 1909) Poet, short story writer and essayist. His best known books, since the Revolution, are *Las Crónicas,* a collection of poems (1961); *Poemas y Cuentos,* poems and stories (1966); and he has written many short pieces, inspired by his recent visit to Vietnam. One appears in this anthology.

PEDRO PÉREZ SARDUY: (b. 1944) Poet and surrealist innovator. He is best known for his book of poems, *Surrealidad.*

LUIS SUARDÍAZ: (b. 1936) Poet, critic and former journalist and director of radio and television current affairs programmes. He is now the Director of Literature in the National Council of Culture in Havana. His most outstanding book is his very recent *Haber Vivido,* a slim volume of popular poems.

# Acknowledgments

Acknowledgements and thanks are due to the translators, the Cuban official literary sources in Havana, and to the Authors for permission to publish the English translations of their poems, short stories and essays in this anthology. Grateful acknowledgement is also made to the following for permitting their published material to be reprinted: the Book Institute and Nicolás Guillén for his poem, *Land in the Sierra and Below,* and the Editors of 'el cornu emplumado' and the same poet for his poem, *Che Comandante;* the Editors of 'el cornu emplumado' and Nancy Morejón for her poem, *Poem,* and the Book Institute and the same poet for her poem, *Central Park, Some People, 3:00 p.m.;* the Editors of 'el cornu emplumado' and Domingo Alfonso for his poem, *Madrigal written in the Year of the Space Rocket, Mariner IV,* and the Book Institute and the same poet for his poems, *A Little Biography, People like me, Señor Julio Osorio* and *Poem;* the Editors of 'La Gaceta de Cuba', Havana, and Pedro Pérez Sarduy for his poem, *Che,* and the Editors of 'Union', Havana, and the same poet for his poem, *The Rebellion of the Warrior;* the Editors of 'el cornu emplumado' and Roberto Fernández Retamar for his poem, *How lucky they are, the normal people,* and the Book Institute and the same poet for his poems, *The Last Station of the Ruins, No word does you justice, For an instant* and *To Whom it may Concern;* the Book Institute and Fayad Jamís for his poems, *For this Liberty, Poem in Minas del Frío* and *The Victory of Playa Girón;* the Book Institute and Miguel Barnet for his poems, *My Country, Che* and *Revolution;* the Book Institute and Guillermo Rodríguez Rivera for his poem, *Working Hours;* the Book Institute and Belkis Cuza Malé for her poems, *I haven't forgotten you* and *Photogenic People;* the Editors of 'el cornu emplumado' and Félix Pita Rodríguez for his poem, *The Guerrillas arrive,* and the Book Institute and the same poet for his poems, *Rifle Number 5767* and *Poetry with a Purpose;* the Editors of 'el cornu emplumado' and Alberto Rocasolano for his poem, *Revolution is not simply a word;* the Editors of 'el cornu emplumado' and Víctor Casaús for his poem, *Moon-9,* and the Book Institute and the same poet for his poem, *We are;* the Editors of 'el cornu emplumado' and Eduardo Lolo for his poems, *Anna* and *If you get up some morning;* the Book Institute and César López for his poem, *Who can be certain?;* the Editors of 'el cornu emplumado' and Orlando Alomá for his poem, *The Militant Angel;* the Book Institute and Luis Suardíaz for his poem, *Witness for the Prosecution;* the Book Institute and Antón Arrufat for his poem, *Playa Girón;* the Book Institute and Manuel Díaz Martínez for his poem, *Bread;* the Book Institute and the following Authors for their short stories: *The Seed* by Félix Pita Rodríguez, *The Philanthropist* by Virgilio Piñera, *Soldier Eloy* by Samuel Feijóo, *Pepe* by Víctor Agostini, *A certain Friday 13th* by Luis Agüero, and *The Chief* by Arnaldo Correa; the Press Office of the Cultural Congress of Havana, 1968, and the following Authors for their essays: *The Secret Weapons* by Edmundo Desnoes, and *The Intellectual in the Revolution* by Ambrosio Fornet; the Book Institute for the following essay-excerpts from the published work of Ernesto Che Guevara: *The Cultural Vanguard* and *'El Patojo';* and the Cuban National radio and television networks, Radio Havana Cuba, the Book Institute and Fidel Castro for his excerpted essay, *On Che's Assassination* and for *On Intellectual Property.*